P9-CFP-010

KATHY REICHS

DEJA DEAD

POCKET STAR BOOKS

New York   London   Toronto   Sydney

A Pocket Star Book published by
POCKET BOOKS, a division of Simon & Schuster, Inc.
1230 Avenue of the Americas, New York, NY 10020

Copyright © 1997 by Kathleen J. Reichs

Originally published in hardcover in 1997 by Scribner

ISBN: 1-4165-1055-9

This Pocket Books printing May 2005

10 9 8 7 6 5 4 3 2 1

POCKET STAR BOOKS and colophon are registered
trademarks of Simon & Schuster, Inc.

Manufactured in the United States of America

For information regarding special discounts for bulk purchases,
please contact Simon & Schuster Special Sales at 1-800-456-6798
or business@simonandschuster.com.

For Karl and Marta Reichs,
the two kindest and most generous people I know.
Paldies par jūsu mīlestību, Vecāmamma un Paps.

Kārlis Reichs 1914–1996

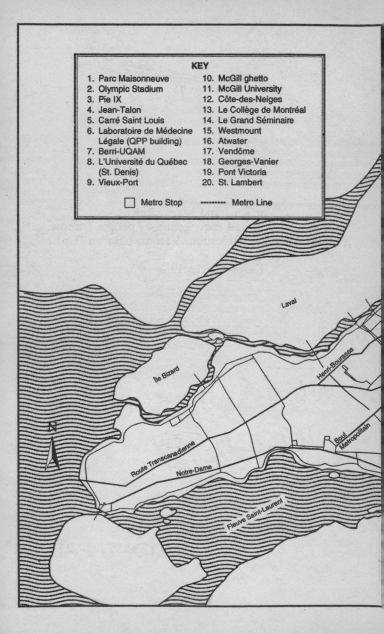

KEY

1. Parc Maisonneuve
2. Olympic Stadium
3. Pie IX
4. Jean-Talon
5. Carré Saint Louis
6. Laboratoire de Médecine Légale (QPP building)
7. Berri-UQAM
8. L'Université du Québec (St. Denis)
9. Vieux-Port
10. McGill ghetto
11. McGill University
12. Côte-des-Neiges
13. Le Collège de Montréal
14. Le Grand Séminaire
15. Westmount
16. Atwater
17. Vendôme
18. Georges-Vanier
19. Pont Victoria
20. St. Lambert

☐ Metro Stop ---------- Metro Line

Laval

Île Bizard

Henri-Bourassa

Boul. Métropolitain

N

Route Transcanadienne

Notre-Dame

Fleuve Saint-Laurent

MONTREAL

ACKNOWLEDGMENTS

In an attempt to create accurate fiction, I consulted experts in many fields. I wish to thank Bernard Chapais for his explanation of Canadian regulations pertaining to the housing and maintenance of laboratory aniamls; Sylvian Roy, Jean-Guy Hébert, and Michel Hamel for their help on serology; Bernard Pommeville for his detailed demonstration of X-ray microfluorescence; and Robert Dorion for his advice on forensic dentistry, bite mark analysis, and proper use of the French language. Last, but far from least, I wish to express my gratitude to Steve Symes for his boundless patience in discussing saws and their effects on bone.

I owe a debt of thanks to John Robinson and Marysue Rucci, without whom *Déjà Dead* may never have come to be. John brought the manuscript to Marysue's attention, and she saw merit in it. My editors, Susanne Kirk, Marysue Rucci, and Maria Rejt waded through the original version of *Déjà Dead*, improving it greatly with their editorial suggestions. A million thanks to my agent, Jennifer Rudolph Walsh. She is amazing.

Finally, on a more personal note, I want to thank the members of my family who read the embryonic work and made valuable comments. I appreciate their support, and their patience with my long absences.

1

I WASN'T THINKING ABOUT THE man who'd blown himself up. Earlier I had. Now I was putting him together. Two sections of skull lay in front of me, and a third jutted from a sand-filled stainless steel bowl, the glue still drying on its reassembled fragments. Enough bone to confirm identity. The coroner would be pleased.

It was late afternoon, Thursday, June 2, 1994. While the glue set, my mind had gone truant. The knock that would break my reverie, tip my life off course, and alter my comprehension of the bounds of human depravity wouldn't come for another ten minutes. I was enjoying my view of the St. Lawrence, the sole advantage of my cramped corner office. Somehow the sight of water has always reju-venated me, especially when it flows rhythmically. Forget Golden Pond. I'm sure Freud could have run with that.

My thoughts meandered to the upcoming week-

KATHY REICHS

end. I had a trip to Quebec City in mind, but my plans were vague. I thought of visiting the Plains of Abraham, eating mussels and crepes, and buying trinkets from the street vendors. Escape in tourism. I'd been in Montreal a full year, working as forensic anthropologist for the province, but I hadn't been up there yet, so it seemed like a good program. I needed a couple of days without skeletons, decomposed bodies, or corpses freshly dragged from the river.

Ideas come easily to me, enacting them comes harder. I usually let things go. Perhaps it's an escape hatch, my way of allowing myself to double back and ease out the side door on a lot of my schemes. Irresolute about my social life, obsessive in my work.

I knew he was standing there before the knock. Though he moved quietly for a man of his bulk, the smell of old pipe tobacco gave him away. Pierre LaManche had been director of the Laboratoire de Médecine Légale for almost two decades. His visits to my office were never social, and I suspected that his news wouldn't be good. LaManche tapped the door softly with his knuckles.

"Temperance?" It rhymed with France. He would not use the shortened version. Perhaps to his ear it just didn't translate. Perhaps he'd had a bad experience in Arizona. He, alone, did not call me Tempe.

"Oui?" After months, it was automatic. I had arrived in Montreal thinking myself fluent in French, but I hadn't counted on *Le Français Québecois.* I was learning, but slowly.

"I have just had a call." He glanced at a pink telephone slip he was holding. Everything about his face was vertical, the lines and folds moving from high to low, paralleling the long, straight nose and

2

ears. The plan was pure basset hound. It was a face that had probably looked old in youth, its arrangement only deepening with time. I couldn't have guessed his age.

"Two Hydro-Quebec workers found some bones today." He studied my face, which was not happy. His eyes returned to the pink paper.

"They are close to the site where the historic burials were found last summer," he said in his proper, formal French. I'd never heard him use a contraction. No slang or police jargon. "You were there. It is probably more of the same. I need someone to go out there to confirm that this is not a coroner case."

When he glanced up from the paper, the change in angle caused the furrows and creases to deepen, sucking in the afternoon light, as a black hole draws in matter. He made an attempt at a gaunt smile and four crevices veered north.

"You think it's archaeological?" I was stalling. A scene search had not been in my pre-weekend plans. To leave the next day I still had to pick up the dry cleaning, do the laundry, stop at the pharmacy, pack, put oil in the car, and explain cat care to Winston, the caretaker at my building.

He nodded.

"Okay." It was not okay.

He handed me the slip. "Do you want a squad car to take you there?"

I looked at him, trying hard for baleful. "No, I drove in today." I read the address. It was close to home. "I'll find it."

He left as silently as he'd come. Pierre La-Manche favored crepe-soled shoes, kept his pockets empty so nothing jangled or swished. Like a croc in a river he arrived and departed unannounced by auditory cues. Some of the staff found it unnerving.

I packed a set of coveralls in a backpack with my rubber boots, hoping I wouldn't need either, and grabbed my laptop, briefcase, and the embroidered canteen cover that was serving as that season's purse. I was still promising myself that I wouldn't be back until Monday, but another voice in my head was intruding, insisting otherwise.

When summer arrives in Montreal it flounces in like a rumba dancer: all ruffles and bright cotton, with flashing thighs and sweat-slicked skin. It is a ribald celebration that begins in June and continues until September.

The season is embraced and relished. Life moves into the open. After the long, bleak winter, outdoor cafés reappear, cyclists and Rollerbladers compete for the bike paths, festivals follow quickly one after another on the streets, and crowds turn the sidewalks into swirling patterns.

How different summer on the St. Lawrence is from summer in my home state of North Carolina, where languid lounging on beach chairs, mountain porches, or suburban decks marks the season, and the lines between spring, summer, and fall are difficult to determine without a calendar. This brash vernal rebirth, more than the bitterness of winter, had surprised me my first year in the North, banishing the homesickness I'd felt during the long, dark cold.

These thoughts were drifting through my mind as I drove under the Jacques-Cartier Bridge and turned west onto Viger. I passed the Molson brewery, which sprawled along the river to my left, then the round tower of the Radio-Canada Building, and thought of the people trapped inside: occupants of industrial apiaries who undoubtedly craved release as much as I did. I imagined them studying the

4

sunshine from behind glass rectangles, longing for boats and bikes and sneakers, checking their watches, bitten by June.

I rolled down the window and reached for the radio.

Gerry Boulet sang *"Les Yeux du Cœur."* I translated automatically in my mind. I could picture him, an intense man with dark eyes and a tangle of curls flying around his head, passionate about his music, dead at forty-four.

Historic burials. Every forensic anthropologist handles these cases. Old bones unearthed by dogs, construction workers, spring floods, grave diggers. The coroner's office is the overseer of death in Quebec Province. If you die inappropriately, not under the care of a physician, not in bed, the coroner wants to know why. If your death threatens to take others along, the coroner wants to know that. The coroner demands an explanation of violent, unexpected, or untimely death, but persons long gone are of little interest. While their passings may once have cried out for justice, or heralded warning of an impending epidemic, the voices have been still for too long. Their antiquity established, these finds are turned over to the archaeologists. This promised to be such a case. Please.

I zigzagged through the logjam of downtown traffic, arriving within fifteen minutes at the address LaManche had given me. Le Grand Séminaire. A remnant of the vast holdings of the Catholic Church, Le Grand Séminaire occupies a large tract of land in the heart of Montreal. Centre-ville. Downtown. My neighborhood. The small, urban citadel endures as an island of green in a sea of high-rise cement, and stands as mute testimony to a once-powerful institution. Stone walls, complete with watchtowers, surround somber gray castles, carefully tended lawns, and open spaces gone wild.

In the glory days of the church, families sent their sons here by the thousands to train for the priesthood. Some still come, but their numbers are few. The larger buildings are now rented out and house schools and institutions more secular in mission where the Internet and fax machine replace Scripture and theological discourse as the working paradigm. Perhaps it's a good metaphor for modern society. We're too absorbed in communicating among ourselves to worry about an almighty architect.

I stopped on a small street opposite the seminary grounds and looked east along Sherbrooke, toward the portion of the property now leased by Le Collège de Montréal. Nothing unusual. I dropped an elbow out the window and peered in the opposite direction. The hot, dusty metal seared the skin on my inner arm, and I retracted it quickly, like a crab poked with a stick.

There they were. Juxtaposed incongruously against a medieval stone tower, I could see a blue-and-white patrol unit with POLICE-COMMUNAUTÉ URBAINE DE MONTRÉAL written on its side. It blocked the western entrance to the compound. A gray Hydro-Quebec truck was parked just ahead of it, ladders and equipment protruding like appendages to a space station. Near the truck a uniformed officer stood talking with two men in work clothes.

I turned left and slid into the westbound traffic on Sherbrooke, relieved to see no reporters. In Montreal an encounter with the press can be a double ordeal, since the media turn out in both French and English. I am not particularly gracious when badgered in one language. Under dual assault I can become downright surly.

6

LaManche was right. I'd come to these grounds the previous summer. I recalled the case—bones unearthed during the repair of a water main. Church property. Old cemetery. Coffin burials. Call the archaeologist. Case closed. Hopefully, this report would read the same.

As I maneuvered my Mazda ahead of the truck and parked, the three men stopped talking and looked in my direction. When I got out of the car the officer paused, as if thinking it over, then moved toward me. He was not smiling. At 4:15 P.M. it was probably past the end of his shift and he didn't want to be there. Well, neither did I.

"You'll have to move on, madame. You may not park here." As he spoke he gestured with his hand, shooing me in the direction in which I was to depart. I could picture him clearing flies from potato salad with the same movement.

"I'm Dr. Brennan," I said, slamming the Mazda door. "Laboratoire de Médecine Légale."

"You're the one from the coroner?" His tone would have made a KGB interrogator sound trusting.

"Yes. I'm the *anthropologiste judiciaire.*" Slowly, like a second-grade teacher. "I do the disinterments and the skeletal cases. I understand this may qualify for both?"

I handed him my ID. A small, brass rectangle above his shirt pocket identified him as Const. Groulx.

He looked at the photo, then at me. My appearance was not convincing. I'd planned to work on the skull reconstruction all day, and was dressed for glue. I was wearing faded brown jeans, a denim shirt, sleeves rolled to the elbows, Topsiders, no socks. Most of my hair was bound up in a barrette. The rest, having fought gravity and lost, spiraled

7

limply around my face and down my neck. I was speckled with patches of dried Elmer's. I must have looked more like a middle-aged mother forced to abandon a wallpaper project than a forensic anthropologist.

He studied the ID for a long time, then returned it without comment. I was obviously not what he wanted.

"Have you seen the remains?" I asked.

"No. I am securing the site." He used a modified version of the hand flip to indicate the two men who stood watching us, conversation suspended.

"They found it. I called it in. They will lead you."

I wondered if Constable Groulx was capable of a compound sentence. With another hand gesture, he indicated the workers once again.

"I will watch your car."

I nodded but he was already turning away. The Hydro workers watched in silence as I approached. Both wore aviator shades, and the late afternoon sun shot orange beams off alternating lenses as one or the other moved his head. Their mustaches looped in identical upside-down U's around their mouths.

The one on the left was the older of the two, a thin, dark man with the look of a rat terrier. He was glancing around nervously, his gaze bouncing from object to object, person to person, like a bee making sorties in and out of a peony blossom. His eyes kept darting to me, then quickly away, as if he feared contact with other eyes would commit him to something he'd later come to regret. He shifted his weight from foot to foot and hunched and unhunched his shoulders.

His partner was a much larger man with a long, lank ponytail and a weathered face. He smiled as

I drew near, displaying gaps that once held teeth. I suspected he'd be the more loquacious of the two.

"Bonjour. Comment ça va?" The French equivalent of "Hi. How are you?"

"Bien. Bien." Simultaneous head nods. Fine. Fine.

I identified myself, asked if they'd reported finding the bones. More nods.

"Tell me about it." As I spoke I withdrew a small spiral notebook from my backpack, flipped back the cover, and clicked a ballpoint into readiness. I smiled encouragingly.

Ponytail spoke eagerly, his words racing out like children released for recess. He was enjoying the adventure. His French was heavily accented, the words running together and the endings swallowed in the fashion of the upriver Québecois. I had to listen carefully.

"We were clearing brush, it's part of our job." He pointed at overhead power lines, then did a sweep of the ground. "We must keep the lines clear."

I nodded.

"When I got down into that trench over there"— he turned and pointed in the direction of a wooded area running the length of the property—"I smelled something funny." He stopped, his eyes locked in the direction of the trees, arm extended, index finger piercing the air.

"Funny?"

He turned back. "Well, not exactly funny." He paused, sucking in his lower lip as he searched his personal lexicon for the right word. "Dead," he said. "You know, dead?"

I waited for him to go on.

"You know, like an animal that crawls in somewhere and dies?" He gave a slight shrug of the shoulders as he said it, then looked at me for confirmation. I did know. I'm on a first-name basis with the odor of death. I nodded again.

"That's what I thought. That a dog, or maybe a raccoon, died. So I started poking around in the brush with my rake, right where the smell was real strong. Sure enough, I found a bunch of bones." Another shrug.

"Uh-huh." I was beginning to get an uneasy feeling. Ancient burials don't smell.

"So I called Gil over . . ." He looked to the older man for affirmation. Gil was staring at the ground. ". . . and we both started digging around in the leaves and stuff. What we found don't look like no dog or raccoon to me." As he said it he folded his arms across his chest, lowered his chin, and rocked back on his heels.

"Why is that?"

"Too big." He rolled his tongue and used it to probe one of the gaps in his dental work. The tip appeared and disappeared between the teeth like a worm testing for daylight.

"Anything else?"

"What do you mean?" The worm withdrew.

"Did you find anything besides bones?"

"Yeah. That's what don't seem right." He spread his arms wide, indicating a dimension with his hands. "There's a big plastic sack around all this stuff, and . . ." He shrugged, turning his palms up and leaving the sentence unfinished.

"And?" My uneasiness was escalating.

"*Une ventouse.*" He said it quickly, embarrassed and excited at the same time. Gil was traveling with me, his apprehension matching mine. His eyes had left the ground and were roving in double time.

"A what?" I asked, thinking perhaps I'd misunderstood the word.

"Une ventouse. A plunger. For the bathroom." He imitated its use, his body thrust forward, hands wrapped around an invisible handle, arms driving upward and downward. The macabre little panto- mime was so out of context it was jarring.

Gil let out a *"Sacré . . ."* and locked his eyes back on to the earth. I just stared at him. This wasn't right. I finished my notes and closed the spiral.

"Is it wet down there?" I didn't really want to wear the boots and coveralls unless it was nec- essary.

"Nah," he said, again looking to Gil for confir- mation. Gil shook his head, eyes never leaving the dirt at his feet.

"Okay," I said. "Let's go." I hoped that I ap- peared calmer than I felt.

Ponytail led the way across the grass and into the woods. We descended gradually into a small ravine, the trees and brush growing thicker as we approached the bottom. I followed into the thicket, taking the larger branches in my right hand as he bent them back for me, then handing them off to Gil. Still small branches tugged at my hair. The place smelled of damp earth, grass, and rotting leaves. Sunlight penetrated the foliage unevenly, dappling the ground with puzzle piece splotches. Here and there a beam found an opening and sliced straight through to the ground. Dust particles danced in the slanted shafts. Flying insects swarmed around my face and whined in my ears, and creep- ers grabbed my ankles.

At the bottom of the trench the worker stopped to get his bearings, then turned to the right. I fol- lowed, slapping at mosquitoes, handing off vegeta- tion, squinting through clouds of gnats around my eyes, and the occasional loner that went straight for the cornea. Sweat beaded my lip and dampened my hair, plastering the escapee strands to my forehead and neck. I needn't have worried about my dress or coiffure.

Fifteen yards from the corpse I no longer needed a guide. Blending with the loamy scent of woods and sunlight I detected the unmistakable smell of death. The odor of decomposing flesh is like no other, and it hung there in the warm afternoon air, faint but undeniable. Step by step, the sweet, fetid stench grew stronger, building in intensity like the whine of a locust, until it ceased blending, and overpowered all other smells. The aromas of moss and humus and pine and sky deferred to the rankness of rotting flesh.

Gil stopped and hung back at a discreet distance. The smell was enough. He didn't need another look. Ten feet farther the younger man halted, turned, and wordlessly pointed to a small heap partially covered by leaves and debris. Flies buzzed and circled around it, like academics at a free buffet.

At the sight my stomach went into a tuck, and the voice in my head started in on "I told you so." With growing dread, I placed my pack at the base of a tree, withdrew a pair of surgical gloves, and picked my way gingerly through the foliage. When I neared the mound I could see where the men had raked away the vegetation. What I saw confirmed my fears.

Protruding from the leaves and soil was an arcade of ribs, their ends curving upward like the framework of an embryonic boat. I bent down for a closer look. Flies whined in protest, the sun iridescent on their blue-green bodies. When I cleared more debris I could see that the ribs were held in place by a segment of spinal column.

Taking a deep breath, I eased on the latex gloves and began to remove handfuls of dead leaves and pine needles. As I exposed the backbone to the sunlight, a knot of startled beetles flew apart. The bugs disentangled themselves and scuttled outward, disappearing one by one over the vertebral edges.

Ignoring the insects, I continued to remove sediment. Slowly, carefully, I cleared an area approximately three feet square. In less than ten minutes I could see what Gil and his partner had discovered. Brushing hair from my face with a latexed hand, I leaned back on my heels and surveyed the emerging picture.

I looked at a partially skeletonized torso, the rib cage, backbone, and pelvis still connected by dried muscle and ligament. While connective tissue is stubborn, refusing to yield its hold on the joints for months or years, the brain and internal organs are not so tenacious. With the aid of bacteria and insects, they decompose quickly, sometimes in a matter of weeks.

I could see remnants of brown and desiccated tissue clinging to the thoracic and abdominal surfaces of the bones. As I squatted there, the flies buzzing and the sunlight dappling the woods around me, I knew two things with certainty. The torso was human, and it hadn't been there long.

I knew also that its arrival in that place wasn't by chance. The victim had been killed and dumped. The remains lay on a plastic bag, the common kitchen variety used for garbage. It was ripped open now, but I guessed the bag had been used to transport the torso. The head and limbs were missing, and I could see no personal effects or objects close by. Except one.

The bones of the pelvis encircled a bathroom plunger, its long wooden handle projecting upward like an inverted Popsicle stick, its red rubber cup pressed hard against the pelvic outlet. Its position suggested deliberate placement. Gruesome as the idea was, I didn't believe the association was spurious.

I stood and looked around, my knees protesting the change to upright posture. I knew from experience that scavenging animals can drag body parts impressive distances. Dogs often hide them in areas of low brush, and burrowing animals drag small bones and teeth into underground holes. I brushed dirt from my hands and scanned the immediate vicinity, looking for likely routes.

Flies buzzed and a horn blared a million miles away on Sherbrooke. Memories of other woods, other graves, other bones skittered through my mind, like disconnected images from old movies. I stood absolutely still, searching, wholly alert. Finally, I sensed, more than saw, an irregularity in my surroundings. Like a sunbeam glinting off a mirror, it was gone before my neurons could form an image. An almost imperceptible flicker caused me to turn my head. Nothing. I held myself rigid, unsure if I'd really seen anything. I brushed the insects from my eyes and noticed that it was growing cooler.

Shit. I continued looking. A slight breeze lifted the damp curls around my face and stirred the leaves. Then I sensed it again. A suggestion of sunlight skipping off something. I took a few steps, unsure of the source, and stopped, every cell of my being intent on sunlight and shadows. Nothing. Of course not, stupid. There can't be anything over there. No flies.

Then I spotted it. The wind puffed gently, flicking over a shiny surface and causing a momentary ripple in the afternoon light. Not much, but it

14

caught my eye. Hardly breathing, I went closer and looked down. I wasn't surprised at what I saw. Here we go, I thought.

Peeking from a hollow in the roots of a yellow poplar was the corner of another plastic bag. A spray of buttercups ringed both the poplar and the bag, tiptoeing off in slender tendrils to disappear into the surrounding weeds. The bright yellow flowers looked like escapees from a Beatrix Potter illustration, the freshness of the blooms in stark contrast to what I knew lay hidden in the bag.

I approached the tree, twigs and leaves snapping beneath my feet. Bracing myself with one hand, I cleared enough plastic to get a grip, took firm hold, and pulled gently. No give. Rewrapping the plastic around my hand, I pulled harder, and felt the bag move. I could tell that its contents had substance. Insects whined in my face. Sweat trickled down my back. My heart drummed like the bass in a heavy metal band.

One more tug and the bag came free. I dragged it forward far enough to allow a view inside. Or maybe I just wanted it away from Ms. Potter's flowers. Whatever it held was heavy, and I had little doubt what that would be. And I was right. As I disentangled the ends of the plastic, the smell of putrefaction was overwhelming. I unwound the edges and looked inside.

A human face stared out at me. Sealed off from the insects that hasten decomposition, the flesh had not fully rotted. But heat and moisture had altered the features, converting them into a death mask bearing scant resemblance to the person it had been. Two eyes, shriveled and constricted, peered out from under half-closed lids. The nose lay bent to one side, the nostrils compressed and flattened against a sunken cheek. The lips curled back, a grin for eternity with a set of perfect teeth. The flesh was pasty white, a blanched and soggy wrapper molding itself closely to the underlying bone. Framing the whole was a mass of dull red hair, the lusterless corkscrew curls plastered to the head by an ooze of liquefied brain tissue.

Shaken, I closed the bag. Remembering the Hydro workers, I glanced over to where I'd left them. The younger was watching me closely. His companion remained some distance behind, shoulders hunched, hands thrust deep into the pockets of his work pants.

Stripping off my gloves, I walked past them, out of the woods and back toward the CUM squad car. They said nothing, but I could hear them following, scraping and rustling in my wake.

Constable Groulx was leaning against his hood. He watched me approach but didn't change position. I'd worked with more amiable individuals.

"May I use your radio?" I could be cool, too.

He pushed himself upright with both hands and circled the car to the driver's side. Leaning in through the open window, he disengaged the mike and looked at me questioningly.

"Homicide," I said.

He looked surprised, regretted it, and put through the call. *"Section des homicides,"* he said to the dispatcher. After the usual delays, transfers, and static, the voice of a detective came over the air.

"Claudel," it said, sounding irritated.

Constable Groulx handed me the mike. I identified myself and gave my location. "I've got a homicide here," I said. "Probable body dump. Probable female. Probable decapitation. You'd better get recovery out here right away."

There was a long pause. No one was finding this good news.

"Pardon?"

I repeated what I'd said, asking Claudel to pass the word along to Pierre LaManche when he called the morgue. There would be nothing for the archaeologists this time.

I returned the mike to Groulx, who'd been listening to every word. I reminded him to get a full report from the two workers. He looked like a man who'd just been sentenced to ten to twenty. He knew he wouldn't be going anywhere for some time. I wasn't terribly sympathetic. I wouldn't be sleeping in Quebec City this weekend. In fact, as I drove the few short blocks to my condo, I suspected that no one would be sleeping much for a long time. As things turned out, I was right. What I couldn't know then was the full extent of the horror we were about to face.

2

THE NEXT DAY BEGAN AS WARM and sunny as its predecessor, a fact that would normally draw me into high spirits. I am a woman whose moods are influenced by the weather, my outlook rising and falling with the barometer. But that day the weather would be irrelevant. By 9 A.M. I was already in autopsy room 4, the smallest of the suites at the Laboratoire de Médecine Légale, and one that is specially outfitted for extra ventilation. I often work here since most of my cases are less than perfectly preserved. But it's never fully effective. Nothing is. The fans and disinfectants never quite win over the smell of ripened death. The antiseptic gleam of the stainless steel never really eradicates the images of human carnage.

The remains recovered at Le Grand Séminaire definitely qualified for room 4. After a quick dinner the previous evening, I'd gone back to the grounds and we'd processed the site. The bones were at the morgue by 9:30 P.M. Now they lay in a body bag on a gurney to my right. Case #26704 had been discussed at the morning staff meeting. Following standard procedure, the body had been assigned to one of the five pathologists working at the lab. Since the corpse was largely skeletonized, the little soft tissue that remained far too decomposed for standard autopsy, my expertise was requested.

One of the autopsy technicians had called in sick this morning, leaving us shorthanded. Bad timing. It'd been a busy night: a teenage suicide, an elderly couple found dead in their home, and a car fire victim charred beyond recognition. Four autopsies. I'd offered to work alone.

I was dressed in green surgical scrubs, plastic goggles, and latex gloves. Fetching. I'd already cleaned and photographed the head. It would be X-rayed this morning, then boiled to remove the putrefied flesh and brain tissue so that I could do a detailed examination of the cranial features.

I'd painstakingly examined the hair, searching for fibers or other trace evidence. As I separated the damp strands, I couldn't help imagining the last time the victim had combed it, wondering if she'd been pleased, frustrated, indifferent. Good hair day. Bad hair day. Dead hair day.

Suppressing these thoughts, I bagged the sample and sent it up to biology for microscopic analysis. The plunger and plastic bags had also been turned over to the Laboratoire des Sciences Judiciaires where they'd be checked for prints, traces of bodily fluids, or other minuscule indicators of killer or victim.

Three hours on our hands and knees the previous night feeling through mud, combing through grass and leaves, and turning over rocks and logs had yielded nothing else. We'd searched until darkness

closed us down, but came away empty. No clothing.
No shoes. No jewelry. No personal effects. The
crime scene recovery team would return to dig and
sift today, but I doubted they'd find anything. I
would have no manufacturer's tags or labels, no
zippers or buckles, no jewelry, no weapons or bind-
ings, no slashes or entrance holes in clothing to
corroborate my findings. The body had been
dumped, naked and mutilated, stripped of everything that linked it to a life.

I returned to the body bag for the rest of its
grisly contents, ready to start my preliminary examination. Later, the limbs and torso would be
cleaned, and I would do a complete analysis of all
the bones. We'd recovered almost the whole skeleton. The killer had made that task easier. As with
the head and torso, he, or she, had placed the arms
and legs in separate plastic bags. There were four
in all. Very tidy. Packaged and discarded like last
week's garbage. I filed the outrage in another place
and forced myself to concentrate.

I removed the dismembered segments and arranged them in anatomical order on the stainless
steel autopsy table in the middle of the room. First,
I transferred the torso and centered it, breast side
up. It held together reasonably well. Unlike the bag
holding the head, those containing the body parts
had not stayed tightly sealed. The torso was in the
worst shape, the bones held together only by leath-
erized bands of dried muscle and ligament. I noted
that the uppermost vertebrae were missing, and
hoped I'd find them attached to the head. Except
for traces, the internal organs were long gone.

Next, I placed the arms to the sides and the legs
below. The limbs hadn't been exposed to sunlight,
and weren't as desiccated as the chest and abdomen. They retained large portions of putrefied soft

tissue. I tried to ignore the seething blanket of pale yellow that made a languid, wavelike retreat from the surface of each limb as I withdrew it from the body bag. Maggots will abandon a corpse when exposed to light. They were dropping from the body to the table, from the table to the floor, in a slow but steady drizzle. Pale yellow grains of rice lay writhing by my feet. I avoided stepping on them. I'd never really gotten used to them.

I reached for my clipboard and began to fill in the form. Name: *Inconnue.* Unknown. Date of autopsy: June 3, 1994. Investigators: Luc Claudel, Michel Charbonneau, *Section des homicides,* CUM. Homicide division, Montreal Urban Community Police.

I added the police report number, the morgue number, and the Laboratoire de Médecine Légale, or LML, number and experienced my usual wave of anger at the arrogant indifference of the system. Violent death allows no privacy. It plunders one's dignity as surely as it has taken one's life. The body is handled, scrutinized, and photographed, with a new series of digits allocated at each step. The victim becomes part of the evidence, an exhibit, on display for police, pathologists, forensic specialists, lawyers, and, eventually, jurors. Number it. Photograph it. Take samples. Tag the toe. While I am an active participant, I can never accept the impersonality of the system. It is like looting on the most personal level. At least I would give this victim a name. Death in anonymity would not be added to the list of violations he or she would suffer.

I selected a form from those on the clipboard. I'd alter my normal routine and leave the full skeletal inventory for later. For now the detectives wanted only the ID profile: sex, age, and race.

Race was pretty straightforward. The hair was

red, what skin remained appeared fair. Decomposition, however, could do strange things. I'd check the skeletal details after cleaning. For now Caucasoid seemed a safe bet.

I already suspected the victim was female. The facial features were delicate, the overall body build slight. The long hair meant nothing.

I looked at the pelvis. Turning it to the side I noted that the notch below the hip blade was broad and shallow. I repositioned it so that I could see the pubic bones, the region in front where the right and left halves of the pelvis meet. The curve formed by their lower borders was a wide arch. Delicate raised ridges cut across the front of each pubic bone, creating distinct triangles in the lower corners. Typical female features. Later I'd take measurements and run discriminant function analyses on the computer, but I had no doubt these were the remains of a woman.

I was wrapping the pubic area in a wet rag when the sound of the phone startled me. I hadn't realized how quiet it was. Or how tense I was. I walked to the desk, zigzagging through maggots like a child playing jacks.

"Dr. Brennan," I answered, pushing the goggles to the top of my head and dropping into the chair. Using my pen, I flicked a maggot from the desktop.

"Claudel," a voice said. One of the two CUM detectives assigned to the case. I looked at the wall clock—ten-forty. Later than I realized. He didn't go on. Obviously he assumed his name was message enough.

"I'm working on her right now," I said. I could hear a metallic grating sound. "I shou—"

"*Elle?*" he interrupted. Female?

"Yes." I watched another maggot contract into

a crescent, then double back on itself and repeat the maneuver in the opposite direction. Not bad.

"White?"

"Yes."

"Age?"

"I should be able to give you a range within an hour."

I could picture him looking at his watch.

"Okay. I'll be there after lunch." Click. It was a statement, not a request. Apparently it didn't matter if it was okay with me.

I hung up and returned to the lady on the table. Picking up the clipboard, I flipped to the next page on the report form. Age. This was an adult. Earlier, I'd checked her mouth. The wisdom teeth were fully erupted.

I examined the arms where they'd been detached at the shoulders. The end of each humerus was fully formed. I could see no line demarcating a separate cap on either side. The other ends were useless—they had been cleanly severed just above the wrists. I'd have to find those fragments later. I looked at the legs. The head of the femur was also completely formed on both right and left.

Something about those severed joints disturbed me. It was a feeling apart from the normal reaction to depravity, but it was vague, ill-formed. As I allowed the left leg to settle back onto the table my guts felt like ice. The cloud of dread that first touched me in the woods returned. I shook it off and forced myself to focus on the question at hand. Age. Fix the age. A correct age estimate can lead to a name. Nothing else will matter until she has a name.

I used a scalpel to peel back the flesh around the knee and elbow joints. It came away easily. Here, too, the long bones were fully mature. I'd verify this on X ray, but knew it meant bone growth had been completed. I saw no lipping or arthritic change in the joints. Adult, but young. It was consistent with the lack of wear I'd observed on the teeth.

But I wanted more precision. Claudel would expect it. I looked at each collarbone where it met the sternum at the base of the throat. Though the one on the right was detached, the joint surface was encased in a hard knot of dried cartilage and ligament. Using a scissors, I snipped away as much of the leathery tissue as I could, then wrapped the bone in another wet rag. I returned my attention to the pelvis.

I removed that rag and, again using a scalpel, began gently sawing through the cartilage connecting the two halves in front. Wetting it down had made it more pliable, easier to cut, but still the process was slow and tedious. I didn't want to risk damaging the underlying surfaces. When the pubic bones were finally separate, I cut the few strips of dried muscle uniting the pelvis to the lower end of the spine in back, freed it, carried it to the sink, and submerged the pubic portion in water.

Next I returned to the body and unwrapped the collarbone. Again, I teased off as much tissue as possible. Then I filled a plastic specimen container with water, positioned it against the rib cage, and stuck the end of the clavicle in it.

I glanced at the wall clock—12:25 P.M. Stepping back from the table, I peeled off my gloves and straightened. Slowly. My back felt like a Pop Warner league had been practicing on it. I placed my hands on my hips and stretched, arching backward and rotating my upper body. It didn't really relieve the pain, but it didn't hurt either. My spine seemed to hurt a lot lately, and bending over an autopsy

24

table for three hours tended to aggravate it. I refused to believe or admit it was age-related. My newly discovered need for reading glasses and the seemingly permanent upgrade from 115 to 120 in my weight were likewise not the result of aging. Nothing was.

I turned to see Daniel, one of the autopsy technicians, watching from the outer office. A tic pulled his upper lip, and his eyes pinched shut momentarily. With a jerk he shifted, placing all his weight on one leg and cocking the other. He looked like a sandpiper waiting out a wave.

"When would you like me to do the radiography?" he asked. His glasses rode low on his nose and he seemed to peer over rather than through them.

"I should finish up by three," I said, tossing my gloves into the biological waste receptacle. I suddenly realized how hungry I was. My morning coffee sat on the counter, cold and untouched. I'd completely forgotten it.

"Okay." He hopped backward, pivoted, and disappeared down the hall.

I flipped the goggles onto the counter, withdrew a white paper sheet from a drawer below the side counter, unfolded it, and covered the body. After washing my hands I returned to my office on the fifth floor, changed into street clothes, and went out for lunch. This was rare for me, but today I needed the sunshine.

Claudel was true to his word. When I returned at one-thirty he was already in my office. He sat opposite my desk, his attention focused on the reconstructed skull on my worktable. He turned his head when he heard me, but said nothing. I hung my coat on the back of the door and moved past him and into my chair.

"Bonjour, Monsieur Claudel. *Comment ça va?"* I smiled at him across my desk.

"Bonjour." Apparently, he was uninterested in how I was doing. Okay. I waited. I would not succumb to his charm.

A folder lay on the desk in front of him. He placed his hand on it and looked at me. His face brought to mind a parrot. The features angled sharply from his ears to the midline, plunging forward into a beaklike nose. Along this apex his chin, his mouth, and the tip of his nose pointed downward in a series of V's. When he smiled, which was rare, the V of his mouth sharpened, and the lips drew in, rather than back.

He sighed. He was being very patient with me. I hadn't worked with Claudel before, but knew his reputation. He thought himself an exceptionally intelligent man.

"I have several names," he said. "Possibles. They all disappeared within the last six months."

We'd already discussed the question of time since death. My morning's work hadn't changed my mind. I was certain she'd been dead less than three months. That would place the murder in March or later. Winters are cold in Quebec, hard on the living but kind to the dead. Frozen bodies do not decay. Nor do they attract bugs. Had she been dumped last fall, before the onset of winter, there would've been signs of insect infestation. The presence of casings or larvae would've indicated an aborted fall invasion. There were none. Given that it had been a warm spring, the abundance of maggots and the degree of deterioration were consistent with an interval of three months or less. The presence of connective tissue along with the virtual absence of viscera and brain matter also suggested a late winter, early spring death.

I leaned back and looked at him expectantly. I could be cagey too. He opened the folder and thumbed through its contents. I waited.

Selecting one of the forms, he read, "Myriam Weider." There was a pause as he sifted through the information on the form. "Disappeared April 4, 1994." Pause. "Female. White." Long pause. "Date of birth 9/6/48."

We both calculated mentally—forty-five years old.

"Possible," I said, gesturing with my hand for him to go on.

He laid the form on the desk and read from the next. "Solange Leger. Reported missing by the husband," he paused, straining to make out the date, "May 2, 1994. Female. White. Date of birth 8/17/28."

"No." I shook my head. "Too old."

He placed the form at the back of the folder and selected another. "Isabelle Gagnon. Last seen April 1, 1994. Female. White. Date of birth 1/15/71."

"Twenty-three. Yeah." I nodded slowly. "Possible." It went on the desk.

"Suzanne St. Pierre. Female. Missing since March 9, 1994." His lips moved as he read. "Failed to return from school." He paused, calculating on his own. "Age sixteen. Jesus Christ."

Again I shook my head. "She's too young. This isn't a kid."

He frowned, pulling out the last form. "Evelyn Fontaine. Female. Age thirty-six. Last seen in Sept Îles on March 28. Oh yeah. She's an Innu."

"Doubtful," I said. I didn't think the remains were those of an Indian.

"That's it," he said. There were two forms on the

desk. Myriam Weider, age forty-five, and Isabelle Gagnon, age twenty-three. Maybe one of them was lying downstairs in room 4. Claudel looked at me. His eyebrows rose in the middle forming yet another V, this one inverted.

"How old *was* she?" he asked, emphasizing the verb and his long-suffering patience.

"Let's go downstairs and see." That'll bring a little sunshine into your day, I thought.

It was petty but I couldn't help it. I knew Claudel's reputation for avoiding the autopsy room, and I wanted to discomfort him. For a moment he looked trapped. I enjoyed his unease. Grabbing a lab coat from the hook on the door, I hurried down the hall and inserted my key for the elevator. He was silent as we descended. He looked like a man on the way to a prostate exam. Claudel rarely rode this elevator. It stopped only at the morgue.

The body lay undisturbed. I gloved and removed the white sheet. From the corner of my eye I could see Claudel framed in the doorway. He'd entered the room just far enough to be able to say he'd been there. His eyes wandered over the steel countertops, the glass-fronted cabinets with their stock of clear plastic containers, the hanging scale, everything but the body. I'd seen it before. Photographs were no threat. The blood and gore were somewhere else. Distant. The murder scene was a clinical exercise. No problem. Dissect it, study it, solve the puzzle. But place a body on an autopsy table and it was a different matter. Claudel had put his face in neutral, hoping to look calm.

I removed the pubic bones from the water and gently pried them apart. Using a probe, I teased around the edges of the gelatinous sheath that covered the right pubic face. Gradually it loosened its hold and came away. The underlying bone was marked with deep furrows and ridges coursing horizontally across its surface. A sliver of solid bone partially framed the outer margin, forming a delicate and incomplete rim around the pubic face. I repeated the process on the left. It was identical.

Claudel hadn't moved from the doorway. I carried the pelvis to the Luxolamp, pulled the extensor arm toward me, and pressed the switch. Fluorescent light illuminated the bone. Through the round magnifying glass, details appeared that hadn't been apparent to the naked eye. I looked at the uppermost curve of each hipbone and saw what I'd been expecting.

"Monsieur Claudel," I said without looking up. "Look at this."

He came up behind me, and I moved over to allow him an unobstructed view. I pointed to an irregularity on the upper border of the hip. The iliac crest was in the process of attaching itself when death had occurred.

I set the pelvis down. He continued looking at it, but didn't touch it. I returned to the body to examine the clavicle, certain of what I'd find. I withdrew the sternal end from the water and began to tease away the tissue. When I could see the joint surface I gestured for Claudel to join me. Wordlessly I pointed to the end of the bone. Its surface was billowy, like the pubic face. A small disk of bone clung to the center, its edges distinct and unfused.

"So?" Sweat beaded his forehead. He was hiding his nervousness with bravado.

"She's young. Probably early twenties."

I could have explained how bone reveals age, but I didn't think he'd be a good listener, so I just waited. Particles of cartilage clung to my gloved hands, and I held them away from my body, palms up, like a panhandler. Claudel kept the same distance he would with an Ebola patient. His eyes stayed on me, but their focus shifted to thoughts inside his head as he ran through the data, looking for a match.

"Gagnon." It was a statement, not a question.

I nodded. Isabelle Gagnon. Age twenty-three.

"I'll have the coroner request dental records," he said.

I nodded again. He seemed to bring it out in me.

"Cause of death?" he asked.

"Nothing apparent," I said. "I may know more when I see the X rays. Or I may see something on the bones when they're cleaned."

With that he left. He didn't say good-bye. I didn't expect it. His departure was mutually appreciated.

I stripped off my gloves and tossed them. On the way out I poked my head into the large autopsy suite and told Daniel I was finished with this case for the day. I asked him to take full body and cranial X rays, A-P and lateral views. Upstairs I stopped by the histology lab and told the head technician that the body was ready for boiling, warning him to take extra care since this was a dismemberment. It was unnecessary. No one could reduce a body like Denis. In two days a skeleton would appear, clean and undamaged.

I spent the rest of the afternoon with the glued-together skull. Though fragmentary, there was, indeed, enough detail to confirm the identity of its owner. He wouldn't drive any more propane tankers.

Returning home, I began to feel the sense of foreboding I'd experienced in the ravine. All day I'd used work to keep it at bay. I'd banished the

apprehension by centering my mind fully on identifying the victim and on piecing together the late
trucker. At lunch the park pigeons had been my
distraction. Unraveling the pecking order could be
all-consuming. Gray was alpha. Brown speckles
seemed to be next. Blackfoot was clearly low on
the list.

Now I was free to relax. To think. To worry. It
started as soon as I pulled into the garage and
turned off the radio. Music off, anxiety on. No, I
admonished myself. Later. After dinner.

I entered the apartment and heard the reassuring
beep of the security system. Leaving my briefcase
in the entry hall, I closed the door and walked
to the Lebanese restaurant on the corner, where I
ordered a Shish Taouk and Shawarma plate to go.
It's what I love most about living downtown—
within a block of my condo are representative samples of all the cuisines of the world. Could the
weight gain . . . ? Nah.

While I waited for the take-out I perused the buffet selections. Homos. Taboule. *Feuilles de vignes.*
Bless the global village. Lebanese gone French.

A shelf to the left of the cash register held bottles
of red wine. My weapon of choice. As I looked at
them, for the thousandth time I felt the craving. I
remembered the taste, the smell, the dry, tangy feel
of the wine on my tongue. I remembered the
warmth that would start in my gut and spread upward and outward, navigating a path through my
body, lighting the fires of well-being along its
course. The bonfires of control. Of vigor. Of invin-
cibility. I could use that right now, I thought. Right.
Who was I kidding? I wouldn't stop there. What
were those stages? I'd move right on to bulletproof
and then to invisible. Or was it the other way
around? No matter. I'd carry it too far, and then

the crash would come. The comfort would be short term, the price heavy. It'd been six years since I'd had a drink.

I took my food home and ate it with Birdie and the Montreal Expos. He slept, curled in my lap, purring softly. They lost to the Cubs by two runs. Neither mentioned the murder. I appreciated that.

I took a long, hot bath and fell into bed at ten-thirty. Alone in the dark and quiet I could no longer suppress the thought. Like cells gone mad, it grew and gathered strength, finally forcing itself into my consciousness, insisting on recognition. The other homicide. The other young woman who'd come to the morgue in pieces. I saw her in vivid detail, remembered my feelings as I'd worked on her bones. Chantale Trottier. Age: sixteen. Strangled, beaten, decapitated, dismembered. Less than a year ago she'd arrived naked and packaged in plastic garbage bags.

I was ready to end the day but my mind refused to clock out. I lay there as mountains formed and the continental plates shifted. Finally, I fell asleep, the phrase ricocheting in my skull. It would haunt me all weekend. Serial murder.

3

GABBY WAS CALLING MY FLIGHT.
I had an enormous suitcase and couldn't maneuver
it down the jetway. The other passengers were annoyed, but no one was helping me. I could see Katy
leaning out to watch me from the front row of first
class. She was wearing the dress we'd chosen for
her high school graduation. Moss green silk. But
she'd told me later she didn't like it, regretted the
choice. She would've preferred the floral print.
Why was she wearing it? Why was Gabby at the
airport when she should have been at the university? Her voice over the loudspeaker was becoming
louder, more strident.

I sat up. It was seven-twenty. Monday morning.
Light illuminated the edges of the window shade,
but little seeped into the room.

Gabby's voice continued. ". . . but I knew I
wouldn't be able to get ya later. Guess you're an
earlier riser than I thought. Anyway, about to . . ."

I picked up the phone. "Hello." I tried to sound less groggy than I was. The voice stopped in midsentence.

"Temp? Is that you?"

I nodded.

"Did I wake ya?"

"Yes." I was not yet up to a witty response.

"Sorry. Should I call back later?"

"No, no. I'm up." I resisted adding that I'd had to get up to answer the phone anyway.

"Butt outa bed, babe. Early worm time. Listen, about tonight. Could we make it se—" A high-pitched screech interrupted her.

"Hang on. I must've left the answering machine on automatic." I set down the receiver and walked to the living room. The red light was flashing. I picked up the portable handset, returned to the bedroom, and replaced that receiver in its cradle.

"Okay." By now I was fully awake and starting to crave coffee. I headed for the kitchen.

"I was calling about tonight." Her voice had an edge to it. I couldn't blame her. She'd been trying to finish one sentence for five minutes now.

"I'm sorry, Gabby. I spent the whole weekend reading a student thesis, and I was up pretty late last night. I was really sound asleep. I didn't even hear the phone ring." That was odd, even for me. "What's up?"

"About tonight. Uh, could we make it seven-thirty instead of seven? This project has me jumpier than a cricket in a lizard cage."

"Sure. No problem. That's probably better for me too." Cradling the phone on my shoulder, I reached into the cabinet for the jar of coffee beans, and transferred three scoops to the grinder.

"Want me to pick ya up?" she asked.

"Either way. I can drive if you want. Where

should we go?" I considered grinding, decided against it. She already sounded a little touchy.

Silence. I could picture her playing with her nose ring as she thought it over. Or today it might be a stud. At first it had bothered me, and I'd had difficulty concentrating in conversations with Gabby. I'd find myself focusing on the ring, wondering how much pain was involved in piercing one's nose. I no longer noticed.

"It should be nice tonight," she said. "How 'bout someplace we can eat outside? Prince Arthur or St. Denis?"

"Great," I said. "No reason for you to come down here, then. I'll be by about seven-thirty. Think of someplace new. I feel like something exotic."

Though it could be risky with Gabby, that was our usual routine. She knew the city much better than I, so the choice of restaurant usually fell to her.

"Okay. *À plus tard.*"

"*À plus tard,*" I responded. I was surprised and a bit relieved. Normally she'd stay on the phone forever. I often had to manufacture excuses to escape.

The telephone has always been a lifeline for Gabby and me. I associate her with the phone as I do no one else. This pattern was set early in our friendship. Our graduate student conversations were a strange relief from the melancholy that enveloped me in those years. My daughter Katy finally fed, bathed, and in her crib, Gabby and I would log hours on the line, sharing the excitement of a newly discovered book, discussing our classes, professors, fellow students, and nothing in particular. It was the only frivolity we allowed ourselves in a nonfrivolous time in our lives.

Though we talk less frequently now, the pattern has altered little in the decades since. Together or apart, we are there for each other's highs and lows. It was Gabby who talked me through the AA days, when need for a drink colored my waking hours and brought me to at night, trembling and sweating. It is me whom Gabby dials, exhilarated and hopeful when love enters her life, lonely and despairing when, once again, it leaves.

When the coffee was ready I took it to the glass table in the dining room. Memories of Gabby were replaying in my mind. I always smiled when I thought of her. Gabby in grad seminar. Gabby at the Pit. Gabby at the dig, red kerchief askew, hennaed dreadlocks swinging as she scraped the dirt with her trowel. At six foot one she understood early that she'd never be a conventional beauty. She didn't try to become thin or tan. She didn't shave her legs or armpits. Gabby was Gabby. Gabrielle Macaulay from Trois-Rivières, Quebec. French mother, English father.

We'd been close in grad school. She'd hated physical anthropology, suffered through the courses I loved. I felt the same about her ethnology seminars. When we left Northwestern I'd gone to North Carolina and she'd returned to Quebec. We'd seen little of each other over the years, but the phone had kept us close. It was largely because of Gabby that I'd been offered a visiting professorship at McGill in 1990. During that year I'd begun working at the lab part time, and had continued the arrangement after returning to North Carolina, commuting North every six weeks as the caseload dictated. This year I had taken a leave of absence from UNC-Charlotte, and was in Montreal full time. I'd missed being with Gabby, and was enjoying the renewal of our friendship.

The flashing light on the answering machine caught my eye. There must've been a call before Gabby. I had it set to answer after four rings unless the tape had already been triggered. Then it would pick up after one. Wondering how I could've slept through four rings and an entire message, I went over and pressed the button. The tape rewound, engaged, and played. Silence, then a click. A short beep followed, then Gabby's voice. It was only a hang-up. Good. I hit rewind and went to dress for work.

The medico-legal lab is located in what is known as the QPP or SQ building, depending on your linguistic preference. To anglophones, it is the Quebec Provincial Police—to francophones, La Sûreté du Québec. The Laboratoire de Médecine Légale, similar to a medical examiner's office in the States, shares the fifth floor with the Laboratoire des Sciences Judiciaires, the central crime lab for the province. Together the LML and the LSJ make up a unit known as La Direction de l'Expertise Judiciaire—DEJ. There is a jail on the fourth and top three floors of the building. The morgue and autopsy suites are in the basement. The provincial police occupy the remaining eight floors.

This arrangement has its advantages. We're all together. If I need an opinion on fibers, or a report on a soil sample, a walk down the corridor takes me directly to the source. It also has its drawbacks in that we are easily accessible. For an SQ investigator, or a city detective dropping off evidence or paperwork, it is a short elevator ride to our offices.

Witness that morning. Claudel was waiting at my office door when I arrived. He was carrying a small brown envelope and repeatedly tapped its edge against the palm of his hand. To say he looked agitated would be like saying Gandhi looked hungry.

"I have the dental records," he said in way of greeting. He flourished the envelope like a presenter at the Academy Awards.

"I picked them up myself."

He read a name scrawled on the outside. "Dr. Nguyen. He's got an office over in Rosemont. I would have been here earlier but the guy's got a real cretin of a secretary."

"Coffee?" I asked. Though I'd never met Dr. Nguyen's secretary I felt empathy for her. I knew she hadn't had a good morning.

He opened his mouth to accept or decline. I don't know which. At that moment Marc Bergeron rounded the corner. Seemingly unaware of our presence, he strode past the row of shiny black office doors, stopping one short of mine. Crooking a knee, he placed his briefcase on the upraised thigh. I thought of the crane maneuver in the *Karate Kid*. Thus poised, he clicked the case open, rummaged among its contents, and withdrew a set of keys.

"Marc?"

It startled him. He slammed the case shut and swung it down, all in one movement.

"Bien fait," I said, suppressing a smile.

"Merci." He looked at Claudel and me, the briefcase in his left hand, the keys in his right.

Marc Bergeron was, by any standard, peculiar-looking. In his late fifties or early sixties, his long, bony frame was slightly stooped, bent forward at midchest as if perpetually ready to absorb a blow to the stomach. His hair started midway back on his scalp and exploded in a corona of white frizz. It brought him to well over six foot three. His wire-rimmed glasses were always greasy and speckled with dust, and he often squinted, as though reading the fine print on a rebate coupon. He looked more like a Tim Burton creation than a forensic dentist.

"Monsieur Claudel has the dental records for Gagnon," I said, indicating the detective. Claudel raised the envelope, as if in proof.

Nothing clicked behind the smudged lenses. Bergeron regarded me blankly. He looked like a tall, confused dandelion, with his long, thin stem and puff of white hair. I realized he knew nothing about the case.

Bergeron was among the professionals employed part time by the LML, each a forensic specialist consulted for specific expertise. Neuropathology. Radiology. Microbiology. Odontology. He normally came to the lab once a week. The rest of the time he saw patients in private practice. He hadn't been here last week.

I summarized. "Last Thursday workers found some bones on the grounds of Le Grand Séminaire. Pierre LaManche thought it was another historic cemetery situation and sent me over. It wasn't."

He set down the briefcase and listened intently.

"I found parts of a dismembered body that had been bagged and dumped, probably within the last couple of months. It's a female, white, probably in her early twenties."

Claudel's envelope tapping had become more rapid. It stopped momentarily as hc looked pointedly at his watch. He cleared his throat.

Bergeron looked at him, then back at me. I continued.

"Monsieur Claudel and I narrowed the possibles to one we think is pretty good. The profile fits and the timing is reasonable. He drove the records in himself. A Dr. Nguyen over in Rosemont. Know him?"

Bergeron shook his head and extended a long, skinny hand. *"Bon,"* he said. "Give them to me. I'll have a look at them. Has Denis done X rays yet?"

"Daniel did them," I said. "They should be on your desk."

He unlocked the door to his office. Claudel followed. Through the open door I could see a small brown envelope lying on his desk. Bergeron picked it up and checked the case number. From where I stood I could see Claudel charting the room, like a monarch, deciding on a place to light.

"You may call me in an hour, Monsieur Claudel," Bergeron said.

The detective stopped in mid-chart. He started to speak, then pressed his lips into a thin, tight line, readjusted his cuffs, and left. For the second time in minutes I suppressed a smile. Bergeron would never tolerate an investigator peering over his shoulder as he worked. Claudel had just learned that.

Bergeron's gaunt face reappeared. "Coming in?" he asked.

"Sure," I said. "Coffee?" I still hadn't had any since getting to work. We often got it for each other, taking turns making the trek to the kitchenette in the other wing.

"Great." He dug out his mug and handed it to me. "I'll get set up here."

I got my own mug and started down the corridor. I was pleased at his invitation. We often worked the same cases, the decomposed, burned, mummified, or skeletonized, the dead who could not be identified by normal means. I thought we worked well together. It seemed he agreed.

When I returned, two sets of small black squares lay on the light box. Each X ray showed a segment of jaw, the dentition bright against a stark black background. I remembered the teeth as I'd first seen them in the woods, their flawlessness in sharp contrast to the grisly context. They looked different now. Sanitized. Neatly lined up in rows, ready for inspection. The familiar shapes of crowns, roots, and pulp chambers were illuminated in differing intensities of gray and white.

Bergeron began by arranging the antemortem radiographs to the right and the postmortem to the left. His long, bony fingers located a small bump on each X ray, and, one by one, he oriented them, placing the dot face up. When he'd finished, each antemortem radiograph lay in identical alignment to its postmortem counterpart.

He compared the two sets for discrepancies. Everything matched. Neither series showed missing teeth. All roots were complete to their tips. The outlines and curvatures on the left mirrored perfectly those on the right. But most noticeable were the stark white globs representing dental restorations. The constellation of shapes on the antemortem films was mimicked in detail on the films Daniel had taken.

After studying the X rays for what seemed an interminable time, Bergeron selected a square from the right, placed it over the corresponding postmortem X ray, and positioned it for my inspection. The irregular patterns on the molars superimposed exactly. He swiveled to face me.

"C'est positif," he said, leaning back and placing an elbow on the table. "Unofficially, of course, until I finish with the written records." He reached for his coffee. He would do an exhaustive comparison of the written records in addition to a more detailed X-ray comparison, but he had no doubt. This was Isabelle Gagnon.

I was glad I wouldn't be the one to face the

KATHY REICHS

parents. The husband. The lover. The son. I'd been
present at such meetings. I knew the look. The
eyes, pleading. Tell me this is a mistake. A bad
dream. Make it end. Say it isn't so. Then, comprehension. In a millisecond, the world changed
forever.

"Thanks for looking at this right away, Marc," I
said. "And thanks for the preliminary."

"I wish they could all be this easy." He took a
sip of coffee, grimaced, and shook his head.

"Do you want me to deal with Claudel?" I tried
to keep the distaste out of my voice. Apparently I
didn't succeed. He smiled knowingly.

"I have no doubt you can handle Monsieur
Claudel."

"Right," I said. "That's what he needs. A
handler."

I could hear him laughing as I returned to my
office.

My grandmother always told me there is good in
everyone. "Just look fer it . . ." she'd say, the
brogue smooth as satin, ". . . and ye'll find it. Everyone has a virtue." Gran, you never met Claudel.

Claudel's virtue was promptness. He was back in
fifty minutes.

He stopped in Bergeron's office, and I could hear
their voices through the wall. My name was repeated several times as Bergeron forwarded him to
me. Claudel's cadence signaled irritation. He
wanted a real opinion, but now he'd have to settle
for me again. He appeared seconds later, his face
hard.

Neither of us offered greeting. He waited at
the door.

"It's positive," I said. "Gagnon."

He frowned, but I could see excitement collecting in his eyes. He had a victim. Now he could begin the investigation. I wondered if he felt anything for the dead woman or if it was all an exercise for him. Find the bad guy. Outwit the perp. I'd heard the banter, the comments, the jokes made over a victim's battered body. For some it was a way to deal with the obscenity of violence, a protective barrier against the daily reality of human slaughter. Morgue humor. Mask the horror in male bravado. For others it went deeper. I suspected Claudel was among the others.

I watched him for several seconds. Down the hall a phone rang. Though I truly disliked the man, I forced myself to admit that his opinion of me mattered. I wanted his approval. I wanted him to like me. I wanted all of them to accept me, to admit me to the club.

An image of Dr. Lentz flashed into my mind, a hologram psychologist, lecturing from the past.

"Tempe," she would say, "you are the child of an alcoholic father. You are searching for the attention he denied you. You want Daddy's approval, so you try to please everybody."

She made me see it, but she couldn't correct it. I had to do that on my own. Occasionally I overcompensated, and many found me a genuine pain in the ass. This had not been the case with Claudel. I realized I'd been avoiding a confrontation.

I took a deep breath and began, choosing my words carefully.

"Monsieur Claudel, have you considered the possibility that this murder is connected to others that have taken place during the past two years?"

His features froze, the lips drawn in so tightly against his teeth as to be almost invisible. A cloud of red began at his collar and spread slowly up his neck and face. His voice was icy.

"Such as?" He held himself absolutely still.

"Such as Chantale Trottier," I continued. "She was killed in October of '93. Dismembered, decapitated, disemboweled." I looked directly at him. "What was left of her was found wrapped in plastic trash bags."

He raised both hands to the level of his mouth, clasped them together, fingers intertwined, and tapped them against his lips. His perfectly chosen gold cuff links, in his perfectly fitted designer shirt, clinked faintly. He looked straight at me.

"Ms. Brennan," he said, emphasizing the English label. "Perhaps you should stick to your area of expertise. I think we would recognize any links which might exist between crimes under our jurisdiction. These murders share nothing in common."

Ignoring the demotion, I forged on. "They were both women. They were both murdered within the past year. Both bodies showed signs of mutilation or attempt—"

His carefully constructed dam of control ruptured, and his anger rushed at me in a torrent.

"Tabernac!" he exploded. "Do you wo—"

His lips pursed to form the despised word, but he stopped himself just in time. With a visible effort, he regained his composure.

"Do you always have to overreact?"

"Think about it," I spat at him. I was trembling in rage as I got up to close the door.

44

4

IT SHOULD HAVE FELT GOOD just to sit in the steam room and sweat. Like broccoli. That had been my intention. Three miles on the StairMaster, a round on the Nautilus, then vegetate. Like the rest of the day, the gym was not living up to my expectations. The workout had dissipated some of my anger, but I was still agitated. I knew Claudel was an asshole. It was one of the names I'd stomped on his chest with each pump of the StairMaster. Asshole. Dickhead. Moron. Two syllables worked best. I'd figured that out, but little else. It distracted me for a while, but now that my mind was idle I couldn't drive the murders out. Isabelle Gagnon. Chantale Trottier. I kept rolling them around, like peas on a dinner plate.

I shifted my towel, and allowed my brain to reprocess the events of the day. When Claudel left, I'd checked with Denis to see when Gagnon's skeleton would be ready. I wanted to go over every inch of it for signs of trauma. Fractures. Gashes. Anything. Something about the way the body had been carved up bothered me. I wanted a close look at those cut marks. There was a problem with the boiling unit. The bones wouldn't be ready until tomorrow.

Next I'd gone to the central files and pulled the jacket for Trottier. I spent the rest of the afternoon poring over police accounts, autopsy findings, toxicology reports, photos. Something lingered in my memory cells, nagging at me, insisting the cases were linked. Some forgotten detail hovered just beyond recall, coupling the victims in a way I didn't understand. Some stored memory that I couldn't access told me it wasn't just the mutilation and bagging. I wanted to find the connection.

I readjusted my towel and wiped sweat from my face. The skin on my fingertips had gathered into little puckers. Everywhere else I was slick as a perch. I was definitely a short-timer. I couldn't take the heat for more than twenty minutes, no matter what the alleged benefits. Five more.

Chantale Trottier had been killed less than a year ago, in the fall of my first year full time at the lab. She was sixteen. I'd spread the autopsy photos on my desk this afternoon, but I didn't need them. I remembered her vividly, remembered in crisp detail the day she'd arrived at the morgue.

October 22, the afternoon of the oyster party. It was a Friday and most of the staff had quit early to drink beer and shuck their way through the crates of Malpeques that are an autumn tradition.

Through the crowd in the conference room I noticed LaManche talking on the phone. He held a hand over his free ear as a barricade against the party noise. I watched him. When he hung up he did a visual sweep of the room. Spotting me, he signaled with one hand, indicating that I should meet him in the hall. When he located Bergeron and got his attention, he repeated the message. In the elevator, five minutes later, he explained. A young girl had just come in. The body was badly beaten and dismembered. A visual ID would be impossible. He wanted Bergeron to look at the teeth. He wanted me to look at the cuts on the bones.

The mood in the autopsy room was in sharp contrast to the gaiety upstairs. Two SQ detectives stood at a distance while a uniformed officer from the identity section took photos. The technician positioned the remains in silence. The detectives said nothing. There were no jokes or wisecracks. The usual banter was completely stilled. The only sound was the click of the shutter as it recorded the atrocity that lay on the autopsy table.

What was left of her had been arranged to form a body. The six bloody pieces had been placed in correct anatomical order, but the angles were slightly off, turning her into a life-size version of those plastic dolls designed to be twisted into distorted positions. The overall effect was macabre.

Her head had been cut off high on the neck, and the truncated muscles looked bright poppy red. The pallid skin rolled back gently at the severed edges, as if recoiling from contact with the fresh, raw meat. Her eyes were half open, and a delicate trail of dried blood meandered from her right nostril. Her hair was wet and lay plastered against her head. It had been long and blond.

Her trunk was bisected at the waist. The upper torso lay with her arms bent at the elbows, the hands drawn in and resting on her stomach. Coffin position, except her fingers were not intertwined.

Her right hand was partially detached, and the

ends of the creamy white tendons jutted out like snapped electrical cords. Her attacker had been more successful with the left. The technician had placed it beside her head, where it lay alone, the fingers drawn in like the legs of a shriveled spider.

Her chest had been opened lengthwise, from throat to belly, and the pendulous breasts drooped downward toward each side of the rib cage, their weight drawing apart the two halves of divided flesh. The lower section of torso extended from her waist to her knees. Her lower legs rested side by side, positioned below their normal points of attachment. Unfettered by union at the knee joint, they lay with the feet rotated far to the sides, the toes pointed outward.

With a stab of pain, I'd noticed that her toenails were painted a soft pink. The intimacy of that simple act had caused me such an ache that I wanted to cover her, to scream at all of them to leave her alone. Instead, I'd stood and watched, waiting for my turn to trespass.

I could still close my eyes and see the jagged edges of the lacerations on her scalp, evidence of repeated blows with a blunt object. I could recall in minute detail the bruises on her neck. I could visualize the petechial hemorrhages in her eyes, tiny spots left by the bursting of small blood vessels. Caused by tremendous pressure on the jugular vessels, they are the classic sign of strangulation.

My gut had recoiled as I'd wondered what else had happened to her, this woman-child so carefully composed and nurtured by peanut butter, Scout leaders, summer camps, and Sunday schools. I'd grieved for the years she wouldn't be allowed to live, for the proms she'd never attend, and the beers she'd never sneak. We think we are a civilized tribe, we North Americans in the last decade of the second millennium. We'd promised her three score years and ten. We'd allowed her but sixteen.

Shutting out the memories of that painful autopsy, I wiped perspiration from my face and shook my head, whipping my soggy hair back and forth. The mental images were liquefying so that I could no longer separate what I was recalling from the past from what I'd seen in the detail photos that afternoon. Like life. I've long suspected that many of my memories of childhood are actually drawn from old pictures, that they are a composite of snapshots, a mosaic of celluloid images reworked into a remembered reality. Kodak cast backward. Maybe it's better to recall the past that way. We rarely take pictures of sad occasions.

The door opened and a woman entered the steam room. She smiled and nodded, then carefully spread her towel on the bench to my left. Her thighs were the consistency of a sea sponge. I gathered my towel and headed for the shower.

Birdie was waiting when I got home. He watched me from across the entrance hall, his white form reflected softly in the black marble floor. He seemed annoyed. Do cats feel such emotions? Perhaps I was projecting. I checked his bowl and found it low, but not empty. Feeling guilty, I filled it anyway. Birdie had adjusted well to the move. His needs were simple. Me, Friskies Ocean Fish, and sleep. Such wants find no impediment in borders and relocate easily.

I had an hour before I was to meet Gabby so I stretched out on the sofa. The workout and steam had taken their toll, and I felt as if major muscle groups had gone off duty. But exhaustion has its rewards. I was physically, if not mentally, relaxed. As usual at such times I really wanted a drink.

Late afternoon sunlight flooded the room, its effect muted by the bleached muslin sheared across each window. It is what I love most about the apartment. The sunlight melds with the pale pastels to create a bright airiness I find soothing. It is my island of tranquillity in a world of tension.

The apartment is on the ground floor of a U-shaped building, which wraps around an inner courtyard. The unit takes up most of one wing and is free of immediate neighbors. On one side of the living room, French doors open to the courtyard garden. A set opposite gives way to my own small yard. It is an urban rarity—grass and flowers in the heart of Centre-ville. I've even planted a small herb garden.

At first I'd wondered if I'd like living by myself. I'd never done it. I'd gone from home to college to marriage with Pete, raising Katy, never the mistress of my own estate. I need not have worried. I love it.

I was drifting on the boundary between sleep and wakefulness when the phone yanked me back. Headachy from a nap interrupted, I spoke into the receiver. I was rewarded by a robotic voice trying to sell me a cemetery plot.

"Merde," I said, swinging my legs outward and rising from the couch. It is the one drawback to living alone. I talk to myself.

The other drawback is being apart from my daughter. I dialed, and she picked up on the first ring.

"Oh, Mom, I'm so glad you called! How are you? I can't talk now, I've got someone on the other line, but can I catch you a little later?"

I smiled. Katy. Always breathless and spinning in a thousand directions.

"Sure, hon. It's nothing important, just wanted

to say hi. I'm going to dinner with Gabby tonight. How about tomorrow?"

"Great. Give her a big kiss for me. Oh, I think I got an A in French if that's what's on your mind."

"Never doubted it," I said, laughing. "Talk to you tomorrow."

Twenty minutes later I parked in front of Gabby's building. By some miracle there was a spot just opposite her door. I killed the engine and got out.

Gabby lives on Carré St. Louis, a charming little square tucked between Rue St. Laurent and Rue St. Denis. The park is surrounded by row houses with unpredictable shapes and elaborate wood trim, relics of an age of architectural whimsy. Their owners have painted them with rainbow eccentricity and filled their yards with riotous bouquets of summer flowers, making them look like a scene in a Disney animation.

There is an air of capriciousness to the park, from its central fountain, rising from the pool like a giant tulip, to the small wrought-iron fence decorating its perimeter. Little more than knee-high, its frivolous spikes and curlicues separate the public green of the plaza from the gingerbread houses encircling its perimeter. It seemed the Victorians, so prim in their sexual prudery, could be playful in their building design. Somehow, I find this reassuring, a quiet confirmation that there is balance in life.

I glanced at Gabby's building. It stands on the north side of the park, the third one in from Rue Henri-Julien. Katy would have called it "wretched excess," like the prom dresses we'd scorned in our annual spring quest. It seemed the architect couldn't stop until he'd incorporated every fanciful detail he knew.

The building is a three-story brownstone, its lower floors bulging into large bay windows, its roof rising to a truncated hexagonal turret. The roof tower is covered with small oval tiles arranged like the scales on a mermaid's tail. It's topped by a widow's walk bordered in wrought iron. The windows are Moorish, their lower edges square, their upper borders ballooning into domed arches. Every door and window is framed by intricately carved woodwork painted a light shade of lavender. Downstairs, to the left of the bay, an iron staircase sweeps from ground level to a second-story porch, the sworls and loops of its banisters echoing those of the park fence. Early June flowers bloomed in window boxes and in oversized pots lining the porch.

She must have been waiting. Before I could cross the street, the lace curtain flicked momentarily, and the front door opened. She waved, then locked the door and double-checked, shaking the handle vigorously. She swooped down the steep iron staircase, her long skirt billowing behind her like a spinnaker on a downwind run. I could hear her as she drew near. Gabby likes things that sparkle or jangle. That night a ring of small silver bells circled her ankle. It jingled with each step. She dressed in what I'd dubbed Nouveau Ashram in grad school. She always would.

"How ya doing?"

"Good," I hedged.

Even as I was saying it, I knew it wasn't true. But I didn't want to discuss the murders, or Claudel, or my lost trip to Quebec City, or my broken marriage, or anything else that had been plaguing my peace of mind lately.

"You?"

"*Bien.*"

She wagged her head from side to side and the dreadlocks flopped. *Bien. Pas bien.* Just like old times. But not quite. I recognized my own behavior. She was hedging also, wanted to keep the conversation light. Feeling a little blue, but suspecting I'd set the mood, I let it go and joined in the conspiracy of mutual avoidance.

"So, where should we eat?"

I wasn't really changing the subject since there hadn't actually been one.

"What do ya feel like?"

I thought about it. I usually make such choices by imagining food on a plate in front of me. My mind definitely prefers a visual mode. I guess you could say, when it comes to food, it's graphics, not menu, driven. Tonight it wanted something red and heavy.

"Italian?"

"Okay." She considered. "Vivaldi's on Prince Arthur? We can sit outside."

"Perfect. And I won't have to waste this parking place."

We angled across the square, passing beneath the large broadleafs that arch above its lawn. Old men sat on benches, talking in groups, surveying their fellow citizens. A woman in a shower cap fed pigeons from a bag of bread, admonishing them like rowdy children. A pair of foot patrolmen strolled one of the paths that crisscross the park, their hands clasped behind them in identical V's. They stopped periodically to exchange pleasantries, ask questions, respond to quips.

We passed the cement gazebo at the west end of the square. I noted the word "Vespasian," and wondered, once again, why the name of a Roman emperor was carved above its door.

We left the square, crossed Rue Laval, and

passed through a set of cement pillars marking the entrance to Rue Prince Arthur. All this time no words were spoken. This was odd. Gabby wasn't this quiet, or this passive. She was usually bursting with plans and ideas. Tonight she'd simply yielded to my suggestion.

I watched her, discreetly, from the corner of my eye. She was scanning the faces we passed while simultaneously chewing on a thumbnail. The scrutiny didn't appear to be absentminded. She seemed edgy, searching the crowded sidewalks.

The evening was warm and humid, and Prince Arthur was jammed. People swirled and eddied in all directions. The restaurants had thrown open their doors and windows, and the tables spilled out helter skelter, as though someone planned to arrange them later. Men in cotton shirts and women with bare shoulders talked and laughed under brightly colored umbrellas. Others stood in lines, waiting to be seated. I joined the line outside Vivaldi's while Gabby walked to the corner dépanneur to buy a bottle of wine.

When we were finally settled Gabby ordered the fettuccine Alfredo. I asked for veal piccata, spaghetti on the side. Though seduced by the lemon, I remained partially loyal to the vision of red. While we waited for our salads, I sipped a Perrier. We spoke some, moving our mouths, forming words, saying nothing. Mostly we sat. It wasn't the comfortable silence of old friends accustomed to each other, but a dialogue of uneasiness.

I'm as familiar with the ebb and flow of Gabby's moods as I was with my own menstrual cycles. I sensed something tense in her demeanor. Her eyes didn't meet mine, but roved restlessly, continuously exploring as they had in the park. She was obviously distracted. She reached for her wine often.

Each time she lifted her glass the early evening light kindled the Chianti, making it blaze like a Carolina sunset.

I knew the signs. She was drinking too much, trying to blunt the anxiety. Alcohol, the opiate of the troubled. I knew because I'd tried it. The ice in my Perrier was slowly melting, and I watched the lemon resuscitate itself. It dropped from one cube to another with a delicate fizzing sound.

"Gabby, what's up?"

The question startled her.

"Up?"

She gave a short, jittery laugh and brushed a dreadlock from her face. Her eyes were unreadable.

Taking her cue, I moved once again to a neutral topic. She would tell me when she was ready. Or perhaps I was being a coward. The price of intimacy would be its loss.

"Do you hear from anyone from Northwestern?"

We'd met as graduate students in the seventies. I'd been married. Katy was a preschooler. I envied Gabby and the others their freedom back then. I'd missed the bonding experience of all-night parties and early morning philosophy sessions. I was their age but lived in a different world. Gabby was the only one with whom I'd grown close. I've never really known why. We look as different as two women can. We did back then. Perhaps it was because Gabby liked Pete, or, at least, pretended to. Flashback: Pete, military-crisp, surrounded by flower children high on grass and cheap beer. He hated my grad school parties, masked his discomfort behind cocky disdain. Only Gabby had made the effort to break through.

I'd lost contact with all but a few of our classmates. They were scattered across the States now, most at universities and museums. Over the years Gabby had been better at maintaining ties. Or perhaps they sought her out more.

"I hear from Joe now and then. He's teaching at some podunk place in Iowa, I think. Or Idaho." American geography had never been Gabby's strong suit.

"Oh yeah?" I encouraged.

"And Vern's selling real estate in Las Vegas. He came through here for some sort of conference a few months ago. He's out of anthropology and happy as a clam."

She sipped.

"Same hair, though."

This time the laugh sounded genuine. Either the wine or my personal charm was relaxing her.

"Oh, and I got an e-mail message from Jenny. She's thinking of getting back into research. You know she married some yo-yo and gave up a ten-ured position at Rutgers to follow him to the Keys?"

Gabby didn't usually mince words.

"Well, she's gotten some sort of adjunct affiliation and is busting her butt on a grant proposal."

Another sip.

"When he lets her. What gives with Pete?"

The question hit me broadside. Up to this point I'd been very cautious in talking about my failed marriage. It was as if the gears of my speech were jammed on the subject, and releasing them would somehow verify the truth. As if the act of arranging words in rows, of forming sentences, would validate a reality I wasn't quite ready to face. I avoided the topic. Gabby was one of the few I'd told.

"He's fine. We talk."

"People change."

"Yes."

The salads arrived and for a few minutes we concentrated on dressings and pepper grinding. When I looked up she was sitting very still, a forkful of lettuce suspended over her plate. She'd withdrawn from me once again, though this time she seemed to be examining an inner world, rather than the one around her.

I tried another tack.

"Tell me how your project is going." I speared a black olive.

"Huh? Oh, the project. Good. It's going good. I've finally gotten their confidence and some of them are really starting to open up to me."

She took a bite of salad.

"Gabby, I know you've explained this, but tell me again. I'm just a physical sciences type. What exactly is the goal of the research?"

She laughed at the familiar demarcation between the physical and cultural anthropology students. Our class had been small but diverse: some studying ethnology, others taking linguistics, archaeology, and biological anthropology. I knew as little about deconstructionism as she did about mitochondrial DNA.

"Remember the ethnographies Ray made us read? The Yanomamo, and the Semai, and the Nuer? Well, it's the same idea. We're trying to describe the world of the prostitute through close observation and interviews with informants. Field work. Up close and personal." She took another bite of salad. "Who are they? Where do they come from? How do they get into hooking? What do they do on a daily basis? What support networks do they have? How do they fit into the legitimate economy? How do they view themselves? Where—"

"I get it."

Perhaps the wine was having its effect, or perhaps I'd tapped into the one passion in her life. She was becoming more animated. Though it had grown dark I could see that her face was flushed. Her eyes glistened with the light of the streetlamp. Or maybe the alcohol.

"Society has just written these women off. No one's really interested in them, except those who are somehow threatened by them and want them gone."

I nodded as we each took a bite of salad.

"Most people think girls hook because they've been abused, or because they're forced into it, or whatever. Actually, a lot of them do it simply for the money. With limited skills for the legitimate job market, they're never going to make a decent living and they know that. They make a decision to hook for a few years because it's the most profitable thing they can do. Peddling ass pays better than slinging burgers."

More salad.

"And, like any other group, they've got their own subculture. I'm interested in the networks they construct, the mental mapping they do, the support systems they rely on, that sort of thing."

The waiter returned with our entrées.

"What about the men who hire them?"

"What?" The question seemed to unnerve her.

"What about the guys who go down there? They must be an important element in the whole thing. Are you also talking to them?" I rolled a forkful of spaghetti.

"I—Yeah, some," she stammered, clearly flustered. After a pause: "Enough about me, Temp. Tell me what you're working on. Any interesting cases?" Her eyes were focused on her plate.

The shift was so abrupt it caught me off-guard. I answered without thinking.

"These murders have me pretty uptight." I regretted saying it immediately.

"What murders?" Her voice was becoming thick, the words rounded and soft on the edges.

"A pretty nasty one came in last Thursday." I didn't go on. Gabby has never wanted to hear about my work.

"Oh?" She helped herself to more bread. She was being polite. She'd told me about her work, now she'd listen to me talk about mine.

"Yeah. Surprisingly there hasn't been much press. Her body was found off Sherbrooke last week. Came in as an unknown. Turns out she was killed last April."

"That sounds like a lot of your cases. So what's rattling ya?"

I sat back and looked at her, wondering if I really wanted to go into this. Maybe it would be better to talk about it. Better for whom? For me? There was no one else with whom I could do that. Did she really want to hear it?

"The victim was mutilated. Then the body was butchered and thrown into a ravine."

She looked at me without commenting.

"I think the MO is similar to another one I worked on."

"Meaning?"

"I see the same"—I groped for the right word—"elements in both."

"Such as?" She reached for her glass.

"Savage battering, disfiguring the body."

"But that's pretty common, isn't it? When women are the victims? Bash our heads in, choke us, then slash us up? Male Violence 101."

"Yes," I admitted. "And I don't really know the

cause of death in this last one since she was so badly decomposed."

Gabby looked ill at ease. Maybe this was a mistake.

"What else?" She held her wine but didn't drink.

"The mutilation. Cutting up the body. Or removing parts of it. Or . . ." I trailed off, thinking of the plunger. I still wasn't sure what it meant.

"So ya think the same bastard did them both?"

"Yes. I do. But I can't convince the idiot who's working the case. He won't even look into the other one."

"The murders could be the work of one of these dirtbags who gets his rocks off butchering women?"

I answered without looking up. "Yes."

"And ya think he'll do it again?"

Her voice was sharp once more, the velvety edges gone. I put my fork down and looked at her. She was peering at me intently, her head thrust slightly forward, her fingers wrapped tightly around the stem of her wineglass. The glass was trembling, its contents rippling gently.

"Gabby, I'm sorry. I shouldn't have talked about this. Gabby, are you all right?"

She straightened in her seat and set the glass down deliberately, holding on to it a moment before letting go. She continued to stare at me. I signaled the waiter.

"Do you want coffee?"

She nodded her head.

We finished dinner, indulging ourselves in cannoli and cappuccino. She seemed to recover her humor as we laughed and mocked the memory of our student selves in the Age of Aquarius, our hair worn long and straight, our shirts tie-dyed, our jeans slung low on our hips and belled at the ankles, a generation following identical escape routes from conformity. It was past midnight when we left the restaurant.

Walking along Prince Arthur, she brought up the murders again.

"What would this guy be like?"

The question took me by surprise.

"I mean, would he be wacko? Would he be normal? Would ya be able to spot him?"

My confusion was annoying her.

"Could ya pick the fucker out at a church picnic?"

"The killer?"

"Yes."

"I don't know."

She pursued it. "Would he be functional?"

"I think so. If one person did kill both these women, and I don't know that for sure, Gab, he's organized. He plans. Many serial killers fool the world for a long time before they're caught. But I'm not a psychologist. That's pure speculation."

We arrived at the car and I unlocked it. Suddenly she reached over and grabbed my arm. "Let me show ya the strip."

I didn't follow. Again the mental leap had left me out. My mind went into bridge building.

"Uh . . ."

"The red-light district. My project. Let's just drive by and I'll show ya the girls."

I glanced over just as the headlights of an oncoming car caught her. Her face looked strange in the shifting illumination. The light moved across her like the beam of a flashlight, accentuating some features, throwing others into shadow. Her eagerness was persuasive. I looked at my watch—twelve-eighteen.

"Okay." It really wasn't. Tomorrow would be

tough. But she seemed so anxious I didn't have the heart to disappoint her.

She folded herself into the car and slid the seat back to its farthest position. It gave her some leg room, but not enough.

We rode in silence for a couple of minutes. Following her instructions I went west several blocks, then turned south onto St. Urbain. We skirted the easternmost edge of the McGill ghetto, a schizoid amalgam of low-rent student housing, high-rise condos, and gentrified brownstones. Within six blocks I turned left onto Rue Ste. Catherine. Behind me lay the heart of Montreal. In the rearview mirror I could see the looming shapes of Complexe Desjardins and Place des Arts challenging each other from their opposite corners. Below them lay Complexe Guy-Favreau and the Palais des Congrès.

In Montreal, the grandeur of downtown gives way quickly to the squalor of the east end. Rue Ste. Catherine sees it all. Born in the affluence of Westmount, it strides through Centre-ville, eastward to Boulevard St. Laurent, the Main, the dividing line between east and west. Ste. Catherine is home to the Forum, Eaton's, and the Spectrum. Downtown it is lined with high-rises and hotels, with theaters and shopping centers. But at St. Laurent it leaves behind the office complexes and condominiums, the convention centers and boutiques, the restaurants and singles' bars. The hookers and the punks take over from there. Their turf stretches eastward, from the Main to the gay village. They share it with the drug dealers and the skinheads. Tourists and suburbanites venture in as visitors, to gawk and avoid eye contact. They see the other side and reaffirm their separateness. But they don't stay long.

We were almost at St. Laurent when Gabby indicated that I should pull to the right. I found a spot in front of La Boutique du Sex, and turned off the engine. Across the street a group of women clustered outside the Hotel Granada. Its sign offered CHAMBRES TOURISTIQUES, but I doubted any tourists frequented its rooms.

"There," she said. "That's Monique."

Monique was wearing red vinyl boots that reached to midthigh. Black spandex, pulled to its tensile limits, struggled to cover her rump. Through it I could see the line of her panties, and a lumpy ridge formed by the hem of her white polyester blouse. Plastic earrings dangled to her shoulders, splashes of dazzling pink against her impossibly black hair. She seemed a caricature of a hooker.

"That's Candy."

She indicated a young woman in yellow shorts and cowboy boots. Her makeup made Bozo look drab. She was painfully young. Except for the cigarette and clown face, she could have been my daughter.

"Do they use their real names?" It was like witnessing a cliché.

"I don't know. Would you?"

She pointed to a girl in black sneakers and short shorts.

"Poirette."

"How old is she?" I was appalled.

"Says she's eighteen. She's probably fifteen."

I leaned back and rested my hands on the steering wheel. As she pointed them out, one by one, I couldn't help thinking of gibbons. Just like the small apes, the women spaced themselves at equal intervals, dividing the field into a mosaic of precise territories. Each worked her patch, excluding others of her gender, and trying to beguile a mate. The seductive poses, the taunts and jeers, were a courtship ritual, *sapiens* style. With these dancers, however, reproduction was not the goal.

I realized Gabby had stopped talking. She'd finished her roll call. I turned to look at her. She was facing in my direction, but her eyes went past me, locked on something outside my window. Perhaps outside my world.

"Let's go."

She said it so quietly I could hardly hear her. "Wha—?"

"Go!"

Her ferocity stunned me. A volley flew to my lips, but the look in her eyes convinced me to say nothing.

Again we rode in silence. Gabby seemed to be deep in thought, as though mentally she'd relocated to a different planet. But as I pulled up to her apartment she blindsided me with another question.

"Are they raped?"

My mind rewound and played the tape of our conversation. No good. I'd missed another bridge.

"Who?" I asked.

"These women."

The hookers? The murder victims?

"Which women?"

For several seconds she didn't answer.

"I'm so sick of this shit!"

She was out of the car and up the stairs before I could react. Then her vehemence slapped me in the face.

5

FOR THE NEXT COUPLE OF WEEKS I heard nothing from Gabby. I was also not on Claudel's dialing list. He'd cut mc out of the loop. I learned about Isabelle Gagnon's life through Pierre LaManche.

She'd lived with her brother and his lover in St. Édouard, a working-class neighborhood northeast of Centre-ville. She worked in a lover's boutique, a small shop off St. Denis specializing in unisex clothes and paraphernalia. Une Tranche de Vie. A Slice of Life. The brother, who was a baker, had thought of the name. The irony of it was depressing.

Isabelle disappeared on Friday, April 1. According to the brother, she was a regular at some of the bars on St. Denis, and had been out late the night before. He thought he'd heard her come in around 2 A.M., but didn't check. The two men left for work early the next morning. A neighbor saw her at 1 P.M. Isabelle was expected at the boutique at 4 P.M. She never showed up. Her remains were discovered nine weeks later at Le Grand Séminaire. She was twenty-three.

LaManche came into my office late one afternoon to see if I'd finished my analysis.

"There are multiple fractures of the skull," I said. "It took quite a bit of reconstructing."

"Oui."

I took the skull from its cork ring.

"She was hit at least three times. This is the first."

I pointed to a small, saucerlike crater. A series of concentric circles expanded outward from its epicenter, like rings on a shooting target.

"The first blow wasn't hard enough to shatter her skull. It just caused a depression fracture of the outer table. Then he hit her here."

I indicated the center of a starburst pattern of fracture lines. Looping through the stellate system was a series of curvilinear fractures. The rays and the circles interlaced to form a spiderweb of damage.

"This blow was much harder, and caused a massive comminuted fracture. Her skull shattered."

It had taken long hours to reassemble the pieces. Traces of glue were visible along the fragment edges.

He listened, absorbed, his eyes driving back and forth from the skull to my face so intently they seemed to burrow a channel through the air.

"Then he hit her here."

I traced a runner from another starburst system toward an arm of the one I'd just shown him. The second linear break came up to the first and stopped, like a country road at a T-intersection.

"This blow came later. New fractures will be arrested by preexisting ones. New lines won't cross old ones, so this one had to have come last."

"Oui."

"The blows were probably delivered from the back and slightly to the right."

"Oui."

He did this to me often. The absence of feedback was no indication of a lack of interest. Or understanding. Pierre LaManche missed nothing. I doubt he ever needed second explanations. The monosyllabic response was his way of forcing you to organize your thoughts. A sort of dry-run jury presentation. I forged on.

"When a skull is hit it acts like a balloon. For a fraction of a second the bone pushes in at the point of impact, and bulges out on the opposite side. So the damage isn't restricted to the place the head was struck."

I looked to see if he was with me. He was.

"Because of the architecture of the skull, the forces caused by a sudden impact travel along certain pathways. The bone fails, or breaks, somewhat predictably."

I pointed to the forehead.

"For example, an impact here can result in damage to the orbits or face."

I indicated the back of the skull.

"A blow here often causes side-to-side fractures of the base of the skull."

He nodded.

"In this case, there are two comminuted fractures and one depressed fracture of the posterior right parietal. There are several linear fractures that start on the opposite side of the skull and travel toward the damage in the right parietal. This suggests she was struck from the back and to her right."

"Three times," he said.

"Three times," I confirmed.

"Did it kill her?" He knew what my answer would be.

"Could have. I can't say."

"Any other signs of cause?"

"No bullets, no stab marks, no other fractures. I've got some odd gashes on the vertebrae, but I'm not really sure what they mean."

"Due to the dismemberment?"

I shook my head. "I don't think so. They're not in the right place."

I replaced the skull in its ring.

"The dismemberment was very clean. He didn't just chop the limbs off. He severed them neatly at the joints. Remember the Gagne case? Or Valencia?"

He thought a minute. In a rare display of movement he tipped his head to the right, then to the left, like a dog cuing in on the crinkle of cellophane.

"Gagne came in, oh, maybe two years ago," I prompted. "He was wrapped in layers of blankets, trussed up with packaging tape. His legs had been sawed off and packaged individually."

At the time it had reminded me of the ancient Egyptians. Before mummification they removed the internal organs and preserved them. The viscera were then bundled separately and placed with the body. Gagne's killers had done the same with his legs.

"Ah, *oui*. I remember the case."

"Gagne's legs were sawed off below the knees. Same with Valencia. His arms and legs were cut several inches above or below the joints."

Valencia had gotten greedy on a drug deal. He came to us in a hockey bag.

"In both those cases the limbs were hacked off

at the most convenient place. In this case the guy neatly disconnected the joints. Look."

I showed him a diagram. I'd used a standard autopsy drawing to indicate the points at which the body had been cut. One line ran through the throat. Others bisected the shoulder, hip, and knee joints.

"He cut the head off at the level of the sixth cervical vertebra. He removed the arms at the shoulder joints, and the legs at the hip sockets. The lower legs were separated at the knee joints."

I picked up the left scapula.

"See how the cuts surround the glenoid fossa?"

He studied the marks, sets of parallel grooves circling the joint surface.

"Same thing with the leg." I switched the scapula for the pelvis. "Look at the acetabulum. He went right into the socket."

LaManche inspected the deep cup that accommodates the head of the femur. Numerous gashes scarred its walls. Silently, I took the pelvis and handed him the femur. Its neck was ringed by pairs of parallel cuts.

He looked at the bone a long time, then returned it to the table.

"The only place he deviated was with the hands. There he just sliced right through the bone."

I showed him a radius.

"Odd."

"Yes."

"Which is more typical? This or the others?"

"The others. Usually you want to cut a body up so it's easier to dispose of, so you do it the fastest way possible. Grab a saw and hack away. This guy took more time."

"Hmm. What does it mean?"

I'd given the question quite a bit of thought.

"I don't know."

Neither of us spoke for a few moments.

"The family wants the body for burial. I'm going to hold off as long as I can, but be sure you've got good pictures and everything you will need if we go to trial on this one."

"I plan to take sections from two or three of the cut marks. I'll look at them under the microscope to see if I can pinpoint the tool type."

I chose my next words carefully, and watched him closely for a reaction.

"If I get any good features I'd like to try comparing these cuts to some I have on another case."

The corners of his mouth twitched almost imperceptibly. I couldn't tell if it was amusement or annoyance. Or perhaps I'd imagined it.

After a pause he said, "Yes. Monsieur Claudel has mentioned this." He looked directly at me. "Tell me why you think these cases are connected."

I outlined the similarities I saw between the Trottier and Gagnon cases. Bludgeoning. Cutting of the body after death. The use of the plastic bags. Dumping in a secluded area.

"Are these both CUM cases?"

"Gagnon is. Trottier is SQ. She was found in the St. Jerome."

As in many cities, questions of jurisdiction can be tricky in Montreal. The city lies on an island in the middle of the St. Lawrence. The Communauté Urbaine de Montréal police handle murders occurring on the island itself. Off the island, they fall to local police departments, or to La Sûreté du Québec. Coordination is not always good.

After a pause he said, "Monsieur Claudel can be"—he hesitated—"difficult. Follow through on your comparison. Let me know if you need anything."

*   *   *

Later that week I'd photographed the cut marks with a photomicroscope, using varying angles, magnifications, and intensities of light. I hoped to bring out details of their internal structure. I'd also removed small segments of bone from several joint surfaces. I planned to view them with the scanning electron microscope. Instead I was up to my neck in bones for the next two weeks.

A partially clothed skeleton was discovered by kids hiking in a provincial park. A badly decomposed body washed up on the shore of Lac St. Louis. While cleaning the basement of their newly purchased home, a couple found a trunk full of human skulls covered with wax, blood and feathers. Each find came to me.

The remains from Lac St. Louis were presumed to be those of a gentleman who died in a boating mishap the previous fall when a competitor took exception to his freelancing as a cigarette smuggler. I was putting his skull back together when the call came.

I'd been expecting it, though not this soon. As I listened my heart raced and the blood below my breastbone felt fizzy, like carbonated soda shaken in a bottle. I felt hot all over.

"She's been dead less than six hours," LaManche was saying. "I think you'd better take a look."

6

MARGARET ADKINS WAS TWENTY-four. She had lived with her common-law husband and their six-year-old son in a neighborhood nestled in the shadow of the Olympic Stadium. She was to have met her sister at ten-thirty that morning for shopping and lunch. She didn't make it. Nor did she take later phone calls after speaking with her husband at ten. She couldn't. She'd been murdered sometime between his call and noon, when her sister discovered her body. That was four hours ago. That's all we knew.

Claudel was still at the scene. His partner, Michel Charbonneau, sat on one of the plastic chairs lining the far wall of the large autopsy suite. LaManche had returned from the murder scene less than an hour ago, the body preceding him by minutes. The autopsy was under way when I arrived. I knew immediately that we'd all work overtime that night.

She lay facedown, her arms straight against her

sides, hands palm up with the fingers curving inward. The paper bags placed on them at the scene
had already been removed. Her fingernails had
been inspected and scrapings taken. She was nude,
and her skin looked waxy against the polished
stainless steel. Small circles dotted her back, pressure points left by drainage holes in the table's surface. Here and there a solitary hair clung to her
skin, estranged forever from the curly tangle on
her head.

The back of her head was distorted, the shape
slightly off, like a lopsided figure in a child's drawing. Blood oozed from her hair and mingled with
the water used to clean her, gathering below the
body in a translucent, red pool. Her sweat suit, bra,
panties, shoes, and socks had been spread across
the adjacent autopsy table. They were saturated
with blood, and the sticky, metallic smell hung
heavy on the air. A Ziploc bag next to the sweats
held an elasticized belt and sanitary pad.

Daniel was taking Polaroids. The white-bordered
squares lay on the desk next to Charbonneau, their
emerging images in varying degrees of clarity.
Charbonneau was inspecting them, one by one,
then carefully returning each to its original place.
He chewed on his lower lip as he studied them.

A uniformed officer from identity was shooting
with a Nikon and flash. As he circled the table,
Lisa, newest of the autopsy technicians, positioned
an old-fashioned screen behind the body. The
painted metal frame, with its shirred white fabric,
belonged to an era when such paraphernalia were
used in hospital rooms to barricade patients during
intimate procedures. The irony was jarring. I wondered whose privacy they were trying to protect
here. Margaret Adkins was past caring.

After several shots the photographer stood down

from his stool and looked questioningly at La-Manche. The pathologist stepped closer to the body and pointed to a scrape on the back of the left shoulder.

"Did you get this?"

Lisa held a rectangular card to the left of the abrasion. On it were written the LML number, the morgue number, and the date: June 23, 1994. Both Daniel and the photographer took close-ups.

At LaManche's direction, Lisa shaved the hair from around the head wounds, spraying the scalp repeatedly with a nozzle. There were five in all. Each showed the jagged edges typical of blunt instrument trauma. LaManche measured and diagrammed them. The cameras captured them in close-up.

At length LaManche said, "That should do it from this angle. Please turn her back over."

Lisa stepped forward, momentarily blocking my view. She slid the body to the far left side of the table, rolled it back slightly, and snugged the left arm tightly against the stomach. Then she and Daniel turned the body onto its back. I heard a soft thunk as the head dropped onto the stainless steel. Lisa lifted the head, placed a rubber block behind the neck, and stepped back.

What I saw made my blood race even faster, as if the thumb had been slipped from the shaken soda bottle in my chest and a geyser of fear allowed to erupt.

Margaret Adkins had been ripped open from her breastbone to her pubis. A jagged fissure ran downward from her sternum, exposing along its course the colors and textures of her mutilated entrails. At its deepest points, where the organs had been displaced, I could see the glistening sheath surrounding her vertebral column.

I dragged my eyes upward, away from the terrible cruelty in her belly. But there was to be no relief there. Her head was turned slightly, revealing a pixie-like face, with upturned nose and delicately pointed chin. Her cheeks were high and sprinkled with freckles. In death, the tiny brown splotches stood out in sharp contrast to the surrounding white in which they floated. She looked like Pippi Longstocking in short brown hair. But the little elf mouth was not laughing. It was stretched wide, and a severed left breast bulged from it, the nipple resting on the delicate lower lip.

I looked up and met LaManche's eyes. The lines paralleling them seemed deeper than usual. There was a tension to the lower lids that caused the sagging parenthesis under each to twitch slightly. I saw sadness, but perhaps something more.

LaManche said nothing and continued the autopsy, his attention shifting back and forth between the body and his clipboard. He recorded each atrocity, noting its position and dimensions. He detailed every scar and lesion. As he worked, the body was photographed from the front as it had been from the back. We waited. Charbonneau smoked.

After what seemed like hours, LaManche finished the external exam.

"*Bon*. Take her for radiography."

He stripped off his gloves and sat down at the desk, hunching over his clipboard like an old man with a stamp collection.

Lisa and Daniel rolled a steel gurney to the right of the autopsy table. With professional agility and detachment they transferred the body and wheeled it off to be X-rayed.

Silently, I moved over and took the chair next to Charbonneau. He half rose, nodding and smiling in my direction, took a long pull on his cigarette, and stubbed it out.

"Dr. Brennan, how goes it?"

Charbonneau always spoke to me in English, proud of his fluency. His speech was an odd mixture of Québecois and Southern slang, born of a childhood in Chicoutimi, embellished by two years in the oil fields of east Texas.

"Good. And you?"

"Can't complain." He shrugged in a way only francophiles have mastered, shoulders hunched, palms raised.

Charbonneau had a wide, friendly face and prickly gray hair that always reminded me of a sea anemone. He was a large man, his neck disproportionately so, and his collars always looked tight. His ties, perhaps in an attempt to compensate, either rolled over and slipped sideways, or disengaged themselves and hung below the level of his first shirt button. He'd loosen them early in the morning, probably hoping to make the inevitable look intentional. Or maybe he just wanted to be comfortable. Unlike most of the CUM detectives, Charbonneau did not try to make a daily fashion statement. Or maybe he did. Today he wore a pale yellow shirt, polyester pants, and a green plaid sports jacket. The tie was brown.

"Seen the prom pics?" he asked, reaching to retrieve a brown envelope from the desk.

"Not yet."

He withdrew a stack of Polaroids and handed them to me. "These are just the backup shots that came in with the body."

I nodded and began going through them. Charbonneau watched me closely. Perhaps he hoped I would recoil from the carnage so he could tell

Claudel I'd blinked. Perhaps he was genuinely interested in my reaction.

The photos were in chronological order, re-creating the scene as the recovery team had found it. The first showed a narrow street lined on both sides by old but well-kept buildings, each three stories high. Parallel rows of trees bordered the curbs on each side, their trunks disappearing into small squares of dirt surrounded by cement. The buildings were fronted by a series of postage-stamp yards, each bisected by a walkway leading to a steep metal staircase. Here and there a tricycle blocked the sidewalk.

The next several shots focused on the exterior of one of the red-brick buildings. Small details caught my attention. Plaques over a pair of second-story doors bore the numbers 1407 and 1409. Someone had planted flowers below one of the ground-floor windows in front. I could make out three forlorn marigolds huddled together, their huge yellow heads shriveled and drooping in identical arcs, solitary blooms coaxed into life and abandoned. A bicycle leaned against the rusted iron fence that surrounded the tiny front yard. A rusty sign angled from the grass, leaning low to the ground, as if to hide the message: À VENDRE. FOR SALE.

Despite the attempts at individualization, the building looked like all the others lining the street. Same stairs, same balcony, same double doors, same lace curtains. I wondered: Why this one? Why did tragedy visit this place? Why not 1405? Or across the street? Or down the block?

One by one the photos took me closer, like a microscope shifting to higher and higher magnification. The next series showed the condo's interior, and, again, it was the minutiae that I found arresting. Small rooms. Cheap furniture. The inevitable TV. A living room. A dining room. A boy's bedroom, walls hung with hockey posters. A book lying on the single bed: *How the World Works.* Another stab of pain. I doubted the book would explain this.

Margaret Adkins had liked blue. Every door and inch of woodwork had been painted a bright, Santorini blue.

Finally, the victim. The body lay in a tiny room to the left of the front entrance. From it, doors gave on to a second bedroom and the kitchen. Through the entrance to the kitchen I could see a Formica table set with plastic place mats. The cramped space where Adkins had died held only a TV, a sofa, and a sideboard. Her body lay centered between them.

She lay on her back, her legs spread wide. She was fully dressed, but the top of her sweat suit had been yanked up, covering her face. The sweatshirt pinned her wrists together above her head, elbows out, hands hanging limp. Third position, like a novice ballerina at her first recital.

The gash in her chest gaped raw and bloody, only partially camouflaged by the darkening film that surrounded the body and seemed to cover everything. A crimson square marked the place where her left breast had been, its borders formed by overlapping incisions, the long, perpendicular slashes crossing each other at ninety-degree angles at the corners. The wound reminded me of trephinations I'd seen on the skulls of ancient Mayans. But this mutilation had not been done to relieve the victim's pain, or to release imagined phantoms from her body. If any imprisoned spirit had been set free, it had not been hers. Margaret Adkins was made the trapdoor through which some stranger's twisted, tormented soul sought relief.

The bottom of her sweats had been pulled down around her spread knees, the elastic waist stretched taut. Blood trickled from between her legs and pooled below her. She'd died still wearing her sneakers and socks.

Wordlessly, I replaced the photos and handed the envelope to Charbonneau.

"It's a nasty one, eh?" he asked. He removed a speck from his lower lip, inspected and flicked it.

"Yes."

"Asshole thinks he's a goddamn surgeon. Real blade cowboy." He shook his head.

I was about to answer when Daniel returned with the X rays and began to clamp them to the light box on the wall. Each made a sound like distant thunder as it bowed in his hand.

We inspected them in sequence, our collective gaze moving from left to right, from her head to her feet. The frontal and lateral X rays of the skull showed multiple fractures. The shoulders, arms, and rib cage were normal. There was nothing extraordinary until we arrived at the radiograph of her abdomen and pelvis. Everyone saw it at once.

"Holy shit," said Charbonneau.

"Christ."

"Tabernouche."

A small human form glowed from the depths of Margaret Adkins's abdomen. We all stared at it, mute. There was but one explanation. The figure had been thrust through the vagina and high into the viscera with enough force to conceal it completely from external view. On seeing it, I felt as if a hot poker had pierced my gut. Involuntarily, I clutched my belly, as my heart hammered against my ribs. I stared at the film. I saw a statue.

Framed by the broad pelvic bones, the silhouette stood out in sharp contrast to the organs in which it was embedded. Surrounded by the grays of her intestines, the stark white figure stood with one foot forward, hands outstretched. It appeared to be a religious statue. The figure's head was bowed, like a paleolithic Venus figurine.

For a few moments no one spoke. The room was absolutely silent.

"I've seen those," Daniel said at last. With a stabbing motion he pushed his glasses back onto the bridge of his nose. A tic squeezed his features like a rubber toy.

"It's our lady of something. You know. The Virgin. Mary."

We all examined the opaque shape on the X ray. Somehow it seemed to compound the offense, making it all the more obscene.

"This sonofabitch's a real sick bastard," said Charbonneau, the practiced nonchalance of the homicide detective overridden by the emotion of the moment.

His vehemence surprised me. I was unsure if the atrocity alone had stirred something in him, or if the religious nature of the offending object was contributing to his reaction. Like most Québecois, Charbonneau had no doubt had a childhood permeated with traditional Catholicism, the rhythm of his daily life inextricably ruled by church dogma. Though many of us throw off the outward trappings, reverence for the symbols often lingers. A man might refuse to wear a scapular, but neither will he burn it. I understood. Different city, different language, but I, too, was a member of the tribe. Atavistic emotions die hard.

There was another long silence. Finally, LaManche spoke, choosing his words carefully. I couldn't tell if he realized the full implications of what we were seeing. I wasn't sure I did. Though he used milder tones than I'd have chosen, he voiced my thoughts perfectly.

"Monsieur Charbonneau, I believe you and your partner need to meet with Dr. Brennan and me. As I am sure you know, there are some unsettling aspects to this case and several others."

He paused to allow that to sink in, and to consult a mental calendar.

"I will have the results of this autopsy by later tonight. Tomorrow is a holiday. Would Monday morning be convenient?"

The detective looked at him, then at me. His face was neutral. I couldn't tell if he understood LaManche's meaning, or if he was truly unaware of the other cases. It was not beyond Claudel to have dismissed my comments without sharing them with his partner. If so, Charbonneau could not admit his ignorance.

"Yeah. Okay. I'll see what I can do."

LaManche held his melancholy eyes on Charbonneau and waited.

"Okay. Okay. We'll be here. Now I better get my ass back on the street and start looking for this shithook. If Claudel turns up, tell him I'll meet him back at headquarters around eight."

He was rattled. He'd failed to switch over to French when addressing LaManche. It was clear he would have a long talk with his partner.

LaManche resumed the autopsy before the door closed behind Charbonneau. The rest was routine. The chest was opened with a Y-shaped incision. The organs were removed, weighed, sliced, and inspected. The statue's position was determined, the internal damage assessed and described. Using a scalpel, Daniel cut the skin across the crown of the head, peeled the face forward and the scalp backward, and removed a section of skullcap with a Stryker saw. I took a step backward and held my breath as the air filled with the whine of the saw and the smell of burnt bone. The brain was structurally normal. Here and there gelatinous globs clung to its surface, like black jellyfish on a slick, gray globe. Subdural hematoma from the blows to her head.

I knew what the essence of LaManche's report would be. The victim was a healthy young woman with no abnormalities or signs of disease. Then, that day, someone had bludgeoned her head with enough force to fracture her skull and cause her cerebral vessels to bleed into her brain. At least five times. He had then rammed a statue into her vagina, partially disemboweled her, and slashed off her breast.

A shudder ran through me as I considered her ordeal. The wounds to her vagina were vital. Her torn flesh had bled extensively. The statue had been inserted while her heart still beat. While she was alive.

". . . tell Daniel what you want, Temperance."

I hadn't been listening. LaManche's voice brought me back to the present. He'd finished, and was suggesting I take my bone samples. The sternum and front portions of the ribs had been removed early in the autopsy, so I told Daniel they were to be sent upstairs for soaking and cleaning.

I stepped close to the body and peered into the thoracic cavity. A number of small gashes meandered up the belly side of the vertebral bodies. They appeared as a trail of faint slits in the tough sheath covering the spine.

"I want the vertebrae from about here to here. Ribs, too." I indicated the segment containing the gashes. "Send it up to Denis. Tell him to soak it, no boiling. And be very careful in removing it. Don't touch it with any kind of blade."

He listened, holding his gloved hands out. His nose and upper lip jumped as he tried to adjust his glasses. He nodded continuously.

When I stopped speaking he looked at LaManche. "Then close?" he asked.

"Close her up after that," LaManche responded.

DÉJÀ DEAD

Daniel set to the task. He would remove the bone segments, then replace the organs and close the midsection. Finally, he would restore the skullcap, reposition the face, and sew the severed borders of the scalp. Save for the Y-shaped seam down her front, Margaret Adkins would appear untouched. She would be ready for her funeral.

I returned to my office, determined to regroup mentally before driving home. The fifth floor was totally deserted. I swiveled my chair, put my feet on the window ledge, and looked out at my river world. On my shore, the Miron complex resembled a Lego creation, its eccentric gray buildings connected by a horizontal latticework of steel. Beyond the cement factory, a boat moved slowly upriver, its running lights barely visible behind the gray veil of dusk.

The building was absolutely still, but the spooky quiet failed to relax me. My thoughts were black as the river. I wondered briefly if there was someone looking back at me from the factory, someone who was equally alone, equally unnerved by the after-hours solitude that rings so loudly in an empty office building.

I was having trouble sleeping and had been up since 6:30 A.M. I should have been tired. Instead I was agitated. I found myself absently playing with my right eyebrow, a nervous gesture that had profoundly irritated my husband. Years of his criticism had never broken me of the habit. Separation has its advantages. I can now fidget to my heart's content.

Pete. Our last year together. Katy's face when we'd told her about the split. Shouldn't be too traumatic, we thought, she's away at college. How wrong we'd been. The tears had almost made me reverse the decision. Margaret Adkins, her hands curled in death. She'd painted her doors blue with those hands. She'd

83

hung her son's posters. The killer. Was he out there right now? Was he relishing what he'd done today? Was his blood lust satiated, or was his need to kill heightened by the act itself?

The phone rang, splitting the silence like a sonic boom and yanking me back from whatever private grotto I'd entered. I was so startled I jumped, upending the pencil holder with my elbow. Bics and Scripto markers went flying.

"Dr. Bren—"

"Tempe. Oh, thank God! I tried your apartment but ya weren't there. Obviously." Her laugh was high and strained. "I thought I'd try this number just for the hell of it. Didn't really think I'd find ya."

I recognized her voice, but it had a quality I'd never heard before. It was stretched taught with fear. The tone was elevated, the cadence spiky. Her words rushed at me, breathy and urgent, like a whisper carried on sharply expelled breath. My stomach muscles contracted once again.

"Gabby, I haven't heard from you in three weeks. Why haven't y—"

"I couldn't. I've been—involved—in something. Tempe, I need help."

A soft scraping and clattering came over the line as she repositioned the receiver. In the background I could hear the hollow sound of a public place. It was punctuated by a staccato of muffled voices and metallic clangs. In my mind's eye I could see her standing at a pay phone, scanning her surroundings, her eyes never resting, broadcasting fear like Radio Free Europe.

"Where are you?" I selected a pen from the Pick-Up Sticks tumble on my desk and began to twirl it.

"I'm at a restaurant. La Belle Province. It's at the corner of Ste. Catherine and St. Laurent. Come get me, Temp. I can't go out there."

DÉJÀ DEAD

The rattling increased. She was becoming more agitated.

"Gabby, it's been a very long day here. You're only a few blocks from your apartment. Couldn't you—"

"He's going to kill me! I can't control it anymore. I thought I could, but I can't. I can't shield him anymore. I have to protect myself. He's not right. He's dangerous. He's—*completement fou!*"

Her voice had been rising steadily, treading upward on a staircase of hysteria. It stopped suddenly, the break accentuated by the abrupt shift to French. I stopped twirling the pen and looked at my watch— 9:15 P.M. Shit.

"Okay. I'll be there in about fifteen minutes. Watch for me. I'll come across Ste. Catherine."

My heart was racing and my hands were trembling. I locked the office and practically ran to the car on wobbly legs. I felt as if I were on an eight-cup coffee high.

7

DURING THE DRIVE MY EMOTIONS did acrobatics. It had turned dark, but the city was fully lit. Apartment windows glowed softly in the east end neighborhood surrounding the SQ building, and here and there a television flickered blue light into the summer night. People sat on balconies and stoops, clustered in chairs dragged outside for summer curtain calls. They talked and sipped cold drinks, having piloted the thick heat of afternoon into the renewing cool of evening.

I coveted their quiet domesticity, just wanted to go home, share a tuna sandwich with Birdie, and sleep. I wanted Gabby to be all right, but I wanted her to take a taxi home. I dreaded dealing with her hysteria. I felt relief at hearing from her. Fear for her safety. Annoyance at having to go into the Main. It was not a good mix.

I took René Lévesque to St. Laurent and hung a right, turning my back on Chinatown. That neighborhood was closing for the night, the last of the shop owners packing up their crates and display bins and dragging them inside.

The Main sprawled ahead of me, stretching north from Chinatown along Boulevard St. Laurent. The Main is a close-packed quarter of small shops, bistros, and cheap cafés, with St. Laurent as its main commercial artery. From there it radiates out into a network of narrow, back streets packed with cramped, low-rent housing. Though French in temperament, the Main has always been a polycultural mosaic, a zone in which the languages and ethnic identities coexist but fail to blend, like the distinct smells that waft from its dozens of shops and bakeries. The Italians, the Portuguese, the Greeks, the Poles, and the Chinese cluster in enclaves along St. Laurent as it climbs its way from the port to the mountain.

The Main was once Montreal's principal switching station for immigrants, the newcomers attracted by the cheap housing and the comforting proximity of fellow countrymen. They settled there to learn the ways of Canada, each group of rookies banding together to ease its disorientation, and to buoy its confidence in the face of an alien culture. Some learned French and English, prospered, and moved on. Others stayed, either because they preferred the security of the familiar, or because they lacked the ability to get out. Today this nucleus of conservatives and losers is joined by an assortment of dropouts and predators, by a legion of the powerless, discarded by society, and by those who prey on them. Outsiders come to the Main in search of many things: wholesale bargains, cheap dinners, drugs, booze, and sex. They come to buy, to gawk, to laugh, but they don't stay.

Ste. Catherine forms the southern boundary of the Main. Here I turned right, and pulled to the curb where Gabby and I had sat almost three weeks before. It was earlier now, and the hookers were just beginning to divvy up their patches. The bikers hadn't arrived.

Gabby must have been watching. When I glanced in the rearview mirror, she was already halfway across the street, running, her briefcase clutched to her chest. Though her terror wasn't enough to launch her into full flight, her fear was evident. She ran in the manner of adults long estranged from the unfettered gallop of childhood, her long legs slightly bent, her head lowered, her shoulder bag swinging in rhythm to her stilted stride.

She circled the car, got in, and sat with eyes closed, chest heaving. She was obviously struggling for composure, clenching her hands tightly in an attempt to stop the trembling. I'd never seen her like this and it frightened me. Gabby had always had a flare for the dramatic as she threaded her way through perpetual crises, both real and imagined, but nothing had ever undone her to this extent before.

For a few moments I said nothing. Though the night was warm, I felt a chill, and my breathing became thin and shallow. Outside on the street, horns blared and a hooker cajoled a passing car. Her voice rode the summer evening like a toy plane, rising and falling in loops and spirals.

"Let's go."

It was so quiet I almost missed it. Déjà vu.

"Do you want to tell me what's going on?" I asked.

She raised a hand as if to ward off a scolding. It trembled, and she placed it flat against her chest. From across the car I could sense the fear. Her body was warm with the smell of sandalwood and perspiration.

"I will. I will. Just give me a minute."

"Don't jerk me around, Gabby," I said, more harshly than I'd intended.

"I'm sorry. Let's just get the hell out of here," she said, dropping her head into her hands.

All right, we'd follow her script. She'd have to calm down and tell me in her own way. But tell me she would.

"Home?" I asked.

She nodded, never taking her face from her hands. I started the car and headed for Carré St. Louis. When I arrived at her building she still hadn't spoken. Though her breathing had steadied, her hands still shook. They had resumed their clasping and unclasping, clutching each other, separating, then linking once again in an odd dance of panic. The choreography of terror.

I put the car in park and killed the engine, dreading the encounter that was to come. I'd counseled Gabby through calamities of health, parental conflict, academics, faith, self-esteem, and love. I'd always found it draining. Invariably, the next time I'd see her, she'd be cheerful and unruffled, the catastrophe forgotten. It wasn't that I was unsympathetic, but I'd been down this route with Gabby many times before. I remembered the pregnancy that wasn't. The stolen wallet that turned up beneath the couch cushions. Nevertheless, the intensity of her reaction disturbed me. Much as I longed for solitude, she didn't look as if she should be alone.

"Would you like to stay with me tonight?"

She didn't answer. Across the square an old man arranged a bundle under his head and settled onto a bench for the night.

The silence stretched for so long I thought she hadn't heard. I turned, about to repeat the invitation, and found she was staring intently in my direction. The jittery movements of a moment ago had been replaced by absolute stillness. Her spine was rigid, and her upper body angled forward, barely touching the seat back. One hand lay in her lap, the other was curled into a fist pressed tightly to her lips. Her eyes squinted, the lower lids quivering almost imperceptibly. She seemed to be weighing something in her mind, considering variables and calculating outcomes. The sudden mood swing was unnerving.

"You must think I'm crazy." She was totally calm, her voice low and modulated.

"I'm confused." I didn't say what I really thought.

"Yeah. That's a kind way to put it."

She said it with a self-deprecating laugh, slowly shaking her head. The dreadlocks flopped.

"I guess I really freaked back there."

I waited for her to go on. A car door slammed. The low, melancholy voice of a sax floated from the park. An ambulance whined in the distance. Summer in the city.

In the dark, I felt, more than saw, Gabby's focus alter. It was as if she'd taken a road up to me, then veered off at the last minute. Like a lens on automatic, her eyes readjusted to something beyond me, and she seemed to seal herself off again. She was having another session with herself, running through her options, deciding what face to wear.

"I'll be okay," she said, gathering her briefcase and bag, and reaching for the handle. "I really appreciate your coming for me."

She'd decided on evasive.

Maybe it was fatigue, maybe it was the stress of the last few days. Whatever. I lost it.

"Wait just a minute!" I exploded. "I want to know what's going on! An hour ago you were talking about someone wanting to kill you! You come sprinting out of that restaurant and across the street, shaking and gasping like the goddamn Night Stalker's on your tail! You can't breathe, your hands are jerking like they're wired for high voltage, and now you're just going to sail out of here with a 'Thank you very much for the ride,' without any explanation?"

I'd never been so furious with her. My voice had risen, and my breath was coming in short gulps. I could feel a tiny throbbing in my left temple.

The force of my anger froze her in place. Her eyes went round and cavernous, like those of a doe caught in high beams. A car passed and her face flickered white then red, amplifying the image.

She held a moment, a catatonic cutout rigid against the summer sky. Then, as if a valve had been released, the tension seemed to drain from her body. She let go of the handle, lowered her briefcase, and settled back into the seat. Again, she turned inward, reconsidering. Perhaps she was deciding where to begin; perhaps she was scouting alternative escape routes. I waited.

At length, she took a deep breath and her shoulders straightened slightly. She'd settled on a course. As soon as she spoke I knew what she'd determined to do. She would let me in, but only so far. She chose her words carefully, threading a guarded path through the emotional quagmire in her mind. I leaned against the door and braced myself.

"I've been working with some—unusual—people lately."

I thought that an understatement, but didn't say so.

"No, no. I know that sounds banal. I don't mean the usual street people. I can handle that."

Her choice of words was tortuous.

91

"If you know the players, learn the rules and the lingo, you're fine down there. It's like anywhere else. You've got to observe the local etiquette and not piss people off. It's pretty simple: Don't trespass on someone else's patch, don't screw up a trick, don't talk to the cops. Except for the hours, it's not hard to work down there. Besides, the girls know me now. They know I'm no threat."

She went mute. I couldn't tell if she was closing me out again, or if she'd gone back to the shelves to continue her sorting. I decided to nudge.

"Is one of them threatening you?"

Ethics had always been important to Gabby, and I suspected she was trying to shield an informant.

"The girls? No. No. They're fine. They're never a problem. I think they kind of like my company. I can be as raunchy as any of them."

Great. We know what the problem isn't. I prodded some more.

"How do you avoid being mistaken for one of them?"

"Oh, I don't try. I just sort of blend in. Otherwise I'd be defeating my own purpose. The girls know I don't turn tricks, so they just, I don't know, go along with it."

I didn't ask the obvious.

"If a guy hassles me, I just say I'm not working right then. Most of them move on."

There was another pause as she continued her mental triage, considering what to tell me, what to keep to herself, and what to scoop into a heap, not tendered, but accessible if probed. She fumbled with a tassle on her briefcase. A dog barked in the square. I was sure she was protecting someone, or something, but this time I didn't goad her.

"Most of them," she continued, "except this one guy lately."

Pause.

"Who is he?"

Pause.

"I don't know, but he has me really creeped out. He's not a john, exactly, but he likes to hang out with prostitutes. I don't think the girls pay much attention to him. But he knows a lot about the street, and he's been willing to talk to me, so I've been interviewing him."

Pause.

"Lately, he's begun following me. I didn't realize it at first, but I've started noticing him in odd places. He'll be at the Métro when I come home at night, or here, in the square. Once I saw him at Concordia, outside the library building where I have my office. Or I'll see him behind me, on a sidewalk, walking in the same direction I am. Last week I was on St. Laurent when I spotted him. I wanted to convince myself it was my imagination, so I tested him. If I slowed down, so did he. If I speeded up, he did the same thing. I tried to shake him by going into a patisserie. When I came out, he was across the street, pretending to window shop."

"You're sure it's always the same guy?"

"Absolutely."

There was a long, laden silence. I waited it out.

"That's not all."

She stared at her hands, which, once again, had found each other. They were tightly clenched.

"Recently he's started talking some really weird shit. I've tried to avoid him, but tonight he showed up at the restaurant. Lately it's like he's equipped with radar. Anyway, he got off on the same stuff, asking me all kinds of sick questions."

She went back inside her head. After a moment she turned to me, as if she'd found an answer there she hadn't seen before. Her voice was tinged with mild surprise.

"It's his eyes, Tempe. His eyes are so weird! They're black and hard, like a viper, and the whites are all pink and flecked with blood. I don't know if he's sick, or if he's hung over all the time, or what. I've never seen eyes like that. They make you want to crawl under something and hide. Tempe, I just freaked! I guess I've been thinking about our last conversation, and this shitfreak you're cleaning up after, and my mind took the first bus outa there."

I didn't know what to say. I couldn't read her face in the darkness, but her body spoke the language of fear. Her torso was rigid and her arms were drawn in, pressing the briefcase to her chest, as if for protection.

"What else do you know about this guy?"

"Not much."

"What do the girls think about him?"

"They ignore him."

"Has he ever been threatening?"

"No. Not directly."

"Has he ever been violent or out of control?"

"No."

"Is he into drugs?"

"I don't know."

"Do you know who he is or where he lives?"

"No. There are some things we don't ask. It's an unspoken rule, sort of a tacit agreement down here."

Again there was a long silence while we both weighed what she'd said. I watched a cyclist pass along the sidewalk, pedaling with unhurried strokes. His helmet seemed to pulsate, blinking on as he passed beneath a streetlamp, then off as he moved back into darkness. He crossed my field of vision then disappeared slowly into the night, a firefly signaling his passage. On. Off. On. Off.

I thought about what she'd said, wondering if I was to blame. Had I set her fears in motion by talking about my own, or had she actually encountered a psychopath? Was she amplifying a set of harmless coincidences, or was she truly in jeopardy? Should I let things ride for a while? Should I do something? Was this a police matter? I was running through my old, practiced loop.

We sat for some time, listening to the sounds of the park and smelling the soft summer night, each of us drifting alone in separate reflections. The quiet interlude had a calming effect. Eventually Gabby shook her head, dropped the briefcase to her lap, and leaned back in the seat. Though her features were obscured, the change in her was visible. When she spoke, her voice was stronger, less shaky.

"I know I'm overreacting. He's just some harmless weirdo who wants to rattle my cage. And I'm playing into his game. I'm letting this fuckhead grab my mind and shake me."

"Don't you run across a lot of 'weirdos,' as you call him?"

"Yeah. Most of my informants aren't exactly the Brooks Brothers crowd." She gave a short, mirthless laugh.

"What makes you think this guy may be different?

She thought about it, worrying a thumbnail with her teeth.

"Ah, it's hard to put into words. There's just a—a line that divides the crackpots from the real predators. It's hard to define, but ya know when it's been crossed. Maybe it's an instinct I've picked up down there. In the business, if a woman feels threatened by someone, she won't go with him. Each one has her own little triggering devices, but they all draw that line on something. Could be eyes, could be some odd request. Hélène won't go with anyone who wears cowboy boots."

She took another time-out to debate with herself.

"I think I just got carried away by all the talk about serial killers and sexual devos."

More introspection. I tried to steal a look at my watch.

"All this guy is trying to do is shock me."

Another pause. She was talking herself down.

"What an asshole."

Or up. Her voice was growing angrier by the minute.

"Goddammit, Tempe, I'm not going to let this turd get his rocks off sniveling trash and showing me his sick pictures. I'm going to tell him to blow it out his ass."

She turned and put her hand on mine.

"I'm so sorry I dragged you down here tonight. I am such a jerk! Will ya forgive me?"

I stared mutely at her. Again, her emotional U-turn had taken me by surprise. How could she be terrified, analytical, angry, then apologetic all within the space of thirty minutes? I was too tired, and it was too late at night to sort it out.

"Gabby, it's late. Let's talk about this tomorrow. Of course I'm not mad. I'm just glad you're all right. I meant it about staying at my place. You're always welcome."

She leaned over and hugged me. "Thanks, but I'll be fine. I'll call ya. I promise."

I watched her climb the stairs, her skirt floating like mist around her. In an instant she disappeared through the purple doorway, leaving the space between us empty and undisturbed. I sat alone, surrounded by the dark and the faint scent of sandalwood. Though nothing stirred, a momentary chill gripped my heart. Like a shadow, it flickered and was gone.

All the way home my mind was at warp speed. Was Gabby constructing another melodrama? Was she genuinely in danger? Were there things she wasn't telling me? Could this man be truly dangerous? Was she nurturing the seeds of paranoia planted by my talk of murder? Should I tell the police?

I refused to allow my concern for Gabby's safety to overpower me. When I got home, I resorted to a childhood ritual that works when I'm tense or overwrought: I ran a hot bath and filled it with herbal salts. I put a Chris Rea CD on full volume, and, as I soaked, he sang to me of the road to hell. The neighbors would have to survive. After my bath, I tried Katy's number, but, once again, got her machine. Then I shared milk and cookies with Birdie, who preferred the milk, left the dishes on the counter, and crawled into bed.

My anxiety was not completely dissipated. Sleep didn't come easily, and I lay in bed for some time, watching the shadows on the ceiling, and fighting the impulse to call Pete. I hated myself for needing him at such times, for craving his strength whenever I felt upset. It was one ritual I'd vowed to break.

Eventually sleep took me down like a whirlpool, swirling all thoughts of Pete, and Katy, and Gabby, and the murders from my consciousness. It was a good thing. It's what got me through the following day.

8

I SLEPT SOUNDLY UNTIL NINE-
fifteen the next morning. I'm not usually a napper,
but it was Friday, June 24, St. Jean Baptiste Day,
La Fête Nationale du Québec, and I was encouraging the holiday languor allowed on such days. Since
the feast of St. John the Baptist is the principal
holiday for the province, almost everything is
closed. There would be no *Gazette* at my door that
morning, so I made coffee, then walked to the corner in search of an alternative paper.

The day was bright and vivid, the world displayed on active matrix. Objects and their shadows
stood out in sharp detail, the colors of brick and
wood, metal and paint, grass and flowers screaming
out their separate places on the spectrum. The sky
was dazzling and absolutely intolerant of clouds,
reminding me of the robin's egg blue on the holy
cards of my childhood, the same outrageous blue.
I was certain St. Jean would have approved.

The morning air felt warm and soft, perfect with the smell of window box petunias. The temperature had climbed gradually but persistently over the past week, with each day's high surpassing its predecessor. Today's forecast: thirty-two degrees Celsius. I did a quick conversion: about eighty-nine degrees Fahrenheit. Since Montreal is built on an island, the surrounding moat of the St. Lawrence ensures constant humidity. Yahoo! It would be a Carolina day: hot and humid. Bred in the South, I love it.

I purchased *Le Journal de Montréal*. The "number one daily French paper in America" was not as fastidious about taking the day off as the English language *Gazette*. As I walked the half block back to my condo, I glanced at the front page. The headline was written in three-inch letters the color of the sky: BONNE FÊTE QUÉBEC!

I thought about the parade and the concerts to follow at Parc Maisonneuve, about the sweat and the beer that would flow, and about the political rift that divided the people of Quebec. With a fall election due, passions were high, and those pushing for separation were hoping fervently that this would be the year. T-shirts and placards already clamored: *L'an prochain mon pays!* Next year my own country! I hoped the day would not be marred by violence.

Arriving home, I poured myself a coffee, mixed a bowl of Müeslix, and spread the paper on the dining room table. I am a news junkie. While I can go several days without a newspaper, contenting myself with a regular series of eleven o'clock TV fixes, before long I have to have the written word. When traveling, I locate CNN first, then unpack. I make it through the hectic days of the work week, distracted by the demands of teaching or casework, soothed by the familiar voices of "Morning Edition" and "All Things Considered," knowing that on the weekend I will catch up.

I cannot drink, loathe cigarette smoke, and was logging a lean year for sex, so Saturday mornings I reveled in journalistic orgies, allowing myself hours to devour the tiniest minutiae. It isn't that there's anything new in the news. There isn't. I know that. It's like balls in a Bingo hopper. The same events keep coming up over and over. Earthquake. Coup d'état. Trade war. Hostage taking. My compulsion is to know which balls are up on any given day.

Le Journal is committed to the format of short stories and abundant pictures. Though not *The Christian Science Monitor,* it would do. Birdie knew the routine, and hoisted himself onto the adjacent chair. I'm never sure if he's attracted by my company, or by hopes of Müeslix leavings. He arched his back, settled with all four feet drawn primly in, and fixed his round yellow eyes on me, as if seeking the answer to some profound feline mystery. As I read, I could feel his gaze on the side of my face.

I found it on page two, between a story about a strangled priest and coverage of World Cup soccer.

VICTIM FOUND MURDERED AND MUTILATED

A twenty-four-year-old woman was found murdered and savagely disfigured in her east end home yesterday afternoon. The victim, identified as Margaret Adkins, was a homemaker and the mother of a six-year-old son. Mme. Adkins was last known to be alive at 10 A.M., when she spoke by phone to her husband. Her brutally beaten and mutilated body was discovered by her sister around noon.

According to CUM police, there were no signs of forced entry, and it is unclear how her attacker gained access to the home. An autopsy was performed at the Laboratoire de Médecine Légale by Dr. Pierre LaManche. Dr. Temperance Brennan, an American forensic anthropologist and expert in skeletal trauma, is examining the bones of the victim for indications of knife marks. . . .

The story continued with a patchwork of speculations on the victim's final comings and goings, a synopsis of her life, a heartrending account of the reaction of her family, and promises that the police were doing everything possible to apprehend the killer.

Several photos accompanied the article, depicting the grizzly drama and its cast of characters. There, in shades of gray, were the apartment and its staircase, the police, the morgue attendants pushing the gurney with its sealed body bag. A scattering of neighbors lined the sidewalk, held back by crime scene tape, their curiosity frozen in grainy black and white. Among the figures inside the tape I recognized Claudel, his right arm raised like the conductor of a high school band. A circular inset presented a close-up of Margaret Adkins, a blurred but happier version of the face I'd seen on the autopsy table.

A second photograph showed an older woman with bleached hair curled tightly around her head, and a young boy in shorts and an Expos T-shirt. A bearded man in wire-rimmed glasses had one arm placed protectively around the shoulders of each. All three stared from the page with grief and puzzlement, the expression common to those left in the wake of violent crime, a look with which I've become all too familiar. The caption identified them as the mother, son, and common-law husband of the victim.

I was dismayed to see the third photo: a shot of me at a disinterment. I was familiar with it. Taken in 1992 and kept on file, it was frequently exhumed and reprinted. I was, as usual, identified as "... *une anthropologiste américaine.*"

"Damn!"

Birdie flicked his tail and looked disapproving. I didn't care. My vow to banish the murders from my mind for the entire holiday weekend had been short-lived. I should have known the story was going to be in today's paper. I finished the last, cold dregs of my coffee and tried Gabby's number. No answer. Though there could be a million explanations, that, too, made me cranky.

I went to the bedroom to dress for Tai Chi. The class normally met on Tuesday nights, but since no one was working, they'd voted to hold a special session today. I hadn't been sure I wanted to go, but the article and the unanswered phone settled it. At least for an hour or two my mind would be clear.

Again, I was wrong. Ninety minutes of "stroking the bird," "waving hands like clouds," and "needle at the bottom of the sea" did nothing to put me in a holiday mood. I was so distracted that I was out of sync the entire workout, and came away more aggravated than before.

Driving home, I turned on the radio, bent on herding my thoughts like a shepherd tends his flock, nurturing the frivolous and driving off the macabre. I was determined that the weekend could still be salvaged.

"... was killed sometime around noon yesterday. Mme. Adkins was expected by her sister, but did not keep the appointment. The body was discovered at 1327 Desjardins. Police could find no evidence of a break-in, and suspect Mme. Adkins may have known her assailant."

I knew I should change the station. Instead, I let the voice suck me in. It stirred what was simmering on my mental back burner, bringing my frustrations to the surface and demolishing with finality any possibility of a weekend furlough.

". . . the results of an autopsy have not been released. Police are scouring east end Montreal, questioning everyone who knew the victim. The incident is the twenty-sixth homicide this year in the CUM. Police are asking anyone with information to call the homicide squad at 555-2052."

Without making a conscious decision, I did an about-face and headed toward the lab. My hands steered and my feet worked the pedals. Within twenty minutes I was there, determined to accomplish something, but unsure what.

The SQ building was quiet, the usual tumult hushed by the desertion of all but an unlucky few. The lobby guards eyed me suspiciously, but said nothing. It may have been the ponytail and spandex, or it may have been a general surliness at having drawn holiday duty. I didn't care.

The LML and LSJ wings were completely abandoned. The empty offices and labs seemed to lie in repose, regrouping for the aftermath of a long, hot weekend. My office was as I'd left it, the pens and markers still scattered across the desktop. As I picked them up I looked around, my eyes roving over unfinished reports, uncataloged slides, and an ongoing project on maxillary sutures. The empty orbits of my reference skulls regarded me blankly.

I still wasn't sure why I was there or what I planned to do. I felt tense and out of sorts. Again

I thought of Dr. Lentz. She'd led me to recognize my alcohol addiction, to face my growing alienation from Pete. Gently but relentlessly her words had picked at the scabs that covered my emotions. "Tempe," she'd say, "must you always be in control? Can no one else be trusted?"

Maybe she was right. Perhaps I was just trying to escape the guilt that always plagued me when I couldn't resolve a problem. Maybe I was simply evading inactivity and the feeling of inadequacy that accompanied it. I told myself the murder investigation really wasn't my responsibility, that the homicide detectives had that duty, and my job was to assist them with complete and accurate technical support. I chided myself for being there simply for lack of alternative invitations. It didn't work.

Although I recognized the logic of my own arguments by the time the pencil clean-up was complete, I still couldn't escape the feeling that there was something I needed to do. It gnawed at me, like a hamster with a carrot. I couldn't shake the nagging sensation that I was missing some tiny element that was important to these cases in a way I didn't yet understand. I needed to do something.

I pulled a file jacket from the cabinet where I keep old case reports, and another from my current case pile, and laid them beside the Adkins dossier. Three yellow folders. Three women yanked from their surroundings and slaughtered with psychopathic malevolence. Trottier. Gagnon. Adkins. The victims lived miles apart and were dissimilar in background, age, and physical characteristics, yet I couldn't shake the conviction that the same hand had butchered all three. Claudel could see only the differences. I needed to find the link that would convince him otherwise.

Tearing off a sheet of lined paper, I constructed

a crude chart, heading the columns with categories
I thought might be relevant. Age. Race. Hair color/
length. Eye color. Height. Weight. Clothing when
last seen. Marital status. Language. Ethnic group/
religion. Place/type of residence. Place/type of em-
ployment. Cause of death. Date and time of death.
Postmortem body treatment. Location of body.

I started with Chantale Trottier, but realized
quickly that my files wouldn't contain all the information I needed. I wanted to see the full police
reports and scene photos. I looked at my watch—
1:45 P.M. Trottier had been an SQ case, so I decided
to drop down to the first floor. I doubted there
would be much activity in the homicide squad
room, so it might be a good time to request what
I wanted.

I was right. The huge room was almost empty,
its colony of regulation gray metal desks largely
uninhabited. Three men clustered together in the
far corner of the room. Two occupied adjoining
desks, facing each other across stacks of file folders
and overflowing in-baskets.

A tall, lanky man with hollow cheeks and hair
the color of hand-rubbed pewter sat with his chair
tipped back, feet propped high and ankles crossed.
His name was Andrew Ryan. He spoke in the hard,
flat French of an anglophone, stabbing the air with
a ballpoint pen. His jacket hung from the chair
back, its empty arms swinging in rhythm to the pen
thrusts. The tableau reminded me of firemen at a
firehouse, relaxed but ready at a moment's notice.

Ryan's partner watched him from across the
desk, head tilted to one side, like a canary inspecting a face outside its cage. He was short and
muscular, though his body was beginning to take
on the bulges of middle age. He had the unlined
tan of a bronzing salon, and his thick black hair

was styled and perfectly combed. He looked like a would-be actor in a promo shot. I suspected even his mustache was professionally coifed. A wooden plaque on his desk said Jean Bertrand.

The third man perched on the edge of Bertrand's desk, listening to the banter and inspecting the tassles on his Italian loafers. When I saw him my spirits dropped like an elevator.

". . . like a goat shitting cinders."

They laughed simultaneously, with the throaty sound men seem to share when enjoying a joke at the expense of women. Claudel looked at his watch.

You're being paranoid, Brennan, I told myself. Get a grip. I cleared my throat and began weaving my way through the labyrinth of desks. The trio fell silent and turned in my direction. Recognizing me, the SQ detectives smiled and rose. Claudel did not. Making no attempt to mask his disapproval, he flexed and lowered his feet, and resumed his tassle inspection, abandoning it only to consult his watch.

"Dr. Brennan. How are you?" Ryan asked, switching to English and extending his hand in my direction. "You been home lately?"

"Not for several months." His grip was firm.

"I've been meaning to ask you, do you pack an AK-47 when you go out down there?"

"No, we keep those mostly for home use. Mounted."

I was used to their quips about American violence.

"They got indoor toilets down there yet?" asked Bertrand. His topic of choice was the South.

"In some of the bigger hotels," I responded.

Of the three men, only Ryan looked embarrassed.

Andrew Ryan was an unlikely candidate for an SQ homicide detective. Born in Nova Scotia, he was the only son of Irish parents. Both were physicians who trained in London, arriving in Canada with English as their sole language. They expected their son to follow into the professional ranks, and, having chafed under the confines of their own unilingualism, vowed to ensure his fluency in French.

It was during his junior year at St. Francis Xavier that things began to go bad. Enticed by the thrill of life on the edge, Ryan got into trouble with booze and pills. Eventually, he was spending little time on campus, preferring the dark, stale beer-smelling haunts of dopers and drunks. He became known to the local police, his benders frequently concluding on the floor of a cell, his finales played facedown in vomit. He ended up one night in St. Martha's Hospital, a cokehead's blade having pierced his neck, nearly severing his carotid artery.

As with a born-again Christian, his conversion was swift and total. Still drawn to life in the underbelly, Ryan merely changed sides. He finished his undergraduate studies in criminology, applied for and got a job with the SQ, eventually rising to the rank of detective lieutenant.

His time on the streets served him well. Though usually polite and soft-spoken, Ryan had the reputation of a brawler who could take the lowlifes on their own terms and match them trick for trick. I'd never worked with him. All this had come to me through the squad room grapevine. I'd never heard a negative comment about Andrew Ryan.

"What are you doing here today?" he asked. He swept his long arm toward the window. "You should be out enjoying the party."

I could see a thin scar winding out of his collar and up the side of his neck. It looked smooth and shiny, like a latex snake.

"Lousy social life, I guess. And I don't know what else to do when the stores are closed."

KATHY REICHS

I said it brushing bangs back from my forehead.
I remembered my gym gear, and felt a bit intimi-
dated by their impeccable tailoring. The three of
them looked like an ad for *GQ*.

Bertrand came from behind his desk, and extended his hand, nodding and smiling. I shook it.
Claudel continued not to look at me. I needed him
here like I needed a yeast infection.

"I wondered if I could take a look at a file from
last year. Chantale Trottier. She was killed in October of '93. The body was found in St. Jerome."

Bertrand snapped his fingers into a pointing gesture, which he aimed at me.

"Yes. I remember that one. The kid in the dump.
We still haven't nailed the bastard that did that
one."

From the corner of my eye I saw Claudel's eyes
go to Ryan. Though the movement was almost imperceptible, it triggered my curiosity. I doubted
Claudel was there on a social call, was certain
they'd talked about yesterday's murder. I wondered
if they'd discussed Trottier or Gagnon.

"Sure," said Ryan, his face smiling but impassive.
"Whatever you need. You think there's something
in there we missed?"

He reached for a pack of cigarettes and shook
one loose. Placing it in his mouth, he extended the
pack toward me. I shook my head.

"No, no. Nothing like that," I said. "I've got a
couple of cases upstairs I'm working on, and they
keep making me think of Trottier. I'm not really
sure what I'm looking for. I'd just like to go over
the scene photos and maybe the incident report."

"Yeah, I know the feeling," he said, blowing a
stream of smoke out the side of his mouth. If he
knew any of my cases were also Claudel's, he didn't

108

let on. "Sometimes you just have to follow a hunch. What do you think you've got?"

"She thinks there's a psychopath out there responsible for every murder since Cock Robin."

Claudel's voice was flat, and I saw that his eyes were back on the tassles. His mouth barely moved when he spoke. It seemed to me that he did not try to disguise his contempt. I turned away and ignored him.

Ryan smiled at Claudel. "Come on, Luc, ease back, it never hurts to take another look. We sure aren't setting any speed records clipping this worm."

Claudel snorted and shook his head. Again he consulted his watch.

Then, to me, "What've you got?"

Before I could answer the door flew open and Michel Charbonneau burst into the far end of the room. He jogged toward us, weaving through the desks and waving a paper in his left hand.

"We've got him," he said. "We've got the sonofabitch." His face was red and he was breathing hard.

"About time," said Claudel. "Let's see." He addressed Charbonneau as one would a delivery boy, his impatience obliterating any pretense of courtesy.

Charbonneau's brow furrowed, but he handed the paper to Claudel. The three men huddled, their heads bent close, like a team consulting the playbook. Charbonneau spoke to their backs.

"The dumb fucker used her bank card an hour after he iced her. Apparently he hadn't had enough fun for the day, so he went to the corner dépanneur to score some change. Only this place don't cater to the quiche and Brie crowd, so they've got a video camera pointed at the money machine.

Ident hammered the transaction and, *voilà,* we've got us a Kodak moment."

He nodded at the photocopy.

"He's a real beauty, eh? I took it by there this morning, but the night clerk didn't know the guy's name. Thought he recognized the face. Suggested we talk to the guy comes in after nine. Apparently our boy's a regular."

"Holy shit," said Bertrand.

Ryan just stared at the picture, his tall, lean frame hunched over that of his shorter partner.

"So this is the cocksucker," said Claudel, scrutinizing the image in his hand. "Let's get this asshole."

"I'd like to ride along."

They'd forgotten I was there. All four turned toward me, the SQ detectives half amused and curious as to what would happen next.

"C'est impossible," said Claudel, the only one now using French. His jaw muscles bunched and his face went taut. There was no smile in his eyes.

Showdown.

"Sergeant Detective Claudel," I began, returning his French and choosing my words carefully. "I believe I see significant similarities in several homicide victims whom I have been asked to examine. If this is so, there may be one individual, a psychopath as you call him, behind all of their deaths. Maybe I'm right, maybe I'm wrong. Do you really want to assume responsibility for ignoring the possibility and risking the lives of more innocent victims?"

I was polite but unyielding. I, too, was unamused.

"Oh hell, Luc, let her ride along," said Charbonneau. "We're just going to do some interviews."

"Go on, this guy's going down whether you cut her in or not," said Ryan.

Claudel said nothing. He took out his keys, stuffed the photo into his pocket, and brushed past me on his way to the door.

"Let's boogie," said Charbonneau.

I had a hunch yet another day might go into overtime.

9

GETTING THERE WAS NO SMALL task. As Charbonneau fought his way west along De Maisonneuve, I sat in the back, gazing out the window and ignoring the bursts of static that erupted from the radio. The afternoon was sweltering. As we inched along, I watched heat rise from the pavement in undulating waves.

Montreal was preening itself with patriotic fervor. The fleur-de-lis was everywhere, hung from windows and balconies, worn on T-shirts, hats, and boxer shorts, painted on faces, and waved on flags and placards. From Centre-ville eastward to the Main, sweaty revelers clogged the streets, choking off traffic like plaque in an artery. Thousands of people filled the streets, ebbing and flowing in streams of blue and white. Though seemingly without orientation, the throng oozed generally northward, toward Sherbrooke and the parade, punks moving next to mothers with strollers. The march-ers and floats had left St. Urbain at 2 P.M., twirling and high-stepping eastward along Sherbrooke. At that moment they were just above us.

Over the hum of the air conditioner I could hear a lot of laughter and sporadic bursts of song. Already there was some fighting. As we waited out the light at Amherst, I watched a lummox push his girlfriend against a wall. He had hair the color of unbrushed teeth, burred on top and long in the back. His chicken-white skin was moving toward grenadine. We pulled away before the scene could play itself out, leaving me with an image of the girl's startled face superimposed on the breasts of a naked woman. Eyes squinting and mouth in an O, she was framed by a poster for a Tamara de Lempicka exposition at the Musée des Beaux Arts. *"Une femme libre,"* it whooped. "A free woman." Another of life's ironies. I took some satisfaction in knowing the oaf wouldn't have a good night. He might even blister.

Charbonneau turned to Claudel. "Lemme see that picture a minute."

Claudel pulled it from his pocket. Charbonneau studied it, shifting his eyes from the traffic to the photo in his hand.

"He sure don't look like much, does he?" he said to no one in particular. Wordlessly he extended the picture to me over the seat back.

What I held was a black-and-white print, a blowup of a single frame taken from high up and to the subject's right. It showed a blurred male figure with face averted, concentrating on the task of inserting or retracting a card at an automatic teller machine.

His hair was short and wispy in front, splayed downward into a fringe on his forehead. The top of his head was almost bare, and he had combed as many long strands as possible from left to right in an attempt to hide his baldness. My favorite male "do." About as attractive as a Speedo bathing suit.

His eyes were shielded by bushy brows, and his ears flared out like petals on a pansy. His skin looked deathly pale. He wore a plaid shirt and what looked like work pants. The graininess and poor angle obscured any other details. I had to agree with Charbonneau. He didn't look like much. It could have been anyone. Silently, I handed the photo back.

Dépanneurs are the convenience stores of Quebec. They are found anywhere shelves and a refrigerator can be packed into a covered space. Scattered throughout the city, dépanneurs survive by providing grocery, dairy, and alcohol essentials. They dot every neighborhood, forming a capillary bed that feeds the needs of locals and foot travelers. They can be counted on for milk, cigarettes, beer, and cheap wine, the remainder of their inventory determined by neighborhood preferences. They provide no glitz and no parking. The upscale version may have a bank machine. It was to one such that we were heading.

"Rue Berger?" Charbonneau asked Claudel.

"*Oui.* It runs south from Ste. Catherine. Take René Lévesque to St. Dominique then go back north. That's a snakepit of one-ways in there."

Charbonneau turned left and began creeping south. In his impatience he kept goosing the gas then tapping the brake, causing the Chevy to lurch like a Ferris wheel seat. Feeling a bit seasick, I focused on the action at the boutiques, bistros, and modern brick buildings of L'Université du Québec, which lined St. Denis.

"Sacré bleu!"

"Ca-lice!" said Charbonneau as a dark green Toyota station wagon cut him off.

"Bastard," he added as he hit the brake then shot up to its bumper. "Look at that oily little freak."

Claudel ignored him, apparently used to his partner's erratic driving. I thought of Dramamine, but held my tongue.

Eventually we reached René Lévesque and turned west, then cut north onto St. Dominique. We doubled back at Ste. Catherine and, once again, I found myself in the Main, less than one block from Gabby's girls. Berger is one of a small checkerboard of side streets sandwiched between St. Laurent and St. Denis. It lay directly ahead.

Charbonneau turned the corner and slid to the curb in front of the Dépanneur Berger. A dingy sign above its door promised *"bière et vin."* Sun-bleached ads for Molson and Labatt covered the windows, the tape yellowed and peeling with age. Rows of dead flies lined the sill below, their bodies stratified according to season of death. Iron bars safeguarded the glass. Two geezers sat on kitchen chairs outside the door.

"Guy's name is Halevi," said Charbonneau, consulting his notebook. "He probably won't have much to say."

"They never do. His memory may improve if we sweat him a little," said Claudel, slamming the car door.

The geezers watched us silently.

A string of brass bells jangled as we entered. The interior was hot and smelled of dust and spices and old cardboard. Two rows of back-to-back shelves ran the length of the store, forming one center and two side aisles. The dusty shelves held an assortment of aging canned and packaged goods.

On the far right a horizontal refrigerator case held vats of nuts, dal, dried peas, and flour. An assembly of limp vegetables lay in its far end. Something from another era, the case no longer refrigerated.

Upright coolers with wine and beer lined the left wall. In the rear, a small, open case, draped with plastic to conserve the cold, held milk, olives, and feta cheese. To its right, in the far corner, was the bank machine. Except for this, the place looked as if it hadn't been renovated since Alaska applied for U.S. statehood.

The counter was directly to the left of the front door. Mr. Halevi sat behind it, speaking heatedly into a cellular phone. He kept running his hand over his naked head, the maneuver a holdover from a hairier youth. A sign on the cash register read SMILE. GOD LOVES YOU. Halevi was not taking his own advice. His face was red, and he was clearly piqued. I stood back and watched.

Claudel positioned himself directly in front of the counter and cleared his throat. Halevi showed him a palm and nodded his head in a "hold on" gesture. Claudel flashed his badge and shook his head. Halevi looked momentarily confused, said something in rapid Hindi, and clicked off. His eyes, huge behind thick lenses, moved from Claudel to Charbonneau and back.

"Yes," he said.

"You Bipin Halevi?" asked Charbonneau in English.

"Yes."

Charbonneau placed the photo face up on the counter. "Take a look. You know this guy?"

Halevi rotated the picture and leaned over it, his jittery fingers holding down the edges. He was nervous and trying hard to please, or at least to give the impression of cooperation. Many dépanneur operators sell smuggled cigarettes or other black market goodies, and police visits are as popular as tax audits.

"No one could recognize a man from this. Is this from the video? Men were here earlier. What did this man do?"

He spoke English with the singsong cadence of northern India.

"Any idea who he is?" said Charbonneau, ignoring the questions.

Halevi shrugged. "With my customers, you don't ask. Besides, this is too fuzzy. And his face is turned away."

He shifted on his stool. He was relaxing somewhat, realizing that he wasn't the object of the inquiry, that it had to do with the security video the police had confiscated.

"He a local?" asked Claudel.

"I tell you, I don't know."

"Does this even remotely remind you of anyone comes in here?"

Halevi stared at the picture.

"Maybe. Maybe, yes. But it's just not clear. I wish I could help. I . . . Maybe this could be a man I've seen."

Charbonneau looked at him hard, probably thinking what I was. Was Halevi trying to please, or did he really see something familiar in the photo?

"Who?"

"I—I don't know him. Just a customer."

"Any pattern to what he does?"

Halevi looked blank.

"Does the guy come at the same time of day? Does he come from the same direction? Does he buy the same stuff? Does he wear a goddamn tutu?" Claudel was becoming annoyed.

"I told you. I don't ask. I don't notice. I sell my stuff. At night I go home. This face is like many others. They come and they go."

"How late is this place open?"

"Till two."

"He come in at night?"

"Maybe."

Charbonneau was taking notes in a leather-bound pad. So far he'd written little.

"You work yesterday afternoon?"

Halevi nodded. "It was busy, the day before the holiday, eh? Maybe people think I won't be open today."

"You see this guy come in?"

Halevi studied the picture again, ran both hands to the back of his head, then scratched his halo of hair vigorously. He blew out a puff of air and raised his hands in a gesture of helplessness.

Charbonneau slipped the photo into his notebook and snapped it shut. He placed his card on the counter.

"If you think of anything else, Mr. Halevi, give us a call. We thank you for your time."

"Sure, sure," he said, his face brightening for the first time since seeing the badge. "I will call."

"Sure, sure," said Claudel when we were outside. "That toad'll call when Mother Teresa screws Saddam Hussein."

"He works a dépanneur. He's got chili for brains," Charbonneau responded.

As we crossed to the car I looked back over my shoulder. The two geezers were still flanking the door. They seemed a permanent fixture, like stone dogs at the entrance to a Buddhist temple.

"Let me have the picture a minute," I told Charbonneau.

He looked surprised but dug it out. Claudel

opened the car door, and baked air rolled out like heat from a smelter. He draped one arm over the door, propped a foot on the frame, and watched me. As I recrossed the street, he said something to Charbonneau. Fortunately, I didn't hear.

I walked over to the old man on the right. He wore faded red running shorts, a tank top, dress socks, and leather oxfords. His bony legs were cobwebbed by varicose veins, and looked as if the pasty, white skin had been stretched over knots of spaghetti. His mouth had the collapsed look of toothlessness. A cigarette jutted from one corner at a downward angle. He watched me approach with unmasked curiosity.

"Bonjour," I said.

"Hey," he said, leaning forward to peel his sweat-slicked back from the cracked vinyl of the chair. He'd either heard us talking or picked up on my accent.

"Hot day."

"I seen hotter." The cigarette jumped as he spoke.

"You live near here?"

He flapped a scrawny arm in the direction of St. Laurent.

"Could I ask you something?"

He recrossed his legs and nodded.

I handed him the photo.

"Have you ever seen this man?"

He held the picture at arm's length in his left hand, and shaded it from the sun with his right. Smoke floated across his face. He studied the image for so long, I thought perhaps he'd drifted off. I watched a gray-and-white cat covered with raw, red patches slither behind his chair, skirt the building, and disappear around the corner.

The second old man placed both hands on his

knees and raised himself with a low grunt. His skin had once been fair, but now looked as if he'd been sitting in that chair a hundred and twenty years. Adjusting first the suspenders and then the belt that held his gray work pants, he shuffled over to us. He brought the rim of his Mets cap to the level of his companion's shoulder, and squinted at the photo. Finally, spaghetti legs handed it back.

"A man's own mother wouldn't know him from this. Picture's shit."

The second geezer was more positive.

"He lives over there somewhere," he said, aiming a yellowed finger down the block at a seedy brick three-flat, and speaking in a joual so thick I could barely understand him. He, too, was without teeth or dentures, and, as he spoke, his chin seemed to reach for his nose. When he paused, I pointed to the photo and then to the building. He nodded his head.

"Souvent?" Often? I asked.

"Mmm, *oui*," he responded, raising his eyebrows and shoulders, thrusting forward his lower lip, and giving the palm up, palm down gesture with his hands. Often. Sort of.

The other geezer shook his head and snorted in disgust.

I signaled to Charbonneau and Claudel to join me, and explained what the old man had said. Claudel looked at me as he might a buzzing wasp, an annoyance that must be dealt with. I met his eyes, daring him to say something. He knew they should have questioned the men.

Without comment, Charbonneau turned his back and focused on the pair. Claudel and I stood and listened. The joual was rapid as gunfire, the vowels so stretched and the endings so truncated, I caught little of the exchange. But the gestures and signals were clear as a headline. Suspenders said he lived down the block. Spaghetti legs disagreed.

At length Charbonneau turned back to us. He tipped his head in the direction of the car, gesturing Claudel and me to follow. As we crossed the street, I could feel two sets of rheumy eyes burning the back of my neck.

10

LEANING ON THE CHEVY, Charbonneau shook free a cigarette and lit it. His body looked as tense as an unsprung trap. For a moment he was quiet, seeming to sort through what the old men had said. Finally he spoke, his mouth a straight line, his lips hardly moving.

"What do you think?" he asked.

"Click and clack look like they spend a lot of time here," I offered. Inside my T-shirt, a rivulet of sweat ran down my back.

"Could be a pair of real head cases," said Claudel.

"Or it could be they've actually seen the prick-ass," said Charbonneau. He inhaled deeply then flicked at the cigarette with his middle finger.

"They weren't exactly star witnesses on details," said Claudel.

"Yeah," said Charbonneau, "but we all agreed. The guy ain't much to remember. And mutants like him usually keep a pretty low profile."

"And grandpa number two seemed pretty sure," I added.

Claudel snorted. "Those two may not be sure of anything but the wine shop and the blood bank. Probably the only two landmarks they can map."

Charbonneau took one last drag, dropped the butt, and ground it with his toe. "It could be nothing, or it could be he's in there. Me, I don't want to guess wrong. I say we take a look, bust his ass if we find him."

I observed yet another of Claudel's shrugs. "Okay. But I'm not about to get my bacon fried. I'll call for backup."

He flicked his eyes to me and back to Charbonneau, brows raised.

"She don't bother me," Charbonneau said.

Shaking his head, Claudel rounded the car and slid in on the passenger side. Through the windshield I could see him reach for his handset.

Charbonneau turned to me. "Stay alert," he said. "If anything breaks, get down."

I appreciated his refraining from telling me not to touch anything.

In less than a minute Claudel's head reappeared above the door frame.

"*Allons-y,*" he said. Let's roll.

I climbed into the backseat, and the two detectives got in front. Charbonneau put the car in gear and we crept slowly up the block. Claudel turned to me.

"Don't touch anything in there. If this is the guy, we don't want anything screwed up."

"I'll try," I said, fighting to suppress the sarcasm in my voice. "I'm one of the nontestosterone gender, and we sometimes have trouble remembering things like that."

He blew out a puff of air and pivoted back in

his seat. I was sure if he'd had an appreciative audience he'd have rolled his eyes and smirked.

Charbonneau pulled to the curb in midblock, and we all considered the building. It sat surrounded by empty lots. The cracked cement and gravel were overgrown with weeds and strewn with the broken bottles, old tires, and the usual debris that accumulates on abandoned urban spaces. Someone had painted a mural on the wall facing the lot. It depicted a goat with an automatic weapon slung from each ear. In its mouth it held a human skeleton. I wondered if the meaning was clear to anyone but the artist.

"The old boy hadn't seen him today," said Charbonneau, drumming his fingers on the steering wheel.

"When did they go on neighborhood watch?" asked Claudel.

"Ten," said Charbonneau. He looked at his watch, and Claudel and I followed suit. Pavlov would have been proud—3:10 P.M.

"Maybe the guy's a late sleeper," said Charbonneau. "Or maybe he's worn out from his little field trip yesterday."

"Or maybe he's not in there at all and these geeks are getting ready to bust their balls laughing."

"Maybe."

I watched a group of girls cross the vacant lot behind the building, their arms intertwined in teenage comraderie. Their shorts formed a row of Quebec flags, a chorus line of fleur-de-lis swaying in unison as they picked their way through the weeds. Each had braided her hair in tiny cornrows and sprayed it bright blue. As I watched them laugh and jostle in the summer heat, I thought how easily such youthful high spirits could be extinguished forever by the act of a madman. I fought back a wave of anger. Was it possible we were sitting not ten yards from such a monster?

At that moment a blue-and-white patrol unit slipped quietly in behind us. Charbonneau got out and spoke to the officers. In a minute he was back.

"They'll cover the back," he said, nodding toward the squad car. His voice had an edge to it, all sarcasm gone. *"Allons-y."*

When I opened the door Claudel started to speak, changed his mind, and walked toward the apartment. I followed with Charbonneau. I noticed that he had unbuttoned his jacket, and his right arm was tense and slightly bent. Reflex readiness. For what? I wondered.

The red-brick building stood alone, its neighbors long since gone. Trash littered the adjacent lots, and large blocks of cement dotted them helter-skelter, like boulders left in a glacial retreat. A rusted and sagging chain-link fence ran along the building's south side. The goat faced north.

Three ancient white doors, side by side, opened onto Berger at street level. In front of them, the ground was covered by a patch of asphalt running to the curb. Once painted red, the pavement was now the color of dried blood.

In the window of the third door, a handwritten sign rested at an angle against a limp and grayed lace curtain. I could barely read through the dirty glass, *"Chambres à louer, #1."* Rooms to rent. Claudel put one foot on the step and pressed on the higher of two buttons next to the door frame. No answer. He rang again, then, after a brief pause, pounded on the door.

"Tabernac!" shrieked a voice directly in my ear. The piercing Québecois expletive sent my heart leaping into my throat.

I turned and saw that the voice came from a first-floor window eight inches to my left. A face scowled through the screen in undisguised annoyance.

"What do you think you're doing? You break that door, *trou de cul,* and you're going to pay for it."

"Police," said Claudel, ignoring the asshole reference.

"Yeah? You show me something."

Claudel held his shield close to the screen. The face leaned forward and I could see it was that of a woman. It was flushed and porcine, its perimeter bordered by a diaphanous lime scarf, knotted with exuberance on the top of her head. The ends sprouted upward, bobbing on the air like chiffon ears. Save for the absence of armaments and ninety extra pounds, she bore a noticeable resemblance to the goat.

"So?" The scarf tips floated as she looked from Claudel to Charbonneau to me. Deciding I was the least threatening, she pointed them in my direction.

"We'd like to ask you a few questions," I said, feeling instantly as if I'd done a Jack Webb imitation. It sounded as clichéd in French as it would have in English. At least I hadn't added "ma'am" at the end.

"Is this about Jean-Marc?"

"We really shouldn't do this in the street," I said, wondering who Jean-Marc was.

The face hesitated then disappeared. In a moment we heard the rattle of locks being turned, and the door was opened by an enormous woman in a yellow polyester housedress. Her underarms and midsection were dark with perspiration, and I could see sweat mixed with grime in the folds that circled her neck. She held the door for us, then turned and waddled down a narrow hall, disappearing through a door on the left. We followed in single file, Claudel leading, me bringing up the rear. The corridor smelled of cabbage and old grease. The temperature inside was at least ninety-five degrees.

Her tiny apartment was rank with the stench of overused cat litter, and was crammed with the dark, heavy furniture mass-produced in the twenties and thirties. I doubted the fabric had been changed from the original. A clear vinyl runner cut diagonally across the living room carpet, which was a threadbare imitation of a Persian original. There wasn't an uncluttered surface in sight.

The woman lumbered to an overstuffed chair by the window and dropped heavily into it. A metal TV table to her right teetered, and a can of diet Pepsi wobbled with the tremor. She settled in and glanced nervously out the window. I wondered if she was expecting someone, or if she simply hated to have her surveillance interrupted.

I handed her the photo. She looked at it, and her eyes took on the shape of larvae, burrowing between their well-padded lids. She raised them to the three of us and realized, too late, that she had placed herself at a disadvantage. Standing, we had the benefit of height. She craned up at us, shifting the larvae from one of us to the other. Her mood seemed to change from belligerent to cautious.

"You are . . . ?" began Claudel.

"Marie-Eve Rochon. What is this all about? Is Jean-Marc in trouble?"

"You are the concierge?"

"I collect the rent for the owner," she answered. Though there wasn't much room, she shifted in the chair. Its protest was audible.

"Know him?" asked Claudel, gesturing at the photo.

"Yes and no. He's staying here but I don't know him."

"Where?"

"Number 6. First entrance, room on the ground level," she said, making a wide gesture with her arm. The loose, lumpy flesh jiggled like tapioca.

"What's his name?"

She thought for a moment, fidgeting absently with a scarf tip. I watched a bead of sweat reach its hydrostatic maximum, burst, and trickle down her face. "St. Jacques. Course, they don't usually use their real names."

Charbonneau was taking notes.

"How long has he been here?"

"Maybe a year. That's a long time for here. Most are vagrants. Course, I don't see him much. Maybe he comes and goes. I don't pay attention." She flicked her eyes down and crimped her lips at the obviousness of her lie. "I don't ask."

"You get any references?"

Her lips fluttered with a loud puff of air, and she shook her head slowly.

"He have any visitors?"

"I told you, I don't see him much." For a time she was silent. Her fidgeting had pulled the scarf to the right, and the ears were now off center on her head. "Seems like he's always alone."

Charbonneau looked around. "The other apartments like this?"

"Mine's the biggest." The corners of her mouth tightened and there was an almost imperceptible lift to her chin. Even in shabbiness there was room for pride. "The others are broken up. Some are just rooms with hot plates and toilets."

"He here now?"

The woman shrugged.

Charbonneau closed his notebook. "We need to talk to him. Let's go."

She looked surprised. *"Moi?"*

"We may need to get into the flat."

She leaned forward in the chair and rubbed both hands on her thighs. Her eyes widened and her nostrils seemed to dilate. "I can't do that. That would be a violation of privacy. You need a warrant or something."

Charbonneau fixed her with a level stare and did not answer. Claudel sighed loudly, as though bored and disappointed. I watched a rivulet of condensed water run down the Pepsi can and join a ring at its base. No one spoke or moved.

"Okay, okay, but this is your idea."

Shifting her weight from ham to ham, she scooted forward in diagonal thrusts, like a sailboat on a series of short tacks. The housedress crept higher and higher, exposing enormous stretches of marbleized flesh. When she had maneuvered her center of gravity to the chair's edge, she placed both hands on the arms and levered herself up.

She crossed to a desk on the far side of the room and gophered around in a drawer. Shortly, she withdrew a key and checked its tag. Satisfied, she held it out to Charbonneau.

"Thank you, madame. We will be happy to check your property for irregularities."

As we turned to leave, her curiosity overcame her. "Hey, what's this guy done?"

"We'll return the key on our way out," said Claudel. Once again, we left with eyes fixed on our backs.

The corridor inside the first entrance was identical to the one we'd just left. Doors opened to the left and right, and, at the rear, a steep staircase led to an upper floor. Number 6 was the first on the left. The building was stifling and eerily quiet.

Charbonneau stood to the left, Claudel and I to the right. Both their jackets hung loose, and Claudel rested his palm on the butt of his .357. He knocked on the door. No answer. He knocked a second time. Same response.

The two detectives exchanged glances, and Claudel nodded. The corners of his mouth were tucked in tightly, beaking his face even more then usual. Charbonneau fitted the key into the lock and swung the door in. We waited, rigid, listening to dust motes settle back into place. Nothing.

"St. Jacques?"

Silence.

"Monsieur St. Jacques?"

Same answer.

Charbonneau raised a palm in my direction. I waited while the detectives entered, then followed, my heart pounding in my chest.

The room held little furniture. In the left-rear corner a pink plastic curtain hung by rusted rings from a semicircular rod, separating the area into a makeshift bathroom. Below the curtain I could see the base of a commode and a set of pipes that probably led to a sink. The pipes were badly rusted and supported a thriving colony of a soft, green life-form. To the right of the curtain, the back wall had been fitted with a Formica-topped counter. It held a hot plate, several plastic tumblers, and an unmatched collection of dishes and pans.

In front of the curtain, an unmade bed ran the length of the left wall. A table fashioned from a large plywood plank was placed along the right. Its base was formed by two sawhorses, each clearly stamped as property of the city of Montreal. The surface was heaped with books and papers. The wall above was covered with maps, photos, and newspaper articles, forming a cut-and-paste mosaic that extended the length of the table. A metal folding chair was tucked below. The room's only window was to the right of the front door, identical to that used by Madame Rochon. Two bare bulbs jutted from a hole in the ceiling.

"Nice place," said Charbonneau.

"Yeah. A thing of beauty. I'd rank it up there with herpes and Burt Reynolds's hairpiece."

Claudel moved to the toilet area, withdrew a pen from his pocket, and gingerly drew back the curtain.

"Defense Ministry might want to take scrapings. This stuff may have potential for biological warfare." He dropped the curtain and moved toward the table.

"Dickhead isn't even here," said Charbonneau, flipping a blanket edge onto the bed with the tip of his shoe.

I was surveying the kitchenware on the Formica counter. Two Expos beer tumblers. A dented saucepan encrusted with something resembling SpaghettiOs. A half-eaten chunk of cheese congealed in the same substance in a blue china bowl. A cup from Burger King. Several cellophane packages of saltine crackers.

It hit me when I leaned over the hot plate. The lingering warmth made my blood turn to ice, and I spun toward Charbonneau.

"He's here!"

My words hit the air at the exact moment a door exploded open in the right-hand corner of the room. It slammed into Claudel, knocking him off balance and pinning his right arm and shoulder against the wall. A figure lunged across the room, body doubled over, legs thrusting toward the open front door. I could hear breath rasping in his throat.

For just an instant in his headlong plunge across the room, the fugitive raised his head, and two flat, dark eyes met mine, peering out from under the orange brim of a cap. In that brief flash I recognized the look of a terrified animal. Nothing more. Then he was gone.

Claudel regained his balance, unsnapped his gun, and bolted out the door. Charbonneau was right behind him. Without thinking, I plunged into the chase.

11

WHEN I SHOT ONTO THE street the sunlight blinded me. I squinted up Berger trying to locate Charbonneau and Claudel. The parade was over, and large numbers of people were drifting down from Sherbrooke. I spotted Claudel shouldering his way through the crowd, his face red and contorted as he demanded passage through the sticky bodies. Charbonneau was close behind. He was holding his badge straight arm in front of him, using it like a chisel to gouge his way forward.

The throng parted on, unaware that anything unusual was taking place. A heavy blonde swayed on her boyfriend's shoulders, her head thrown back, her arms held high, wagging a bottle of Molson's at the sky. A drunken man wearing a Quebec flag like a Superman cape hung from a lamppost. He prompted the crowd in chanting, *"Québec pour les Québecois!"* I noticed the chorus had a stridence that hadn't been there earlier.

I veered into the vacant lot, climbed onto a cement block, and stood on tiptoe to scan the crowd. St. Jacques, if that's who it had been, was nowhere to be seen. He had the home-court advantage, and had used it to put as much geography as possible between himself and us.

I could see one of the backup team replacing his handset and joining the chase. He'd radioed for reinforcements, but I doubted a cruiser could penetrate the mob. He and his partner were elbowing their way toward Berger and Ste. Catherine, well behind Claudel and Charbonneau.

Then I spotted the orange baseball cap. It was ahead of Charbonneau, who had turned east on Ste. Catherine, unable to see it through the mass of bodies. St. Jacques was heading west. As quickly as I saw him, he disappeared. I waved my arms for attention, but it was useless. I'd lost sight of Claudel, and neither of the patrolmen could see me.

Without thinking, I jumped from the block and plunged into the crowd. The smell of sweat, suntan lotion, and stale beer seemed to seep from the bodies around me, forming a bubble of human smog. I lowered my head and plowed through the swarm with less than my usual courtesy, bulldozing a path toward St. Jacques. I had no badge to excuse my roughness, so I pushed and shoved and avoided eye contact. Most people took the jostling with good humor, others paused to fling insults at my back. The majority were gender specific.

I tried to see St. Jacques's baseball cap through the hundreds of heads surrounding me, but it was impossible. I set a course toward the point where I'd spotted him, driving through the bodies like an icebreaker on the St. Lawrence.

It almost worked. I was close to Ste. Catherine

when I was grabbed roughly from behind. A hand the size of a Prince tennis racket wrapped itself around my throat and my ponytail was yanked sharply downward. My chin shot up, and I felt, or heard, something snap in my neck. The hand jerked me backward, and pressed me flat against the chest of a Yeti construction worker. I could feel his heat and smell his perspiration as it soaked my hair and back. A face came close to my ear, and I was enveloped in the odor of sour wine, cigarette smoke, and stale nacho chips.

"Hey, *plotte,* who the fuck you shoving?"

I could not have answered were I inclined. This seemed to anger him further and he released my hair and neck, placed both hands on my back, and shoved violently. My head snapped forward like a catapult launcher, and the force of the movement propelled me into a woman in short shorts and stiletto heels. She screamed, and the people around us separated slightly. I threw my hands out in an attempt to regain my balance, but it was too late. I went down, bouncing hard off someone's knee.

As I hit the pavement I slid and scraped my cheek and forehead, and threw my arms over my head in a reflex of self-preservation. The blood was pounding in my ears. I could feel surface gravel grinding into my right cheek, and knew I had lost some of the skin. As I attempted to push off the pavement with my hands, a boot came down hard on my fingers, mashing them. I could see nothing but knees, legs, and feet as the crowd rolled over me, seeming not to see me until the instant of tripping over me.

I rolled onto my side and tried again to come to my hands and knees. Unintended blows from feet and legs kept me from righting myself. No one stopped to shield me or help me up.

Then I heard an angry voice, and felt the crowd recede slightly. A small pocket of space formed around me, and a hand appeared at my face, its fingers gesturing impatiently. I grasped it and pulled myself up, rising, unbelievably, to sunlight and oxygen.

The hand was attached to Claudel. He held back the crowd with his other arm as I got painfully to my feet. I saw his lips move but couldn't understand what he was saying. As usual, he seemed to be annoyed. Nonetheless, he'd never looked so good. He finished speaking, paused, and looked me over. He took in the jagged tear in my right knee and the abrasions on my elbows. His eyes came to rest on my right cheek. It was scraped and bleeding, and the eye on that side was beginning to swell shut.

Dropping my hand, he withdrew a handkerchief from his pocket and gestured at my face. When I reached for it my hand was trembling. I blotted away blood and gravel, refolded to a clean surface, and held the linen against my cheek.

Claudel leaned close and shouted in my ear, "Stay with me!"

I nodded.

He worked his way toward the west side of Berger, where the crowd was a little thinner. I followed on rubbery legs. Then he turned and began to worm his way in the direction of the car. I lunged and grabbed his arm. He stopped and looked a question at me. I shook my head vehemently, and his eyebrows went from a deep V to a Stan Laurel imitation.

"He's over there!" I screamed, pointing in the opposite direction. "I saw him."

A man in a Tweedledee costume brushed past me. He was eating a snow cone, and the drops from

DÉJÀ DEAD

the melt-off werc painting a red trail down his belly. It looked like a blood-spatter pattern.

Claudel's brows dived in the midline. "You are going to thc car," he said.

"I saw him on Ste. Catherine!" I repeated, thinking perhaps he hadn't heard. "Outside Les Foufounes Électriques! He was going toward St. Laurent!" Even to me, my voice was sounding a bit hysterical.

It got his attention. He hesitated a second, assessing the damage to my cheek and limbs.

"You're okay?"

"Yeah."

"You will go to the car?"

"Yes!" He turned to go. "Wait." One by one I lifted my trembling legs over a rusted metal cable that looped knee-high around the edge of the lot, crossed to another cement block, and stepped onto it. I scanned the sea of heads, looking for the orange baseball cap. Nothing. Claudel watched impatiently as I surveyed the crowd, shifting his eyes from me to the intersection then back again. He reminded me of a sled dog waiting for the gun.

Finally, I shook my head and raised my hands.

"Go. I'll keep looking."

Skirting the open lot, he began elbowing his way in the direction I'd indicated. The mob on Ste. Catherine was bigger than ever, and, in a few minutes, I watched his head disappear into it. The swarm seemed to absorb him, like an army of antibodies seeking out and surrounding a foreign protein. One moment he was an individual, the next a dot in the pattern.

I searched until my vision blurred, but hard as I tried I couldn't locate Charbonneau or St. Jacques. Beyond St. Urbain, I could see a squad car nibbling its way into the edge of the crowd, its lights flashing

137

KATHY REICHS

red and blue. The revelers ignored its whining insistence on right of way. Once I caught a flash of orange, but it turned out to be a tiger wearing tails and high-top sneakers. Moments later she passed closer, carrying her costume head and drinking a Dr Pepper.

The sun was burning, and my head pounded. I could feel a crust hardening on my abraded cheek. I kept scanning and rescanning, sweeping the crowd. I refused to quit until Charbonneau and Claudel returned. But I knew it was farce. St. Jean and the day had smiled on our quarry, and he had escaped.

An hour later we were gathered around the car. Both detectives had removed their jackets and ties and tossed them in the backseat. Beads of sweat glistened on their faces and flowed into their collars. Their underarms and backs were saturated, and Charbonneau's face was the color of a raspberry tart. His hair stood on end in front, reminding me of a schnauzer with a bad clip. My T-shirt hung limp, and my spandex workout pants felt as if I'd put them on straight from the washer. Our breathing had slowed to normal, and "fuck" had been said at least a dozen times, with everyone contributing.

"Merde," said Claudel. It was an acceptable alternative.

Charbonneau leaned into the car and extracted a pack of Players from his jacket pocket. He slumped against a fender, lit up, and blew the smoke out the corner of his mouth.

"Bastard can cut a crowd like a cockroach through shit."

"He knows his way around here," I said, resisting

138

the urge to explore the damage to my cheek. "That helps him."

He smoked for a moment.

"Think it was our guy from the cash machine?"

"Hell, I don't know," I said. "I didn't get a look at his face."

Claudel snorted, then pulled a handkerchief from his pocket and began wiping the perspiration from the back of his neck.

I locked my one good eye on him. "Were you able to ID him?"

Another snort.

I looked at him shaking his head, and my plan of zero commentary evaporated.

"You're treating me like I'm not quite bright, Monsieur Claudel, and you're starting to piss me off."

He gave another in his series of smirks.

"How's your face feel?" he asked.

"Peachy!" I shot back between clenched teeth. "At my age free dermabrasion is a bonus."

"Next time you decide to go on a wild-assed crime fighting spree, don't expect me to scrape you up."

"Next time do a better job of controlling an arrest scene and I won't have to." The blood was pounding in my temples, and my hands were clenched so tightly the nails were digging small crescents into the flesh of my palms.

"Okay. Knock this shit off," said Charbonneau, flipping his cigarette in a wide arc. "Let's toss the apartment."

He turned to the patrolmen, who had been standing by quietly.

"Call in recovery."

"You got it," said the taller, moving toward the squad car.

Silently, the rest of us followed Charbonneau to the red-brick building and reentered the corridor. The other patrolman waited outside.

In our absence someone had closed the outer door, but the one leading to number 6 still stood wide. We entered the room and spread out as before, like characters in a stage play following directions for blocking.

I moved toward the back. The hot plate was cold now, and the SpaghettiOs had not improved with age. A fly danced on the edge of the pan, reminding me of other, grislier leftovers that may have been abandoned by the occupant. Nothing else had changed.

I walked over to the door in the far right corner of the room. Small chunks of plaster littered the floor, the result of a doorknob slammed against the wall with great force. The door was half open, revealing a wooden staircase descending to a lower floor. It dropped one step to a small landing, made a ninety-degree turn to the right, and disappeared into darkness. The landing was lined with tin cans where it met the back wall. Rusted hooks jutted from the wood at eye level. I could see a light switch on the wall to the left. The plate was missing, and the exposed wires looped around themselves like worms in a bait carton.

Charbonneau joined me and eased the door back with his pen. I indicated the switch, and he used the pen to flip it. A bulb went on somewhere below, casting the bottom steps into shadowy relief. We listened to the gloom. Silence. Claudel came up behind us.

Charbonneau stepped onto the landing, paused, and descended slowly. I followed, feeling each riser protest softly under my feet. My battered legs trembled as though I'd just run a marathon, but I resisted the temptation to touch the walls. The passage was narrow, and all I could see were Charbonneau's shoulders ahead of me.

At the bottom, the air was dank and smelled of mildew. Already my cheek felt like molten lava, and the coolness was a welcome relief. I looked around. It was a standard basement, roughly half the size of the building. The back wall was constructed of unfinished cinder blocks, and must have been added later to subdivide a larger area. A metal washtub stood ahead and to the right, with a long wooden workbench snugged up against it. Pink paint was peeling from the bench. Below it lay a collection of cleaning brushes, their bristles yellowed and covered in cobwebs. A black garden hose was coiled neatly on the wall.

A behemoth furnace filled the space to the right, its round metal ducts branching and rising like the limbs of an oak. A midden of trash circled its base. In the dim light I could identify broken picture frames, bicycle wheels, bent and twisted lawn chairs, empty paint cans, and a commode. The cast-offs looked like offerings to a Druid god.

A bare bulb hung in the middle of the room, throwing about one watt of light. That was it. The rest of the cellar was empty.

"Sonofabitch must've been waiting at the top," said Charbonneau, gazing up the stairs, hands on his hips.

"Madame Fatass might have told us the guy had this little hidey-hole," said Claudel, teasing at the trash pile with the tip of his shoe. "Regular Salman Rushdie down here."

I was impressed by the literary reference, but having returned to my original plan of neutral observation, said nothing. My legs were beginning to ache, and something was very wrong in my neck.

"Fucker could've scrambled us from behind that door."

Charbonneau and I didn't reply. We'd had the same thought.

Dropping his hands, Charbonneau crossed to the stairs and started up. I followed, beginning to feel a bit like Tonto. When I emerged into the room, the heat rolled over me. I crossed to the makeshift table and started examining the collage on the wall above.

The central piece was a large map of the Montreal area. Cutouts from magazines and newspapers surrounded it. Those on the right were standard issue pornography shots, the progeny of *Playboy* and *Hustler*. Young women stared from them, their bodies in distorted positions, their clothes absent or in disarray. Some pouted, some invited, and some feigned looks of orgasmic bliss. None was very convincing. The collagist was eclectic in his taste. He exhibited no preference as to body type, race, or hair color. I noted that the edges of each picture were carefully trimmed. Each was set equidistant from its neighbors and stapled in place.

A grouping of newspaper articles occupied the space to the left of the map. Although a few were in English, the majority were drawn from the French press. I noticed that those in English were always accompanied by pictures. I leaned close and read a few sentences about a groundbreaking at a church in Drummondville. I moved to a French article on a kidnapping in Senneville. My eyes shifted to an ad for Videodrome, claiming to be the largest distributor of pornographic films in Canada. There was a piece from *Allo Police* on a nude dance bar. It showed "Babette" dressed in leather cross garters and draped with chains. There was another on a break-in in St.-Paul-du-Nord in which the burglar had constructed a dummy of his victim's nightclothes, stabbed it repeatedly, then left it on her bed. Then I spotted something that again turned my blood to ice.

In his collection St. Jacques had carefully clipped and stapled three articles side by side. Each described a serial killer. Unlike the others, these appeared to be photocopies. The first described Léopold Dion, "The Monster of Pont-Rouge." In the spring of 1963 police had discovered him at home with the bodies of four young men. They had all been strangled.

The second recounted the exploits of Wayne Clifford Boden, who strangled and raped women in Montreal and Calgary beginning in 1969. When arrested in 1971, his final count was four. In the margin someone had written "Bill *l'étrangleur.*"

The third article covered the career of William Dean Christenson, alias Bill *l'éventreur,* Montreal's own Ripper. He'd killed, decapitated, and dismembered two women in the early 1980s.

"Look at this," I said to no one in particular. Though the room was stifling, I felt cold all over.

Charbonneau came up behind me. "Oh, baby, baby," he intoned flatly, as his eyes swept over the arrangement to the right of the map. "Love in wide angle."

"Here," I said, pointing at the articles. "Look at these."

Claudel joined us and the two men scanned them wordlessly. They smelled of sweat and laundered cotton and aftershave. Outside I could hear a woman calling to Sophie, and wondered briefly if she beckoned a pet or a child.

"Holy fuck," breathed Charbonneau, as he grasped the theme of the stories.

"Doesn't mean he's Charlie Manson," scoffed Claudel.

"No. He's probably working on his senior thesis."

For the first time I thought I detected a note of annoyance in Charbonneau's voice.

"The guy could have delusions of grandeur," Claudel went on. "Maybe he watched the Menendez brothers and thought they were keen. Maybe he thinks he's Dudley DoRight and wants to fight evil. Maybe he's practicing his French and finds this more interesting than Tin Tin. How the fuck do I know? But it doesn't make him Jack the Ripper." He glanced toward the door. "Where the hell is recovery?"

Sonofabitch, I thought, but held my tongue.

Charbonneau and I turned our attention to the desktop. A stack of newspapers leaned against the wall. Charbonneau used his pen to rifle through them, lifting the edges then allowing the sections to drop back into place. The stack contained only want ads, most from *La Presse* and the *Gazette*.

"Maybe the toad was looking for a job," said Claudel sardonically. "Thought he'd use Boden as a reference."

"What was that underneath?" I'd seen a flash of yellow as the bottom section was lifted briefly.

Charbonneau nudged the pen under the last section in the pile and levered it upward, tipping the stack toward the wall. A yellow tablet lay under it. I wondered briefly if pen manipulation was required training for detectives. He allowed the newspapers to drop back to the desktop, slid the pen to the back of the stack, and pushed at the tablet, sliding it forward and into view.

It was a lined yellow pad, the type favored by attorneys. We could see that the top page was partially filled with writing. Bracing the stack with the back of his hand, Charbonneau teased the tablet out and slid it into full view.

The impact of the serial killer stories was nothing compared to the jolt I felt on seeing what was scrawled there. The fear that I'd kept down deep in its lair lunged out and grabbed me in its teeth.

Isabelle Gagnon. Margaret Adkins. Their names leapt out at me. They were part of a list of seven that ran along the bound edge of the tablet. Beside each, running sideways across the page, was a series of columns separated by vertical lines. It looked like a crude spreadsheet containing personal data on each of the individuals listed. It did not look unlike my own spreadsheet, except I didn't recognize the other five names.

The first column listed addresses, the second phone numbers. The next held brief notations on the residence. Apt. w/ outsd. entr., condo, 1st flr.; house w/ yd. The next column contained sets of letters behind some names, for others it was blank. I looked at the Adkins entry. Hu. So. The combinations looked familiar. I closed my eyes and ran a key word search. Kinship charts.

"Those are people they live with," I said. "Look at Adkins. Husband. Son."

"Yeah. Gagnon's got Br and Bf. Brother, boyfriend," said Charbonneau.

"Big fag," added Claudel. "What's Do mean?" he asked, referring to the last column. St. Jacques had written it behind some names, left no notation for others.

No one had an answer.

Charbonneau flipped back the first sheet and everyone fell silent reading the next set of notations. The page was divided in half with one name at the top and another halfway down. Below each was another set of columns. That on the left was headed "Date," the next two were marked "In" and "Out." The empty spaces were filled with dates and times.

"Jesus H. Christ, he stalked them. He picked them out and tracked them like goddamn quail or something," exploded Charbonneau.

Claudel said nothing.

"This sick sonofabitch hunted women," repeated Charbonneau, as if rephrasing it would somehow make it more believable. Or less.

"Some research project," I said softly. "And he hasn't turned it in yet."

"What?" asked Claudel.

"Adkins and Gagnon are dead. These dates are recent. Who are the others?"

"Shit."

"Where the fuck is recovery?" Claudel strode over to the door and disappeared into the corridor. I could hear him swearing at the patrolman.

My eyes wandered back to the wall. I didn't want to think about the list anymore today. I was hot and exhausted and in pain, and there was no satisfaction in the realization that I was probably right, and that now we would work together. That even Claudel would come on board.

I looked at the map, searching for something to divert myself. It was a large one showing in rainbow detail the island, the river, and the jumble of communities comprising the CUM and surrounding areas. The pink municipalities were crisscrossed by small white streets, and linked by red arterial roads and large blue autoroutes. They were dotted by the green of parks, golf courses, and cemeteries, the orange of institutions, the lavender of shopping centers, and the gray of industrial areas.

I found Centre-ville and leaned closer to try to

locate my own small street. It was only one block long and, as I searched for it, I began to understand why taxis had so much difficulty finding me. I vowed to be more patient in the future. Or at least more specific. I traced Sherbrooke west to intersect Guy, but found I'd gone too far. It was then I had my third shock of the afternoon.

My finger hovered above Atwater, just outside the orange polygon demarcating Le Grand Séminaire. My eye was drawn to a small symbol sketched in pen at its southwest corner, a circle enclosing an X. It lay close to the site where Isabelle Gagnon's body had been discovered. With my heart pounding, I shifted to the east end and tried to find the Olympic Stadium.

"Monsieur Charbonneau, look at this," I said, my voice strained and shaky.

He came closer.

"Where's the stadium?"

He touched it with his pen and looked at me.

"Where's Margaret Adkins's condo?"

He hesitated a minute, leaned in, and started to point to a street running south from Parc Maisonneuve. His pen rested in midair as we both stared at the tiny figure. It was an X drawn and circled in pen.

"Where did Chantale Trottier live?"

"Ste. Anne-de-Bellevue. Too far out."

We both stared at the map.

"Let's search it systematically, sector by sector," I suggested. "I'll start in the upper left-hand corner and work down, you start with the lower right and work up."

He found it first. The third X. The mark was on the south shore, near St. Lambert. He knew of no homicides in that district. Neither did Claudel. We looked for another ten minutes, but found no other X's.

We were just starting a second search when the crime scene van pulled up in front.

"Where the fuck have you been?" asked Claudel as they came through the door with their metal cases.

"It's like driving through Woodstock out there," said Pierre Gilbert, "only less mud." His round face was completely encircled by curly beard and curlier hair, reminding me of a Roman god. I could never remember which one. "What've we got here?"

"Girl killed over on Desjardins? Pussbag that lifted her card calls this little hole home," said Claudel. "Maybe."

He indicated the room with a sweep of his arm. "Put a lot of himself into it."

"Well, we'll take it out," said Gilbert with a smile. His hair was clinging in circles to his wet forehead. "Let's dust."

"There's a basement, too."

"*Oui.*" Save for the inflection, dropping then rising, it sounded more like a question than an assent. *Whyyyy?*

"Claude, why don't you start down below? Marcie, take the counter back there."

Marcie moved to the back of the room, removed a canister from her metal suitcase, and began brushing black powder on the Formica counter. The other technician headed downstairs. Pierre put on latex gloves and began removing sections of newspaper from the desktop and placing them in a large plastic sack. It was then I had my final shock of the day.

"*Qu'est-ce que c'est?*" he said, lifting a small square from what had been the middle of the stack. He studied it a long time. "*C'est toi?*"

I was surprised to see him look at me.

Wordlessly I walked over and glanced at what he had. I was unnerved to see my own familiar jeans, my "Absolutely Irish" T-shirt, my Bausch and Lomb aviator sunglasses. In his gloved hand he held the photo which had appeared in *Le Journal* that morning.

For the second time that day I saw myself locked at an exhumation two years in the past. The picture had been cut and trimmed with the same careful precision as those on the wall. It differed in only one respect. My image had been circled and recircled in pen, and the front of my chest was marked with a large X.

12

I SLEPT A LOT OF THE WEEKend. Saturday morning I had tried getting up, but that was short-lived. My legs trembled, and if I turned my head long fingers of pain shot up my neck and grabbed the base of my skull. My face had crusted over like crème brûlée, and my right eye looked like a purple plum gone bad. It was a weekend of soup, aspirin, and antiseptic. I spent the days dozing on the couch, keeping abreast of O. J. Simpson's escapades. At night I was asleep by nine.

By Monday the jackhammer had stopped pounding inside my cranium. I could walk stiffly and rotate my head somewhat. I got up early, showered, and was in my office by eighty-thirty.

There were three requisitions on my desk. Ignoring them, I tried Gabby's number, but got only her machine. I made myself a cup of instant coffee and uncurled the phone messages I'd taken from my slot. One was from a detective in Verdun, another from Andrew Ryan, the third a reporter. I threw the last away and set the others by the phone. Neither Charbonneau nor Claudel had called. Nor had Gabby.

I dialed the CUM squad room and asked for Charbonneau. After a pause I was told he wasn't there. Neither was Claudel. I left a message, wondering if they were out on the street early or starting the day late.

I dialed Andrew Ryan but his line was busy. Since I was accomplishing nothing by phone, I decided to drop by in person. Maybe Ryan would discuss Trottier.

I rode the elevator to the first floor and wound my way back to the squad room. The scene was much livelier than during my last visit. As I crossed to Ryan's desk I could feel eyes on my face. It made me vaguely uncomfortable. Obviously they knew about Friday.

"Dr. Brennan," said Ryan in English, unfolding from his chair and extending a hand. His elongated face broke into a smile when he saw the scab that was my right cheek. "Trying out a new shade of blush?"

"Right. Crimson cement. I got a message you called?"

For a moment he looked blank.

"Oh yeah. I pulled the jacket on Trottier. You can take a look if you want."

He leaned over and fiddled with some folders on his desk, spreading them out in a fan-shaped heap. He selected one and handed it to me just as his partner entered the room. Bertrand strode toward us wearing a light gray sports jacket monochromatically blended to darker gray pants, a black shirt, and a black-and-white floral tie. Save for the tan, he looked like an image from 1950s TV.

"Dr. Brennan, how goes it?"

"Great."

"Wow, nice effect."

"Pavement is impersonal," I said, looking around for a place to spread the file. "May I . . ." I gestured to an empty desk.

"Sure, they're out already."

I sat down and began sorting the contents of the folder, leafing through incident reports, untangling interviews, and turning over photos. Chantale Trottier. It was like walking barefoot across hot asphalt. The pain came back as though it had happened yesterday, and I had to keep looking away, allowing my mind breaks from the surging sorrow.

On October 16, 1993, a sixteen-year-old girl rose reluctantly, ironed her blouse, and spent an hour shampooing and preening. She refused the breakfast her mother offered, and left her suburban home to join friends for the train ride to school. She wore a plaid uniform jumper and knee socks and carried her books in a backpack. She chatted and giggled, and ate lunch after math class. At the end of the day she vanished. Thirty hours later her butchered body was found in plastic garbage bags forty miles from her home.

A shadow fell across the desk and I looked up. Bertrand held two mugs of coffee. The one he offered me said "Monday I Start My Diet." Gratefully, I reached out and took it.

"Anything interesting?"

"Not much." I took a sip. "She was sixteen. Found in St. Jerome."

"Yup."

"Gagnon was twenty-three. Found in Centreville. Also in plastic bags," I mused aloud.

He tipped his head.

"Adkins was twenty-four, found at home, over by the stadium."

"She wasn't dismembered."

"No, but she was cut up and mutilated. Maybe the killer got interrupted. Had less time."

He sipped his coffee, slurping loudly. When he lowered the mug, milky brown beads clung to his mustache.

"Gagnon and Adkins were both on St. Jacques's list." I assumed the story had spread by now. I was right.

"Yeah but the media went snake over those cases. The guy had clipped *Allo Police* and *Photo Police* articles on both of them. With pictures. He could just be a maggot that feeds on that kind of crap."

"Could be." I took another sip, not really believing it.

"Didn't he have a whole dungheap of stuff?"

"Yeah," said Ryan from behind us. "Dickhead had clippings on all kinds of weird shit. Francoeur, didn't you catch some of those dummy cases when you were with property?" This to a short, fat man with a shiny brown head who was eating a Snickers bar four desks over.

Francoeur put down the candy, licking his fingers and nodding. His rimless glasses blinked as his head moved up and down.

"Um. Hum. Two." Lick. "Damnedest thing." Lick. "This squirrel creeps the place, rifles the bedroom, then makes a big doll with a nightgown or a sweat suit, something that belongs to the lady of the house. He stuffs it, dresses it up in her underwear, then lays it out on the bed and slashes it. Probably makes him harder than a math final."

Lick. Lick. "Then he gets his sorry ass out of there. Doesn't even take anything."

"Sperm?"

"Nope. Believes in safe sleaze, I guess."

"What's he use?"

"Probably a knife, but we never found it. He must bring it with him."

Francoeur peeled back the wrapper and took another bite of Snickers.

"How's he get in?"

"Bedroom window." It came out through caramel and peanuts.

"When?"

"Night, usually."

"Where's he put on these little freak shows?"

Francoeur chewed slowly for a moment, then, using a thumbnail, removed a speck of peanut from his molar. He inspected and flicked it.

"One was in St. Calixte, and I think the other was St. Hubert. The one this guy clipped went down a couple of weeks ago in St. Paul-du-Nord." His upper lip bulged as he ran his tongue over his incisors. "And I think one fell to the CUM. I sort of remember a call about a year ago from someone over there."

Silence.

"They'll pop him, but this squirrcl isn't exactly high priority. He doesn't hurt anybody and he doesn't take anything. He's just got a twisted idea of a cheap date."

Francoeur crumbled the Snickers wrapper and arced it into the wastebasket beside his desk.

"I hear the concerned citizen in St. Paul-du-Nord refused to follow up with a complaint."

"Yeah," said Ryan, "those cases are about as rewarding as a lobotomy with a Scout knife."

"Our hero probably clipped the story because

he gets a hard-on reading about busting someone's bedroom. He had a story on that girl out in Senneville and we know he wasn't the one grabbed her. Turned out the father had the kid stashed the whole time." Francoeur leaned back in his chair. "Maybe he just identifies with a kindred pervert."

I listened to this exchange without really looking at the participants. My eyes drifted over a large city map behind Francoeur's head. It was similar to the one I'd seen in the Berger apartment, but drawn to a smaller scale, extending out to include the far eastern and western suburbs off the island of Montreal.

The discussion snaked around the squad room, scooping up anecdotes of Peeping Toms and other sexual perverts. As it meandered from desk to desk, I rose quietly and crossed to the map for a closer view, hoping to draw as little attention to myself as possible. I studied it, replaying the exercise Charbonneau and I had gone through on Friday, mentally plotting the location of the X's. Ryan's voice startled me.

"What are you thinking?" he asked.

I took a container of pins from a ledge below the map. Each was topped by a large, brightly colored ball. Choosing a red one, I placed it at the southwest corner of Le Grand Séminaire.

"Gagnon," I said.

Next I placed one below the Olympic Stadium.

"Adkins."

The third went in the upper-left corner, near a broad expanse of river known as Lac des Deux-Montagnes.

"Trottier."

The island of Montreal is shaped like a foot with its ankle dipping in from the northwest, its heel to the south, and its toes pointing northeast. Two pins marked the foot, just above the sole, one in the heel of Centre-ville, another to the east, halfway up the toes. The third lay up the ankle, on the far western end of the island. There was no apparent pattern.

"St. Jacques marked this one and this one," I said, pointing to one of the downtown pins, then to the one on the east end.

I searched the south shore, following the Victoria Bridge across to St. Lambert, then dropping south. Finding the street names I'd seen on Friday, I took a fourth pin and pushed it in on the far side of the river, just below the arch of the foot. The scatter made even less sense. Ryan looked at me quizzically.

"That was his third X."

"What's there?"

"What do you think?" I asked.

"Hell if I know. Could be his dead dog Spike." He glanced at his watch. "Look, we've got this ..."

"Don't you think it would be a good idea to find out?"

He looked at me for a long time before he answered. His eyes were neon blue, and I was mildly surprised that I'd never noticed them before. He shook his head.

"It just doesn't feel right. It isn't enough. Right now your serial killer idea's got more holes than the Trans-Canada. Fill them in. Get me something else, or get Claudel to do a request for an SQ search. So far, this isn't our baby."

Bertrand was signaling to him, pointing at his watch, then hitching his thumb at the door. Ryan looked at his partner, nodded, then turned the neon back on me.

I said nothing. My eyes roved over his face, rummaging for a sign of encouragement. If it was there, I couldn't find it.

"Gotta go. Just leave the file on my desk when you're done."

"Right."

"And . . . Uh . . . Keep your head up."

"What?"

"I heard what you found in there. This prick could be more than just your average dirtbag." He reached into his pocket, withdrew a card, and wrote something on it. "You can get me at this number just about any time. Call if you need help."

Ten minutes later I was sitting at my desk, frustrated and antsy. I was trying to concentrate on other things, but having little success. Every time a phone rang in an office along the corridor, I reached for mine, willing it to be Claudel or Charbonneau. At ten-fifteen I called again.

A voice said, "Hold, please." Then.

"Claudel."

"It's Dr. Brennan," I said.

The silence was deep enough to scuba.

"Oui."

"Did you get my messages?"

"Oui."

I could tell he was going to be as forthcoming as a bootlegger at a tax audit.

"I wondered what you dug up on St. Jacques?"

He gave a snort. "Yeah, St. Jacques. Right."

Though I felt like reaching across the line to rip out his tongue, I decided the situation called for tact, rule number one in the care and handling of arrogant detectives.

"You don't think that's his real name?"

"If that's his real name, I'm Margaret Thatcher."

"So, where are you?"

There was another pause, and I could see him turning his face to the ceiling, deciding how best to rid himself of me.

"I'll tell you where we are, we're nowhere. We didn't get piss all. No dripping weapons. No home movies. No rambling confession notes. No souvenir body parts. Zip."

"Prints?"

"None usable."

"Personal effects?"

"The guy's taste falls somewhere between severe and stark. No decorative touches. No personal effects. No clothes. Oh yeah, one sweatshirt and an old rubber glove. A dirty blanket. That's it."

"Why the glove?"

"Maybe he worried about his nails."

"What *do* you have?"

"You saw it. His collection of Miss Show Me Your Twangie shots, the map, the newspapers, the clippings, the list. Oh, and some Franco-American spaghetti."

"Nothing else?"

"Nothing."

"No toiletries? Drugstore items?"

"*Nada.*"

I picked through that for a moment.

"Doesn't sound like he really lives there."

"If he does, he's the filthiest sonofabitch you'll ever meet. He doesn't brush his teeth or shave. No soap. No shampoo. No floss."

I gave that some thought.

"How do you read it?"

"Could be the little freak just uses the place as a hidey-hole for his true crime and porno hobby. Maybe his old lady doesn't like his taste in art. Maybe she doesn't let him jack off at home. How should I know?"

"What about the list."

"We're checking out the names and addresses."

"Any in St. Lambert?"

Another pause.

"No."

"Any more information on how he might have gotten Margaret Adkins's bank card?"

This time the pause was longer, more palpably hostile.

"Dr. Brennan, why don't you stick to what you do and let us catch the killers?"

"Is he?" I couldn't resist asking.

"What?"

"A killer?"

I found myself listening to a dial tone.

I spent what was left of the morning estimating the age, sex, and height of an individual from a single ulna. The bone was found by children digging a fort near Pointe-aux-Trembles, and probably came from an old cemetery.

At twelve-fifteen I went upstairs for a Diet Coke. I brought it back to my office, closed the door, and took out my sandwich and peach. Swiveling to face the river, I encouraged my thoughts to wander. They didn't. Like a Patriot missile, they homed in on Claudel.

He still rejected the idea of a serial killer. Could he be right? Could the similarities be coincidental? Could I be manufacturing associations that weren't there? Could St. Jacques merely have a grotesque interest in violence? Of course. Movie producers and publishing houses make millions off the same theme. Maybe he wasn't a killer himself, maybe he just charted the murders or played some kind of voyeuristic tracking game. Maybe he found Margaret Adkins's bank card. Maybe he stole it before

KATHY REICHS

her death and she hadn't yet missed it. Maybe.
Maybe. Maybe.

No. It didn't tally. If not St. Jacques, there was
someone out there responsible for several of these
deaths. At least some of the murders were linked.
I didn't want to wait for another butchered body
to prove me right.

What would it take to convince Claudel I wasn't
a dimwit with an overactive imagination? He resented my involvement in his territory, thought I
was overstepping my bounds. He'd told me to stick
to what I do. And Ryan. What had he said? Pot-
holes. Not enough. Find stronger evidence of a link.

"All right, Claudel, you sonofabitch, that's exactly what you'll get."

I said it aloud, snapping my chair into full upright
position and tossing my peach pit into the wastebasket.

So.

What do I do?

I dig up bodies. I look at bones.

13

IN THE HISTOLOGY LAB I asked Denis to pull out cases 25906-93 and 26704-94. I cleared the table to the right of the operating scope and placed my clipboard and pen. I took out two tubes of vinyl polysiloxane and positioned them, along with a small spatula, a tablet of coated papers, and a digital caliper accurate to .0001 inch.

Denis placed two cardboard boxes on the end of the table, one large and one small, each sealed and carefully labeled. I eased the lid from the larger box, selected portions of Isabelle Gagnon's skeleton, and laid them out on the right half of the table.

Next I opened the smaller box. Though Chantale Trottier's body had been returned to her family for burial, segments of bone had been retained as evidence, a standard procedure in homicide cases involving skeletal injury or mutilation.

I removed sixteen Ziploc bags and put them on the left side of the table. Each was marked as to body part and side. Right wrist. Left wrist. Right knee. Left knee. Cervical vertebrae. Thoracic and lumbar vertebrae. I emptied each bag and arranged the contents in anatomical order. The two segments of femur went next to their corresponding portions of tibia and fibula to form the knee joints. Each wrist was represented by six inches of radius and ulna. The ends of the bones sawed at autopsy were clearly notched. I would not confuse these cuts with those made by the killer.

I pulled the mixing pad toward me, opened one of the tubes, and squeezed a bright blue ribbon of dental impression material onto the top sheet. Next to it I squirted a white ribbon from the second tube. Selecting one of Trottier's arm bones, I placed it in front of me and picked up the spatula. Working quickly, I mixed the blue catalyst and the white base, kneading and scraping the two squiggles into a homogenous goo. I scraped the compound into a plastic syringe, then squeezed it out like cake decoration, carefully covering the joint surface.

I laid the first bone down, cleaned the spatula and syringe, tore off the used sheet, and began the process anew with another bone. As each mold hardened I removed it, marked it as to case number, anatomical site, side, and date, and placed it next to the bone on which it had been formed. I repeated the procedure until a rubbery blue mold sat next to each of the bones in front of me. It took over two hours.

Next I turned to the microscope. I set the magnification and adjusted the fiber-optic light to angle across the viewing plate. Starting with Isabelle Gagnon's right femur I began a meticulous examination of each of the small nicks and scratches I had just cast.

The cut marks seemed to be of two types. Each arm bone had a series of trench-like troughs lying parallel to its joint surfaces. The walls of the troughs were straight and dropped to meet their floors at ninety-degree angles. Most of the trench-like cuts were less than a quarter of an inch in length and averaged five hundredths of an inch across. The leg bones were circled by similar grooves.

Other marks were V-shaped, narrower, and lacked the squared-off walls and floors of the trench-like grooves. The V-shaped cuts lay parallel to the trenches on the ends of the long bones, but were unaccompanied in the hip sockets and on the vertebrae.

I diagrammed the position of each mark, and recorded its length, width, and, in the case of the trenches, depth. Next I observed each trench and its corresponding mold from above and in cross-section. The molds allowed me to see minute features not readily apparent when viewing the trenches directly. Tiny bumps, grooves, and scratches marking the walls and floors appeared as three-dimensional negatives. It was like viewing a relief map, the islands, terraces, and synclines of each trench replicated in bright blue plastic.

The limbs had been separated at the joints, leaving the long bones intact. With one exception. The bones of the lower arms had been severed just above the wrists. Turning to the bisected ends of the radius and ulna, I noted the presence and position of breakaway spurs, and analyzed the cross-sectional surface of each cut. When I'd finished with Gagnon, I repeated the whole process for Trottier.

At some point Denis asked if he could lock

something up, and I agreed, paying no attention to his question. I didn't notice the lab grow quiet.

"What are you still doing here?"

I almost dropped the vertebra I was removing from the microscope.

"Jesus Christ, Ryan! Don't do that!"

"Don't go bughouse, I just saw the light and thought I'd drop in to see if Denis was putting in overtime slicing up something entertaining."

"What time is it?" I gathered the other cervical vertebrae and placed them in their bag.

Andrew Ryan looked at his watch. "Five-forty." He watched me lift the bags into the smaller cardboard box and set the cover on top.

"Find anything useful?"

"Yup."

I tapped the cover into place and picked up Isabelle Gagnon's pelvic bones.

"Claudel doesn't put much stock in this cut-mark business."

It was precisely the wrong thing to say. I put the pelvic bones in the larger box.

"He thinks a saw's a saw."

I laid the two scapulae in the box and reached for the arm bones.

"What do you think?"

"Shit, I don't know."

"You are of the carpentry and grout gender. What do you know about saws?" I continued laying bones in the box.

"They cut things."

"Good. What things?"

"Wood. Shrubbery. Metal." He paused. "Bone."

"How?"

"How?"

"How."

He thought a minute. "With teeth. The teeth go back and forth and cut through the material."

"What about radial saws?"

"Oh well, they go around."

"Do they slice through the material or chisel through it?"

"What do you mean?"

"Are the teeth sharp on the edge or flat? Do they cut the material or rip their way through it?"

"Oh."

"And do they cut when they go back or when they go forth?"

"What do you mean?"

"You said the teeth go back and forth. Do they cut on the back or on the forth? On the push stroke or on the pull stroke?"

"Oh."

"Are they designed to cut on the grain or across the grain?"

"Does that matter?"

"How far apart are the teeth? Are they evenly spaced? How many are on the blade? What's their shape? How are they angled front to back? Is their edge pointed or squared off? How are they set relative to the plane of the blade? What kind of . . ."

"Okay, okay, I see. So, tell me about saws."

As I spoke, I placed the last of Isabelle Gagnon's bones in the box and tapped on the cover.

"There must be hundreds of different kinds of saws. Crosscut saws. Ripsaws. Pruning saws. Hacksaws. Keyhole saws. Kitchen and meat saws. Ryoba saws. Gigli and rod saws. Bone and metacarpal saws. And those are just the hand-powered ones. Some run on muscle, and some are powered by electricity or gas. Some move with a reciprocating action, some use continuous action, some move back and forth, some use a rotating blade. Saws are designed to cut different types of materials and to do different things as they cut. Even if we just stick to handsaws, which is what we've got here, they vary as to blade dimensions, and the size, spacing, and set of their teeth."

I looked to see if he was still with me. He was, eyes as blue as the flame in a gas burner.

"What all this means is that saws leave characteristic marks in materials such as bone. The troughs they leave are of different widths and contain certain patterns in their walls and floors."

"So if you've got a bone you can tell the specific saw that cut it?"

"No. But you *can* determine the most likely class of saw that made the cuts."

He digested that. "How do you know this is a handsaw?"

"Power saws don't depend on muscle, so they tend to leave more consistent cuts. The scratches in the cuts, the striae, are more evenly patterned. The direction of the cut is also more uniform; you don't see a lot of directional changes like you do with a handsaw." I thought for a minute. "Since there isn't a lot of human energy required, people using power saws often leave a lot of false starts. And deeper false starts. Also, because the saw is heavier, or sometimes because the person working it is putting pressure on the object being cut, power saws tend to leave larger breakaway spurs when the bone finally gives."

"What if a really strong person is working a handsaw?"

"Good point. Individual skill and strength can be factors. But power saws often leave scratches at the start of the cut, since the blade is already moving when it makes contact. Exit chipping is also more marked with a power saw." I paused, but this time he waited me out. "The greater transfer of energy with power saws can also leave a sort of polish on the cut surface. Handsaws don't usually do that."

I took a breath. He waited to be sure I was actually through.

"What's a false start?"

"When the blade first enters the bone it forms a trough, or kerf, with corners at the initial striking surface. As the saw moves deeper and deeper into the bone, the initial corners become walls and the kerf develops a distinct floor. Like a trench. If the blade jumps out, or is pulled out, before going all the way through the bone, the kerf that's left is known as a false start. A false start contains all kinds of information. Its width is determined by the width of the saw blade and the set of its teeth. A false start will also have a characteristic shape in cross-section, and the teeth of the blade may leave marks on its walls."

"What if the saw goes straight through the bone?"

"If the cut progresses all the way through the bone, the kerf floor can still partially be seen in a breakaway spur. That's a spike that's left at the edge of the bone where it finally breaks. Also, individual tooth marks may be left on the cut surface."

I dug Gagnon's radius back out, found a partial false start on the breakaway spur, and angled the fiber-optic beam across it.

"Here, look at this."

He leaned over and squinted into the eyepiece, fiddling with the focus knob.

"Yeah. I see it."

"Look at the kerf floor. What do you see?"

"It looks lumpy."

"Right. Those lumps are bone islands. They mean that the teeth were set at alternating angles from the saw blade. That kind of set causes a phenomenon known as blade drift."

He raised his head from the microscope and looked at me blankly. The eyepiece had left double rings, grooving his face like that of a swimmer with tight goggles.

"When the first tooth cuts into the bone it tries to align itself to the plane of the blade. It seeks the midline, and the blade goes along with that. When the next tooth enters the bone it tries to do the same thing, but it's set in the opposite direction. The blade readjusts. This happens as each tooth comes along, so the forces acting on the blade change constantly. As a result, it sort of drifts back and forth in the kerf. The more set to the teeth, the more the blade is forced to drift. A very wide set causes successive teeth to drift so much that material is actually left in the midline of the kerf. Bone islands. Lumps."

"So they tell you the teeth were angled."

"Actually, they tell more than that. Since each directional change of a tooth is caused by the introduction of a new tooth, the distance between these directional changes can tell the distance between teeth. Since islands represent the widest points of bone drift, the distance from island to island is equal to the distance between two teeth. Let me show you something else."

I withdrew the radius and inserted the ulna so that the cut surface at its wrist end was illuminated, then I stepped back from the microscope.

"Can you see those wavy lines on the cut surface?"

"Yeah. Looks kind of like a washboard, only curvy."

"That's called harmonics. Blade drift leaves those peaks and valleys on the wall of the cut just as it leaves bone islands on the floor. The peaks and islands correspond to the wide points in drift; the valleys and narrow aspects of the floor correspond to the points in drift when the blade is closest to the midline."

"So you can measure these peaks and valleys like you do the islands?"

"Exactly."

"How come I don't see anything farther down in the kerf?"

"Drift occurs mostly at the beginning or end of a cut, when the blade is free, not embedded in bone."

"Makes sense." He looked up. The goggles were back.

"Can you tell anything about direction?"

"Of blade stroke or blade progress?"

"What's the difference?"

"Direction of stroke has to do with whether the blade is cutting on the push or the pull. Most Western saws are designed to cut on the push. Some Japanese saws cut on the pull. Some can cut on both. Progress has to do with the direction the blade moves through the bone."

"Can you determine that?"

"Yup."

"So what do you have?" he asked, rubbing his eyes and trying to look at me at the same time.

I took my time answering, kneading the small of my back, then reaching for my clipboard. I flipped through my notes, selecting relevant points.

"Isabelle Gagnon's bones have quite a few false starts. The kerfs measure about .05 inches in width and have floors that, in most cases, have some dip to them. Harmonics are present, and there are bone islands. Both are measurable." I flipped a page. "There's some exit chipping."

He waited for me to go on. When I didn't, he said, "What does all that mean?"

"I think we're dealing with a handsaw with alternating set teeth, probably a TPI of 10."

"TPI?"

"Teeth per inch. In other words, tooth distance is about a tenth of an inch. The teeth are chisel type, and the saw cuts on the push stroke."

"I see."

"The blade drift is extreme and there's a lot of exit chipping, but the blade seems to cut efficiently by chiseling the material clear. I think it's probably a saw designed like a very large hacksaw. The islands mean the set has to be pretty wide, to avoid binding."

"That narrows it to what?"

I was pretty sure I knew what had made the cuts, but wasn't ready to share my thoughts.

"There's someone else I want to talk to before I reach a conclusion."

"Anything else?"

I flipped to the first page of my notes, and summarized the observations I'd made.

"The false starts are on the anterior surfaces of the long bones. Where there are breakaway spurs, they're on the posterior aspects. That means the body was probably lying on its back when it was cut up. The arms were detached at the shoulders, and the hands were cut off. The legs were removed at the hips and the knee joints were severed. The head was removed at the level of the fifth cervical vertebra. The thorax was opened with a vertical slash that penetrated all the way to the vertebral column."

He shook his head. "Guy was a real whiz with a saw."

"It's more complicated than that."

"*More* complicated?"

"He also used a knife."

I adjusted the ulna and refocused. "Take another look."

He bent over the scope, and I couldn't help noticing his nice, tight butt. Jesus, Brennan . . .

"You don't have to press quite so hard against the eyepieces."

His shoulders relaxed somewhat, and he shifted his weight.

"See the kerfs we've been talking about?"

"Uh-huh."

"Now, look to the left. See the narrow slash?"

He was silent for a moment as he adjusted the focus. "Looks more like a wedge. Not square. It's not as wide."

"Right. That's made by a knife."

He stood up. Goggles.

"The knife marks have a definite pattern. A lot of them parallel the saw false starts, some even cross them. Also, they're the only kind I see in the hip joint and on the vertebrae."

"Meaning?"

"Some of the knife marks overlie saw marks and some are underneath, so the cutting probably came before and after the sawing. I think he cut the flesh with the knife, separated the joints with the saw, then finished with the knife, maybe disconnecting any muscles or tendons that still held the bones together. Except for the wrists, he went right into the joints. For some reason he just sawed the hands off above the wrists, going right through the lower arm bones."

He nodded.

"He decapitated Isabelle Gagnon and opened her chest using just the knife. There are no saw marks on any of the vertebrae."

We were both silent for a few moments thinking about that. I wanted all this to sink in before I dropped the bombshell.

"I also examined Trottier."

The brilliant blue eyes met mine. His gaunt face looked tense, stretched, as he prepared it to receive what I was about to say.

"It's identical."

He swallowed and took a deep breath. Then he spoke very quietly. "This guy must run Freon through his veins."

Ryan pushed off from the counter just as a janitor poked his head through the door. We both turned to look at him, and, seeing our somber expressions, the man left quickly. Ryan's eyes reengaged mine. His jaw muscles flexed.

"Run this by Claudel. You're getting there."

"I've got a couple of other things I want to check out first. Then I'll approach Capitaine Congenial."

He departed without saying good-bye, and I finished repacking the bones. I left the boxes on the table and locked the lab behind me. As I passed through the main reception area, I noted the clock above the elevators: 6:30 P.M. Once again it was me and the cleaning crew. I knew it was too late to accomplish either of the last two things I'd planned to do, but decided to try anyway.

I walked past my own office and down the corridor to the last door on the right. A small plaque said, INFORMATIQUE, with the name LUCIE DUMONT printed neatly below.

It had been long in arriving, but the LML and LSJ were finally coming on-line. Complete computerization had been achieved in the fall of '93, and data were continually being fed into the system. Current cases could now be tracked, with reports from all divisions coordinated into master files.

Cases from years past were gradually being entered into the database. L'Expertise Judiciaire had roared into the computer age, and Lucie Dumont was leading the charge.

Her door was closed. I knocked, knowing there would be no answer. At 6:30 P.M. even Lucie Dumont was gone.

I trudged back to my office, pulled out my membership directory for the American Academy of Forensic Sciences, and found the name I was looking for. I glanced at my watch, quickly calculating. It would be only four-forty there. Or would it be five-forty? Was Oklahoma on Mountain or Central time?

"Oh hell," I said, punching in the area code and number. A voice answered and I asked for Aaron Calvert. I was told, in a friendly, twangy way, that I was speaking with the night service, but that they'd be glad to take a message. I left my name and number and hung up, still not knowing into what time zone I'd been speaking.

This was not going well. I sat a moment, regretful that my burst of resolve hadn't come earlier in the day. Then, undaunted, I reached for the receiver again. I dialed Gabby's number and got no response. Apparently, even the answering machine had dropped out. I tried her office at the university, and listened to the line roll over after four rings. As I was about to hang up, the phone was answered. It was the departmental office. No, they hadn't seen her. No, she hadn't picked up her mail for a few days. No, that wasn't unusual, it was summer. I thanked them and hung up.

"Strike three," I said to the empty air. No Lucy. No Aaron. No Gabby. God, Gabby, where are you? I wouldn't let myself think about it.

I tapped the blotter with a pen.

"High and outside."

I tapped some more.

"Fourth and long," I added, ignoring the mixed metaphor. Tap. Tap.

"D.Q."

I leaned back and flipped the pen end on end into the air.

"Double fault."

I caught the pen and sent it airborne again.

"Personal foul."

Another launch.

"Time to switch to a new game plan."

Catch. Launch.

"Time to dig in and hold the line."

I caught the pen and held it. Dig in. I looked at the pen. Dig in. That's it.

"Okay," I said, pushing back my chair and reaching for my purse.

"Try batting from the other side of the plate."

I slung the purse over my shoulder and turned out the light.

"In your face, Claudel!"

14

WHEN I GOT TO THE MAZDA
I tried resuming my sports cliché soliloquy. It was
no good. The genius was gone. Anticipation of
what I had planned for the evening had me too
wired for creative thought. I drove to the apartment, stopping only at Kojax to pick up a souvlaki plate.

Arriving home, I ignored Birdie's accusatory
greeting, and went directly to the refrigerator for a
Diet Coke. I set it on the table next to the grease-
stained bag containing my dinner, and glanced at
the answering machine. It stared back, silent and
unblinking. Gabby hadn't called. A growing sense
of anxiety was wrapping itself around me and, like
a conductor high on his music, my heart was beating prestissimo.

I went to the bedroom and rifled through the
bedside stand. What I wanted was buried in the
third drawer. I took it to the dining room, spread

it on the table, and opened my drink and carry-out. No go. The sight of greasy rice and overcooked beef made my stomach withdraw like a sand crab. I reached for a slice of pita.

I located my street on the now familiar foot, and traced a route out of Centre-ville and across the river onto the south shore. Finding the neighbor-hood I wanted, I folded the map with the cities of St. Lambert and Longueuil showing. I tried another bite of souvlaki as I studied the landmarks, but my stomach hadn't altered its negativism. It would accept no input.

Birdie had oozed to within three inches of me. "Knock yourself out," I said, sliding the aluminum container in his direction. He looked astounded, hesitated, then moved toward it. The purring had already begun.

In the hall closet I found a flashlight, a pair of garden gloves, and a can of insect repellent. I threw them into a backpack along with the map, a tablet and a clipboard. I changed into a T-shirt, jeans, and sneakers, and braided my hair back tightly. As an afterthought, I grabbed a long-sleeved denim shirt and stuffed it into the pack. I got the pad from beside the phone and scribbled: "Gone to check out the third X—St. Lambert." I looked at my watch: 7:45 P.M. I added the date and time, and laid the tablet on the dining room table. Probably unnecessary, but in case I got into trouble I had at least left a trail.

Slinging the pack over my shoulder, I punched in the code for the security system, but in my building excitement I got the numbers wrong and had to start over. After messing up a second time, I stopped, closed my eyes, and recited every word of "I Wonder What the King Is Doing Tonight." Clear the mind with an exercise in trivia. It was a

DÉJÀ DEAD

trick I'd learned in grad school, and, as usual, it
worked. The time-out in Camelot helped me rees-
tablish control. I entered the code without a slip,
and left the apartment.

Emerging from the garage, I circled the block,
took Ste. Catherine east to De la Montagne, and
wound my way south to the Victoria Bridge, one
of three linking the island of Montreal with the
south shore of the St. Lawrence River. The clouds
that had tiptoed across the afternoon sky were now
gathering for serious action. They filled the horizon,
dark and ominous, turning the river a hostile,
inky gray.

I could see Île Notre-Dame and Île Ste. Hélène
upriver, with the Jacques-Cartier Bridge arching
above them. The little islands lay somber in the
deepening gloom. They must have throbbed with
activity during Expo '67, but were idle now,
hushed, dormant, like the site of an ancient
civilization.

Downriver lay Île des Soeurs. Nuns' Island. Once
the property of the church, it was now a Yuppie
ghetto, a small acropolis of condos, golf courses,
tennis courts, and swimming pools, the Champlain
Bridge its lifeline to the city. The lights of its high-
rise towers flickered, as if in competition with the
distant lightning.

Reaching the south shore, I exited onto Sir Wil-
fred Laurier Boulevard. In the time it took to cross
the river, the evening sky had turned an eerie
green. I pulled over to study the map. Using the
small emerald shapes that represented a park and
the St. Lambert golf course, I fixed my location,
then replaced the map on the seat beside me. As
I shifted into gear, a snap of lightning electrified
the night. The wind had picked up, and the first fat
drops began to splatter on the windshield.

I crept along through the spooky, prestorm darkness, slowing at each intersection to crane forward and squint at the street signs. I followed the route I'd plotted in my head, turning left here, right there, then two more lefts . . .

After ten more minutes I pulled over and put the car in park. My heart sounded like a Ping-Pong ball in play. I rubbed my damp palms on my jeans and looked around.

The sky had deepened and the darkness was almost total. I'd come through residential neighborhoods of small bungalows and tree-lined streets, but now found myself on the edge of an abandoned industrial park, marked as a small gray crescent on the map. I was definitely alone.

A row of deserted warehouses lined the right side of the street, their lifeless shapes illuminated by a single functioning streetlamp. The building closest to the lamppost stood out in eerie clarity, like a stage prop under studio lights, while its neighbors receded into ever-deepening murkiness, the farthest disappearing into pitch blackness. Some of the buildings bore realtors' signs offering them for sale or rent. Others had none, as if their owners had given up. Windows were broken, and the parking lots were cracked and strewn with debris. The scene was an old black-and-white of London during the Blitz.

The view to the left was no less desolate. Nothing. Total darkness. This emptiness corresponded to the unmarked green space on the map where St. Jacques had placed his third X. I'd hoped to find a cemetery or a small park.

Damn.

I put my hands on the wheel and stared into the blackness.

Now what?

I really hadn't thought this through.

Lightning flashed, and for a moment the street was aglow. Something flew out of the night and slapped against the windshield. I jumped and gave a yelp. The creature hung there a moment, beating a spastic tattoo against the glass, then flew off into the dark, an erratic rider on the mounting wind.

Cool it, Brennan. Deep breath. My anxiety level was in the ionosphere.

I reached for the backpack, put on the denim shirt, shoved the gloves into my back pocket and the flashlight into my waistband, leaving the notepad and pen.

You won't be taking any notes, I told myself.

The night smelled of rain on warm cement. The wind was chasing debris along the street, swirling leaves and paper upward into small cyclones, dropping them into piles, then stirring them up anew. It caught my hair and grabbed at my clothes, snapping my shirttails like laundry on a line. I tucked in the shirt and took the flashlight in my hand. The hand trembled.

Sweeping the beam in front of me, I crossed the street, then stepped up the curb onto a narrow patch of grass. I'd been right. A rusted iron fence, about six feet high, ran along the edge of the property. On the far side of the fence, trees and bushes formed a thick tangle, a wildwood forest that stopped abruptly, held in check by the iron barrier. I aimed the light straight ahead, trying to peer through the trees, but I couldn't tell how far they extended or what lay beyond them.

As I followed the fence line, overhanging branches dipped and rose in the wind, shadows dancing across the small, yellow circle of my flashlight. Raindrops slapped the leaves above my head, and a few penetrated to strike my face. The downpour was not far off. Either the dropping temperature or the hostile setting was making me shiver. More like both. I cursed myself for bringing the bug spray instead of a jacket.

Three quarters of the way up the block I stepped down hard at a drop in elevation. I swept the light along what seemed to be a driveway or service road leading forward to a break in the trees. At the fence, a set of gates was held shut by a length of chain and a combination padlock.

The entrance didn't look recently used. Weeds grew in the gravel roadbed, and the border of litter that ran the length of the fence was uninterrupted at the gate. I aimed the light through the opening, but it penetrated the darkness only a little. It was like using a Bic to light the Astrodome.

I inched along for another fifty yards or so until I reached the end of the block. It took a decade. At the corner I looked around. The street I'd been following ended at a T-intersection. I peered into the gloom on the far side of the intersecting, equally dark and deserted street.

I could make out a sea of asphalt running the length of the block and surrounded by a chain-link fence. I guessed it had been a parking area for a factory or warehouse. The crumbling compound was lit by a single bulb suspended from a makeshift arch on a telephone pole. The bulb was hooded by a metal shade, and threw light for approximately twenty feet. Debris skittered across the empty pavement, and here and there I could see the silhouette of a small shack or storage shed.

I listened for a moment. A cacophony. Wind. Raindrops. Distant thunder. My pounding heart. The light from across the way compromised the blackness just enough to reveal my unsteady hands

Okay, Brennan, I chided myself, cut the crap. No pain, no gain.

"Hmm. Good one," I said aloud. My voice sounded strange, muffled, as if the night were swallowing my words before they could reach my ears.

I turned back to the fence. At the end of the block it rounded the corner and took a hard left, paralleling the street I'd just reached. I turned with it. Within ten feet the iron uprights ended at a stone wall. I stepped back and played the light over it. The wall was grayish, about eight feet high, topped by a border of stones jutting six inches laterally from the face. As best I could see in the darkness, it ran the length of the street, with an opening near midblock. It looked to be the front of the property.

I followed the wall, noting the soggy paper, broken glass, and aluminum containers that had collected at its base. I stepped on a variety of objects I didn't care to identify.

Within fifty yards the wall gave way, once again, to rusted iron grillwork. More gates, secured like the set at the side entrance. When I held the flashlight close to inspect the chain and padlock, the metal links gleamed. This chain looked new.

I tucked the flashlight into my waistband, and yanked the chain sharply. It held. I tried again, with the same result. I stepped back, retrieved the light, and began passing the beam slowly up and down the bars.

Just then something grabbed my leg. As I clawed at my ankle, I dropped the flashlight. In my mind I could see red eyes and yellow teeth. In my hand I felt a plastic sack.

"Shit," I said, my mouth dry, my hands shakier than before as I disentangled myself from the bag. "Assaulted and battered by a Pharmaprix sack."

I released the bag and it went whipping off in the wind. I could hear it rustling as I groped for my flashlight. It had gone out when it hit the ground. I found it but it was reluctant to serve. At first nothing. I pounded it against the palm of my hand, and the bulb flicked on, then died. Another tap and the beam stayed on, but the light looked shaky and uncertain. I had little confidence in its long-term commitment.

I hovered a moment in the dark, considering my next move. Did I really want to go further with this? What in God's name did I hope to accomplish? Home to a hot bath and bed seemed the better plan.

I closed my eyes and concentrated on sound, straining to filter any signs of human presence from the bustle of the elements. Later, in the many times I would replay that scene in my mind, I would ask myself if there wasn't something I missed. The crunch of tires on gravel. The creak of a hinge. The hum of a car engine. Perhaps I was sloppy, perhaps the building storm was a co-conspirator, but I noticed nothing.

I took a deep breath, squared my shoulders, and peered into the darkness beyond the wall. Once in Egypt I had been in a tomb in the Valley of the Kings when the lights failed. I remember standing in that small space, engulfed not just in darkness, but in a total absence of light. I had felt as if the world had been snuffed out. As I tried to tease something from the void beyond the fence, that feeling returned. What held darker secrets? The pharaoh's tomb or the blackness inside that wall?

The X marks something. It's in there. Go.

I retraced my steps to the corner and down the fence to the side gate. How could I disengage the lock? I was playing the light over the metal bars, searching for an answer, when lightning lit the scene like a camera flash. I smelled ozone in the air and felt a tingling in my scalp and hands. In the brief burst of light I spied a sign to the right of the gates.

By the flashlight beam it looked to be a small metal plaque bolted to the bars. Though rusted and obscured, the message was clear. *Entrée interdite.* Entrance forbidden. Keep out. I held the light close and tried to make out the smaller print below. Something de Montreal. It looked like Archduke. Archduke de Montreal? I didn't think there was one.

I peered at a tiny circle below the writing. Gently, I dislodged some rust with my thumbnail. An emblem began to appear, resembling a crest or coat of arms that looked vaguely familiar. Then it hit me. Archdiocese. Archdiocese of Montreal. Of course. This was church property, probably an abandoned convent or monastery. Quebec was peppered with them.

Okay, Brennan, you're Catholic. Protected on church property. Full-court press. Where were these clichés coming from? Pumping out with the rushes of adrenaline that alternated with the trembling apprehension.

I stuck the flashlight into my jeans, took the chain in my right hand, and grasped a rusty metal upright with my left. I was about to yank, but there was no resistance. Link by link the chain slithered through the bars, looping over my wrist like a snake coiling onto a branch. I let go of the gate and reeled in the chain with both hands. It didn't come loose completely, but stopped when the padlock wedged between the bars. I looked at it in disbelief. It was hooked through the last link, but the prongs had been left unclasped.

I unhooked the lock, pulled the rest of the chain through the bars, and stared at them both. The wind had stopped during my labors, leaving an unsettling hush. The quiet pounded on my ears.

I looped the chain over the right gate, and pulled the left one toward me. The hinges seemed to scream in the void left by the wind. No other sound breached the silence. No frogs. No crickets. No distant train whistles. It was as if the universe were holding its breath, awaiting the storm's next move.

The gate moved grudgingly and I passed through, easing it closed behind me. I followed a roadbed, my shoes making soft crunching sounds on the gravel. I kept the light roving from the road to the thicket of trees on each side. After ten yards I stopped and directed the beam upward. The branches, ominously still, were interlaced in an arch above my head.

Here's the church. Here's the steeple. Great. My mind had switched to children's rhymes. I was shivering from tension and wound up with enough energy to repaint the Pentagon. You're losing it, Brennan, I warned myself. Think about Claudel. No. Think about Gagnon and Trottier and Adkins.

I turned to my right and swept the beam as far as it would reach, allowing it to linger briefly on each of the trees bordering the road. They marched along in endless rank. When I did the same on my left, I thought I saw a narrow break about ten yards up.

I kept the beam focused on that spot and crept forward. What looked like a gap wasn't. The trees didn't break rank, yet the place looked different somehow, disturbed. Then it struck me. It wasn't the trees, it was the underbrush. The ground cover was sparse and patchy, and the vines and creepers looked stunted compared with those nearby. Like a clearing partly overgrown again.

They're younger, I thought. More recent. I shone the light in all directions. The undersized vegetation seemed to flow in a narrow strip, like a stream meandering through the trees. Or a path. I gripped the flashlight tighter and followed the diversion. As I took my first step, the storm broke.

The steady drizzle gave way to a sudden torrent, and the trees burst into motion, leaping and diving like a thousand kites. Lightning flashed and thunder responded, over and over, like demon creatures seeking each other. Snap. Where are you? Boom. Over here. The wind returned with full fury, driving the water sideways.

Water soaked my clothes and plastered my hair to my head. It streamed down my face, blurred my vision, and stung the abrasion on my cheek. Blinking, I tucked some loose hair behind my ears and ran a hand over my eyes. I pulled out a shirttail and held it over the flashlight to try to keep the water from getting inside the casing.

Hunching my shoulders, I edged up the path, oblivious of everything beyond the ten-foot diameter of my pale yellow beacon. I swung the beam back and forth across the path, allowing it to probe the woods on either side, like a dog on a leash, sniffing and poking its way along.

In about fifty feet I spotted it. Looking back, I realize that an instant synapse occurred, that in a nanosecond my brain linked the visual input of the moment to a past experience recently stored. At some level of awareness I knew what I was seeing before my conscious mind developed the picture.

As I closed in and the beam teased its find from the covering darkness, recognition broke the surface. I could taste my stomach contents in my throat.

In the wobbling shaft of light I saw a brown plastic garbage bag poking through the dirt and leaves, its open end twisted and tied back onto itself. The knot rose from the earth like a sea lion surfacing for air.

I watched rain pound down on the bag and the surrounding soil. The water nibbled at the edges of the shallow burial, turning the dirt to mud and slowly but persistently uncovering the hole. I could feel a weakness at the back of my knees as more of the bag was exposed.

A flash of lightning snapped me out of my reverie. I jumped more than stepped toward the bag, and bent down to examine it. Tucking the flashlight back into my jeans, I grabbed the knotted end of the bag and pulled. It was still buried too deep to budge. I tried to undo the knot, but my wet fingers got a poor grip on wet plastic. It wouldn't give. I placed my nose close to the sealed opening and inhaled. Mud and plastic. No other smell.

I made a small perforation in the bag with my thumbnail and sniffed again. Though faint, the odor was identifiable. The sweet, fetid smell of rotted flesh and damp bone. Before I could decide on flight or fury, a twig snapped and I sensed movement behind me. As I tried to leap sideways, lightning flashed inside my head, sending me plunging back into that pharaoh's tomb.

15

I HADN'T BEEN THIS HUNG-over in a very long time. As usual, I was too sick to remember much. When I moved, harpoons of pain shot into my brain and forced me to be still. I knew if I opened my eyes I'd vomit. My stomach also recoiled at the thought of motion, yet I had to get up. Above all, I was cold. My body was gripped by a chill that had taken over its core. I began to shake uncontrollably, and thought I needed another blanket.

I sat up with my eyes still tightly shut. The pain in my head was so fierce I retched up a small quantity of bile. I lowered my head to my knees and waited for the nausea to pass. Still unable to open my eyes, I spit the bile into my left hand, and felt for my comforter with my right.

Through the throbbing and shivering, I began to realize I wasn't in my bed. My groping hand encountered twigs and leaves. That got my eyes open, pain or no pain.

I was sitting in a wood, in wet clothes and covered with mud. The ground around me was littered with leaves and small branches, and the air was heavy with the smell of earth and things that would become earth. Above me I could see a latticework of branches, their dark, spidery fingers intertwining against a black velvet sky. Behind them, a million stars flickered through the leafy cover.

Then memory logged in. The storm. The gates. The path. But how had I come to be lying here? This was not a hangover night, only a parody of one.

I ran an exploratory hand over the back of my head. A knob the size of a lime was palpable beneath my hair. Great. Bashed twice in one week. Most boxers are punched less often.

But *how* had I been bashed? Had I tripped and fallen? Had a tree limb struck me? The storm had been churning things up pretty well, but no large branches lay next to me. I couldn't remember, and I didn't care. I just wanted to be gone.

Fighting back nausea, on my hands and knees I fumbled for the flashlight. I found it half buried in mud, wiped it clean, and flicked the switch. Amazingly, it worked. Controlling my trembling legs, I stood and more fireworks exploded in my head. I braced myself against a tree and retched again.

The taste of bile filled my mouth and triggered more questions by my consciousness. When did I eat? Last night? Tonight? What time is it? How long have I been here? The storm had ended and stars emerged. And it was still night. And I was freezing. That's all I knew.

When the abdominal contractions stopped, I straightened slowly and played the flashlight around me, looking for the path. The beam dancing across the ground cover tripped another cognitive wire. The buried bag. The burst of memory brought with it a wave of fear. I gripped the flashlight tighter, and turned a complete rotation, assuring myself that no one was behind me. Back to the bag. Where had it been? Recall was creeping back, but in still frames. I could see the bag in my mind, but couldn't fix a location on the ground.

I probed in the adjacent vegetation searching for the burial. My head pounded and nausea kept rising in my throat, but there was nothing left, and the dry heaving made my sides ache and my eyes tear. I kept stopping and bracing against a tree, waiting for the spasms to subside. I noted crickets warming up for a post-storm gig, and their music had the feel of gravel sucked into my ears and dragged across my brain.

The bag was not ten feet away when I finally found it. Shaking so I could hardly hold the flashlight steady, I saw it as I remembered, though with more plastic exposed. A moat of rainwater circled its perimeter, and small pools had collected in the folds and creases of the bag itself.

In no condition to recover it, I just stood staring. I knew the scene had to be processed correctly, but was afraid someone might disturb it, or remove the remains before a unit could get there. I wanted to cry in frustration.

Oh, there's a good idea, Brennan. Weep. Maybe someone will come and rescue you.

I stood, trembling from cold and whatever, trying to think but my brain cells not cooperating, slamming their doors and refusing all callers. Phone it in. That thought got through.

I identified the borders of the brushy path and picked my way out of the woods. Or hoped I was. Couldn't remember coming in and had only a vague notion of the way out. My sense of direction had left with my short-term memory. Without warning, the flashlight died, and I was plunged into the near darkness of filtered starlight. Shaking the flashlight did not help, nor swearing at it.

"Shit!" At least I tried.

I listened for some audible direction finder. All I heard were crickets from every direction. Chirping in the round. That wouldn't work.

I tried to distinguish shadowy small growth from shadowy larger growth, and crept forward in the direction my face was pointing. As good a plan as any. Unseen branches grabbed my hair and clothing, and vines and creepers tugged at my feet.

You're off the path, Brennan. This stuff's getting thicker.

I was deciding which way to veer when one foot met air and dropped off the earth. I followed it forward, landing hard on my hands and one knee. My feet were trapped, and my forward knee pressed against what felt like loose earth. The flashlight had flown from my hand and jarred to life when it hit the ground. It had tumbled and was now casting an eerie yellow glow back toward me. I looked down and saw my feet disappearing into a tight, dark space.

My heart in my throat, I clawed my way out and scrambled toward the light, sideways like a crab on a beach. Pointing the beam to where I'd fallen, I saw a small crater. It gaped fresh and raw, like an unhealed wound in the earth. Loose dirt rimmed its perimeter and gathered in a small mound behind it.

I shone the light into the opening. It was not large, perhaps two feet across and three feet deep. In my stumbling, I planted a foot too close to the rim, sending a stream of soil dribbling into the pit. Like Grape-Nuts pouring from a box, I thought. They joined those I'd dislodged by my fall.

I stared at the soil as it collected in a small heap at the bottom of the hole. Something about it. Then realization. The dirt was practically dry. Even to my scrambled brain the inference was clear. This hole had either been covered, or dug since the rain.

An involuntary tremor seized me, and I wrapped my arms across my chest for warmth. I was still soaking and the storm had left cold air in its wake. The arm movement didn't really warm me, and drew the light away from the pit. I unfolded my arms and readjusted the beam. Why would someone . . .

The real question slammed home, making my stomach recoil like a .45 caliber pistol. *Who?* Who had come here to dig, or empty, this hole? Is he, or she, here now? That thought jolted me into action. I spun and swept the flash around in a 360. A geyser of pain vented in my head and my heartbeat tripled.

I don't know what I expected to see. A slathering Doberman? Norman Bates with his mother? Hannibal Lecter? A George Burns god in a baseball cap? None of them showed. I was alone with the trees and the creepers and the star-pierced darkness.

What I did see in the rotating light was the path. I left the fresh hole and staggered back to the half-buried bag. I kicked a blanket of leaves over it. The crude camouflage wouldn't fool the person who brought it there, but it might conceal the bag from casual eyes.

When satisfied with my ground cover, I took the can of insect repellent from my pocket and jammed it into the fork of an adjacent tree as a marker. Moving down the path, I tripped on weeds and roots and barely kept my feet. My legs felt as if they'd been deadened with drugs, and I moved in slow motion.

At the junction of the path with the roadbed, I stuck each of my gloves into a tree fork, and plunged on toward the gate. I was sick and exhausted, and feared I might pass out. The adrenaline would soon give out, and collapse would come. When it did, I wanted to be elsewhere.

My old Mazda was parked where I'd left it. Looking neither left nor right, I stumbled headlong across the street, mindless of who might be waiting for me. Almost past feeling, I plunged my hands into pocket after pocket, groping for keys. On finding them I cursed myself for carrying so many on the same ring. Shaking, cursing, and dropping the keys twice, I disentangled the car key, opened the door, and threw myself behind the wheel.

Locking the door, I draped my arms across the steering wheel and rested my head. I felt a need to sleep, to escape my circumstances by drifting out of them. I knew I had to fight the urge. Someone could be out there, watching me, deciding on a course of action.

Another mistake, I reminded myself, as my eyelids drifted toward each other, would be to just rest here a second.

My mind went into random scan. George Burns appeared again and said, "I'm always interested in the future. I plan to spend the rest of my life there."

I sat up smartly and dropped my hands to my lap. The stab of pain helped clear my mind. I didn't throw up. Progress.

"If you're going to *have* a future, you'd better get your ass out of here, Brennan."

My voice sounded heavy in the closed space, but it, too, helped orient me to the present reality. I started the engine, and the digits on the console clock glowed green: 2:15 A.M. When had I set out?

Still shivering, I flicked the heat to high, though I wasn't sure it would help. The chill I was feeling was only partly due to the wind and the night air. There was a deeper cold in my soul that would not be warmed by a mechanical heater. I pulled away without a backward glance.

I slid the soap over my breasts, circling each again and again, willing the sweet-smelling lather to cleanse me of the night's events. I raised my face to the spray that was pounding my head and coursing over my body. The water would grow cold soon. I'd been showering for twenty minutes, trying to drive out the cold and silence the voices in my head.

The heat and the steam and the scent of jasmine should have relaxed me, loosened the tension in my muscles and carried away the soreness. They hadn't. The whole time I was listening for a sound outside my rectangle of steam. I was waiting for the phone to ring. Fearful I'd miss Ryan's call, I had brought the handset into the bathroom.

I'd called the station immediately on reaching home, even before stripping off my wet clothes. The dispatcher had been skeptical, reluctant to disturb a detective in the middle of the night. She'd been adamant in her refusal to give me Ryan's home number, and I'd left his card at work. Standing in my living room, shivering, my head still pounding and my stomach regrouping for another attack, I'd been in no mood for discussion. My words, as well as my tone, persuaded her. I would apologize tomorrow.

That had been half an hour ago. I felt the back of my head. The lump was still there. Under my wet hair it felt like a hard-boiled egg, and was tender to the touch. Before getting into the shower I'd gone through the instructions I'd been given following previous thumps on the head. I checked my pupils, rotated my head hard right and hard left, and pricked my hands and feet to test for feeling. All parts seemed to be in their proper places and in working order. If I'd suffered a concussion, it was a mild one.

I turned off the water and stepped from the shower. The phone lay where I'd left it, mute and disinterested.

Damn. Where is he?

I dried myself, slipped into my ratty old terry cloth robe, and wrapped a towel around my hair. I checked the answering machine to be sure I hadn't missed a call. No red light. Damn. Retrieving the handset, I clicked it on to see if it was working. Dial tone. Of course it was working. I was just agitated.

I lay down on the couch and placed the phone on the coffee table. Surely he'd call soon. No point going to bed. I closed my eyes, planning to rest a few minutes before making something to eat. But the cold and the stress and the fatigue and the jolt to my brain melded into a tidal wave of exhaustion that rose up and crashed over me, plunging me into a deep but troubled sleep. I didn't drift off, I passed out.

I was outside a fence, watching someone dig with an enormous shovel. Each time the blade came out of the ground it seethed with rats. When I looked down, there were rats everywhere. I had to keep kicking at them to keep them off my feet. The figure wielding the shovel was shadowy, but when it turned I could see it was Pete. He pointed at me and said something, but I couldn't make out the words. He started to shout and beckon to me, his mouth a round, black circle that grew larger and larger, engulfing his face and turning it into a hideous clown mask.

Rats ran across my feet. One was dragging Isabelle Gagnon's head. Its teeth were clamped onto her hair as it yanked the head across the lawn.

I tried to run, but my legs didn't move. I'd sunk into the earth, and was standing in a grave. Dirt was trickling in around me. Charbonneau and Claudel were peering down at me. I tried to speak, but words wouldn't come. I wanted them to pull me out. I held my hands out to them, but they ignored me.

Then they were joined by another figure, a man in long robes and an odd hat. He looked down and asked me if I'd been confirmed. I couldn't answer. He told me I was on church property, and had to leave. He said only those who worked for the church could enter its gates. His cassock flapped in the wind, and I worried that his hat would fall into the grave. He tried to restrain his vestments with one hand, and dial a flip phone with the other. It started to ring, but he ignored it. It rang and rang.

So did the phone on my coffee table, which I eventually distinguished from the phone in my dream. Awakening through layers of resistance, I reached for the handset.

"Um. Hm," I said, groggily.

"Brennan?"

Anglophone. Gruff. Familiar. I fought to clear my head.

"Yes?" I looked at my wrist. No watch.

"Ryan. This better be good."

"What time is it?" I had no idea if I'd been asleep five minutes or five hours. This was getting old.

"Four-fifteen."

"Just a sec."

I set the phone down and stumbled to the bathroom. I threw cold water on my face, sang one chorus of "The Drunken Sailor" as I jogged in place. Rewrapping my turban, I returned to Ryan. I didn't want to increase his annoyance by making him wait, but, even more, I didn't want to sound groggy, or to ramble. Better to take a minute to slap myself into shape.

"Okay, I'm back. Sorry."

"Was someone singing?"

"Hm. I went out to St. Lambert tonight," I began. I wanted to tell him enough, but didn't want to go into the details at 4:15 A.M. "I found the spot where St. Jacques put the X. It's some sort of abandoned church property."

"You called to tell me this at four in the morning?"

"I found a body. It's badly decomposed, probably already skeletal from the smell. We need to get out there right away before someone stumbles on it, or the neighborhood dogs organize a church supper."

I took a breath and waited.

"Are you fucking crazy?"

I wasn't sure if he was referring to what I'd found, or to my going out alone. Since he was probably right about the latter, I went for the former.

"I know a body when I find one."

There was a long silence, then, "Buried or surface?"

"Buried, but very shallow. The portion I saw was exposed, and the rain was making it worse."

"You sure this isn't another pissant cemetery eroding out?"

"The body's in a plastic bag." Like Gagnon. And Trottier. It didn't need saying.

"Shit." I could hear a match being struck, then the long expulsion of breath that meant a cigarette had been lit.

"Think we should go now?"

"No fucking way." I could hear him pull on the cigarette. "And what is this 'we'? You have something of a reputation as a freelancer, Brennan, which doesn't particularly impress me. Your go-to-hell attitude may work with Claudel, but it's not going to slice with me. The next time you feel an urge to go waltzing around a crime scene, you might just politely inquire as to whether someone in the homicide squad has an opening on his dance card. We do still fit that sort of thing into our busy schedules."

I hadn't expected gratitude, but I was unprepared for the vehemence of his response. I was starting to get angry, and it was causing the hammering in my head to escalate. I waited, but he didn't go on.

"I appreciate your calling back so soon."

"Hm."

"Where are you?" With my brain fully functional, I would never have asked. I regretted it immediately.

After a pause, "With a friend."

Good move, Brennan. No wonder he was annoyed.

"I think someone was out there tonight."

"What?"

"While I was looking at the burial, I thought I heard something, then I took a shot to the head that knocked me out. All hell was breaking loose with the storm, so I can't be sure."

"Are you hurt?"

"No."

Another pause. I could almost hear him turning things over in his head.

"I'll send a squad to secure the site until morning. Then I'll get recovery out there. Think we'll need the dogs?"

"I only saw the one bag, but there must be more. Also, it looked like there'd been other digging going on in the area. It's probably a good idea."

I waited for a response. There was none.

"What time will you pick me up?" I asked.

"I won't be picking you up, *Doctor* Brennan. This is real life homicide, as in the jurisdiction of the homicide squad, not *Murder She Wrote.*"

Now I was furious. My temples were pounding and I could feel a small cloud of heat directly between them, deep in my brain.

" 'More holes than the TransCanada,' " I spat at him. " 'Get me something else.' Those are your words, Ryan. Well, I got it. And I can take you right to it. Besides, this involves skeletal remains. Bones. That's *my* jurisdiction, unless I'm mistaken."

The line was silent for so long I thought he might have hung up. I waited.

"I'll come by at eight."

"I'll be ready."

"Brennan?"

"Yeah?"

"Maybe you should invest in a helmet."

The line went dead.

16

RYAN WAS TRUE TO HIS word, and by eight forty-five we were sliding in behind the recovery van. It sat not ten feet from where I'd parked the night before. But it was a different world from the one I'd visited hours earlier. The sun was shining and the street throbbed with activity. Cars and police cruisers lined both curbs, and at least twenty people, in plainclothes and uniform, stood talking in clumps.

I could see DEJ, SQ, and cops from St. Lambert scattered here and there, each wearing a different uniform and distinctive insignia. The assemblage reminded me of the mixed flocks birds will sometimes form, spontaneous jamborees of twittering and chirping, each bird declaring its species by the color of its plumage and the stripes on its wings.

A woman with a large shoulder bag and a young man draped with cameras smoked and leaned against the hood of a white Chevy. Yet another species: the press. Further up the block, on the grassy strip adjacent to the fence, a German shepherd panted and sniffed around a man in a dark blue jumpsuit. The dog kept bolting off on short forays, nose to the ground, then darting back to its handler, tail wagging and face upturned. It seemed anxious to go, confused by the delay.

"The gang's all here," said Ryan, putting the car in park and releasing his seat belt.

He hadn't apologized for his rudeness on the phone, and I hadn't expected it. No one is at his best at 4 A.M. He'd been cordial throughout the ride, almost jocular, pointing out places where incidents had occurred, recounting anecdotes of blunder and humiliation. War stories. Here, in this three-flat, a woman assaulted her husband with a frying pan, then turned it on us. There, in that Poulet Kentucky Frites, we found a nude man stuck in the ventilator shaft. Cop talk. I wondered if their cognitive maps were based on sites of police happenings chronicled in incident reports, rather than on the names of rivers and streets and the numbers on buildings that the rest of us use.

Ryan spied Bertrand and headed toward him. He was part of a clump composed of an SQ officer, Pierre LaManche, and a thin, blond man in dark aviator glasses. I followed him across the street, scanning the crowd for Claudel or Charbonneau. Though this was officially an SQ party, I thought they might be here. Everyone else seemed to be. I saw neither.

As we drew close I could tell the man in the sunglasses was agitated. His hands never rested, but continuously worried a wispy fringe of mustache that crawled across his upper lip. His fingers kept teasing out a few sparse hairs, then stroking them back into place. I noticed that his skin was peculiarly gray and unblemished, having neither color nor texture. He wore a leather bomber jacket and black boots. He could have been twenty-five or sixty-five.

I could feel LaManche's eyes on me as we joined the group. He nodded, but said nothing. I began to have doubts. I'd choreographed this circus, brought all these people here. What if they found nothing? What if someone had removed the bag? What if it did turn out to be just another "pissant cemetery" burial? Last night was dark, I was hyped. How much had I imagined? I could feel a growing tightness in my stomach.

Bertrand greeted us. As usual, he looked like a short, stocky version of a men's fashion model. He'd chosen earth colors for the exhumation, ecologically correct tans and browns, no doubt made without chemical dyes.

Ryan and I acknowledged those we knew, then turned to the man in the shades. Bertrand introduced us.

"Andy. Doc. This is Father Poirier. He's here representing the diocese."

"*Arch*diocese."

"Pardon me. Archdiocese. Since this is church property." Bertrand jerked his thumb toward the fence behind him.

"Tempe Brennan," I volunteered, offering my hand.

Father Poirier fixed his aviators on me and accepted it, wrapping my palm in a weak, spiritless grip. If people were graded on handshakes, he'd get a D-minus. His fingers felt cold and limp, like carrots kept too long in a cooler bin. When he released my hand, I resisted the urge to wipe it on my jeans.

He repeated the ritual with Ryan, whose face

revealed nothing. Ryan's early morning joviality had flown, replaced by stark seriousness. He'd gone into cop mode. Poirier looked as if he wanted to speak, but, seeing Ryan's face, reconsidered and crimped his lips into a tight line. Somehow, with nothing said, he recognized that authority had shifted, that Ryan was now in charge.

"Has anyone been in there yet?" asked Ryan.

"No one. Cambronne got here about 5 A.M.," said Bertrand, indicating the uniformed officer to his right. "No one's gone in or out. Father tells us that only two people have access to the grounds, himself and a caretaker. The guy's in his eighties, been working here since Mamie Eisenhower made bangs popular." In French it came out Eesenhure, and sounded comical.

"The gate could not have been open," said Poirier, turning his aviators back on me. "I check it every time I am here."

"And when is that?" asked Ryan.

The shades released me and fastened on Ryan. They rested there a full three seconds before he responded.

"At least once a week. The Church feels a responsibility for all its properties. We do not simp—"

"What is this place?"

Again, the pause. "Le Monastère St. Bernard. Closed since 1983. The Church felt the numbers did not warrant its continued operation."

I found it strange that he spoke of the Church as an animate being, an entity with feelings and will. His French was also odd, subtly different from the flat, twangy form I'd grown used to. He wasn't Québecois, but I couldn't place the accent. It wasn't the precise but throaty sound of France, what

North Americans call Parisian. I suspected he was Belgian or Swiss.

"What goes on here?" Ryan pursued.

Another pause, as if the sound waves had to travel a long distance to strike a receptor.

"Today, nothing."

The priest stopped speaking and sighed. Perhaps he recalled happier times when the Church thrived and the monasteries bustled. Perhaps he was collecting his thoughts, wanting to be precise in his statements to the police. The aviator lenses hid his eyes. An odd candidate for a priest, with his pristine skin, leather jacket, and biker footwear.

"Now, I come to check the property," he continued. "A caretaker keeps things in order."

"Things?" Ryan was taking notes in a small spiral.

"The furnace, the pipes. Shoveling the snow. We live in a very cold place." Poirier made a sweeping gesture with one thin arm, as if to take in the whole province. "The windows. Sometimes boys like to throw rocks." He looked at me. "The doors and the gates. To make certain they remain locked."

"When did you last check the padlocks?"

"Sunday at 6 P.M. They were all secure."

His prompt answer struck me. He hadn't stopped to think on this one. Maybe Bertrand had already posed the question, or maybe Poirier just anticipated it, but the speed of his response made it sound precooked.

"You noticed nothing out of the ordinary?"

"*Rien.*" Nothing.

"When does this caretaker—what's his name?"

"Monsieur Roy."

"When does he come?"

"He comes on Fridays, unless there is some special task for him."

Ryan didn't speak, but continued looking at him.

"Like clearing snow, or repairing a window."

"Father Poirier, I believe Detective Bertrand has already questioned you about the possibility of burials on the grounds?"

Pause. "No. No. There are none." He wagged his head from side to side and the sunglasses shifted on his nose. A bow popped off one ear and the frames came to rest at a twenty-degree angle. He looked like a tanker listing to port.

"This was a monastery, always a monastery. No one is buried here. But I have called our archivist and asked her to check the records to be absolutely certain." As he spoke, he moved both hands to his temples and adjusted the glasses, realigning them carefully.

"You're aware of why we're here?"

Poirier nodded and the glasses tilted again. He started to speak, then said nothing.

"Okay," said Ryan, closing the spiral and sliding it into his pocket. "How do you suggest we do this?" He directed that question to me.

"Let me take you in, show you what I found. After we remove it, bring in the dog to see if there's anything else." I was hoping my voice conveyed more confidence than I felt. Shit. What if there was nothing there?

"Right."

Ryan strode over to the man in the jumpsuit. The shepherd bounded up to him and nuzzled his hand for attention. He stroked its head as he spoke to the handler. Then he rejoined us and led the whole group to the gate. As we walked I scanned my surroundings discreetly, looking for signs showing I'd been there the night before. Nothing.

We waited at the gate as Poirier withdrew an enormous ring of keys from his pocket and selected one. He grasped the padlock and yanked, making a show of testing it against the bars. It clanged softly in the morning air, and a shower of rust drifted to the ground. Had I locked it hours earlier? I couldn't remember.

Poirier released the mechanism, unhooked the padlock, and swung the gate open. It creaked softly. Not the piercing screech of metal I recalled. He stepped back to clear the way for me, and everyone waited. LaManche still hadn't spoken.

I hitched the backpack higher onto my shoulder, brushed past the priest, and started up the roadbed. In the clear, crisp light of morning the woods seemed friendly, not malevolent. The sun shone through broad leaves and conifer needles, and the air was thick with the smell of pine. A collegial smell that evoked visions of lake houses and summer camps, not corpses and night shadows. I moved slowly, examining every tree, every inch of ground for broken branches, displaced vegetation, disturbed soil, anything to attest to human presence. Especially mine.

My anxiety level rose with every step, and my heart slipped in extra beats. What if I hadn't locked the gate? What if someone had been here after me? What had been done after I'd left?

The atmosphere was that of a place I'd never visited, but which seemed familiar because I'd read about it, or seen it in photographs. I tried to sense by time and distance where the path should be. But I had heavy misgivings. My recollection was jumbled and fuzzy, like a dream partly remembered. Major events were vivid, but details as to sequencing and duration were muddy. Let me see something to serve as a prompt, I prayed.

The prayer was answered in the form of gloves. I'd forgotten them. There, on the left side of the roadbed, just at eye level, three white fingertips poked from the fork of a tree. Yes! I scanned the adjacent trees. The second glove showed in a notch in a small maple about four feet off the ground. An image flashed of me, trembling, probing in the darkness to jam the gloves into place. I gave myself high marks for forethought, and low for recall. I thought I'd put them higher. Perhaps, like Alice, I'd had a size-altering experience in these woods.

I veered off between the gloved trees, on what I could barely make out as a path. Its impact on the thicket was so subtle that, without the markers, I might not have spotted it. In the daylight, the trail was little more than a change in texture, the vegetation along its length stunted and more sparse than that to either side. In a narrow line the ground cover did not intertwine. Weeds and small bushes stood alone, isolated from neighbors, exposing the coarse, burnt sienna of dead leaves and soil on which they stood. That was all.

I thought of the jigsaw puzzles I'd worked as a child. Gran and I pored over the pieces, searching for the right one, our eyes and brains calibrating minute variations in grain and shade. Success depended on the ability to perceive subtle differences in tone and texture. How the hell had I spotted this path in the dark?

I could hear the rustling of leaves and the snapping of twigs behind me. I didn't point out the gloves, but let them be impressed with my land navigational skills. Brennan the Pathfinder. Within a few yards I spotted the can of insect repellent. No subtlety there. The bright orange cap shone like a beacon in the foliage.

And there was my camouflaged mound. Below a white oak the ground swelled into a small protuberance covered by leaves and bordered by bare earth.

In the exposed soil I could see the marks left by my fingers as I'd scratched up leaves and dirt to conceal the plastic. The results of my hurried camouflage job may have revealed more than concealed, but it seemed the thing to do at the time.

I've done many body recoveries. Most hidden corpses are found because of a tip or a lucky break. Informants rat out their accomplices. Excited kids point out their finds. *It smelled awful so we started poking around, and there it was!* It felt odd to be one of the kids.

"There." I indicated the leafy hump.

"You sure?" Ryan asked.

I just looked at him. The others said nothing. I set down my backpack and withdrew another pair of garden gloves. Crossing to the mound, I placed my feet carefully to minimize the disturbance. Absurd, in light of my thrashing about the night before, but at an official scene proper technique is expected.

I squatted down and brushed back enough leaves to expose a small portion of the plastic bag. The bulk of it was still embedded in the earth, and the irregular contour suggested that the contents were secure within. It looked undisturbed. When I turned, Poirier was crossing himself.

Ryan spoke to Cambronne. "Let's get some shots for the travel brochure."

I rejoined the others and waited silently as Cambronne followed his ritual. He unpacked his equipment, filled out a marker board, and photographed the mound and the bag from several distances and directions. Finally, he lowered his camera and stepped back.

Ryan turned to LaManche. "Doc?"

LaManche said his first word since I'd arrived. "Temperance?"

Taking a trowel from the backpack, I crossed back to the mound. I swept away the remaining leaves, carefully uncovering as much of the bag as possible. It looked as I remembered it. I could even see the small perforation I'd made with my thumbnail.

Using the trowel, I scraped soil upward and outward around the periphery, slowly exposing more and more of the bag. The dirt smelled ancient and musty, as if bound in its molecules it held a minute part of everything it had nurtured since the glaciers released it from their icy grip.

I heard voices drifting from the law enforcement carnival on the street, but where I worked, the only sounds came from the birds, insects, and the steady scraping of my trowel. Branches lifted and fell in the breeze, a gentler version of the dance they'd done the night before. The night theater had been Masai warriors leaping and lunging in mock battle. The morning show was the "Anniversary Waltz." Shadows moved across the bag, and across the faces of the solemn group witnessing its emergence. I watched the shapes move on the plastic, like puppets in a shadow play.

Within fifteen minutes the mound had become a pit, with more than half the bag visible. I suspected the contents had rearranged themselves as decomposition progressed and bones were freed of their anatomical responsibilities. If there were bones.

Thinking I'd removed enough soil to free the bundle, I put down my trowel, took hold of the twisted plastic, and slowly pulled. It wouldn't budge. Last night all over again. Was someone underground, holding the other end of the bag, challenging me to a macabre game of tug-of-war?

Cambronne had photographed as I dug, and was now behind me, positioned to fix on Kodachrome the moment of the bag's release. The phrase popped into my mind: Capture the moments of our lives. And deaths, I thought.

I brushed my gloves along the sides of my jeans, grabbed the sack as far down as I could, and gave a short, sharp yank. Movement. The pit wouldn't yield its cache with ease, but I'd weakened its grip. I felt the bag shift and the contents relocate slightly. I took a breath and pulled again, harder. I wanted to dislodge the bag, but not rip it. It gave way and then resettled.

Bracing my feet, I gave one more tug, and my underground opponent gave up the contest. The sack started to slide free. I rewrapped my fingers around the twisted plastic, and, inching backward, step by step, teased the bag out of the pit.

When I'd pulled it free of the rim, I released my grip and stepped back. A common garbage bag, the kind found in kitchens and garages across North America. Intact. The contents made it lumpy. It wasn't heavy. That was not a good sign, or was it? Would I rather find the remains of someone's dog and be humiliated, or the remains of a human body and be vindicated?

Cambronne snapped into action. He placed his placard and took a series of shots. I removed one glove, and dug my Swiss army knife from my pocket.

When Cambronne finished, I knelt beside the bag. My hands shook slightly, but I finally got my thumbnail into the small crescent of the blade and opened it. The stainless steel glinted as sunlight struck it. I selected a spot at the bound end for my incision. I felt five sets of eyes on me.

I glanced at LaManche. His features changed shape as the shadows shifted. I wondered, briefly, how my own sullied face looked in the light. La-

Manche nodded, and I placed pressure on the blade.

Before the steel could pierce the plastic, my hand stopped, checked by a sound like an invisible tether. We all heard it at once, but Bertrand voiced our collective thought.

"What the fuck?" he said.

17

THE SUDDEN DIN WAS A CA-
cophony of sounds. The frantic barking of a dog
mingled with human voices raised in excitement.
Shouts rang back and forth, tense and clipped, but
too indistinct to make out the words. The bedlam
was within the monastery grounds, somewhere off
to our left. My first thought was that the night
prowler had returned, and that every cop in the
province, and at least one German shepherd, were
in pursuit.

I looked at Ryan and the others. Like me, they
were frozen in place. Even Poirier had stopped
fidgeting with his mustache and stood with hand
fixed to upper lip.

Then the approaching sound of a body tunneling
swiftly and indiscriminately through foliage broke
the spell. Heads turned simultaneously, as if operated by one switch. From somewhere in the trees,
a voice called out.

"Ryan? You over there?"

"Here."

We oriented in the direction of the voice.

"Sacré bleu." More thrashing and crunching. "Aiee."

An SQ officer came into view, wrestling back branches and muttering audibly. His beefy face was red, and his breathing was noisy. Sweat beaded his brow and flattened the fringe of hair circling his mostly bald head. Spotting us, he planted a hand on each knee, and bent to catch his breath. I could see scratches where twigs had dragged across the top of his exposed scalp.

After a moment he raised up and jerked a thumb in the direction from which he'd come. In a wheezy voice, like air through a clogged filter, he panted, "You better get over there, Ryan. The goddamn dog's acting like a crackhead with a bad load."

Out of the corner of my eye I saw Poirier's hand jerk to his forehead and slide to his chest. The sign of the cross called upon once more.

"What?" Ryan's eyebrows rose in puzzlement.

"DeSalvo took him around the grounds, like you said, and the sonofabitch started circling this one spot and barking like he thinks Adolf Hitler and the whole goddamn German army's buried there." He paused. "Listen to him!"

"And?"

"And??? The little bastard's about to blow a vocal chord. You don't get over there pretty quick he's going to circle right up his own asshole."

I suppressed a smile. The image was pretty comical.

"Just hold him back a few more minutes. Give him a Milk-Bone or pop him a Valium if you have to. We've got something here we need to finish."

He looked at his watch. "Get back here in ten minutes."

The officer shrugged, released the branch he was holding, and turned to go.

"Eh, Piquot."

The corpulent face swiveled back.

"There's a path here."

"Sacrifice," Piquot hissed, picking his way through the tangle toward the trail Ryan had indicated. I was sure he'd lose it within fifteen yards.

"And Piquot . . ." Ryan continued.

The face looked back again.

"Don't let Rin Tin Tin disturb anything."

He turned back to me. "You waiting to have a birthday, Brennan?"

We heard Piquot thrashing his way out of earshot as I slit the bag from end to end.

The odor didn't leap out and grab me as it had with Isabelle Gagnon. Freed of its confines, it spread outward slowly, asserting itself. My nose identified soil and plant decay, and an overlay of something else. It wasn't the fetid smell of putrefaction, but a more primeval scent. It was a smell that spoke of passing, of origins and extinctions, of life recycled. I had smelled it before. It told me the sack held something dead, and not newly dead.

Don't let it be a dog or a deer, I thought, as my gloved hands separated the opening. My hands shook again and the plastic quivered in them. Yes, I changed my mind, let it be a dog or a deer.

Ryan, Bertrand, and LaManche pressed in as I laid back the severed plastic. Poirier stood like a headstone, rooted to the spot.

First I saw a scapula. Not much, but enough to confirm this was no hunter's cache or family pet. I looked at Ryan. I could see pinching at the corners of his eyes and tension in his jaw muscles.

"It's human."

Poirier's hand flew to his forehead for another go-around.

Ryan reached for his spiral and turned a page. "What have we got?" he asked. His voice was as sharp as the blade I'd just used.

I gently moved the bones. "Ribs . . . shoulder blades . . . collarbones . . . vertebrae," I ticked off. "Looks like they're all thoracic."

"Sternum," I added, on finding the breastbone.

I probed among the bones, looking for more body parts. The others watched in silence. When I reached into the back of the bag, a large brown spider skittered across my hand and up my arm. I could see its eyes rising on stalks, tiny periscopes seeking the cause of this intrusion. Its fuzzy legs felt light and delicate, like a lace hanky brushing across my skin. I jerked back, flinging the spider into space.

"That's it," I said, straightening and stepping back. My knees popped in protest. "Upper torso. No arms." My skin was crawling, but not from the spider.

My gloved hands hung at my sides. I felt no joy in the vindication of my judgment, just a dulling numbness, like someone in shock. My emotional being had shut down, hung up a sign and gone to lunch. It's happened again, I thought. Another human being dead. A monster is out there.

Ryan scribbled in his spiral. His neck tendons bulged.

"Now what?" Poirier's voice was little more than a squeak.

"Now we find the rest," I said.

Cambronne was positioning for photos when we heard the return of Piquot. Again, he came cross country. He joined us, looked at the bones, and released a whispered expletive.

Ryan turned to Bertrand. "Can you take over here while we check out the dog?"

Bertrand nodded. His body was as rigid as the pines around us.

"Let's bag what we've got, then recovery can go over this whole area. I'll send them."

We left Bertrand and Cambronne and followed Piquot toward the barking. The animal sounded almost distraught.

Three hours later I sat on a grassy strip examining the contents of four body bags. The sun was high and hot on my shoulders, but did little to warm the chill inside me. Fifteen feet away the dog lay near its handler, its head angled across enormous brown paws. It had finished a big morning.

Conditioned to respond to the smell of decomposed or decomposing body tissue, body dogs ferret out hidden corpses like infrared systems pinpoint heat. Even after its removal they detect the former resting places of decaying flesh. They are the bloodhounds of the dead. This dog had performed well, zeroing in on three more burial sites. At each strike it announced its find with zeal, barking and snapping and circling the spot in a frenzied display. I wondered if all cadaver dogs were as passionate about their work.

Two hours were needed to excavate, process, and bag the remains. A preliminary inventory before removal, and now a more detailed list, logging every fragment of bone.

I glanced at the dog. It looked as tired as I felt. Only its eyes moved, the chocolate orbs revolving like radar dishes. It shifted its gaze without moving its head.

The dog had a right to be exhausted, but so did I. When it finally raised its head, a long, thin tongue dropped into view and hung quivering. I kept my tongue in my mouth and turned back to the inventory.

"How many?"

I hadn't heard him approach, but I knew the voice. I braced myself.

"Bonjour, Monsieur Claudel. *Comment ça va?"*

"How many?" he repeated.

"One," I answered, never raising my eyes.

"Anything missing?

I finished writing and turned to look at him. He was standing with his feet spread, jacket hung from one arm, peeling the cellophane from a vending machine sandwich.

Like Bertrand, Claudel had chosen natural textiles, cotton for the shirt and pants, linen for the jacket. He'd stayed with the greens, however, preferring a more verdant look. The only color contrast was in the pattern of his tie. Here and there it introduced a tasteful splash of tangerine.

"Can you tell what we've got?" He gestured with bread and lunch meat.

"Yes."

"Yes?"

Less than thirty seconds since his arrival and I wanted to rip the sandwich from his hand and insert it forcefully up his nose, or any other orifice. Claudel did not bring out the best in me when I was relaxed and rested. This morning I was neither. Like the dog, I'd had it. I lacked the energy or the inclination to play games.

"What *we* have is a partial human skeleton. There's almost no soft tissue. The body was dismembered, placed in garbage bags, and buried in four separate locations in there." I pointed to the monastery grounds. "I found one bag last night. The dog smelled out the other three this morning."

He took a bite, and gazed in the direction of the trees.

"What's missing?" The words garbled in ham and Muenster.

I stared at him without speaking, wondering why I found a routine question so annoying. It was his manner. I played myself a variation on my Claudel lecture. Ignore it. This is Claudel. The man is a reptile. Expect condescension and arrogance. He knows you were right. He's heard the story by now. He's not going to say 'bully for you.' It must be killing him. That's good enough. Let it go.

When I didn't answer he returned his attention to me.

"Anything missing?

"Yes."

I put down the skeletal inventory sheet and looked him full in the eye. He squinted back, chewing. I wondered briefly why he had no sunglasses.

"The head."

He stopped chewing.

"What?"

"The head is missing."

"Where is it?"

"Monsieur Claudel, if I knew that, it wouldn't be missing."

I saw his jaw muscles bunch, then release, not from mastication.

"Anything else?"

"Anything else what?"

"Missing?"

"Nothing significant."

His mind gnawed on those facts while his teeth gnawed on the sandwich. As he chewed, his fingers crumpled the cellophane, compressing it into a tight ball. Placing the ball in his pocket, he wiped each corner of his mouth with an index finger.

"I don't suppose you will tell me anything else?" More a statement than a question.

"When I have had time to examine the . . ."

"Yes." He turned and walked away.

Cursing under my breath, I zipped each of the body bags. The dog's head snapped up at the sound. Its eyes followed me as I stuffed the clipboard into my pack and crossed the street toward a morgue attendant with a waist the size of an inner tube. I told him I'd finished, that the remains could be loaded, and that then they should wait.

Up the street, I could see Ryan and Bertrand talking with Claudel and Charbonneau. The SQ meets the CUM. My paranoia made me suspicious of their talking. What was Claudel saying to them? Was it disparaging of me? Most cops are as territorial as howler monkeys, jealous of *their* turf, guarding *their* cases, wanting *their own* collars. Claudel was worse than the others, but why so specifically disdainful of me?

Forget it, Brennan. He's a bastard, and you've embarrassed him in his own backyard. You're not at the top of his hit parade. Stop worrying about feeling and think about the job. You haven't been innocent of possessive casework either.

The talk stopped as I neared. Their manner removed some of the punch from the peppy approach I'd planned, but I hid my discomfort.

"Hey, Doc," said Charbonneau.

I nodded and smiled in his direction.

"So, where are we?" I asked.

"Your boss took off about an hour ago. So did the good father. Recovery is finishing up," said Ryan.

"Anything?"

He shook his head.

"Metal detector hits?"

"Every bloody pop top tab in the province." Ryan sounded exasperated. "Oh, and we're good for one parking meter. How 'bout you?"

"I'm done. I told the morgue boys they could load up."

"Claudel says you've got no head."

"That's right. The skull, jaw, and first four neck vertebrac are missing."

"Meaning?"

"Meaning the victim was decapitated and the killer put the head somewhere. He might've buried it here, but separately, like he did with the other body parts. They were pretty scattered."

"So we've got another bag out there?"

"Maybe. Or he could've disposed of it somewhere else."

"Like where?"

"In the river, down a latrine, in his furnace. How the hell would I know?"

"Why would he do that?" asked Bertrand.

"Maybe so the body couldn't be identified."

"Could it?"

"Probably. But it's a hell of a lot easier with teeth and dental records. Besides, he left the hands."

"So?"

"If a corpse is mutilated to prevent identification, usually the hands are removed too."

He looked at me blankly.

"Prints can be taken from badly decomposed bodies, as long as there's still some preserved skin. I've gotten prints from a five-thousand-year-old mummy."

"Did you get a match?" Claudel's voice was flat.

219

"The guy wasn't entered," I responded with equal lack of mirth.

"But this is just bones," said Bertrand.

"The killer wouldn't know that. He couldn't be sure when the body would be found." Like Gagnon, I thought. Only this one he buried.

I stopped for a minute, and pictured the killer prowling the dark woods, distributing the bags and their grisly contents. Had he carved the victim elsewhere, bagged the bloody pieces, and brought them here by car? Did he park where I had parked, or was he able, somehow, to drive onto the grounds? Had he dug the holes first, planning the location of each? Or had he just carried in bags of body parts, digging one pit here and another there on four trips from his car? Was the dismemberment a panicky attempt to conceal a passion crime, or had both the murder and the mutilation been coldly premeditated?

An appalling possibility struck me. Had he been here with me last night? Back to the present.

"Or . . ."

They all looked at me.

"Or, he could still have it."

"Still have it?" scoffed Claudel.

"Shit," said Ryan.

"Like Dahmer?" asked Charbonneau.

I shrugged.

"We better take Fang back for another sweep," said Ryan. "They never brought him near the torso site."

"Right," I said. "He'll be pleased."

"Mind if we watch?" Charbonneau asked. Claudel shot him a look.

"Not as long as you think happy thoughts," I said. "I'll get the dog. Meet me at the gate."

Striding off, I heard the word "bitch" in

Claudel's nasal tone. No doubt a reference to the animal, I told myself.

The dog leapt to its feet when I approached, its tail wagging slowly. It looked from me to the man in the blue jumpsuit, seeking permission to approach the newcomer. I could see "DeSalvo" stamped on the jumpsuit.

"Fido ready for another go?" I asked, extending a hand, palm down, toward the dog. DeSalvo gave an almost imperceptible nod, and the animal leapt forward and wetly nuzzled my fingers.

"Her name's Margot," he said, speaking in English, but giving the name the French pronunciation.

His voice was low and even, and he moved with the fluid, unhurried ease of those who spend their days with animals. His face was dark and deeply lined, a fan of small creases radiating from the corner of each eye. He looked like a man who'd lived outdoors.

"French or English?"

"She's bilingual."

"Hey, Margot," I said, crouching on one knee to scratch behind her ears. "Sorry about the gender thing. Big day, eh?"

Margot's tail picked up velocity. When I rose, she leapt back, pivoted full circle, then froze, studying my face intently. She tilted her head from side to side, and the crease between her eyes furrowed and unfurrowed.

"Tempe Brennan," I said, offering my hand to DeSalvo.

He clipped one end of Margot's lead to a belt at his waist and grasped the other end with one hand. He reached out his other hand to me. It felt hard and rough, like distressed metal. His grip was an uncontested A.

"David DeSalvo."

"We think there may be more in there, Dave. Margot good for another go-round?"

"Look at her."

On hearing her name Margot pricked her ears, crouched with head down, hips in the air, then sprang forward in a series of short hops. Her eyes were glued to DeSalvo's face.

"Right. What've you covered so far?"

"We zigzagged the whole grounds, 'cept where you were working."

"Any chance she missed something?"

"Nah, not today." He shook his head. "Conditions are perfect. Temperature's just right, it's nice and moist from the rain. Plenty of breeze. And Margot's in top form."

She nuzzled his knee and was rewarded by strokes.

"Margot don't miss much. She wasn't trained to nothing but corpse scent, so she won't get sidetracked by nothing else."

Like trackers, cadaver dogs are taught to follow specific scents. In their case, it's the smell of death. I remembered an Academy meeting at which an exhibitor had given away samples of bottled corpse scent. Eau de putrefaction. A trainer I knew used extracted teeth, bummed from his dentist and aged in plastic vials.

"Margot's 'bout the best I've worked with. Something else's out there, she'll scent it."

I looked at her. I could believe it.

"Okay. Let's take her over to that first site."

DeSalvo clipped the lead's free end to Margot's harness and she led us to the gate where the four detectives waited. We moved along the now familiar route, Margot in the lead, straining at her leash. She sniffed her way along, exploring nooks and crannies with her nose the way my flashlight had with its beam. Occasionally she stopped, inhaled rapidly, then expelled the air in a burst that sent dead leaves eddying around her snout. Satisfied, she'd move on.

We stopped where the path branched off into the woods.

"The part we haven't done is just off here."

DeSalvo gestured in the general direction of our first find.

"I'm gonna swing her around, bring her in downwind. She scents better that way. She thinks she's got something, I'll let her have her head."

"Will we bother her if we go into the area?" I asked.

"Nah. Your smell don't do nothing for her."

Dog and trainer continued up the roadbed for about ten yards, then disappeared into the woods. The detectives and I took the path. The crush of feet had made it more obvious. In fact, the burial site itself could now qualify as a tiny clearing. The vegetation was trampled and some of the overhead branches had been clipped.

At the center, the abandoned hole gaped dark and empty, like a plundered grave. It was much larger than when we'd left it, and the surrounding earth was bare and scuffed. A mound of dirt lay off to the side, an earthen cone with sloping sides and truncated top, its particles unnaturally uniform. Backdirt from the screening.

In less than five minutes we heard barking.

"He behind us?" asked Claudel.

"She," I corrected.

He opened his mouth, then crimped it shut. I could see a small vein pulsing in his temple. Ryan shot me a look. All right, maybe I was goading him.

Wordlessly, we moved back down the path. Margot and DeSalvo were off to the left, rustling through the leaves. In less than a minute they came into view. Margot's body was as tense as a violin string, her shoulder muscles bulging, her chest straining against the leather harness. She held her head high, jerking it from side to side, testing the air in all directions. Her nostrils twitched feverishly.

Suddenly, she stopped and grew rigid, ears extended, tips trembling. A noise started somewhere deep inside her, faint at first, then building, half growl, half whine, like the keening of a mourner in some primordial ritual. As it grew in intensity, I felt the hairs rise on the back of my neck and a chill travel down my body.

DeSalvo reached down and released the lead. For a moment Margot held her stance, as though confirming her position, recalibrating her heading. Then she bolted.

"What the fuck . . ." said Claudel.

"Where the . . ." said Ryan.

"Hot damn!" said Charbonneau.

We'd expected her to scent on the burial site behind us. Instead, she cut straight across the path and tore into the trees below. We watched in silence.

Six feet in, she stopped, lowered her snout, and inhaled several times. Exhaling sharply, she moved to her left and repeated the maneuver. Her body was tense, every muscle taut. As I watched her, images formed in my mind. Flight through darkness. A hard fall. A flash of lightning. An empty hole.

Margot recaptured my attention. She'd stopped at the base of a pine, her whole being focused on the ground in front of her. She lowered her snout and inhaled. Then, as if triggered by some feral instinct, the fur rose along her spine, and her mus-

DÉJÀ DEAD

cles twitched. Margot raised her nose high in the air, blew out one last puff of air, and flew into a frenzy. She lunged forward and jerked back, tail between her legs, snarling and snapping at the ground in front of her.

"Margot! *Ici!*" ordered DeSalvo. He plunged through the branches and grabbed her harness, dragging her back from the source of her agitation.

I didn't have to look. I knew what she'd found. And what she hadn't. I remembered staring at the dry earth and the empty hole. Dug with intent to bury or intent to uncover? Now I knew.

Margot was yapping and growling at the pit I'd fallen into last night. It was still empty, but her nose told me what it had held.

18

THE BEACH. ROLLING SURF.
Sandpipers skittering on spindly legs. Pelicans gliding like paper airplanes, then folding their wings to plummet into the sea. Gone to Carolina in my mind. I could smell the brackish inland marshes, the ocean's salt spray, wet sand, beached fish, and drying seaweed. Hatteras, Ocracoke, and Bald Head to the north. Pawley's, Sullivan's, and Kiawah to the south. I wanted to be home, and which island didn't matter. I wanted palmetto palms and shrimp boats, not butchered women and body parts.

I opened my eyes to pigeons on a statue of Norman Bethune. The sky was graying, yielding pink and yellow remains of a departing sunset to the advance guard of approaching darkness. Streetlights and store signs announced evening's arrival with neon winks. Cars streamed by on three sides, a four-wheeled motorized herd grudgingly parting for the small triangle of green at Guy and De Maisonneuve.

I sat sharing a bench with a man in a Canadiens jersey. His hair flowed to his shoulders, neither blond nor white. Backlit by passing cars, it haloed his head like spun glass. His eyes were the color of denim that's been washed a thousand times, red-rimmed, a yellow crust trickling from each corner. He picked at the crust with pasty, white fingers. From a chain around his neck hung a metal cross the size of my hand.

I'd gotten home by late afternoon, switched the phone to the answering machine, and slept. Ghosts of people I knew alternated with unrecognized figures in a parade without a theme. Ryan chased Gabby into a boarded building. Pete and Claudel dug a hole in my courtyard. Katy lay on a brown plastic bag on the deck of the beach house, burning her skin and refusing lotion. A menacing figure stalked me on St. Laurent.

I woke several times, finally rising at 8 P.M., headachy and famished. A reflection on the wall near the phone pulsed red, red, red, dim; red, red, red, dim. Three messages. I stumbled to the machine and hit play.

Pete was considering an offer with a law firm in San Diego. Terrific. Katy was thinking of dropping out of school. Wonderful. One hang up. At least that wasn't bad news. Still no word from Gabby. Great.

Twenty minutes of talking with Katy did little to ease my mind. She was polite, but noncommittal. Finally, a long silence, then, "Talk to you later." Dial tone. I'd closed my eyes and stood very still. An image of Katy at thirteen filled my mind. Ear to ear with her Appaloosa, her blond hair mingled with his dark mane. Pete and I had gone to visit her at camp. On seeing us her face lit up and she'd left the horse to throw her arms around me. We'd been so close then. Where had the intimacy gone? Why was she unhappy? Why did she want to leave school? Was it the separation? Were Pete and I to blame?

Burning with parental inadequacy, I tried Gabby's apartment. No answer. I remembered a time Gabby had disappeared for ten days. I was crazy worrying about her. Turned out she'd gone on retreat to discover her inner self. Maybe I couldn't get in touch with her because she was getting in touch with herself again.

Two Tylenol relieved my head, and a #4 special at the Singapore sated my hunger. Nothing calmed my discontent. Neither pigeons nor park bench strangers distracted me from the constant themes. Questions crashed and rebounded like bumper cars inside my head. Who was this killer? How did he choose his victims? Did they know him? Did he gain their confidence, worm his way into their homes? Adkins was killed at home. Trottier and Gagnon? Where? At a predesignated place? A place chosen for death and dismemberment? How did the killer get around? Was it St. Jacques?

I stared at the pigeons without seeing them. I imagined the victims, imagined their fear. Chantale Trottier was only sixteen. Had he forced her at knife point? When had she known she was going to die? Had she begged him not to hurt her? Begged for her life? Another image of Katy. Other people's Katys. Empathy to the point of pain.

I focused on the present moment. In the morning, lab work on the recovered bones. Dealing with Claudel. Tending the scabs on my face. So Katy aspired to a career as an NBA groupie, and nothing I said would dissuade her. Pete might split for the Coast. I was horny as Madonna, with no relief in sight. And where the *hell* was Gabby?

"That's it," I said, startling the pigeons and the man beside me. I knew one thing I could do.

I walked home, went directly to the garage, and drove to Carré St. Louis. I parked on Henri-Julien and rounded the corner to Gabby's apartment. Sometimes her building made me think of Barbie's Dreamhouse. Tonight it was Lewis Carroll. I almost smiled.

A single bulb lit the lavender porch, casting shadow petunias across the boards. The looking-glass windows stared at me darkly. "Alice isn't home," they said.

I rang the bell to number 3. Nothing. I rang again. Silence. I tried number 1, then 2 and 4. No response. Wonderland had closed for the night.

Circling the park, I looked for Gabby's car. Not there. Without plan, I drove south, then east toward the Main.

After twenty frustrating minutes looking for a parking place, I left the car on one of the unpaved alleys that feed St. Laurent. The alley was remarkable for flattened beer cans and the stink of stale urine. Piles of trash abounded, and I could hear jukebox noise through the brick on the left. It was a setting which called for that popularly advertised auto security device known as the Club. Lacking one, I entrusted the Mazda to the god of parking, and joined the flow on the strip.

Like a rain forest, the Main is inhabited by sympatric breeds, populations living side by side but occupying different niches. One group is active by day, the other exclusively nocturnal.

In the hours from dawn to dusk the Main is the realm of deliverymen and shopkeepers, of school-children and housewives. The sounds are those of commerce and play. The smells are clean, and speak of food: fresh fish at Waldman's, smoked

meat at Schwartz's, apples and strawberries at War-
shaw's, baked goods at La Boulangerie Polonaise.

As shadows lengthen and streetlamps and bar
lights come on, as shops close and taverns and porn
mills open, the day crowd surrenders the sidewalks
to different creatures. Some are harmless. Tourists
and college kids who come for bargain booze and
cheap thrills. Others are more toxic. Pimps, dealers,
hookers, and crackheads. The users and the used,
the predators and prey in a food chain of human
misery.

At eleven-fifteen, the night shift was in full control. The streets were thronged and the low-rent
bars and bistros were packed. I walked to Ste.
Catherine and stood on the corner, La Belle Province at my back. It seemed a good place to start.
Entering, I walked past the pay phone where
Gabby had made her panicky call.

The restaurant smelled of Pine-Sol, grease, and
overfried onions. It was too late for dinner and too
early for the aprés booze set. Only four booths
were occupied.

A couple with identical Mohawks stared glumly
at each other over half-eaten bowls of chili. Their
spiny hackles were an identical inky black, as if
they'd split the cost of the Clairol. They wore
enough studded leather to open a combination ken-
nel and motorcycle outfitter.

A woman with arms the size of Number 2 pencils
and platinum bouffant hair smoked and drank coffee in a booth at the back. She wore a red tube
top and what my mother would've called capri
pants. She'd probably had that look since she
dropped out of school to join the war effort.

As I watched, she drained the last of her coffee,
took a long pull on her cigarette, and stubbed the
butt into the small metal disk that served as an

ashtray. Her painted eyes surveyed the room list-lessly, not really expecting to find a mark, but pre-pared to dance the dance. Her face displayed the joyless look of someone who'd been on the street a long time. No longer able to compete with the young, she probably specialized in alley quickies and backseat blow jobs. Late night bliss at bargain prices. She hiked the tube higher on her bony chest, picked up her bill, and walked to the counter. Rosie the Riveter hitting the streets again.

Three young men occupied a booth near the door. One lay sprawled across the table, an arm cradling his head, another disappearing limply into his lap. All three wore T-shirts, cutoffs, and base-ball caps. Two had their bills turned backward. The third, in a defiant disregard for fashion, wore his brim planted firmly across his forehead. The up-right pair downed cheeseburgers, seemingly uncon-cerned about their companion. They looked about sixteen.

The only other patron was a nun. No Gabby.

I left the restaurant and looked up and down Ste. Catherine. The bikers had been drifting in, and Harleys and Yamahas lined both sides of the street to the east. Their owners straddled them, or drank and talked in packs, leathered and booted despite the warm evening.

Their women sat behind them, or formed conver-sational clusters of their own. It reminded me of junior high. But these women chose a world of vio-lence and male dominance. Like hamadryas ba-boons, the females in the troop were herded and controlled. Worse. They were pimped and swapped, tattooed and burned, beaten and killed. And yet they stayed. If this was improvement, it was hard to imagine what they'd left behind.

I scanned to the west of St. Laurent. Right away

I saw what I was looking for. Two hookers lounged outside the Granada, smoking cigarettes and playing the crowd. I recognized Poirette, but wasn't sure about the other.

I fought an impulse to give this up and head for home. What if I'd guessed wrong on the dress? I'd chosen a sweatshirt, jeans, and sandals, hoping they'd be nonthreatening, but I didn't know. I'd never done this kind of fieldwork.

Cut the crap, Brennan, you're stalling. Get your sorry butt up there. The worst that can happen is they blow you off. Won't be the first time.

I moved up the block and planted myself in front of the two women.

"*Bonjour.*" My voice sounded quavery, like a cassette tape stretched and rewound. I was annoyed with myself, and coughed to create a cover.

The women stopped talking and inspected me much as they would an unusual insect, or something odd found in a nostril. Neither spoke. Their faces were flat and devoid of emotion.

Poirette shifted her weight, thrusting one hip forward. She was wearing the same black high-tops she'd had on when I first saw her. Wrapping an arm across her waist and resting the opposite elbow on it, she regarded me with veiled eyes. Pulling hard on her cigarette, she breathed the smoke deep into her lungs, then pooched out her lower lip and blew it upward in a stream. The smoke looked like haze in the pulsating neon glow of the hotel sign. The sign's blinking cast nets of red and blue across her cocoa skin. Wordlessly, her dark eyes left my face and returned to the sidewalk parade.

"What you wantin', chère?"

The street woman's voice was deep and raspy, as if the words were formed by particles of sound with empty gaps floating among them. She addressed me in English, with a cadence that spoke of hyacinths and cypress swamps, of gumbo and zydeco bands, of cicadas droning on soft summer nights. She was older than Poirette.

"I'm a friend of Gabrielle Macaulay. I'm trying to find her."

She shook her head. I wasn't sure if she meant she didn't know Gabby, or was unwilling to answer.

"She's an anthropologist? She works down here?"

"Sugar, we all work down here."

Poirette snorted and shifted feet. I looked at her. She was wearing shorts and a bustier made of shiny black vinyl. I was certain she knew Gabby. She'd been one of the women we'd seen that night. Gabby had pointed her out. Up close she looked even younger. I concentrated on her companion.

"Gabby's a large woman," I went on. "About my age. She has"—I groped for a color term—"reddish dreadlocks?"

Blank indifference.

"And a nose ring."

I was hitting a brick wall.

"I haven't been able to reach her for a while. I think her phone's out of order, and I'm a little worried about her. Surely y'all must know her?"

I drew out my vowels and emphasized the Southern version of *vous*. Appeal to regional loyalties. Daughters of Dixie unite.

Louisiana shrugged, a fluid, Cajun version of the universal French response. More shoulder, less palm.

So much for the Daughters of Dixie approach. This was going nowhere. I was beginning to understand what Gabby had meant. You don't ask questions on the Main.

"If you run into her, will you tell her Tempe's looking for her?"

"That a Southern name, chère?"

She slipped a long, red nail into her hair, and scratched her scalp with the tip. The updo was so lacquered, it would've held in a hurricane. It moved as one mass, creating the illusion that her head was changing shape.

"Not exactly. Can you think of anywhere else I might look?"

Another shrug. She withdrew her nail and inspected it.

I pulled a card from my back pocket.

"If you think of anything, this is where you can get in touch with me." As I walked away I could see Poirette reaching for the card.

Approaches to several streetwalkers along Ste. Catherine yielded much the same result. Their reactions ranged from indifference to contempt, uniformly leavened by suspicion and distrust. No information. If Gabby had ever existed down here, no one would admit it.

I went from bar to bar, moving through the seedy haunts of the night people. One was as the next, brainchildren of a single warped decorator. Ceilings were low, and walls cinder block. All painted with Day-Glo murals, or covered with fake bamboo or cheap wood. Dark and dank, they smelled of stale beer, smoke, and human sweat. In the better ones, the floors were dry and the toilets flushed.

Some bars had raised platforms on which strippers writhed and slithered, their teeth and G-strings glowing purple in the black lights, their faces fixed in boredom. Men in tank tops and five o'clock shadows drank beer from bottles and watched the dancers. Imitation elegant women sipped cheap wine, or nursed soft drinks disguised to look like highballs, rousing themselves to smile at passing men, hoping to lure a trick. Aiming for seductive, they looked mostly tired.

The saddest were the women at the borders of this flesh trade life, those just crossing the start and finish lines. There were the painfully young, some still flying the colors of puberty. Some were out for fun and a quick buck, others were escaping some private hell at home. Their stories had a central theme. Hustle long enough to make a stake, then on to a respectable life. Adventurers and runaways, they'd arrive by bus from Ste. Thérèse and Val d'Or, from Valleyfield and Pointe-du-Lac. They came with gleaming hair and fresh faces, confident of their immortality, certain of their ability to control the future. The pot and the coke were just a lark. They never recognized them as the first rungs on a ladder of desperation until they were too high up to get off except by falling.

Then there were those who'd managed to grow old. Only the truly canny and exceptionally strong had prospered and gotten out. The ill and weak were dead. The strong-bodied but weak-willed endured. They saw the future, and accepted it. They would die in the streets because they knew nothing else. Or because they loved or feared some man enough to peddle ass to buy his dope. Or because they needed food to eat and a place to sleep.

I appealed to those entering or those leaving the sisterhood. I avoided the senior generation, the hardened and street smart, still able to rule their patches just as they in turn were ruled by their pimps. Perhaps the young, naive and defiant, or the old, jaded and spent, might be more open. Wrong. In bar after bar they turned away from me, allowing my questions to dissolve into the smoky air. The code of silence held. No access to strangers.

By three-fifteen I'd had it. My hair and clothes smelled of tobacco and reefer, and my shoes of beer. I'd downed enough Sprite to reclaim the Kalahari, and my eyes were seeded with gravel. Leaving yet another loony on yet another bar, I gave up.

19

THE AIR HAD THE TEXTURE
of dew. A mist had risen from the river, and tiny
droplets sparkled like glitter in the streetlights. The
chill and damp felt good against my skin. A knot
of pain between my neck and shoulder blades made
me suspect I'd been tensed for hours, coiled and
ready to bolt. Maybe I had been. If so, the tension
came only in part from my search for Gabby. Approaching the hookers had grown routine. So had
their rejection. Fending off the cruisers and the
gropers had become a reflex response.

It was the battle inside that was wearing me
down. I'd spent four hours fighting off an old lover,
a lover from whom I'd never be free. All night I'd
gazed temptation in the face—the chestnut glow of
scotch on ice, the amber beer poured from bottles
into throats. I'd smelled my moonshine sweetheart
and seen his light in the eyes around me. I'd loved
it once. Hell, I loved it still. But the enchantment

would destruct. For me, any trifling dalliance and the affair would consume and overpower. So I'd walked away from it, with twelve slow steps. And I had stayed away. Having been lovers, we could never be friends. Tonight we'd almost been thrown into each other's arms.

I breathed deeply. The air was a cocktail of motor oil, wet cement, and fermenting yeast from the Molson brewery. Ste. Catherine was almost deserted. An old man in a tuque and parka slumbered against a storefront, a scruffy mongrel at his side. Another sorted through trash on the far side of the street. Perhaps there was a third shift on the Main.

Discouraged and exhausted, I headed toward St. Laurent. I'd tried. If Gabby was in trouble, these folks would not help me reach her. This club was as closed as the Junior League.

I passed the My Kinh. A sign above the window advertised CUISINE VIETNAMIENNE, and promised it all night. I glanced through the grimy glass with little interest, then stopped. Seated at a rear booth was Poirette's companion, her hair still frozen in an apricot pagoda. I watched her for a moment.

She dipped an egg roll into a cherry red sauce, then raised it to her mouth and licked the tip. After a moment she inspected the roll, then nibbled at the wrapping with her front teeth. She dipped again, and repeated the maneuver without hurry. I wondered how long she'd been working that egg roll.

No. Yes. It's too late. Hell. One last shot. I pushed open the door, and entered.

"Hi."

Her hand jumped at the sound of my voice. She looked puzzled at first, then relieved, as recognition surfaced.

"Hey, chère. You still out?" She returned to her roll.

"May I join you?"

"Suit yourself. You're not working my ground, sugar, I got no grievance with you."

I slid into the booth. She was older than I'd thought, late thirties, maybe early forties. Though the skin on her throat and forehead was taut and there were no bags under her eyes, in the harsh fluorescent light I could see small creases radiating from her lips. Her jawline was beginning to sag.

The waiter brought a menu and I ordered Soupe Tonqinoise. I wasn't hungry, but I wanted an excuse to stay.

"You find your friend, chère?" She reached for her coffee, and the plastic bracelets on her wrist clacked. I could see gray scar lines across her inner elbow.

"No."

We waited while an Asian boy of about fifteen brought water and a paper place mat.

"I'm Tempe Brennan."

"I remember. Jewel Tambeaux may hawk pussy, darlin', but she's not stupid." She licked at the egg roll.

"Ms. Tambeaux, I—"

"You call me Jewel, baby."

"Jewel, I just spent four hours trying to find out if a friend is all right, and no one will even admit they've heard of her. Gabby's been coming down here for *years* so I'm sure they know who I'm talking about."

"Might be they do, chère. But they got no idea why you askin'." She put down the roll, and drank the coffee with a soft slurping sound.

"I gave you my card. I'm not hiding who I am."

She looked at me hard for a moment. The smell

of drugstore cologne, smoke, and unwashed hair floated from her and filled the small booth. The neck of her halter was rimmed with makeup.

"Who *are* you, Miss 'Person with a Card Says Tempe Brennan'? You heat? You inta some kind of weird hustle?" It came out sounding like "wired." "You someone got a grudge?" As she spoke she raised one long, red talon from her cup and pointed it at me, emphasizing each possibility.

"Do I look like a threat to Gabby?"

"All folks know, chère, is you're down here in your Charlotte Hornets sweatshirt and Yuppie sandals, and you're asking a lot of questions, trying real hard to shake someone loose. You ain't pussy on the hoof and you ain't trying to score rock. Folks don't know where to put you."

The waiter brought my soup and we sat in silence while I squeezed small cubes of lime and added red pepper paste with a tiny china spoon. As I ate, I watched Jewel nibble her egg roll. I decided to try humble.

"I guess I went about it all wrong."

She raised hazel eyes to me. One false lash had loosened, and it curved upward on her lid, like a millipede rising to test the air. Dropping her eyes, she laid down the remains of the egg roll, and slid her coffee directly in front of her.

"You're right. I shouldn't have just charged up to people and started asking questions. It's just that I'm worried about Gabby. I've called her apartment. I've stopped by. I've called her at school. No one seems to know where she is. It's not like her."

I took a spoonful of soup. It tasted better than I'd anticipated.

"What's your friend Gabby do?"

"She's an anthropologist. She studies people. She's interested in life down here."

"Coming of Age on the Main."

She laughed to herself, watching carefully for my response to the Margaret Mead reference. I gave none, but began to agree that Jewel Tambeaux was no dummy. I sensed I was being tested.

"Maybe she doesn't want to be found right now."

You may open your exam booklets.

"Maybe."

"So what's the problem?"

You may pick up your pencils.

"She seemed very troubled the last time I was with her. Scared, almost."

"Troubled 'bout what, sugar?"

Ready.

"Some guy she thought was following her. Said he was strange."

"Lot of strange ones down here, chère."

Okay, class, begin.

I told her the whole story. As she listened, she swirled the dregs in her cup, watching the black-brown liquid intently. When I'd finished, she continued with the cup, as if scoring my answer. Then she signaled for a refill. I waited to find out my grade.

"I don't know his name, but I most likely know who you talkin' about. Skinny dude, personality of a mealworm. He's strange, all right, and whatever's ailing him ain't no small thing. But I don't think he's dangerous. I doubt he's got the brains to read a ketchup label."

I'd passed.

"Most of us avoid him."

"Why?"

"I'm only passing on the word from the street, 'cause I don't do business with him myself. The guy makes my skin crawl like a gator in mud." She grimaced and gave a small shudder. "Word is he's got peculiar wants."

"Peculiar?"

She put her cup on the table and looked at me, evaluating.

"He pays for it, but he doesn't want to fuck."

I scooped noodles from my soup and waited.

"Girl named Julie goes with him. No one else will. She's about as smart as a runner bean, but that's another story. She told me it's the same show every time. They go to the room, our hero brings a paper bag with a nightie inside. Nothing kinky, lacy kinds of stuff. He watches her put it on, then tells her to lie on the bed. Okay, no big deal. Then he strokes the nightie with one hand and his dick with the other. Pretty soon he gets hard as an oil derrick and blows a gusher, grunting and groaning like he's off in some other creation. Then he makes her take off the gown, thanks her, pays her, and leaves. Julie figures it's easy money."

"What makes you think this is the guy worrying my friend?"

"One time, he's stuffing Granny's nightie back in the ditty bag, Julie sees a big ol' knife handle. She tells him, you want more pussy, cowboy, lose the knife. He tells her it's his sword of righteousness or some damned thing, goes on about the knife, and his soul, and ecological balance, and crap like that. Scares the shit out of her."

"And?"

Another shrug.

"He still around?"

"Haven't seen him for a while, but that don't mean much. I never did see him regular. He'd kind of drift in and drift out."

"Did you ever talk to him?"

"Cutie, we've all talked to him. When he's

around he's like a case of the drips, irritating as hell but you can't shake it. That's how I know he's got the personality of roach larvae."

"Ever see him with Gabby?" I slurped some more noodles.

She sat back and laughed. "Nice try, sugar."

"Where could I find him?"

"Hell if I know. Wait long enough, he'll show up."

"How about Julie?"

"It's a free trade zone here, chère, folks come and go. I don't keep track."

"Have you seen her lately?"

She gave it some thought. "Can't say as I have."

I studied the noodles at the bottom of the bowl and I studied Jewel. She had lifted the lid a tiny crack, allowed a peek inside. Could I raise it farther? I took the chance.

"There may be a serial killer out there, Jewel. Someone murdering women and slicing them up."

Her expression never changed. She just looked at me, a stony gargoyle. Either she hadn't understood, or she was dulled to thoughts of violence and pain, even death. Or perhaps she'd thrown on a mask, a facade to conceal a fear too real to validate by speech. I suspected the latter.

"Jewel, is my friend in danger?"

Our eyes locked.

"She female, chère?"

I motored my way home, letting my thoughts drift, paying little attention to my driving. De Maisonneuve was deserted, the traffic lights playing to an empty house. Suddenly, a pair of headlights appeared in my rearview mirror and bore down on me.

I crossed Peel and slid to my right to allow the

vehicle to pass. The lights moved with me. I shifted back to the inner lane. The driver followed, shifting to high beam.

"Asshole."

I sped up. The car stayed on my bumper.

A prickle of fear. Maybe it wasn't just a drunk. I squinted into the rearview mirror, trying to make out the driver. All I could see was a silhouette. It looked large. A man? I couldn't tell. The lights were blinding. The car unidentifiable.

Hands slick on the wheel, I crossed Guy, turned left around the block, ignoring red lights, shot up my street, and dived underground into the garage of my building.

I waited until the electric door had settled, then bolted, key ready, ears alert for the sound of footsteps. No one followed. As I passed through the first-floor lobby, I peeked through the curtains. A car idled at the curb on the far side of the street, lights burning, its driver a black profile in the pre-dawn dimness. Same car? I couldn't be certain. Was I losing it?

Thirty minutes later I lay watching the curtain of darkness outside my window fade from charcoal to mourning dove gray. Birdie purred in the crook of my knee. I was so exhausted I'd pulled off my clothes and fallen into bed, skipping the preliminaries. Not like me. Usually I'm compulsive about teeth and makeup. Tonight, I didn't care.

20

WEDNESDAY IS GARBAGE day on my block. I slept through the sound of the sanitation truck. I slept through Birdie's nudging. I slept through three phone calls.

I woke at ten-fifteen feeling sluggish and headachy. I was definitely not twenty-four anymore. All-nighters took their toll, and it made me cranky to admit it.

My hair, my skin, even the pillow and sheets smelled of stale smoke. I bundled the linens and last night's clothes into the washer, then took a long, sudsy shower. I was spreading peanut butter on a stale croissant when the phone rang.

"Temperance?" LaManche.

"Yes."

"I have been trying to reach you."

I glanced at the phone machine. Three messages.

"Sorry."

"*Oui.* We will be seeing you today? Already Monsieur Ryan is calling."

"I'll be there within the hour."

"Bon."

I played the messages. A distraught graduate student. LaManche. A hang-up. I wasn't up to student problems, so I tried Gabby. No answer. I dialed Katy and got her machine.

"Leave a short message, like this one," it chirped cheerily. I did, not cheerily.

In twenty minutes I was at the lab. Stuffing my purse in a desk drawer, and ignoring the pink slips scattered across the blotter, I went directly downstairs to the morgue.

The dead come first to the morgue. There, they are logged in and stored in refrigerated compartments until assigned to an LML pathologist. Jurisdiction is coded by floor color. The morgue opens directly onto the autopsy rooms, the red floor of each morgue bay stopping abruptly at the autopsy room threshold. The morgue is run by the coroner, the LML controls the operatories. Red floor: coroner. Gray floor: LML. I do my initial examinations in one of the four autopsy rooms. Afterward, the bones are sent up to the histology lab for final cleaning.

LaManche was making a Y incision in the chest of an infant, her tiny shoulders propped on a rubber headrest, her hands spread at her sides as if poised to make a snow angel. I looked at LaManche.

"Secouée," was all he said. Shaken.

Across the room Nathalie Ayers bent over another autopsy as Lisa lifted the breastplate from a young man. Below a shock of red hair his eyes bulged purple and swollen, and I could see a small, dark hole on his right temple. Suicide. Nathalie was a new pathologist at the LML, and didn't yet do homicides.

Daniel put down the scalpel he was sharpening. "Do you need the bones from St. Lambert?"

"*S'il vous plaît*. In number 4?"

He nodded and disappeared into the morgue.

The skeletal autopsy took several hours, and I confirmed my initial impression that the remains were of one individual, a white female around thirty years of age. Though little soft tissue remained, the bones were in good condition and retained some fat. She'd been dead two to five years. The only oddity was an unfused arch on her fifth lumbar vertebra. Without the head, a positive ID would be tough.

I asked Daniel to transfer the bones to the histo lab, washed, and went upstairs. The pile of pink slips had grown. I phoned Ryan and gave him my summary. He was already working missing persons reports with the St. Lambert police.

One of the calls was from Aaron Calvert in Norman, Oklahoma. Yesterday. When I tried his number, a syrupy voice told me he was away from his desk. She assured me she was devastatingly sorry, and guaranteed that he'd get the message. Professionally affable. I set the other messages aside and went to see Lucie Dumont.

Lucie's office was crammed with terminals, monitors, printers, and computer paraphernalia of all kinds. Cables climbed walls to disappear into the ceiling, or were taped in bundles along the floor. Stacks of printouts drooped on shelves and file cabinets, fanning out like alluvium seeking the lowest point.

Lucie's desk faced the door, the control panel of cabinets and hardware forming a horseshoe behind her. She worked by rolling from station to station, sneakered feet propelling her chair across the gray tile. To me, Lucie was the back of a head silhouetted against a glowing green screen. I rarely saw her face.

Today the horseshoe held five Japanese in business suits. They circled Lucie, arms held close to their bodies, nodding gravely as she pointed to something on a terminal and explained its significance. Cursing my timing, I went on to the histo lab.

The St. Lambert skeleton had arrived from the morgue, and I set about analyzing the cuts the same way I had with Trottier and Gagnon. I described, measured, and plotted the location of each mark, and made impressions of the false starts. As with the others, the tiny gashes and trenches suggested a knife and a saw. Microscopic details were similar, and placement of cuts almost identical to those in the earlier cases.

The woman's hands had been sawed at the wrists, the rest of her limbs detached at the joints. Her belly had been slashed along the midline deep enough to leave cuts on the spine. Although the skull and upper neck bones were missing, marks on the sixth cervical vertebra told me that she had been decapitated at the midthroat. The guy was consistent.

I repacked the bones, gathered my notes, and returned to my office, diverting up the corridor to see if Lucie was free. She and her Japanese suits were nowhere to be seen. I left a Post-it note on her terminal. Maybe she'd thank me for an excuse to bolt.

In my absence Calvert had called. Naturally. As I dialed his number, Lucie appeared in my doorway, her hands clasped tightly in front of her.

"You left me a message, Dr. Brennan?" she

asked, flashing a quick smile. She spoke not a word of English.

She was thin as soup in a homeless shelter, with a burr haircut that accentuated the length of her skull. The absence of hair and pale skin magnified the effect of her eyeglasses, making her seem little more than a mannequin for the oversized frames.

"Yes, Lucie, thank you for stopping by," I said, rising to clear a chair.

She tucked her feet behind the chair leg, one behind the other, as she slid into her seat. Like a cat oozing onto a cushion.

"Did you get stuck with tour duty?"

She twitched a smile, then looked blank.

"The Japanese gentlemen."

"Yes. They are from a crime lab in Kobe, chemists mostly. I do not mind."

"I'm not sure you can help me, but I wanted to ask," I began.

Her lenses focused on a row of skulls I keep on the shelf behind my desk.

"For comparison," I explained.

"Are they real?"

"Yes, they're real."

She shifted her gaze and I could see a distorted version of myself in each pink lens. The corners of her lips jumped and resettled. Her smiles came and went like light from a bulb with a bad connection. Reminded me of my flashlight in the woods.

I explained what I wanted. When I'd finished, she tipped her head and stared upward, as if the answer might be on the ceiling. Taking her time. I listened to the whir of a printer somewhere down the hall.

"There won't be anything before 1985, I know that." Facial flicker. On. Off.

"I realize it's a bit unusual, but see what you can do."

"Quebec City, also?"

"No, just the LML cases for now."

She nodded, smiled, and left. As if on cue, the phone rang. Ryan.

"How about someone younger?"

"How much younger?"

"Seventeen."

"No."

"Maybe someone with some sort of—"

"No."

Silence.

"I've got one sixty-seven."

"Ryan, this woman belongs neither to the Clearasil nor the Geritol set."

He continued with the relentlessness of a busy signal. "What if she had some kind of bone condition or something? I read abou—"

"Ryan, she was between twenty-five and thirty-five."

"Right."

"She probably went missing somewhere between '89 and '92."

"So you've said."

"Oh. One other thing. She probably had kids."

"What?"

"I found pitting on the inside of the pubic bones. You're looking for someone's mother."

"Thanks."

In less time than he could have punched the numbers, the phone rang again.

"Ryan, I—"

"It's me, Mom."

"Hi, darlin', how are you?"

"Good, Mom." Pause. "Are you mad about our conversation last night?"

"Of course not, Katy. I'm just worried about you."

Long pause.

"So. What else is new? We didn't really talk about what you've been up to this summer." There was so much I wanted to say, but I'd let her take the lead.

"Not much. Charlotte's boring as ever. Nothing to do."

Good. Another dose of adolescent negativity. Just what I needed. I tried to hold my annoyance in check.

"How's the job?"

"Okay. Tips are good. I made ninety-four dollars last night."

"That's great."

"I'm getting a lot of hours."

"Terrific."

"I want to quit."

I waited.

She waited.

"Katy, you're going to need that money for school." Katy, don't mess up your life.

"I told you. I don't want to go back right away. I'm thinking of taking a year off to work."

Here we go again. I had an idea what was coming, and launched my offensive.

"Honey, we've gone over this. If you don't like the University of Virginia, you could try McGill. Why don't you take a couple of weeks, come up here, check it out?" Talk fast, Mom. "We could make a vacation of it. I'll take some time off. Maybe we could drive out to the Maritimes, bum around Nova Scotia for a few days." God. What was I saying? How could I work that? No matter. My daughter comes first.

She didn't answer.

"It's not grades, is it?"

"No, no. They were fine."

"Then your credits should transfer. We coul—"

"I want to go to Europe."

"Europe?"

"Italy."

"Italy?"

I didn't have to think that one through.

"Is that where Max is playing?"

"Yes." Defensive. "So?"

"So?"

"They're giving him a lot more money than the Hornets."

I said nothing.

"And a house."

Nothing.

"And a car. A Ferrari."

Nothing.

"Tax free." Her tone was becoming more defiant.

"That's great for Max, Katy. He gets to play a sport he loves and gets paid for it. But what about you?"

"Max wants me to come."

"Max is twenty-four and has a degree. You're nineteen and have one year of college."

She heard the irritation in my voice.

"You got married when you were nineteen."

"Married?" My stomach did a triple gainer.

"Well, you did."

She had a point. I held my tongue, anxious with concern for her but knowing I was helpless to do anything.

"I just said that. We're not getting married."

We sat and listened to the air between Montreal and Charlotte for what seemed like forever.

"Katy, will you think about coming up here?"

"Okay."

"Promise you won't do anything without talking to me?"

More silence.

"Katy?"

"Yes, Mom."

"I love you, sweetheart."

"I love you, too."

"Say hi to your dad for me."

"Okay."

"I'll leave something on your e-mail tomorrow, okay?"

"Okay."

I hung up with an unsteady hand. What next? Bones were easier to read than kids. I got a cup of coffee, then dialed.

"Dr. Calvert, please."

"May I ask who's calling?" I told her. "Just a minute, please." Put on hold.

"Tempe, how are you? You spend more time on the phone than an MCI salesman. You surely are hard to reach." He out-twanged both the day and night shifts.

"I'm sorry, Aaron. My daughter wants to drop out of school and run off with a basketball player," I blurted.

"Can he go to his left or shoot the three?"

"I guess."

"Let her go."

"Very funny."

"Nothing funny about someone who can go left or shoot from outside the arc. Money in the bank."

"Aaron, I've got another dismemberment." I'd called Aaron about cases past. We often bounced ideas off each other.

I heard him chuckle. "You may not have guns up there, but you sure do like to cut."

"Yes. I think this sicko has cut several. They're all women, otherwise there doesn't seem to be much linking them. Except the cut marks. They're going to be critical."

"Serial or mass?"

"Serial."

He digested that for a second. "So. Tell me."

I described the kerfs and the cut ends of the arm bones. He interrupted occasionally to ask a question, or to slow me down. I could picture him taking notes, his tall, gaunt frame bent over some scrap of discarded paper, finding every usable millimeter of blank space. Though Aaron was forty-two, his somber face and dark, Cherokee eyes made him look about ninety. Always had. His wit was as dry as the Gobi, and his heart about that size.

"Any really deep false starts?" he asked, all business.

"No. They're pretty superficial."

"Harmonics are clear?"

"Very."

"You said blade drift in the kerf?"

"Uh. Huh. Yes."

"Are you confident in the tooth distance measures?"

"Yeah. The scratches were distinct in several places. So were some of the islands."

"Otherwise you got pretty flat floors?"

"Yeah. It's really obvious on the impressions."

"And exit chipping," he mumbled, more to himself than me.

"Lots."

A long pause while his mind picked its way through the information I'd given him, sorting the possibilities. I watched people drift past my door. Phones rang. Printers clicked to life, whirred, then rested. I swiveled and gazed out. Traffic rolled across the Jacques-Cartier Bridge, Lilliputian Toyotas and Fords. Minutes ticked by. Finally.

"I'm kinda workin' blind here, Tempe. I'm not sure how you get me to do this. But here goes."

I swiveled back and leaned my elbows on the desk.

"I'd bet the farm this isn't a power saw. Sounds like some kinda specialty handsaw. Probably a kitchen saw of some type."

Yes! I slapped my hand on the desktop, raised a clenched fist, and lowered it sharply, like an engineer pulling the whistle cord. Pink slips sailed up, then fluttered down.

Aaron went on, oblivious to my theatrics. "Kerfs're too big to be any kinda fine-toothed bow saw, or a serrated knife. Besides, sounds like there's too much set to the teeth. With those floor shapes I doubt you're talking about any kinda cross cut. Got to be chisel. All that, 'thout seein' 'em, of course, tells me chef's saw or meat saw."

"What's it look like?"

"Kinda like a big hacksaw. Teeth set pretty wide, so as not to bind. That's why sometimes you get the islands you're describing in the false starts. Usually there's a lotta drift, but the blade chisels through bone just fine and cuts real clean. They're mighty efficient little saws. Cut right through bone, gristle, ligaments, whatever."

"Anything else that might be consistent?"

"Well, there's always the chance you can get something doesn't fit the regular pattern. These saws don't read the books, you know. But right offhand, I can't think of anything else fits all you've told me."

"You are fantastic. That's exactly what I was thinking, but I wanted to hear it from you. Aaron,

I can't tell you how much I appreciate your doing this."

"Ah."

"You want to see the photos and impressions?"

"Sure."

"I'll send them out tomorrow."

Aaron's second passion in life was saws. He cataloged written and photographic descriptions of features produced in bone by known saws, and spent hours poring over cases sent to his lab from all over the world.

A hitch in his breathing told me he had something more to say. As I waited, I gathered pink slips.

"Did you say the only completely sectioned bones are in the lower arms?"

"Yep."

"Went into the joints for the others?"

"Yep."

"Neat?"

"Very."

"Hm."

I stopped gathering. "What?"

"What?" Innocent.

"When you say 'Hm' like that, it means something."

"Just a mighty interesting association."

"Which is?"

"Guy uses a chef's saw. And he goes about cuttin' up a body like he knows what he's doing. Knows what's where, how to get at it. And does it the same way every time."

"Yeah. I thought of that."

A few seconds ticked off.

"But he just whacks off the hands. What about that?"

"That, Dr. Brennan, is a question for a psychologist, not a saw man."

I agreed and changed the subject. "How're the girls?"

Aaron had never married, and, though I'd known him for twenty years, I'm not sure I'd ever seen him with a date. His horses were his first passion. From Tulsa to Chicago to Louisville, and back to Oklahoma City, he traveled where the quarter horse circuit took him.

"Pretty excited. I bid a stallion this past fall and got 'im. The ladies been actin' like yearlings ever since."

We exchanged news of our lives and small talk about mutual friends, and we agreed to get together at the Academy meeting in February.

"Well, good luck nailin' this guy, Tempe."

"Thanks."

My watch read four-forty. Once again the offices and corridors had grown quiet around me. I jumped at the sound of the phone.

Too much coffee, I thought.

As I answered, the receiver was still warm against my ear.

"I saw you last night."

"Gabby?"

"Don't do that again, Tempe."

"Gabby, where are you?"

"You're just going to make things worse."

"Goddammit, Gabby, don't play with me! Where are you? What's going on?"

"Never mind that. I can't be seeing you right now."

I couldn't believe she was doing this again. I could feel the anger rising in my chest.

"Stay away, Tempe. Stay away from me. Stay away from my—"

Gabby's self-centered rudeness ignited my pent-up anger. Fueled by Claudel's arrogance, the inhumanity of a psychopathic killer, and by Katy's youthful folly, I exploded with the fury of a flash fire, rolling over Gabby and charring her.

"Who the hell do you think you are?" I seethed into the phone, my voice cracking. Squeezing the receiver with enough force to break the plastic, I raved on.

"I'll leave you alone! I'll leave you alone, all right! I don't know what bugass little game you're playing, Gabby, but I'm out! Gone! Game, set, match, finished! I'm not buying into your schizophrenia! I'm not buying into your paranoia! And I'm not, repeat *not,* playing Masked Avenger to your damsel in and out of distress!"

Every neuron in my body was overcharged, like a 110 appliance in a 220 socket. My chest was heaving, and I could feel tears behind my eyes. Tempe's temper.

From Gabby, a dial tone.

I sat for a moment, doing nothing, thinking nothing. I felt giddy.

Slowly, I replaced the receiver. I closed my eyes, ran through the sheet music, and made a selection. This one's going out to me. In a low, throaty voice I hummed the tune:

Busted flat in Baton Rouge . . .

21

AT 6 A.M. A STEADY RAIN drummed against my windows. An occasional car made soft shishing sounds as it passed on some predawn journey. For the third time in as many days I saw daybreak, an event I embrace as eagerly as Joe Montana welcomes an all-out blitz. While not a day napper, neither am I an early riser. Yet three mornings this week I'd seen the sun come up, twice as I fell asleep, today as I tossed and turned after eleven hours in bed, feeling neither sleepy nor rested.

Home after Gabby's call, I'd gone on an eating binge. Greasy fried chicken, rehydrated mashed potatoes with synthetic gravy, mushy corn on the cob, and soggy apple pie. *Merci,* Colonel. Then a hot bath and a long pick at the scab on my right cheek. The microsurgery didn't help. I still looked like I'd been dragged. Around seven I turned on the Expos game, and fell asleep to the play-by-play.

I switched on my computer—6 A.M. or 6 P.M., it was alert and ready to perform. I had sent a message to Katy, relaying through the e-mail system at McGill to my mail server at UNC-Charlotte. She could access the message with her laptop and modem, and reply right from her bedroom. Yahoo! Hop aboard the Internet.

The screen's cursor blinked at me, insisting there was nothing in the document I'd created. It was right. The spreadsheet I had started on paper had only column headings but no content. When had I begun this? The day of the parade. Just one week, but it seemed like years. Today was the thirtieth. Four weeks to the day since Isabelle Gagnon's body was found, one week since Margaret Adkins had been murdered.

What had we accomplished since then except discover another body? A stakeout on the Rue Berger apartment confirmed that its occupant had not returned. Big surprise. The bust had turned up nothing useful. We had no leads on the identity of "St. Jacques," and we hadn't identified the latest body. Claudel still wouldn't acknowledge the cases were linked, and Ryan thought of me as a "freelancer." Happy day.

Back to the spreadsheet. I expanded the column headings. Physical characteristics. Geography. Living arrangements. Jobs. Friends. Family members. Dates of birth. Dates of death. Dates of discovery. Times. Places. I entered everything I could think of that might reveal a link. At the far left I entered four row headings: Adkins, Gagnon, Trottier, *"Inconnue."* I'd replace the unknown designation when we tied a name to the St. Lambert bones. At seven-thirty I closed the file, packed the laptop, and got ready for work.

Traffic was clogged, so I cut down to the Ville-

Marie tunnel. Full morning, but dark, heavy clouds trapped the city in murky gloom. The streets were covered with a wet sheen that reflected the brake lights of the morning rush hour.

My wipers beat a monotonous refrain, slapping water from two fan-shaped patches on the windshield. I leaned forward, bobbing my head like a palsied tortoise, searching for clear glass between the streaks. Time for new wipers, I told myself, knowing I wouldn't get them. It took a good half hour to reach the lab.

I wanted to get right to the files, to dig out minutiae and enter them into the spreadsheet, but there were two requisitions on my desk. A baby boy had been found in a municipal park, his tiny body wedged in the rocks of a creek bed. According to LaManche's note, the tissue was desiccated and the internal organs unrecognizable, but otherwise the corpse was well preserved. He wanted an opinion on the infant's age. That wouldn't take long.

I looked at the police report attached to the other form. *"Ossements trouvés dans un bois."* Bones found in the woods. My most common case. Could mean anything from a multiple ax murder to a dead cat.

I called Denis and requested radiographs of the infant, then went downstairs to look at the bones. Lisa brought a cardboard box from the morgue and placed it on the table.

"C'est tout?"

"C'est tout." That's all.

She handed me gloves, and I withdrew three clods of hard clay from the box. Bones protruded from each clump. I chipped at the soil, but it was hard as cement.

"Let's get photos and radiographs, then put these in a screen and get them soaking. Use dividers to keep the chunks separate. I'll be back down after the meeting."

The four other pathologists at the LML meet with LaManche each morning to review cases and receive autopsy assignments. On the days I'm present, I attend. When I got upstairs LaManche, Nathalie Ayers, Jean Pelletier, and Marc Bergeron were already seated around the small conference table in LaManche's office. From the activity board in the corridor, I knew that Marcel Morin was in court, and Emily Santangelo had taken a personal day.

Everyone shifted to make room, and a chair was shuffled into the circle. *Bonjour*'s and *Comment ça va*'s were exchanged.

"Marc, what brings you in on a Thursday?" I asked.

"Holiday tomorrow."

I'd completely forgotten. Canada Day.

"Going to the parade?" asked Pelletier, poker-faced. His French wore the trappings of the Quebec back country, making it difficult for me to unravel his words. For months I hadn't understood him at all, and had missed his wry comments. Now, after four years, I caught most of what he said. I had no trouble following his drift this morning.

"I think I'll skip this one."

"You could just get your face painted at one of those booths. It might be easier."

Chuckles all around.

"Or maybe a tattoo. Less painful."

"Very funny."

Feigned innocence, eyebrows raised, shoulders hoisted, palms up. What? Settling back, he clamped the last two inches of an unfiltered cigarette between yellowed fingers, and inhaled deeply. Someone once told me that Pelletier had never traveled outside Quebec Province. He was sixty-four years old.

"There are only three autopsies," LaManche began, distributing the list of that day's cases.

"Pre-holiday lull," said Pelletier, reaching for his printout. His dentures clicked softly when he spoke. "Things'll get busier."

"Yes." LaManche picked up his red marker. "At least the weather is cooler. Perhaps that will help."

He went over the day's melancholy roster, supplying additional information on each case. A suicide by carbon monoxide. An old man found dead in his bed. A baby tossed into a park.

"The suicide looks pretty straightforward." LaManche scanned the police report. "White male . . . Age twenty-seven . . . Found behind the wheel in his own garage . . . fuel tank empty, key in the ignition, turned to the 'on' position."

He laid several Polaroids on the table. They showed a dark blue Ford centered in a one-car garage. A length of flexible tubing, the type used to vent clothes dryers, ran from the exhaust pipe into the car's right rear window. LaManche read on.

"History of depression . . . *Note d'adieu.*" He looked at Nathalie. "Dr. Ayers?"

She nodded and reached for the paperwork. He marked "Ay" in red on the master list, and picked up the next set of forms.

"Number 26742 is a white male . . . Age seventy-eight . . . Controlled diabetic." His eyes skipped through the summary report, pulling out the pertinent information. "Hadn't been seen for several days . . . Sister found him . . . No signs of trauma." He read to himself for a few seconds. "Curious thing is there was a delay between the time she found him and the time she called for help. Appar-

ently the lady did some housecleaning in between."
He looked up. "Dr. Pelletier?"

Pelletier shrugged and extended his hand. La-
Manche placed a red "Pe" on his list, then passed
him the forms. They were accompanied by a plastic
bag full of prescription and over-the-counter drugs.
Pelletier took the materials, making a wisecrack
which I missed.

My attention was turned to the stack of Polaroids
accompanying the baby case. Taken from several
angles, they showed a shallow creek with a small
footbridge arching across it. A little body lay
among the rocks, its tiny muscles shriveled, its skin
yellowed like old parchment. A fringe of fine hair
floated round its head, another rimmed its pale
blue eyelids. The child's fingers were splayed wide,
as if grasping for help, for something to cling to.
He was nude, and lay half in and half out of a
dark green plastic bag. He looked like a miniature
pharaoh, exposed and discarded. I was beginning
to dislike plastic bags intensely.

I returned the photos to the table and listened
to LaManche. He'd finished his summary, and was
marking "La" on the master sheet. He would do
the autopsy, I would narrow the age range by assessing skeletal development. Bergeron would have
a go at the teeth. Nods all around. There being no
further discussion, the meeting broke up.

I got coffee and returned to my office. A large
brown envelope lay on the desk. I opened it and
slipped the first of the baby's X rays onto the light
box. Withdrawing a form from the drawer in my
worktable, I started my survey. Only two carpals
were present in each hand. No caps at the ends of
the finger bones. I looked at the lower arms. No
cap on either radius. I finished with the upper body,

listing on my inventory sheet those bony elements that were present, and noting which had not yet formed. Then I did the same for the lower body, shifting from film to film to be sure of my observations. The coffee grew cold.

An infant is born with its skeleton incomplete. Some bones, such as the carpals in the hand, are absent at birth, appearing months, or even years later. Other bones lack knobs and ridges that will eventually give them their adult form. The missing parts emerge in predictable succession, allowing for fairly accurate age estimates for very young children. This baby had lived only seven months.

I summarized my conclusions on yet another form, placed all the paperwork in a yellow file folder, and dropped it on the stack for the secretarial pool. It would come back with the report typed in my preferred format, with all supporting materials and diagrams duplicated and assembled. They would also polish my French. I made a verbal report to LaManche. Then I moved on to my clumps.

The clay hadn't dissolved, but had softened enough to allow me to pry out the contents. After fifteen minutes of scraping and teasing, the matrix yielded eight vertebrae, seven long bone fragments, and three chunks of pelvis. All showed evidence of butchering. I spent thirty minutes washing and sorting the mess, then cleaned up and jotted a few notes. On my way upstairs, I asked Lisa to photograph the partial skeletons of the three victims: two white-tailed deer and one medium-sized dog. I filled out another report form and dropped this folder on top of the earlier one. Odd, but not a forensic problem.

Lucie had left a note on my desk. I found her in her office, back to the door, eyes shifting between a terminal screen and an open dossier. She typed with one hand and held her place in the dossier with the other, her index finger moving slowly from entry to entry.

"Got your note," I said.

She raised the finger, typed a few more strokes, then laid a ruler across the file. Pivoting and thrusting in one motion, she rolled to her desk.

"I pulled up what you asked for. Sort of."

She dug through one stack of paper, shifted to another, then returned to the first, searching more slowly. Finally she withdrew a small stack of papers stapled at the corner, scanned a few pages, then extended the collection to me.

"Nothing before '88."

I leafed through the pages, dismayed. How could there be so many?

"First I tried calling up cases with 'dismemberment' as my key word. That's the first list. The long one. I got all the people who threw themselves in front of trains, or fell into machinery and had limbs ripped off. I didn't think you wanted that."

Indeed. It seemed to be a list of every case in which an arm, leg, or finger had been traumatically severed at or even near the time of death.

"Then I tried adding 'intentional,' to limit the selections to cases in which the dismemberment was done on purpose."

I looked at her.

"I got nothing."

"None?"

"That doesn't mean there weren't any."

"How come?"

"I didn't enter this data. Over the past two years we've had special funding to hire part-time workers to get historical data on-line as quickly as possible." She gave an exasperated sigh and shook her head.

"The ministry dragged its heels for years getting computerized, now they want everything up to date overnight. Anyway, the data entry people have standard codes for the basics: date of birth, date of death, cause of death, and so on. But for something that's odd, something that occurs only rarely, they're pretty much on their own. They make up a code."

"Like a dismemberment."

"Right. Someone might call it an amputation, someone else might use the term disjointing, usually they just use the same word the pathologist put in the report. Or they might just enter it as cutting or sawing."

I looked back at the lists, thoroughly discouraged.

"I tried all of those, and a few others. No go."

So much for this idea.

" 'Mutilation' brought up the other really long list." She waited while I turned to the second page. "That was even worse than 'dismemberment.' "

"Then I tried 'dismemberment' in combination with 'postmortem' as a limiter, to select out the cases in which the"—she turned her palms upward and made a scratching motion with her fingers, as if trying to tease the word from the air—"the event took place after death."

I looked up, hopeful.

"All I got was the guy with his dick chopped off."

"Computer took you literally."

"Huh?"

"Never mind." Another joke that didn't travel.

"Then I tried 'mutilation' in combination with the 'postmortem' limiter, and . . ." She reached across the desk and displayed the last printout. "Bango! Is that what you say?"

"Bingo."

"Bingo! I think this may be what you want. You can ignore some of it, like those drug things where they used acid." She pointed to several lines she'd penciled out. "Those are probably not what you want."

I nodded absently, totally absorbed by page three. It listed twelve cases. She'd drawn lines through three of them.

"But I think maybe some of the others might be of interest to you."

I was hardly hearing her. My eyes had been drifting through the list, but were now riveted on the sixth name down. A tingle of uneasiness passed through me. I wanted to get back to my office.

"Lucie, this is great," I said. "This is better than I'd hoped for."

"Anything you can use?"

"Yes. Yes, I think so," I said, trying to sound casual.

"Do you want me to call these cases up?"

"No. Thanks. Let me look this over, then I think I'd rather pull the complete files." Let me be wrong on this one, I prayed to myself.

"Bien sûr."

She took off her glasses and began polishing a lens on the hem of her sweater. Without them she looked incomplete, wrong somehow, like John Denver after he switched to contacts.

"I'd like to know what happens," she said, the pink rectangles back flanking the bridge of her nose.

"Of course. I'll tell you if anything breaks."

As I walked away I heard the wheels of her chair gliding across the tile.

In my office, I laid the printout on my desk and looked at the list. One name stared at me. Francine Morisette-Champoux. Francine Morisette-Champoux.

I'd forgotten all about her. Stay cool, I told myself.
Don't jump to conclusions.

I forced myself to go over the other entries.
Gagne and Valencia were in there, a pair of drug
dealers with a lousy business sense. So was Chantale Trottier. I recognized the name of a Honduran
exchange student whose husband had put a shotgun
to her face and pulled the trigger. He had driven
her from Ohio to Quebec, cut off her hands, and
dumped her nearly headless body in a provincial
park. As a parting gesture, he'd carved his initials
on her breasts. I didn't recognize the other four
cases. They were before 1990, before my time. I
went to the central files and pulled them, along
with the jacket on Morisette-Champoux.

I stacked the files according to their LML numbers, thus achieving chronological order. I'd go
about this systematically. Violating that resolution
as soon as I made it, I went right to the Morisette-
Champoux folder. Its contents made my anxiety
rocket.

22

FRANCINE MORISETTE-CHAM-poux was beaten and shot to death in January 1993. A neighbor had seen her walking her small spaniel around ten one morning. Less than two hours later her husband discovered her body in the kitchen of their home. The dog was in the living room. Its head was never found.

I remembered the case, though I wasn't involved in the investigation. I'd commuted to the lab that winter, flying north for one week of every six. Pete and I were at each other constantly, so I'd agreed to spend the whole summer of '93 in Quebec, optimistic the three-month separation might rejuvenate the marriage. Right. The brutality of the attack on Morisette-Champoux had shocked me then and did still. The crime scene photos brought it all back.

She was lying half under a small wooden table, her arms and legs spread wide, white cotton panties stretched taut between her knees. A sea of blood surrounded her, giving way at its perimeter to the geometric pattern of the linoleum. Dark smears covered the walls and counter fronts. From off camera, the legs of an upturned chair seemed to point at her. You are here.

Her body looked ghostly white against the crimson background. A pencil-thin line looped across her abdomen, a happy-face smile just above her pubis. She was slit from this scar upward to her breastbone, and her innards protruded from the opening. The handle of a kitchen knife was barely visible at the apex of the triangle formed by her legs. Five feet from her, between a work island and the sink, lay her right hand. She'd been forty-seven years old.

"Jesus," I whispered softly.

I was picking my way through the autopsy report when Charbonneau appeared in my doorway. I guessed his mood was not congenial. His eyes looked bloodshot and he didn't bother with greetings. He entered without asking and took the chair opposite my desk.

Watching him, I felt a momentary sense of loss. The lumbering walk, the looseness in his movement, just the *largeness* of him touched something I thought I'd abandoned. Or been abandoned by.

For a moment I saw Pete sitting across from me, and my mind flew backward in time. What an intoxicant his body had been. I never knew if it was his size, or the relaxed way he had of moving it. Maybe it was *his* fascination with *me*. That had seemed genuine. I could never get enough of him. I'd had sexual fantasies, damn good ones, but from the moment I saw him standing in the rain outside the law library they'd always involved Pete. I could use one right now, I thought. Jesus, Brennan. Get a grip. I snapped back to the present.

I waited for Charbonneau to begin. He was staring down at his hands.

"My partner can be a sonofabitch." He spoke in English. "But he's not a bad guy."

I didn't respond. I noticed that his pants had four-inch hems, hand sewn, and wondered if he'd done the job himself.

"He's just—set in his ways. Doesn't like change."

"Yes."

He wouldn't meet my eyes. I felt unease.

"And?" I encouraged.

He leaned back and picked at a thumbnail, still avoiding eye contact. From a radio down the hall Roch Voisine sang softly of Hélène.

"He says he's going to file a complaint." He dropped both hands and shifted his gaze to the window.

"A complaint?" I tried to keep my voice flat.

"With the minister. And the director. And La-Manche. He's even looking up your professional board."

"And what is Monsieur Claudel unhappy about?" Stay calm.

"He says you're overstepping your bounds. Interfering in stuff you got no business in. Messing up his investigation." He squinted into the bright sunlight.

I felt my stomach muscles tighten, and a hotness spread upward.

"Go on." Flat.

"He thinks you're . . ." He fumbled for a word, no doubt seeking a substitute for the one Claudel had actually used. ". . . overreaching."

"And what exactly does that mean?"

He still avoided eye contact.

"He says you're trying to make the Gagnon case into a bigger deal than it really is, seeing all kinds of shit that isn't there. He says you're trying to turn a simple murder into an American-style psycho extravaganza."

"And why am I trying to do that?" My voice wavered slightly.

"Shit, Brennan, this isn't my idea. I don't know." For the first time his eyes met mine. He looked miserable. It was obvious he didn't want to be there.

I stared back, not really seeing him, just using the time to quell the alarm call going out to my adrenals. I had some idea of the type of inquiry a letter of complaint could set in motion, and I knew it wouldn't be good. I'd investigated such charges when I sat on the board's ethics committee. Regardless of outcome, it was never pretty. Neither of us spoke.

"Hélène the things you do. Make me crazy 'bout you," crooned the radio.

Don't kill the messenger, I told myself. My eyes dropped to the dossier on my desk. A body with skin the color of milk reproduced in a dozen glossy rectangles. I considered the photos, then looked at Charbonneau. I hadn't wanted to broach this yet, didn't feel ready, but Claudel was forcing my hand. What the hell. Things couldn't get worse.

"Monsieur Charbonneau, do you remember a woman named Francine Morisette-Champoux?"

"Morisette-Champoux." He repeated the name several times, twirling through his mental Rolodex. "That was several years ago, eh?"

"Almost two. January of 1993." I handed him the photos.

He thumbed through them, nodding his head in recognition. "Yeah, I remember. So?"

"Think, Charbonneau. What do you recall about the case?"

"We never got the turd that did it."

"What else?"

"Brennan, tell me you're not trying to hook this one in, too?"

He went through the photos again, the nodding transformed to negative shaking.

"No way. She was shot. Doesn't fit the pattern."

"The bastard slit her open and cut her hand off."

"She was old. Forty-seven, I think."

I gave him an icy stare.

"I mean, older than the others," he mumbled, reddening.

"Morisette-Champoux's killer drove a knife up her vagina. According to the police report there was extensive bleeding."

I let that sink in.

"She was still alive."

He nodded. I didn't need to explain that a wound inflicted after death will bleed very little since the heart is no longer pumping and blood pressure is gone. Francine Morisette-Champoux had bled profusely.

"With Margaret Adkins it was a metal statue. She was also alive."

Silently, I reached behind me and pulled the Gagnon file. I withdrew the scene photos and spread them in front of him. There was the torso lying on its plastic bag, dappled by the four o'clock sunlight. Nothing had been moved but the covering of leaves. The plunger lay in place, its red rubber cup snug against the pelvic bones, its handle projecting toward the body's severed neck.

"I believe Gagnon's killer shoved that plunger into her with enough force to drive the handle through her belly and clear up to her diaphragm."

He studied the photos for a long time.

"Same pattern with all three victims," I hammered on. "Forceful penetration with a foreign object while the victim is alive. Body mutilation after death. Coincidence, Monsieur Charbonneau? How many sadists do we want out there, Monsieur Charbonneau?"

He ran his fingers through the bristle on his head, then drummed them on the arm of the chair.

"Why didn't you tell us this sooner?"

"I just realized the Morisette-Champoux connection today. With only Adkins and Gagnon, it seemed a bit thin."

"What does Ryan say?"

"Haven't told him."

Unconsciously I fingered the scab on my cheek. I still looked like I'd gone to a TKO with George Foreman.

"Shit." He said it with little force.

"What?"

"I think I'm beginning to agree with you. Claudel's going to bust my balls about this." More drumming. "What else?"

"The saw marks and pattern of dismemberment are almost identical for Gagnon and Trottier."

"Yeah. Ryan told us that."

"And the unknown from St. Lambert."

"A fifth?" It came out "fit."

"You're very quick."

"Thanks." Back to drumming. "Know who she is yet?"

I shook my head. "Ryan's working on it."

He ran a meaty hand over his face. His knuckles were covered with patches of coarse gray hair, miniature versions of the crop on his head.

"So what do you think about victim selection?"

I gave a palm up gesture. "They're all female."

"Great. Ages?"

"Sixteen to forty-seven."

"Physicals?"

"A mix."

"Locations?"

"All over the map."

"So what's the sicko bastard go for? The way they look? The boots they wear? The place they shop?"

I replied with silence.

"You find *anything* common to all five?"

"Some sonofabitch beat the crap out of them, then killed them."

"Right." Tilting forward, he placed his hands on his knees, hunched and lowered his shoulders, and gave a deep sigh. "Claudel's going to shit flaming bullets."

When he'd gone I called Ryan. Neither he nor Bertrand was in, so I left a message. I went through the other dossiers, but found little of interest. Two drug dealers blasted and sawed up by former friends in crime. A man killed by his nephew, dismembered with a power saw, then stored in the basement freezer. A power failure had brought him to the attention of the rest of the family. A female torso washed up in a hockey bag, with head and arms found downriver. The husband was convicted.

I closed the last file and realized I was starving— 1:50 P.M. No wonder. I bought a ham and cheese croissant and a Diet Coke in the cafeteria on the eighth floor, and returned to my office, ordering myself to take a break. Ignoring the order, I tried Ryan again. Still out. A break it would be. I bit the sandwich and allowed my thoughts to meander. Gabby. Nope. Out of bounds. Claudel. Veto. St. Jacques. Off limits.

Katy. How could I get through to her? Right now, no way. By default, back to Pete, and I felt a familiar flutter in my stomach. Remember the tingling skin, the pounding blood, the warm wetness between my legs. Yes, there had been passion. You're just horny, Brennan. I took another bite of my sandwich.

The other Pete. The nights of anger. The arguments. The dinners alone. The cold shroud of resentment that had smothered the lust. I took a swig of Coke. Why was I thinking about Pete so often? If we had a chance to do it all again . . . Thanks, Ms. Streisand.

Relaxation therapy wasn't working. I reread Lucie's printout, careful not to drip mustard on it. I reviewed the list on page three, trying to read the items Lucie had crossed out, but her pencil marks obscured the letters. Out of curiosity, I erased each of her lines and read the entries. Two cases involved bodies stuffed into barrels then doused with acid. A new twist on the ever-popular drug burn.

The third item puzzled me. Its LML number indicated a 1990 case, and that Pelletier had been the pathologist. No coroner was listed. In the name field it read: Singe. The data fields for date of birth, date of autopsy, and cause of death were empty. The entry *"démembrement/postmortem"* had prompted the computer to include the case in Lucie's list.

Finishing the croissant, I went to the central files and pulled the jacket. It contained only three items: a police incident report, a one-page opinion by the pathologist, and an envelope of photographs. I thumbed through the pictures, read the reports, then went in search of Pelletier.

"Got a minute?" I said to his hunched back.

He turned from the microscope, glasses in one hand, pen in the other. "Come in, come in," he urged, sliding the bifocals onto his face.

My office had a window; his had space. He strode

across it and gestured to one of two chairs flanking a low table in front of his desk. Reaching into his lab coat, he withdrew a pack of du Maurier's and extended it to me. I shook my head. We'd been through the ritual a thousand times. He knew I didn't smoke, but would always offer. Like Claudel, Pelletier was set in his ways.

"What can I help you with?" he said, lighting up.

"I'm curious about an old case of yours. Goes back to 1990."

"Ah, *Mon Dieu,* can I remember that far back? I can barely remember my own address sometimes." He leaned forward, cupped his mouth, and looked conspiratorial. "I write it on matchbooks, just in case."

We both laughed. "Dr. Pelletier, I think you remember just about everything you want to remember."

He shrugged and wagged his head, all innocence.

"Anyway, I brought the file." I held it up, then opened it. "Police report says the remains were found in a gym bag behind the Voyageur bus station. Wino opened it, thinking maybe he could find the owner."

"Right," said Pelletier. "Honest rubbies are so common they should form their own fraternal organization."

"Anyway, he didn't like the aroma. Said"—I skimmed the incident report to find the exact phrase—" 'the smell of Satan rose up out of the bag and surrounded my soul.' Unquote."

"A poet. I like that," said Pelletier. "Wonder what he'd say about my shorts."

I ignored that and read on. "He took the bag to a janitor, who called the police. They found a collection of body parts wrapped up in some sort of tablecloth."

"Ah, *oui*. I remember that one," he said, pointing a yellowed finger at me. "Grisly. Horrible." He had that look.

"Dr. Pelletier?"

"The case of the terminal monkey."

"Then I read your report correctly?"

He raised his eyebrows questioningly.

"It really was a monkey?"

He nodded gravely. "Capucin."

"Why did it come here?"

"Dead."

"Yes." Everyone's a comedian. "But why a coroner case?"

The look on my face must have prompted a straight answer. "Whatever was in there was small, and someone had skinned it and cut it up. Hell, it could have been anything. Cops thought it might be a fetus or a neonate, so they sent it to us."

"Was there anything odd about the case?" I wasn't sure what I was looking for.

"Nah. Just another sliced-up monkey." The corners of his mouth twitched slightly.

"Right." Dumb question. "Anything strike you about the way the monkey was cut up?"

"Not really. These monkey dismemberments are all the same."

This was going nowhere.

"Did you ever find out whose monkey it was?"

"Actually, we did. A blurb appeared in the paper, and some guy called from the university."

"UQAM?"

"Yeah, I think so. A biologist or zoologist or something. Anglophone. Ah. Wait."

He went to a desk drawer, pushed the contents around, then withdrew a stack of business cards bound with a rubber band. Rolling the band off, he flicked through the cards and handed one to me.

"That's him. I saw him when he came to ID the deceased."

The card read: Parker T. Bailey, Ph.D., Professeur de Biologie, Université du Québec à Montréal, and gave e-mail, telephone, and fax numbers, along with an address.

"What was the story?" I asked.

"The gentleman keeps monkeys at the university for his research. One day he came in and found one less subject."

"Stolen?"

"Stolen? Liberated? Escaped? Who knows? The primate was AWOL." The expression sounded odd in French.

"So he read about the dead monkey in the paper and called here?"

"C'est ça."

"What happened to it?"

"The monkey?"

I nodded.

"We released it to . . ." He gestured at the card.

"Dr. Bailey," I supplied.

"Oui. There were no next of kin. At least, not in Quebec." Not a twitch.

"I see."

I looked at the card again. This is nothing, my left brain said, while at the same time I heard myself asking, "May I keep this?"

"Of course."

"One other thing." I laid the trap for myself. "Why do you call it the case of the terminal monkey?"

"Well, it was," he answered, surprised.

"Was what?"

"The monkey. It was terminal."

"Yes. I see."

"Also, that's *where* it was."

"Where?"

"The terminal. The bus terminal."

Some things do translate. Unfortunately.

For the rest of the afternoon I pulled details from the four principal files and entered them into the spreadsheet I'd created. Color of hair. Eyes. Skin. Height. Religion. Names. Dates. Places. Signs of the Zodiac. Anything and everything. Doggedly, I plugged it in, planning to search for links later. Or perhaps I thought the patterns would form by themselves, the interconnecting bits of information drawn to each other like neuropeptides to receptor sites. Or maybe I just needed a rote task to occupy my mind, a mental jigsaw puzzle to give the illusion of progress.

At four-fifteen I tried Ryan again. Though he wasn't at his desk, the operator thought she'd seen him, and reluctantly began a search. While I waited, my eye fell on the monkey file. Bored, I dumped out the photos. There were two sets, one of Polaroids, the other of five-by-seven color prints. The operator came back on to tell me Ryan was not in any of the offices she'd rung. Yes, sigh, she'd try the coffee room.

I thumbed through the Polaroids. Obviously taken when the remains arrived in the morgue. Shots of a purple and black nylon gym bag, zipped and unzipped, the latter showing a bundle in its interior. The next few showed the bundle on an autopsy table, before and after it was unrolled.

The remaining half dozen featured the body parts. The scale on the ID card confirmed that the subject was, indeed, tiny, smaller than a full-term fetus or newborn. Putrefaction was advancing nicely. The flesh had begun to blacken and was smeared with something that looked like rancid tapioca. I thought I could identify the head, the torso, and the limbs. Other than that, I couldn't tell squat. The pictures had been taken from too far away, and the detail was lousy. I rotated a few, looking for a better angle, but it was impossible to make out much.

The operator came back with resolve in her voice. Ryan was not there. I'd have to try tomorrow. Denying her the opportunity to launch the argument she'd prepared, I left another message, and hung up.

The five-by-seven close-ups had been taken following cleaning. The detail that had escaped the Polaroids was fully captured in the prints. The tiny corpse had been skinned and disjointed. The photographer, probably Denis, had arranged the pieces in anatomical order, then carefully photographed each in turn.

As I worked my way through the stack, I couldn't help noting that the butchered parts looked vaguely like rabbit about to become stew. Except for one thing. The fifth print showed a small arm ending in four perfect fingers and a thumb curled onto a delicate palm.

The last two prints focused on the head. Without the outer covering of skin and hair it looked primordial, like an embryo detached from the umbilicus, naked and vulnerable. The skull was the size of a tangerine. Though the face was flat and the features anthropoid, it didn't take Jane Goodall to know that this was no human primate. The mouth contained full dentition, molars and all. I counted. Three premolars in each quadrant. The terminal monkey had come from South America.

It's just another animal case, I told myself, returning the pictures to their envelope. We'd get them occasionally, because someone thought the remains to be human. Bear paws skinned and left behind by hunters, pigs and goats slaughtered for meat, the unwanted portions discarded by a roadside, dogs and cats abused and thrown in the river. The callousness of the human animal always astounded me. I never got used to it.

So why did this case hold my attention? Another look at the five-by-sevens. Okay. The monkey had been cut up. Big deal. So are a lot of animal carcasses that we see. Some asshole probably got his jollies tormenting and killing it. Maybe it was a student, pissed off at his grade.

With the fifth photo I stopped, my eyes cemented to the image. Once again, my stomach muscles knotted. I stared at the photo, then reached for the phone.

23

THERE'S NOTHING EMPTIER than a classroom building after hours. It's how I imagine the aftermath of a neutron bomb. Lights burn. Water fountains spew forth on command. Bells ring on schedule. Computer terminals glow eerily. The people are absent. No one quenching a thirst, scurrying to class, or clicking on keyboards. The silence of the catacombs.

I sat on a folding chair outside Parker Bailey's office at the Université du Québec à Montréal—UQAM. Since leaving the lab, I'd worked out at the gym, bought groceries at the Provigo, and fed myself a meal of vermicelli and clam sauce. Not bad for a quick and dirty. Even Birdie was impressed. Now I was impatient.

To say the biology department was quiet would be like saying a quark is small. Up and down the corridor every door was closed. I'd perused the bulletin boards, read the graduate school brochures, the field school announcements, the offers to do word processing or tutoring, the notices announcing guest speakers. Twice.

I looked at my watch for the millionth time—9:12 P.M. Damn. He should be here by now. His class ended at nine. At least, that's what the secretary had told me. I got up and paced. Those who wait must pace—9:14. Damn.

At 9:30 I gave up. As I slung my purse over my shoulder, I heard a door open somewhere out of sight. In a moment a man with an enormous stack of lab books hurried around the corner. He kept adjusting his arms to keep the books from falling. His cardigan looked as if it had left Ireland before the potato famine. I guessed his age at around forty.

He stopped when he saw me, but his face registered nothing. I started to introduce myself when a notebook slipped from the stack. We both lunged for it. Not a good move by him. The better part of the pile followed, scattering across the floor like confetti on New Year's Eve. We gathered and restacked for several minutes, then he unlocked his office and dumped the books on his desk.

"Sorry," he said in heavily accented French. "I—"

"No problem," I responded in English. "I must have startled you."

"Yes. No. I should have made two trips. This happens a lot." His English was not American.

"Lab books?"

"Yeah. I just taught a class in ethological methodology."

He was brushed with all the shades of an Outer Banks sunset. Pale pink skin, raspberry cheeks, and hair the color of a vanilla wafer. His mustache and eyelashes were amber. He looked like a man who'd burn, not tan.

"Sounds intriguing."

"Wish more of them thought so. Can I—"

"I'm Tempe Brennan," I said, reaching into my bag and offering him a card. "Your secretary said I could catch you now."

As he read the card, I explained my visit.

"Yeah, I remember. I hated losing that monkey. It really cheesed me off at the time." Suddenly, "Would you like to sit?"

Without waiting for a reply, he began shoveling objects from a green vinyl chair and heaping them onto the office floor. I stole a peek around. His tiny quarters made mine look like Yankee Stadium.

Every inch of wall space that wasn't covered with shelves was blanketed with pictures of animals. Sticklebacks. Guinea fowl. Marmosets. Warthogs. Even an aardvark. No level of the Linnaean hierarchy had been neglected. It reminded me of the office of an impressario, with celebrity associations displayed like trophies. Only these photos weren't signed.

We both sat, he behind his desk, feet propped on an open drawer, I in the recently cleared visitor's chair.

"Yeah. It really cheesed me off," he repeated, then switched the topic suddenly. "You're an anthropologist?"

"Um. Hm."

"Do much with primates?"

"No. Used to, but not anymore. I'm on the anthropology faculty at the University of North Carolina at Charlotte. Occasionally I teach a course on primate biology or behavior, but I'm really not involved in that work anymore. I'm too busy with forensic research and consulting."

"Right." He waved the card. "What did you do with primates?"

I wondered who was interviewing who. Whom.

"I was interested in osteoporosis, especially the interplay between social behavior and the disease process. We worked with animal models, rhesus mostly, manipulating the social groups, creating stress situations, then monitoring the bone loss."

"Do any work in the wild?"

"Just island colonies."

"Oh?" The amber eyebrows arched with interest.

"Cayo Santiago in Puerto Rico. For several years I taught a field school on Morgan Island, off the coast of South Carolina."

"Rhesus monkeys?"

"Yes. Dr. Bailey, I wonder if you can tell me anything about the monkey that disappeared from your facility?"

He ignored my not so smooth segue. "How'd you get from monkey bones to corpses?"

"Skeletal biology. It's the crux of both."

"Yeah. True."

"The monkey?"

"The monkey. Can't tell you much." He rubbed one Nike against the other, then leaned over and flicked at something. "I came in one morning and the cage was empty. We thought maybe someone had left the latch unhooked and that Alsa, that was her name, maybe she let herself out. They'll do that, you know. She was smart as a pistol and had phenomenal manual dexterity. She had the most amazing little hands. Anyway, we searched the building, alerted campus security, jumped through all the hoops. But we never found her. Then I saw the article in the paper. The rest is history."

"What were you doing with her?"

"Actually, Alsa wasn't my project. A graduate student was working with her. I'm interested in animal communication systems, particularly, but not exclusively, those relying on pheromones and other olfactory signals."

The change in cadence, along with the shift to jargon, clued me that he'd given this synopsis before. He'd launched into his "my research is" spiel, the scientist's oral abstract for public consumption. "The spiel" is based on the KISS principle: Keep It Simple Stupid. It is trotted out for cocktail parties, fund-raisers, first meetings, and other social occasions. We all have one. I was hearing his.

"What was the project?" Enough about you.

He gave a wry smile and shook his head. "Language. Language acquisition in a New World primate. That's where she got her name. L'Apprentissage de la Langue du Singe Americain. ALSA. Marie-Lise was going to be Quebec's answer to Penny Patterson, and Alsa would be the KoKo of South American monkeys." He flourished a pen above his head, gave a derisive snort, then let his arm drop heavily. It made a soft thud against the desk. I studied his face. He looked either tired or discouraged, I couldn't tell which.

"Marie-Lise?"

"My student."

"Was it working?"

"Who knows? She didn't really have enough time. The monkey disappeared five months into the project." More wry. "Followed shortly thereafter by Marie-Lise."

"She left school?"

He nodded.

"Do you know why?"

He paused a long time before answering. "Marie-Lise was a good student. Sure, she had to start over on her thesis, but I have no doubt she could have completed her master's. She loved what she was doing. Yeah, she was devastated when Alsa was killed, but I don't think that was it."

"What do you think it was?"

He drew small triangles on one of the lab books. I let him take his time.

"She had this boyfriend. He'd hassle her all the time about being in school. Badgered her to quit. She only talked to me about it once or twice, but I think it really got to her. I met him at a couple of department parties. I thought the guy was spooky."

"How so?"

"Just . . . I don't know, antisocial. Cynical. Antagonistic. Rude. Like he had never absorbed the basic . . . skills. He always reminded me of a Harlow monkey. You know? Like he was raised in isolation and never learned to deal with other beings. No matter what you said to him, he'd roll his eyes and smirk. God, I hated that."

"Did you ever suspect him? That maybe he killed Alsa to sabotage Marie-Lise's work, to get her to quit school?"

His silence told me that he had. Then, "He was supposedly in Toronto at the time."

"Could he verify that?"

"Marie-Lise believed him. We didn't pursue it. She was too upset. What was the point? Alsa was dead."

I wasn't sure how to ask the next question. "Did you ever read Marie-Lise's project notes?"

He stopped doodling and looked at me sharply. "What do you mean?"

"Is there any chance of something she wanted to cover up? Some reason to want to dump the project?"

"No. Absolutely not." His voice held conviction. His eyes did not.

"Does she keep in touch?"

"No."

"Is that common?"

"Some do, some don't." The triangles were spreading.

I changed tack. "Who else had access to the . . . is it a lab?"

"Just a small one. We keep very few animal subjects here on campus. We just don't have the space. Every species has to be kept in a separate room, you know."

"Oh?"

"Yes. The CCAC has specific guidelines for temperature control, space, diet, social and behavioral parameters, you name it."

"The CCAC?"

"The Canadian Council on Animal Care. They publish a guide for the care and use of experimental animals. It's our bible. Everyone using research animals has to conform to it. Scientists. Breeders. Industry. It also covers the health and safety of personnel working with animals."

"What about security?"

"Oh yeah. The guidelines are very specific."

"What security measures did you follow?"

"I'm working with sticklebacks right now. Fish."

He swiveled and waved his pen at the fish on the wall.

"They don't require a whole lot. Some of my colleagues keep lab rats. They don't either. The animal activists don't usually get wrought up over fish and rodents."

His face did the World Cup of wry.

"Alsa was the only other mammal, so security wasn't all that stringent. She had her own little room, which we kept locked. And, of course, we locked her cage. And the outer lab door."

He stopped.

"I've gone over it in my mind. I can't remember

who was the last to leave that night. I know I didn't have a night class, so I don't think I was here late. Probably one of the grad students did the last check. The secretary won't check those doors unless I specifically ask her to."

He paused again.

"I suppose an outsider could have gotten in. It's not impossible someone left the doors unlocked. Some of the students are less dependable than others."

"What about the cage?"

"The cage was certainly no big deal. Just a padlock. We never found it. I suppose it could have been cut."

I tried to broach the next topic delicately. "Were the missing parts ever found?"

"Missing parts?"

"Alsa had been"—now I groped for a word. KISS—"cut up. Parts of her weren't in the bundle that was recovered. I wondered if anything showed up here."

"Like what? What was missing?" His pastel face looked puzzled.

"Her right hand, Dr. Bailey. Her right hand had been severed at the wrist. It wasn't there."

There was no reason to tell him about the women who'd suffered the same violation, about the real reason I was there.

He was silent. Linking his fingers behind his head, he leaned back and focused on something above me. The raspberry in his cheeks moved toward rhubarb. A small clock radio hummed quietly on his file cabinet.

After a decade, I broke the silence.

"In retrospect, what do you think happened?"

He didn't answer right away. Then, when I was convinced he never would, "I think it was probably one of the mutant life-forms that are spawned in the cesspool around this campus."

I thought he'd finished. The source of his breathing seemed to have moved deeper into his chest. Then he added something, almost in a whisper. I didn't catch it.

"Sorry?" I asked.

"Marie-Lise deserved better."

I found it an odd thing to say. So did Alsa, I thought, but held my tongue. Without warning, a bell split the silence, firing a current through every nerve in my body. I looked at my watch—10:00 P.M.

Sidestepping his question about my interest in a monkey dead four years, I thanked him for his time and asked him to call me should he think of anything else. I left him sitting there, refocusing on whatever had floated above my head. I suspected he was gazing into time, not space.

Not too familiar with the territory, I'd parked in the same alley as the night I'd cruised the Main. Stick with what works. I'd come to think of that outing as the Great Gabby Grope. It seemed like eons ago. It had been two days.

Tonight was cooler, and a soft rain still fell. I zipped my jacket and started back to my car.

Leaving the university, I walked north on St. Denis, past a cavalcade of upscale boutiques and bistros. Though just a few blocks east, St. Denis is a galaxy away from St. Laurent. Frequented by the young and affluent, St. Denis is the place to go seeking—a dress, silver earrings, a mate, a one-night stand. The street of dreams. Most cities have one. Montreal has two: Crescent for the English, St. Denis for the French.

I thought about Alsa as I waited for the light at De Maisonneuve. Bailey was probably right. Ahead and to my right sat the bus station. Whoever had killed her hadn't gone far to ditch the body. That suggested a local.

I watched a young couple emerge from the Berri-UQAM Métro station. They ran through the rain, clinging together like socks just out of the dryer.

Or it could have been a commuter. Right, Brennan, grab a monkey, take the Métro home, whack it, cut it up, then haul it back on the Métro and leave it at the bus station. Great thinking.

The light turned green. I crossed St. Denis and walked west on De Maisonneuve, still thinking about my conversation with Bailey. What was it about him that bothered me? Did he show too much emotion for his student? Too little for the monkey? Why had he seemed so—what?—negative about the Alsa project? Why didn't he know about the hand? Hadn't Pelletier told me Bailey inspected the cadaver? Wouldn't he have noticed the missing hand? The remains had been released to him, and he'd taken them from the lab.

"Shit," I said aloud, mentally smacking my forehead.

A man in coveralls turned to look at me, registering apprehension. He wore no shirt or shoes and carried a shopping bag in both arms, its torn paper handles pointing at odd angles. I smiled to reassure him, and he shuffled on, shaking his head at the state of humanity and the universe.

You're a regular Columbo, I berated myself. You didn't even ask Bailey what he did with the body! Good job.

Having chastised myself, I made amends by proposing consumption of a hot dog.

Knowing I wouldn't sleep anyway, I accepted. That way I could blame it on the food. I went into the Chien Chaud on St. Dominique, ordered a dog all dressed, fries, and a Diet Coke. "No Coke, Pepsi," I was told by a John Belushi look-alike with thick black hair and a heavy accent. Life really does imitate art.

I ate my food in a red-and-white plastic booth, contemplating travel posters peeling from the walls. That would do, I thought, gazing at the too blue skies and blindingly white buildings of Paros, Santorini, Mykonos. Yes. That would do nicely. Cars began to crowd the wet pavement outside. The Main was revving up.

A man arrived and engaged Belushi in loud conversation, presumably Greek. His clothes were damp and smelled of smoke and fat and a spice I didn't recognize. Droplets sparkled in his thick hair. When I glanced over he smiled at me, cocked one bushy eyebrow and ran his tongue slowly along his upper lip. He might as well have shown me his hemorrhoid. Matching his maturity level, I showed him middle man, and turned my attention to the scene outside the window.

Through rain-streaked glass I could make out a row of shops across the street, dark and silent on the eve of a holiday. La Cordonnerie la Fleur. Why would a shoemaker call his shop "The Flower"?

La Boulangerie Nan. I wondered if that was the name of the bakery, the name of the owner, or just an ad for Indian bread. Through the windows I could see empty shelves, ready for the morning's harvest. Do bakers bake on national holidays?

La Boucherie St. Dominique. Its windows were covered with news of weekly specials. *Lapin frais. Boeuf. Agneau. Poulet. Saucisse.* Fresh rabbit. Beef. Lamb. Chicken. Sausage. Monkey.

That's it. You're out of here. I wadded the wrapper into the paper tray that had held my hot dog.

The things for which we kill trees. I added my Pepsi can, threw the whole mess into the trash, and left.

The car was where I'd left it and as I'd left it. Driving, my brain looped back to the murders.

Each slap of the wipers brought up a new image. Alsa's truncated arm. Slap. Morisette-Champoux's hand lying on her kitchen floor. Slap. Chantale Trottier's tendons. Slap. Arm bones with cleanly cut lower ends. Slap.

Was it always the same hand? Couldn't remember. Have to check. No human hand had been missing. Just coincidence? Was Claudel right? Was I getting paranoid? Maybe Alsa's abductor collected animal paws. Was he just an over-zealous Poe fan? Slap. Or she?

At eleven-fifteen I pulled into my garage. Even my bone marrow was exhausted. I'd been up over eighteen hours. No hot dog would keep me awake tonight.

Birdie hadn't waited up. As was his habit when alone, he'd curled up in the small wooden rocker by the fireplace. He looked up when I came in, blinking round yellow eyes at me.

"Hey, Bird, how was it being a cat today?" I purred, scratching under his chin. "Does anything ever keep you up?"

He closed his eyes and stretched his neck, either ignoring or enhancing the feel of my stroking. When I withdrew my hand he yawned widely, nestled his chin back onto his paws, and regarded me from under heavy lids. I went to the bedroom, knowing he'd follow eventually. Unclasping the barrettes in my hair and dumping my clothes in a heap on the floor, I threw back the covers and dropped into bed.

In no time I fell into a dense and dreamless sleep. I hosted no phantom apparitions, no menacing stage plays. At one point I sensed a warm heaviness against my leg, and knew that Birdie had joined me, but I slept on, enveloped in a black void.

Then, my heart was pounding and my eyes were open. I was wide awake, felt alarm, and didn't know why. The transition was so abrupt I had to orient myself.

The room was pitch black. The clock read one twenty-seven. Birdie was gone. I lay in the dark holding my breath, listening, straining for a clue. Why had my body gone to red alert? Had I heard something? What blip had my personal radar detected? Some sensory receptor had sent a signal. Had Birdie heard something? Where was he? It was unlike him to prowl at night.

I relaxed my body and listened harder. The only sound was my heart hammering against my chest. The house was eerily silent.

Then I heard it. A soft clunk followed by a faint metallic rattle. I waited, rigid, not breathing. Ten. Fifteen. Twenty seconds. A glowing digit changed shape on the clock. Then, when I thought I might have imagined it, I heard it again. Clunk. Rattle. My molars compressed like a Black & Decker vise, and my fingers curled into fists.

Was someone in the apartment? I'd grown accustomed to the ordinary sounds of the place. This sound was different, an acoustic intruder. It didn't belong.

Silently, I eased back the quilt and swung my legs out of bed. Blessing last night's sloppiness, I reached for my T-shirt and jeans and slipped them on. I stole across the carpet.

I stopped at the bedroom door to look back in search of a possible weapon. Nothing. There was no moon, but light from a streetlamp oozed through the window in the other bedroom and partly lit the hall with a faint glow. I stole forward, past the bathroom, toward the hall with the court-yard doors. Every few steps I stopped to listen, breath frozen, eyes wide. At the entrance to the kitchen, I heard it again. Clunk. Rattle. It was coming from somewhere near the French doors.

I turned right into the kitchen and peered toward the French doors on the patio side of the apartment. Nothing moved. Silently cursing my aversion to guns, I scanned the kitchen for a weapon. It wasn't exactly an arsenal. Noiselessly, I slid my trembling hand along the wall, feeling for the knife holder. Choosing a bread knife, I wrapped my fingers around the handle, pointed the blade backward, and dropped my arm into full extension.

Slowly, testing with one bare foot at a time, I tiptoed forward far enough to see into the living room. It was as dark as the bedroom and kitchen.

I made out Birdie in the gloom. He was sitting a few feet from the doors, his eyes fixed on something beyond the glass. The tip of his tail twitched back and forth in jittery little arcs. He looked tense as an unshot arrow.

Another clunk-rattle stopped my heart and froze my breath. It came from outside. Birdie's ears went horizontal.

Five tremorous steps brought me alongside Birdie. Unconsciously, I reached out to pat his head. He recoiled at the unexpected touch and went tearing across the room with such force that his claws left divots in the carpet. They looked like small, black commas in the murky darkness. If a cat could be said to scream, Birdie did it.

His flight totally unnerved me. For a moment I was paralyzed, frozen in place like an Easter Island statue.

Do like the cat and get yourself out of here! the voice of panic told me.

I took a step backward. Clunk. Rattle. I stopped, clutching the knife as if it were a lifeline. Silence. Blackness. Da-dum. Da-dum. I listened to my heartbeat, searching my mind for a sector still able to think critically.

If someone is in the apartment, it told me, he is behind you. Your escape route is forward, not backward. But if someone is just outside, don't provide him with a way in.

Da-dum. Da-dum.

The noise is outside, I argued. What Birdie heard is outside.

Da-dum. Da-dum.

Take a look. Flatten yourself against the wall next to the courtyard doors and move the curtains just enough to peer outside. Maybe you can see a shape in the darkness.

Reasonable logic.

Armed with my Chicago Cutlery, I unglued one foot from the carpet, inched forward, and reached the wall. Breathing deeply, I moved the curtain a few inches. The shapes and shadows in the yard were poorly defined but recognizable. The tree, the bench, some bushes. Nothing identifiable as movement, except for branches pushed by wind. I held my position for a long moment. Nothing changed. I moved toward the center of the curtains and tested the door handle. Still locked.

Knife at the ready, I sidled along the wall toward the main entrance door. Toward the security system. The warning light glowed evenly, indicating no breach. On impulse I pressed the test button.

A noise split the silence, and despite my anticipating it, I jumped. My hand jerked upward, bringing the knife into readiness.

Stupid! the functioning brain fragment told me. The security system is operating and it hasn't been breached! Nothing has been opened! No one has entered.

Then he's out there! I responded, still quite shaken.

Maybe, said my brain, but that's not so bad. Turn on some lights, show some activity, and any prowler with sense will beat it out of here.

I tried to swallow, but my mouth was too dry. In a gesture of bravado, I switched on the hall light rapidly followed by every light between there and my bedroom. No intruders anywhere. As I sat on the edge of my bed holding the knife I heard it again. A muffled clunk, rattle. I jumped and almost cut myself.

Emboldened by my conviction that no intruder was inside, I thought, All right you bastard, let me catch just one glimpse, and I'm gonna call the cops.

I moved back to the French doors adjacent to the side yard, quickly this time. That room was still unlit, and I moved the curtain edge once more and peered out, bolder than before.

The scene was the same. Vaguely familiar shapes, some moved by the wind. Clunk, rattle! I started involuntarily, then thought, That noise is back from the doors, not at the doors.

I remembered the side yard floodlight, and moved to find the switch. This was no time to worry about annoying the neighbors. With the light on I returned to my curtain edge. The floodlight was not powerful, but it displayed the yard's features well enough.

The rain had stopped but a breeze had picked up. A fine mist danced in the beam of the light. I listened for a while. Nothing. I scanned my available field of vision several times. Nothing. Recklessly, I deactivated the security system, opened the French door, and stuck my head outside.

To the left, against the wall, the black spruce lived up to its name, but no foreign shape mingled with its branches. The wind gusted slightly, and the branches moved. Clunk. Rattle. A new surge of fright.

The gate. The noise was coming from the gate. My gaze whipped to it in time to catch a slight movement as it settled into place. As I watched, the wind surged again and the gate moved slightly within the boundaries of its latch. Clunk. Rattle.

Chagrined, I marched into the yard and up to the gate. Why had I never noticed that sound? Then I flinched once more. The lock was gone. The padlock that prevented any movement of the latch was missing. Had Winston neglected to replace it after cutting the grass? He must have.

I gave the gate a sharp shove to secure the latch as tightly as I could and turned back toward the door. Then I heard the other sound, more delicate and muffled.

Looking toward it, I saw a foreign object in my herb garden. Like a pumpkin impaled on a stick coming out of the ground. The wispy rustle was that of a plastic covering, moved by the wind.

A horrifying realization overtook me. Without knowing why I knew, I sensed what was beneath that plastic cover. My legs trembled as I crossed the grass and yanked the plastic upward.

At the sight, nausea overcame me and I turned to retch. Wiping my hand across my mouth, I charged back inside, slammed and locked the door, and reset my security alarm.

I fumbled for a number, lurched to the phone, and willed myself to punch the correct buttons. The call was answered on the fourth ring.

"Get over here, please. Right now!"

"Brennan?" Groggy. "What the f—"

"This goddamn minute, Ryan! *Now!*"

24

A GALLON OF TEA LATER I
was curled in Birdie's rocker, dully observing Ryan.
He was on his third call, this one personal, assuring
someone he'd be a while. Judging by his end, the
call's recipient wasn't happy. Tough.

Hysteria has its rewards. Ryan had arrived within
twenty minutes. He searched the apartment and
yard, then contacted the CUM to arrange for a
patrol unit to stake out the building. Ryan had
placed the bag and its grisly contents into another,
larger bag, sealed it, and put it in a corner of the
dining room floor. He would take it to the morgue
tonight. The recovery team would come in the
morning. We were in the living room, me sitting
and sipping tea, Ryan pacing and talking.

I wasn't sure which had the more calming effect,
the tea or Ryan. Probably not the tea. What I really
wanted was a serious drink. Want didn't really describe it. Crave came closer. Actually, I wanted

many drinks. A bottle I could pour from until there was no more. Forget it, Brennan. The cap's on and it's going to stay on.

I sipped my tea and watched Ryan. He wore jeans and a faded denim shirt. Good choice. The blues lit his eyes like colorizing on old film. He finished his calls and sat down.

"That should do it," he said, tossing the phone onto the couch and running a hand over his face. His hair was disheveled and he looked tired. But, then, I probably didn't look like Claudia Schiffer.

Do what? I wondered.

"I appreciate your coming," I said. "I'm sorry I overreacted." I'd already said this, but repeated myself.

"No. You didn't."

"I don't usually—"

"It's okay. We're going to get this psycho."

"I could've just—"

He leaned forward and rested his elbows on his knees. The blue lasers grabbed my eyes and held them. A fleck of lint rode one of his lashes, like a pollen grain clinging to a pistil.

"Brennan, this is serious. There's a guy out there that's some sort of mental mutant. He's psychologically malformed. He's like the rats that tunnel under garbage heaps and slink through sewer pipes in this city. He's a predator. His wiring's twisted, and now he's fed you into whatever degenerate nightmare he's spinning for himself. But he's made a mistake, and we're going to flush him out and squash him. That's what you do with vermin."

The intensity of his response startled me. I could think of nothing to say. Pointing out his mixed metaphors seemed unwise.

He took my silence for skepticism.

"I mean it, Brennan. This asshole has dog food

for brains. Which means you can't pull any more of your stunts."

His comment turned me churlish, a swing that didn't need much of a push. I was feeling vulnerable and dependent and hating myself for it, so I turned my frustration on him.

"Stunts?" I spat at him.

"Shit, Brennan, I don't mean tonight."

We both knew what he did mean. He was right, which increased my annoyance and made me even more contentious. I swirled my tea, now cold, and held my silence.

"This animal's obviously been stalking you," he drummed on, persistent as a jackhammer. "He knows where you live. He knows how to get in."

"He didn't really get in."

"He planted a goddamn human head in your backyard!"

"I know!" I screamed, my composure developing a major fault line.

My eyes slid to the dining room corner. The thing from the garden lay there, silent and inert, an artifact waiting to be processed. It could have been anything. A volleyball. A globe. A melon. The round object in its shiny black bag looked harmless inside the clear plastic into which Ryan had sealed it.

I stared at it, and images of the grisly contents washed over my mind. I saw the skull rising on its scrawny, picket neck. I saw empty orbits staring straight ahead and pink neon glinting off the white enamel in the gaping mouth. I imagined the intruder cutting the lock and boldly crossing the yard to plant his gruesome memento.

"I know," I repeated, "you're right. I'll have to be more careful."

I swirled my cup again, looking for answers in the leaves.

"Want some tea?"

"No. I'm fine." He got up. "I'll check to see if the unit's here."

He disappeared into the back of the apartment, and I made myself another cup. I was still in the kitchen when he returned.

"There's one unit parked in the alley across the street. There'll be another one around back. I'll check with them when I leave. No one should be able to get near this building without being seen."

"Thanks." I took a sip and leaned against the counter.

He took out a pack of du Maurier's and raised his eyebrows at me.

"Sure."

I hated smoke in the apartment. But, then, he probably hated being there. Life is compromise. I thought about searching out my one ashtray, but didn't bother. He smoked and I sipped without speaking, leaning against the counter, each lost in thought. The refrigerator hummed.

"You know, it wasn't really the skull that freaked me. I'm used to skulls. It was just so . . . so out of context."

"Yeah."

"It's a cliché, I know, but I feel so violated. Like some alien creature breached my personal space, rooted about, and left when he lost interest in anything more."

I gripped the mug tightly, feeling vulnerable and hating it. Also feeling stupid. He'd no doubt heard some version of that speech many times. If so, he didn't mention it.

"Do you think it's St. Jacques?"

He looked at me, then flicked his ash into the

sink. Leaning back against the counter, he took a deep pull. His legs stretched almost to the refrigerator.

"I don't know. Hell, we can't even pin down who it is we rousted. St. Jacques is probably an alias. Whoever was using that shithole probably didn't really live there. Turns out the landlady only saw him twice. We've staked the place for a week, and no one's gone in or out."

Hummm. Pull, exhale. Swirl.

"He had my picture in his collection. He'd cut it out and marked it."

"Yep."

"Be straight with me."

He paused a minute, then, "He'd be my pick. Coincidence is just too improbable."

I knew it, but didn't want to hear it. Even more, I didn't want to think about what it meant. I gestured toward the skull.

"From the body we found in St. Lambert?"

"Whoa, that's your country."

He took a last drag, ran tap water over the butt, and looked around for someplace to put it. I pushed off the counter and opened a cabinet containing a trash bag. As he raised up, I laid a hand on his forearm.

"Ryan, do you think I'm crazy? Do you think this serial killer idea is just in my head?"

He straightened and fixed his eyes on me.

"I don't know. I just don't know. You could be right. Four dead women over a two-year period who've all been sliced up or dismembered or both. Maybe a fifth. Maybe some similarities with the mutilation. The object insertion. But that's all. So far, no other tie. Maybe they're linked. Maybe they're not. Maybe there's a truckload of sadists out there operating independently. Maybe St.

Jacques did all of them. Maybe he just likes to collect stories about the exploits of others. Maybe it's only one person, but that person is someone else. Maybe he's fantasizing his next outing right now. Maybe the bastard just planted a skull in your yard, maybe he didn't. I don't know. But I do know some sicko asshole parked a skull in your petunias tonight. Look, I don't want you taking chances. I want your word you'll be careful. No more expeditions."

Again the paternalism. "It was parsley."

"What?" The edge on his voice was sharp enough to cut off any more flippant remarks.

"Just what *do* you want me to do?"

"For now, no more secret sorties." He hooked a thumb at the evidence bag. "And tell me who that is over there."

He looked at his watch.

"Christ. It's three-fifteen. You going to be all right?"

"Yes. Thanks for coming."

"Right."

He checked the phone and the security system again, collected the plastic bag, and I let him out the front. As I watched his retreat I couldn't help noticing that his eyes weren't the only feature the jeans showed off well. Brennan! Too much tea. Or too little of something else.

At exactly four twenty-seven the nightmare started again. At first I thought I was dreaming, replaying earlier events. But I'd never really fallen asleep. I'd been lying there, urging myself to relax, allowing my thoughts to fragment and reassemble like shapes in a kaleidoscope. But the sound I now heard was present and real. I recognized what it was and what it meant. The beep of the security alarm told me a door or window had been opened. The intruder was back and had gotten inside.

My heart rate launched into orbit and I felt the fear return, first suffocating and paralyzing, then triggering a rush of adrenaline that left me alert but uncertain. What to do? Fight? Flight? My fingers gripped the edge of the blanket, and my mind flew in a thousand directions. How had he gotten past the police units? Which room was he in? The knife! It was on the kitchen counter! I lay there, rigid, gauging options. Ryan had checked the phones, but I wanted to sleep undisturbed and had unplugged the one in the bedroom. Could I find the cord, locate the little triangular plug, and make a call before being overpowered? Where had Ryan said the police cars were parked? If I threw open the bedroom window and screamed, could the police hear me and react in time?

I strained to hear every movement in the darkness around me. There! A soft click. In the entrance hall? I stopped breathing. My front teeth clamped my lower lip.

A scrape against the marble floor. Near the entrance hall. Could it be Birdie? No, this sound had weight behind it. Again! A gentle brushing, as though against a wall, not the floor. Too high for a cat.

An image from Africa jumped into my head. A night drive in the Amboseli. A leopard, frozen in the jeep headlights, crouched, muscles taut, nostrils sucking the night air, soundlessly closing in on the unsuspecting gazelle. Was my stalker similarly in command of the darkness, picking a deliberate path to my bedroom? Cutting off escape routes? What was he doing? Why had he come back? What should I do? Something! Don't lie there and wait. Do something!

The phone! I'd try for the phone. There were police units right outside. The dispatcher would reach them. Could I reach it without giving myself away? Did it really matter?

Slowly, I raised the blankets and rolled flat on my back. The rustling of the sheets sounded like thunder in my ears.

Something brushed the wall again. Louder. Closer. As if the intruder was more sure of himself, less inclined to be cautious.

Every muscle and tendon tense, I inched toward the left side of the bed. The pitch black of the room made it hard to get my bearings. Why had I drawn the shade? Why had I unplugged that phone for a little extra sleep? Stupid. Stupid. Stupid. Find the cord, find the plug, punch 911 in the dark. I made a mental inventory of the objects on the nightstand, mapping the route my hand would take. I would have to slide down to the floor to reach the telephone jack.

At the left side of the bed, I raised onto my elbows. My eyes probed the darkness, but it was too deep to distinguish features except for the bedroom door. It was faintly backlit by some appliance with a glowing dial. There was no silhouette in the doorway.

Encouraged, I eased my left leg clear of the bed and slowly, blindly, groped for the floor. Then a shadow crossed the doorway, freezing my leg in midair and locking my muscles in catatonic fear.

This is the end, I thought. In my own bed. Alone. Four cops outside, oblivious. I pictured the other women, their bones, their faces, their gutted bodies. The plunger. The statue. No! screamed a voice in my head. Not me. Please. Not me. How many screams could I manage before he was on me? Before he silenced them with one sweep of his blade across my throat? Enough to alert the police outside?

My eyes darted back and forth, frantic, like those of an animal in a trap. A dark mass filled the doorway. A human figure. I lay speechless, motionless, unable even to launch my final screams.

The figure hesitated, as though uncertain of its next move. No features. Only a silhouette framed in the entrance. The only entrance. The only exit. God! Why didn't I keep a gun?

Seconds dragged by. Maybe the figure could not make out my outline on the very edge of the bed. Maybe the room looked empty from the doorway. Did he have a flashlight? Would he turn on the wall switch?

My mind snapped out of its paralysis. What had they taught in self-defense class? Run if you can. I can't. If cornered, fight to win. Bite. Gouge. Kick. Hurt him! First rule: Don't let him get on top! Second rule: Never let him pin you down! Yes. Surprise him. If I could get to any exit door, the cops outside could save me.

My left foot was already on the floor. Still on my back, I eased my right leg toward the edge of the bed, millimeter by millimeter, pivoting on my buttocks. I had both feet on the floor when the figure made a jerky motion and I was blinded by the glare of light.

My hand flew to my eyes and I lurched forward in a desperate effort to knock the figure aside and escape the bedroom. My right foot caught the sheet, sending me headlong onto the carpet. I rolled quickly to my left and scrambled onto my knees, turning to face my attacker. Third rule: Never turn your back.

The figure remained on the far side of the room, hand on the light switch. Only now it had a face.

A face distorted by some inner turmoil at which I could only guess. A face I knew. My own face was fast forwarding through a series of expressions. Terror. Recognition. Confusion. Our eyes locked and held. Neither moved. Neither spoke. We stared at each other across the air in my bedroom.

I screamed.

"Goddamn you, Gabby! You stupid bitch! What are you doing? What have I done to you? You bitch! You goddam bitch!"

I sat back on my heels, hands on my thighs, making no attempt to control the tears bathing my face or the sobs racking my body.

25 I ROCKED BACK AND FORTH from my knees to heels, sobbing and shouting. My words made little sense and when mingled with the sobbing became incoherent. I knew the voice was mine, but I had no power to stop it. Gibberish I didn't recognize flew from my mouth as I rocked and sobbed and shrieked.

Soon the sobbing won out over the shrieking and receded to a muffled sucking sound. With one last shudder, I stopped my rocking and focused on Gabby. She, too, was crying.

She stood across the room, one hand clutching the light switch, the other pressed to her chest. Her fingers twitched open then closed. Her chest heaved with each intake of breath, and tears ran down her face. She wept silently, and seemed frozen in place except for that one clutching hand.

"Gabby?" My voice broke, and it came out "—by?"

She gave a tight nod, her dreadlocks bobbing about her ashen face. She started making little sucking sounds, as if trying to pull back her tears. Speech seemed beyond her capabilities.

"Jesus Christ, Gabby! Are you crazy?" I whispered, reasonably controlled. "What are you doing here? Why didn't you call?"

She seemed to consider the second question, but attempted to answer the first.

"I needed to . . . talk to you."

I just stared at her. I'd been trying to find this woman for three weeks. She'd avoided me. It was four-thirty in the morning, she'd just broken into my home, and aged me at least a decade.

"How did you get in here?"

"I still have a key." More gulping sounds, but quieter, slower. "From last summer."

She moved a trembling hand from the light switch and displayed a key dangling from a small chain.

I felt anger rising in me, but my exhaustion held it in check.

"Not tonight, Gabby."

"Tempe, I . . ."

I gave her a look intended to freeze her in place once more. She stared back, not comprehending, plaintive.

"Tempe, I can't go home."

Her eyes were dark and round, her body rigid. She looked like an antelope cut from the herd and cornered. A very large antelope, but terrified nonetheless.

Wordlessly, I pushed to my feet, got towels and linens from the hall closet and dropped them on the guest room bed.

"We'll talk in the morning, Gabby."

"Tempe, I . . ."

"In the morning."

As I fell asleep I thought I heard her dial the phone. It didn't matter. Tomorrow.

And talk we did. For hours and hours. Over bowls of cornflakes and plates of spaghetti. Sipping endless cappuccinos. We talked curled on the couch and on long walks up and down Ste. Catherine. It was a weekend of words, most of them pouring from Gabby. At first I was convinced she had come unglued. By Sunday night I wasn't so sure.

The recovery team came by late Friday morning. In deference to me, they called ahead, arrived without fanfare, and worked quickly and efficiently. They accepted Gabby's presence as a natural development. The comfort of a friend after a night of fright. I told Gabby there had been an intruder in the garden, leaving out mention of the head. She had enough on her mind. The team left with encouraging words. "Don't worry, Dr. Brennan. We'll get the bastard. You hang in there."

Gabby's situation was as harrowing as mine. Her former informant had become her stalker. He was everywhere. Sometimes she'd see him on a bench in the park. Other times he'd follow her on the street. At night he'd hang around St. Laurent. Though she now refused to talk to him, he was always there. He kept his distance, but his eyes never left her. Twice she thought he'd been in her apartment.

I said, "Gabby, are you sure?" I meant, Gabby are you losing it?

"Did he take anything?"

"No. At least, I don't think so. Nothing I've noticed. But I know he went through my things. You know how you can tell. Nothing was gone, but things were a bit off. Just sort of rotated in place."

"Why didn't you return my calls?"

"I stopped answering the phone. It rang a dozen times a day and no one would be on the other end. Same with the answering machine. Lots of hangups. I just stopped using it."

"Why didn't you call me?"

"And say what? I'm being stalked? I've made myseif a victim? I can't handle my own life? I thought if I treated him like the maggot he is he'd lose interest. Slither away and pupate somewhere else."

Her eyes looked tortured.

"And I knew what you'd say. You're losing it, Gabby. You're letting your paranoia control you, Gabby. You need help, Gabby."

I felt a stab of guilt, remembering the way I'd hung up with her last. She was right.

"You could have called the police. They'd give you protection." Even as I said it I didn't believe it.

"Right." And then she told me about Thursday night.

"I got home about 3:30 A.M. and I could tell someone had entered the apartment. I'd used the old trick of stretching a thread across the lock. Well, seeing it gone totally unnerved me. I had been in a pretty good mood since I hadn't seen the creep all night. Also, I'd just had the locks changed, so I was feeling secure about the apartment for the first time in months. Seeing that thread on the floor just destroyed me. I couldn't believe he'd gotten in again. I didn't know if he was still inside and I didn't want to find out. I bolted and came here."

Bit by bit she talked of the past three weeks, recounting incidents as they came into her head. As her narrative unfolded over the weekend, my mind rearranged the disjointed episodes into a chronology. Though the man harassing her had done nothing overtly aggressive, I saw a pattern of increasing boldness. By Sunday I began to share her fear.

We decided she would stay with me for the time being, though I wasn't so sure what score my place would earn in a safety check. Late Friday Ryan had called to tell me the patrol unit would be there through Monday. I'd nod to them as we set out on our walks. Gabby thought they were a response to the garden intruder. I didn't suggest otherwise. I needed to bolster her newborn sense of safety, not wreck it.

I suggested we contact the police about her stalker, but she adamantly refused, fearing their involvement would compromise her girls. I also suspected she was afraid of losing their trust and her access to them. Reluctantly, I agreed.

On Monday I left her and went to work. She planned to gather some things from her apartment. She'd agreed to stay off the Main for a while, and meant to spend time writing. For that she needed her laptop and files.

When I got to my office it was past nine. Ryan had already phoned. The scrawled message read: "Got a name. AR." He was out when I returned his call, so I went to the histo lab to check on my garden memento.

It was drying on the counter, cleaned and marked, the absence of soft tissue having made boiling unnecessary. It looked like a thousand other skulls, with its empty orbits and neatly penned LML number. I stared at it, recalling the terror it had triggered three nights earlier.

"Location. Location. Location," I said to the empty lab.

"Pardon?"

I hadn't heard Denis come in.

"Something a realtor once told me."

"Oui?"

"It isn't *what* something is, so much as *where* it is that often shapes our reaction."

He looked blank.

"Never mind. You took soil samples before you washed this?"

"Oui." He held up two small plastic vials.

"Let's get them over to trace."

He nodded.

"Have X rays been done?"

"Oui. I just gave the bitewings and apicals to Dr. Bergeron."

"He's here on a Monday?"

"He's going on holiday for two weeks so he came to finish some reports."

"Happy day." I put the skull in a plastic tub. "Ryan thinks he's got a name."

"Ah, *oui?*" His eyebrows shot up.

"He must have been up with the birds today. The message was taken by the night service."

"For the St. Lambert skeleton or for your chum there?"

He indicated the skull. Apparently the story had already made the rounds.

"Maybe both. I'll let you know."

I headed for my office, stopping by Bergeron's on the way. He'd spoken with Ryan. The detective had found a missing person match promising enough to request a *mandat du coroner* for the antemortem records, and was on his way.

"Know anything about her?"

"Rien." Nothing.

"I'll finish with the skull before lunch. If you need it, just come by."

I spent the next two hours assessing the sex, race, and age of the skull. I observed features of the face and braincase, took measurements, and ran discriminant functions on my computer. We agreed. The skull was that of a white female. Like the St. Lambert skeleton.

Age was frustrating. All I had to go on was closure of the cranial sutures, a notoriously untrustworthy system for evaluating age. The computer couldn't help. I estimated she'd been in her late twenties to mid-thirties when she died. Maybe forty. Again, consistent with the bones from St. Lambert.

I looked for other indicators of congruity. Overall size. Robusticity of muscle attachments. Degree of arthritic change. Condition of the bone. State of preservation. Everything matched. I was convinced this was the head missing from the Monastère St. Bernard skeleton, but I needed more. Then I turned the skull over and examined the base.

Coursing across the occipital bone, close to the point where the skull sits on the vertebral column, I could see a series of slashes. They were V-shaped in cross-section and ran from high to low, following the contour of the bone. Under the Luxolamp they looked similar to the marks I'd observed on the long bones. I wanted to be sure.

I took the skull back to the histo lab, set it next to the operating scope, and got out the headless skeleton. I withdrew the sixth cervical vertebra, placed it under the scope, and reexamined the cuts I'd described the week before. Then I switched to the skull, focusing on the gashes scoring its back and base. The marks were identical, the contours and cross-sectional dimensions matching perfectly.

"Grace Damas."

I switched off the fiber-optic light and turned toward the voice.

"Qui?"

"Grace Damas," repeated Bergeron. "Age thirty-two. According to Ryan, she went missing in February of '92."

I calculated. Two years and four months. "That fits. Anything else?"

"I really didn't ask. Ryan said he'd stop in after lunch. He's tracking something else down."

"Does he know the ID's positive?"

"Not yet. I just finished." He looked at the bones. "Anything?"

"They're a match. I want to see what the trace evidence folks have to say about the soil samples. Maybe we can get a pollen profile. But I'm convinced. Even the cut marks are the same. I wish I had the upper neck vertebrae, but it's not critical."

Grace Damas. All through lunch the name echoed in my head. Grace Damas. Number five. Or was it? How many more would we find? Each of the names was burned into my mind, like a brand on a heifer's rump. Morisette-Champoux. Trottier. Gagnon. Adkins. Now another. Damas.

At one-thirty Ryan came to my office. Bergeron had already given him the positive on the skull. I told him it was good for the skeleton as well.

"What do you know about her?" I asked.

"She was thirty-two. Three kids."

"Christ."

"Good mother. Faithful wife. Active in the church." He glanced at his notes. "St. Demetrius, over on Hutchison. Near Avenue du Parc and Fairmont. Sent the kids off to school one day. Never seen again."

"Husband?"

"Looks clean."

"Boyfriend?"

He shrugged. "It's a very traditional Greek family. If you don't talk about it, those things can't be true. She was a good girl. Lived for her husband. They've got a friggin' shrine set up for her in the living room." Another shrug. "Maybe she was a saint. Maybe she wasn't. We're not going to find out from Mama or Hubby. It's like talking to barnacles. You mention hanky-panky, they pull in and slam shut."

I told him about the cut marks.

"Same as Trottier. And Gagnon."

"Hm."

"Hands were cut off. Like Gagnon, and one each for Morisette-Champoux and Trottier."

"Hm."

When he'd gone I turned on the computer and pulled up my spreadsheet. I erased *"Inconnue"* from the name column and typed in Grace Damas, then entered the scanty information Ryan had given me. In a separate file I summarized what I knew about each of the women, arranging them by date of death.

Grace Damas had disappeared in February of 1992. She was thirty-two, married, the mother of three. She lived in the near northeast part of the city, in an area known as Parc Extension. Her body had been dismembered and buried in a shallow grave at the St. Bernard Monastery in St. Lambert, where it was found in June of 1994. Her head showed up in my garden several days later. Cause of death was unknown.

Francine Morisette-Champoux was beaten and shot in January of 1993. She was forty-seven. Her body was found less than two hours later, just south of Centre-ville, in the condo she shared with her husband. Her killer had slit her belly, cut off her right hand, and forced a knife into her vagina.

Chantale Trottier disappeared in October of 1993. She was sixteen. She lived with her mother off the island, in the lake community of Ste. Anne-de-Bellevue. She'd been beaten, strangled, and dismembered, her right hand partially severed, her left one completely detached. Her body was found two days later in St. Jerome.

Isabelle Gagnon disappeared in April of 1994. She'd lived with her brother in St. Édouard. In June of this year her dismembered body was found on the grounds of Le Grand Séminaire in Centreville. Though cause of death could not be determined, marks on her bones indicated she'd been dismembered, her belly slit. Her hands had been removed, and her killer had inserted a plunger in her vagina. She was twenty-three.

Margaret Adkins was killed on June 23, just over a week ago. She was twenty-four, had one son, and lived with her common-law husband. She'd been beaten to death. Her belly was slit and one breast had been sliced off and forced into her mouth. A metal statue had been rammed up her vagina.

Claudel was right. There was no pattern in MO. They were all beaten, but Morisette-Champoux was also shot. Trottier was strangled. Adkins was bludgeoned. Hell, we didn't even have a cause for Damas and Gagnon.

I went over and over what had been done to each of them. There was variation, but there was also a theme. Sadistic cruelty and mutilation. It had to be one person. One monster. Damas, Gagnon, and Trottier were dismembered and dumped in plastic bags. Their bellies had been slit. Gagnon and Trottier had had their hands severed. Morisette-Champoux was slashed and had a hand cut off, but she wasn't dismembered. Adkins, Gagnon, and Morisette-Champoux had suffered genital penetration with a foreign object. The others hadn't. Adkins's breast was mutilated. No one else was disfigured in that way. Or were they? There hadn't been enough of Damas and Gagnon to say.

I stared at the screen. It has to be here, I told myself. Why can't I see it? What's the link? Why these women? Their ages are up and down the charts. It's not that. They're all white. Big deal, this is Canada. Francophone. Anglophone. Allophone. Married. Single. Common law. Choose another category. Let's try geography.

I got out a map and plotted where each of the bodies had been found. It made even less sense than when I'd done it with Ryan. Now there were five points in the scatter. I tried plotting their homes. The pins looked like paint flung at a canvas by an abstract artist. There was no pattern.

What did you expect, Brennan, an arrow pointing to a flat on Sherbrooke? Forget place. Try time.

I looked at the dates. Damas was the first. In early 1992. I calculated in my head. Eleven months between Damas and Morisette-Champoux. Nine months later, Trottier. Six months to Gagnon. Two months between Gagnon and Adkins.

The intervals were decreasing. Either the killer was growing bolder, or his blood lust was growing stronger. My heart pounded hard against my ribs as I considered the implication. Over a week had passed since Margaret Adkins died.

26

I FELT TRAPPED INSIDE MY skin. Anxious and frustrated. The visions in my head annoyed me, but I couldn't turn them off. I watched a candy wrapper dance on the wind outside my window, tossed by puffs of shifting air.

That piece of paper is you, Brennan, I chided myself. Can't control your own fate, much less anyone else's. There's nothing on St. Jacques. No word on who put the skull in your yard. Gabby's nut case is still out there. Claudel is probably lodging a complaint against you. Your daughter is about to drop out of school. And five dead women are living in your head, and likely to be joined by a sixth or seventh at the rate your investigation is going.

I looked at my watch—2:15 P.M. I couldn't stand my office another minute. I had to do something.

But what?

I glanced at Ryan's incident report. An idea began to form.

They'll be furious, I told myself.

Yes.

I checked the report. The address was there. I pulled up my spreadsheet on the computer screen. They were all there, along with the phone numbers.

You would do better to go to the gym and work off your frustration there.

Yes.

Solo sleuthing won't help the situation with Claudel.

No.

You may lose Ryan's support.

True.

Tough.

I printed the data from the screen, made a choice, and dialed. A man answered on the third ring. He was surprised but agreed to see me. Grabbing my purse, I fled into the summer sunshine.

It was hot again, the air so thick with humidity you could take your finger and write your initials in it. The haze refracted the sun's glare and spread it all around like a cloak. I drove toward the home Francine Morisette-Champoux had shared with her husband. I'd chosen her case for no other reason than proximity. She had lived just below Centreville, not ten minutes from my condo. If I bombed, well, I was on my way home.

I found the address and pulled to a stop. The street was lined with brick town houses, each with its iron balcony, below-ground garage, and brightly colored door.

Unlike most communities in Montreal, this one had no name. Urban renewal had transformed what had been part of the Canadian National yards, replacing tracks and toolsheds with residences, barbecue grills, and tomato plants. The neighborhood was neat and middle class, but suffered from an identity crisis. It was too close to the city core to be truly suburban, but just a hair outside the arc defining trendy downtown. It wasn't old and it wasn't new. Functional and convenient, it lacked bouquet.

I rang the bell and waited. Fresh-cut grass and ripe garbage tinged the hot air. Two doors down a sprinkler arced water across a Chiclet-sized lawn. A central air compressor hummed to life, its sound challenging the sprinkler's steady click.

When he opened the door I thought of the Gerber baby grown up. His hair was blond and receding, the center patch swirling into a curl on his forehead. His cheeks and chin were round and padded, his nose short and angled upward. He was a large man, not yet gone to fat, but moving down that road. Though it was ninety degrees, he wore jeans and a sweatshirt. Calgary Stampede—1985.

"Monsieur Champoux, I'm . . ."

He pulled the door wide and stepped back, ignoring the ID I held for his inspection. I followed him down a narrow hall to a narrow living room. Fish tanks lined one wall, tinting the room an eerie aquamarine. At the far end I could see a counter stacked with small nets, boxes of food, and other fish paraphernalia. Louvered doors opened onto the kitchen. I recognized the kitchen work island and looked away.

Monsieur Champoux cleared a spot on the sofa and indicated I should sit. He dropped into a recliner.

"Monsieur Champoux," I began again, "I'm Dr. Brennan from the Laboratoire de Médecine Légale."

I left it at that, hoping to avoid further explanations about my precise role in the investigation. I didn't really have any.

"Have you found something? I . . . It's been so long I don't let myself think about it anymore." He spoke to the parquet floor. "It's been a year and a half since Francine died, and I haven't heard from you people in over a year."

I wondered where he thought I fit in with "you people."

"I answered so many questions, talked to so many people. The coroner. The cops. The press. I even hired my own investigator. I really wanted to nail this guy. Didn't do any good. They never found a clue. We can pinpoint the time he killed her to within an hour, you know. The coroner said she was still warm. This maniac kills my wife, walks out, and disappears without a trace." He shook his head in disbelief. "Have you finally got something?"

His eyes held a mixture of anguish and hope. Guilt sliced to my core.

"No, Monsieur Champoux, not really." Except four other women may have been killed by the same animal. "I just want to go over a few details, see if there's anything we overlooked."

The hope vanished and resignation surfaced. He leaned back in his chair and waited.

"Your wife was a nutritionist?"

He nodded.

"Where did she work?"

"All over, really. She was paid by the MAS, but on any given day she could have been anywhere."

"The MAS?"

"Ministère des Affaires Sociales."

"She moved around?"

"Her job was to advise food cooperatives, immigrant groups mostly, about how to buy stuff. She'd help them form these collective kitchens, then teach them how to make whatever it is thcy like to eat so it would be cheap, but still healthy. She'd help them get produce and meat and things. Usually in bulk. She was always visiting the kitchens to be sure they were running okay."

"Where were these collectives?"

"All over the place. Parc Extension. Côte des Neiges. St. Henri. Little Burgundy."

"How long had she been working for the MAS?"

"Maybe six, seven years. Before that she worked at the Montreal General. Had much better hours."

"Did she enjoy her work?"

"Oh yeah. She loved it." The words caught briefly in his throat.

"Were her hours irregular?"

"No, they were regular. She worked all the time. Mornings. Evenings. Weekends. There was always a problem and Francine was the one to fix it." His jaw muscles clenched and unclenched.

"Had you and your wife disagreed about her work?"

He fell silent for a moment. Then, "I wanted to see more of her. I wished she was still at the hospital."

"What do you do, Monsieur Champoux?"

"I'm an engineer. I build things. Only no one wants much built these days." He gave a mirthless smile and tipped his head to one side. "I was downsized." He used the English phrase.

"I'm sorry. Do you know where your wife was going the day she was killed?"

He shook his head. "We'd hardly seen each other that week. There was a fire in one of her kitchens and she'd been there day and night. She may have been going back there, or she may have been heading for another one. She didn't keep any kind of journal or log that I know of. They never found one in her office and I never saw one here.

She'd been talking about getting her hair cut. Hell, she may have been going to do that."

He looked at me, his eyes tortured.

"Do you know what that feels like? I don't even know what my wife was planning to do on the day she died."

The circulating water of the tanks murmured softly in the background.

"Had she spoken about anything unusual? Odd phone calls? A stranger at the door?" I thought of Gabby. "Someone on the street?"

Another head shake.

"Would she have?"

"Probably, if we'd spoken. We really hadn't had time those last few days."

I tried a new tack.

"It was January. Cold. The doors and windows would have been closed. Was your wife in the habit of keeping them locked?"

"Yes. She never liked living here, didn't like being right on the street. I talked her into buying this place, but she preferred high-rise buildings with security systems or guards. We get some pretty seedy characters down here, and she was always on edge. That's why we were leaving. She liked the extra space, and the little yard out back, but she never really got used to being here. Her work took her to some rough areas, and when she came home she wanted to feel safe. Untouchable. That's what she said. Untouchable. You know?"

Yes. Oh yes.

"When was the last time you saw your wife, Monsieur Champoux?"

He breathed deeply, exhaled. "She got killed on a Thursday. She'd worked late the night before, because of the fire, so I'd already gone to bed when she got home."

He dropped his head and talked again to the parquet. A patch of tiny vessels colored each of his cheeks.

"She came to bed full of her day, trying to tell me where she'd been and what she'd been doing. I didn't want to hear it."

I saw his chest rise and fall under the sweatshirt.

"The next day I got up early and left. Didn't even say good-bye."

We were quiet a moment.

"That's what I did and there's no way out. I don't get another shot." He raised his eyes and stared into the turquoise of the tanks. "I resented her working when I couldn't, so I froze her out. Now I live with it."

Before I could think of a response he turned to me, his face taut, his voice harder than it had been.

"I went to see my brother-in-law. He had some job leads for me. I was there all morning, then I fou—Then I came back here around noon. She was already dead. They checked all that out."

"Monsieur Champoux, I'm not suggesting y—"

"I don't see that this is going anywhere. We're just rehashing old words."

He rose. I was being dismissed.

"I'm sorry to bring up painful memories."

He regarded me without comment, then moved toward the hall. I followed.

"Thanks for your time, Monsieur Champoux." I handed him my card. "If there's anything you think of later, please give me a call."

He nodded. His face had the numbed look of a person swept into a calamity who can't forget that his last words and last acts toward the wife he loved were petty and far from a proper good-bye. Is there ever a proper good-bye?

As I left I could feel his eyes on my back.

Through the heat I felt cold inside. I hurried to my car.

The interview with Champoux left me shaken. As I drove toward home, I asked myself a thousand questions.

What right had I to dredge up this man's pain? I pictured Champoux's eyes.

Such sorrow. Brought on by my forced reminders?

No. I wasn't the architect of his house of regret. Champoux was a man living with remorse of his own construction.

Remorse for what? For harming his wife?

No. That was not his character.

Remorse for ignoring her. For leaving her thinking she was not important. Simple as that. On the eve of her death, he rejected conversation, turned his back and went to sleep. He didn't say good-bye in the morning. Now he never would.

I turned north onto St. Marc, passing into the shadow of the overpass. Would my inquiries do anything but drag memories to the surface where they would again cause pain?

Could I really help where an army of professionals had failed, or was I just on a personal quest to show up Claudel?

"No!"

I banged the steering wheel with the heel of my hand.

No, dammit, I thought to myself. That is not my goal. No one but me is convinced that there is a single killer and that he will kill again. If I am to prevent more deaths, I have to dig up more facts.

I emerged from shadow into sunlight. Instead of turning east, toward home, I crossed Ste. Catherine, doubled back on Rue du Fort, and merged onto the 20 West. Locals called it the 2 and 20, but I'd yet to find anyone who could explain or locate the 2.

I edged out of the city, drumming my impatience on the steering wheel. It was three-thirty and traffic was already backed up at the Turcot Interchange. Bad timing.

Forty-five minutes later I found Geneviève Trottier weeding tomatoes behind the faded green house she had shared with her daughter. She looked up when I pulled onto the drive, and watched me cross the lawn.

"Oui?" Friendly, sitting back on her heels, squinting up at me.

She wore bright yellow shorts and a halter too big for her small breasts. Sweat glistened on her body and curled her hair tightly around her face. She was younger than I'd expected.

When I explained who I was and why I was there, the friendliness turned somber. She hesitated, put down her trowel, then rose, brushing dirt from her hands. The smell of tomatoes hung heavy around us.

"We'd better go inside," she said, dropping her eyes. Like Champoux she didn't question my right to ask.

She started across the yard and I followed, hating the conversation about to ensue. The knotted halter hung loose across the knobs on her spine. Blades of grass stuck to the backs of her legs and rode the tops of her feet.

Her kitchen gleamed in the afternoon sunlight, its porcelain and wood surfaces testimony to years of care. Potted kalanchoe lined the windows, framed by yellow gingham. Yellow knobs dotted the cabinets and drawers.

"I've made some lemonade," she said, her hands already moving to the task. Comfort in the familiar.

"Yes, thank you. That would be nice."

I sat at a scrubbed wooden table and watched her twist ice cubes from a plastic tray, drop them into glasses, and add the lemonade. She brought the drinks and slid in across from me, her eyes avoiding mine.

"It's hard for me to talk about Chantale," she said, studying her lemonade.

"I understand, and I am so sorry for your loss. How are you doing?"

"Some days it's easier than others."

She folded her hands and tensed, her thin shoulders rising under the halter.

"Have you come to tell me something?"

"I'm afraid not, Madame Trottier. And I don't really have any specific questions for you. I thought there might be something you've remembered, perhaps something you didn't think important earlier?"

Her eyes stayed on the lemonade. A dog barked outside.

"Has anything occurred to you since you last spoke with the detectives? Any detail about the day Chantale disappeared?"

No response. The air in the kitchen was hot and dense with humidity. It smelled faintly of lemon disinfectant.

"I know this is awful for you, but if we're to have any hope of finding your daughter's killer, we still need your help. Is there anything that's been bothering you? Anything you've been thinking about?"

"We fought."

Again. The guilt of nonclosure. The wish to take back words and substitute others.

"She wouldn't eat. She thought she was getting fat."

I knew all this from the report.

"She wasn't fat. You should have seen her. She was beautiful. She was only sixteen." Her eyes finally met mine. A single tear spilled over each lower lid, and trickled down each cheek. "Like the English song."

"I'm so sorry," I said, gently as I could. Through the screened window I could smell sun on geraniums. "Was Chantale unhappy about anything?"

Her fingers tightened around her glass.

"That's what's so hard. She was such an easy child. Always happy. Always full of life, bubbling with plans. Even my divorce didn't seem to upset her. She took it in stride and never missed a step."

Truth or retrospective fantasy? I remembered the Trottiers had divorced when Chantale was nine. Her father was living somewhere in the city.

"Can you tell me anything about those last few weeks? Had Chantale altered her routine in any way? Had any odd calls? Made any new friends?"

Her head moved slowly in continuous negation. No.

"Did she have trouble making friends?"

No.

"Were you uneasy about any of her friends?"

No.

"Did she have a boyfriend?"

No.

"Did she date?"

No.

"Did she have problems at school?"

No.

Poor interrogation technique. Need to get the witness to do the talking instead of me.

"What about that day? The day Chantale disappeared?"

She looked at me, her eyes unreadable.

"Can you tell me what took place that day?"

She took a sip of lemonade, swallowed deliberately, set the glass back on the table. Deliberately.

"We got up around six. I made breakfast." She clutched the glass so tightly I feared it would shatter. "Chantale left for school. She and her friends rode the train since the school is in Centre-ville. They say she went to all her classes. And then she . . ."

A breeze teased the gingham off the window frame.

"She never came home."

"Did she have any special plans that day?"

"No."

"Did she normally come right home after classes?"

"Usually."

"Did you expect her home that day?"

"No. She was going to see her father."

"Did she do that often?"

"Yes. Why do I have to keep answering these questions? It's useless. I've told all this to the detectives. Why do I have to keep repeating the same things over and over? It doesn't do any good. It didn't then, it won't now."

Her eyes fixed on mine, the pain almost palpable.

"You know what? All the time I was filling out missing persons forms and answering questions, Chantale was already dead. She was lying in pieces in a dump. Already dead."

She dropped her head and the thin shoulders shuddered. She was right. We had nothing. I was fishing. She was learning to bury the pain, to plant tomatoes and live, and I'd ambushed her and forced an exhumation.

Be kind. Get out.

"It's all right, Madame Trottier. If you can't remember further details, they are probably not important."

I left my card and standard request. Call if you think of anything. I doubted she would.

Gabby's door was closed when I got home, her room quiet. I thought of looking in, resisted. She could be so touchy about her privacy. I got into bed and tried to read, but Geneviève Trottier's words kept jamming my mind. *Déjà mort*. Already dead. Champoux had used the same phrase. Yes. Déjà dead. Five. That was the chilling truth. Like Champoux and Trottier, I too had thoughts that would not lie quiet in my mind.

27

I WOKE TO THE SOUND OF the morning news. July 5. I'd slipped through Independence Day and not even noticed. No apple pie. No "Stars and Stripes Forever." Not a single sparkler. Somehow the thought depressed me. Every American anywhere on the globe should stand up and strut on the Fourth. I had allowed myself to become a Canadian spectator of American culture. I made plans to go to the ball park at the next opportunity and cheer for whichever American team was in town.

I showered, made coffee and toast, and scanned the *Gazette*. Endless talk of separation. What would happen to the economy? To aboriginals? To English speakers? The want ads embodied the fear. Everyone selling, no one buying. Maybe I should go home. What was I accomplishing here?

Brennan. Stow it. You're surly because you have to take the car in.

It was true. I hate errands. I hate the minutiae of making do in a techno-nation-state in the closing years of the second millennium. Passport. Driver's license. Work permit. Income tax. Rabies shot. Dry cleaning. Dental appointment. Pap smear. My pattern: put it off until unavoidable. Today the car had to be serviced.

I am a daughter of America in my attitude toward the automobile. I feel incomplete without one, cut off and vulnerable. How will I escape an invasion? What if I want to leave the party early, or stay after the Métro stops? Go to the country? Haul a dresser? Gotta have wheels. But I am not a worshiper. I want a car that will start when I turn the key, get me where I want to go, keep doing it for at least a decade, and not require a lot of pampering.

Still no sounds from Gabby's room. Must be nice. I packed my gear and left.

The car was in the shop and I was on the Métro by nine. The morning rush was over, the railcar relatively empty. Bored, I grazed through the ads. See a play at Le Théâtre St. Denis. Improve your job skills at Le Collège O'Sullivan. Buy jeans at Guess, Chanel perfume at La Baie, color at Benetton.

My eyes drifted to the Métro map. Colored lines crossed like the wiring on a motherboard, white dots marked the stops.

I traced my route eastward along the green line from Guy-Concordia to Papineau. The orange line looped around the mountain, north-south on its eastern slope, east-west below the green line, then north-south again on the west side of the city. Yellow dived below the river, emerging on Île Ste. Hélène and at Longueuil on the south shore. At

Berri-UQAM the orange and yellow lines crossed the green. Big dot. Major switching point.

The train hummed as it slithered through its underground tunnel. I counted my stops. Seven dots.

Compulsive, Brennan. Want to wash your hands?

My eyes moved north along the orange line, visualizing the changing landscape of the city. Berri-UQAM. Sherbrooke. Mount Royal. Eventually, Jean-Talon near St. Édouard. Isabelle Gagnon had lived in that neighborhood.

Oh?

I looked for Margaret Adkins's neighborhood. Green line. Which station? Pie IX. I counted from Berri-UQAM. Six stops east.

How many was Gagnon? Back to orange. Six.

Tiny hairs tingled at the back of my neck.

Morisette-Champoux. Georges-Vanier Métro. Orange. Six stops west from Berri-UQAM.

Jesus.

Trottier? No. The Métro doesn't go to Ste. Anne-de-Bellevue.

Damas? Parc Extension. Close to the Laurier and Rosemont stations. Third and fourth stops from Berri-UQAM.

I stared at the map. Three victims lived exactly six stops from the Berri-UQAM station. Coincidence?

"Papineau," said a mechanical voice.

I grabbed my things and bolted onto the platform.

Ten minutes later I heard the phone as I unlocked my office door.

"Dr. Brennan."

"What the hell are you doing, Brennan?"

"Good morning, Ryan. What can I help you with?"

337

"Claudel's trying to nail my butt to the wall because of you. Says you've been running around bothering victims' families."

He waited for me to say something but I didn't.

"Brennan, I've been defending you because I respect you. But I can see what's shaping up here. Your prying could really hang me up on this case."

"I asked a few questions. That's not illegal." I did nothing to defuse his anger.

"You didn't tell anyone. You didn't coordinate. You just went off knocking on doors." I could hear breath being drawn through nostrils. They sounded clenched.

"I called first." Not quite true for Geneviève Trottier.

"You're not an investigator."

"They agreed to see me."

"You're confusing yourself with Mickey Spillane. It's not your job."

"A well-read detective."

"Christ, Brennan, you are pissing me off!"

Squad room noise.

"Look." Controlled. "Don't get me wrong. I think you're solid. But this isn't a game. These people deserve better." His words were hard as granite.

"Yes."

"Trottier is my case."

"What exactly is being done on *your* case?"

"Bren—"

"And what about the others? Where are they going?"

I was on a roll.

"These investigations aren't exactly heading everyone's agenda right now, Ryan. Francine Morisette-Champoux was killed over eighteen months ago. It's been eight months since Trottier. I have this bizarre notion that whoever killed these women ought to be reeled in and locked up. So I take an interest. I ask a few questions. What happens? I'm told to butt out. And because Mr. Claudel thinks I'm about as helpful as a boil, these cases will drop lower and lower until they're off the charts and out of everyone's minds. Again."

"I didn't tell you to butt out."

"What are you saying, Ryan?"

"I understand Claudel wants your ass in a sling. You want to fry his balls. I might too if he'd stone-walled me. I just don't want you two screwing up my case."

"What's that supposed to mean?"

He took a long time to answer.

"I'm not saying I don't want your input. I just want the priorities in this investigation perfectly clear."

For a long time no one spoke. Anger rushed the line in both directions.

"I think I've found something."

"What?" He hadn't expected that.

"I may have a connection."

"What do you mean?" A little of the edge was gone from his voice.

I wasn't sure what I meant. Maybe I just wanted to derail him.

"Meet me for lunch."

"This better be good, Brennan." Pause. "I'll see you at Antoine's at noon."

Fortunately I had no new cases, so I was able to get right to work. So far nothing had fit together. Maybe the Métro was the tie.

I opened the computer and pulled up the file to check addresses. Yes. I had the right stops. I dug out a map and plotted the stations, just as Ryan and I had done with the victims' homes. The three pins formed a triangle, with Berri-UQAM in the center. Morisette-Champoux, Gagnon, and Adkins had each lived within six stops of the station. St. Jacques's apartment was a short walk away.

Could that be it? Catch a train at Berri-UQAM. Pick a victim who gets off six stops away. Hadn't I read about that type of behavior? Fixate on a color. A number. A series of actions. Follow a pattern. Never deviate. Be in control. Wasn't careful planning characteristic of serial killers? Could our boy take it one step further? Could he be a serial killer with some sort of compulsive behavior pattern into which the killings fit?

But what about Trottier and Damas? They didn't fit. It couldn't be that simple. I stared at the map, willing an answer to materialize. The feeling that something lurked just over the wall of my conscious nagged stronger than ever. What? I hardly heard the tap.

"Dr. Brennan?"

Lucie Dumont stood in my doorway. That's all it took. The wall was breached.

"Alsa!"

I'd forgotten all about the little monkey.

My outburst startled Lucie. She jerked, almost dropping her printout.

"Shall I come back?"

I was already digging for Lucie's earlier printout. Yes. Of course. The bus terminal. It's practically next to the Berri-UQAM station. I plotted Alsa. Her pin went right in the center of the triangle.

Was that it? The monkey? Did she tie in? If so, how? Another victim? An experiment? Alsa died two years before Grace Damas. Hadn't I read about that pattern also? Teenage peeping and fantasy escalating to animal torture and, finally, human rape and murder? Wasn't that Dahmer's chilling progression?

I sighed and sat back. If that was the bulletin my subconscious was trying to post, Ryan wouldn't be impressed.

Out the door and down to the central files. Lucie had vanished. I'd apologize later. I was doing that a lot lately. Back to my desk.

The Damas folder held little save my report. I opened the jacket marked Adkins and leafed through. The contents were beginning to look archival, I'd handled them so often. Nothing clicked. On to Gagnon. Morisette-Champoux. Trottier.

I spent an hour pouring over the files. Gran's puzzle pieces again. Jumbled bits of information. Feed them in, let your mind rotate and arrange. It was the arranging **that** wasn't going well. Coffee time.

I brought it back, along with the morning's *Journal.* Sip and read. Regroup. The news varied little from the English language *Gazette,* the editorials enormously. What did Hugh MacLennan call it? The Two Solitudes.

I sat back. There it was again. The subliminal itch. I had the pieces, but wasn't making the fit.

Okay, Brennan. Be systematic. The feeling started today. What have you been doing? Not much. Read the paper. Took the car in. Rode the Métro. Reviewed files.

Alsa? My mind wasn't satisfied. There's more.

Car?

Nothing.

Paper?

Maybe.

I leafed back through it. Same stories. Same editorials. Same want ads.

I stopped.

Want ads. Where had I seen want ads? Stacks of them.

St. Jacques's room.

I went through them slowly. Jobs. Lost and found. Garage sales. Pets. Real estate.

Real estate? Real estate!

I pulled the Adkins folder and withdrew the pictures. Yes. There it was. The tilting, rusty sign, barely visible in the untended yard. *À Vendre.* Someone was selling a condo in Margaret Adkins's building.

So?

Think.

Champoux. What had he said? She didn't like it there. That's why we were leaving. Something like that.

I reached for the phone. No answer.

What about Gagnon? Didn't the brother rent? Perhaps the landlord was selling the building.

I checked the photos. No sign. Damn.

I tried Champoux again. Still no answer.

I dialed Geneviève Trottier. It was answered on the second ring.

"Bonjour." Cheerful.

"Madame Trottier?"

"Oui." Curious.

"This is Dr. Brennan. We spoke yesterday."

"Oui." Fearful.

"I have one question, if I may?"

"Oui." Resigned.

"Did you have your home on the market when Chantale disappeared?"

"Pardonnez-moi?"

"Were you trying to sell your home in October of last year?"

"Who told you that?"

"No one. I was just curious."

"No. No. I have lived here since my husband and I separated. I have no intention of leaving. Chantale . . . I . . . it was our home."

"Thank you, Madame Trottier. I'm sorry to have disturbed you." Again I'd violated the accord she'd reached with her memories.

This is going nowhere. Maybe it's a stupid idea.

I tried Champoux. A male voice answered as I was about to hang up.

"Oui."

"Monsieur Champoux?"

"Un instant."

"Oui." A second male voice.

"Monsieur Champoux?"

"Oui."

I explained who I was and posed my question. Yes, they had been trying to sell the property. It was listed with ReMax. When his wife was killed he took it off the market. Yes, he thought ads had run, but he couldn't be sure. I thanked him and hung up.

Two out of five. Could be. Maybe St. Jacques used want ads.

I called recovery. The materials from the Berger Street apartment were in property.

I glanced at my watch—eleven forty-five. Time to meet Ryan. He wouldn't bite. I needed more.

Once again I spread the Gagnon photos and studied them, one by one. This time I saw it. Grabbing a magnifying glass, I moved the lens until the object came into focus. I leaned closer, adjusting and readjusting to be sure.

"Hot damn."

I scooped the pictures into their envelope, stuffed them into my briefcase, and almost ran to the restaurant.

Le Paradis Tropique is directly across from the

SQ building. The food is lousy, the service slow, but the tiny restaurant is always crowded at noon, due largely to the effervescence of its owner, Antoine Janvier. Today's greeting was typical.

"Ah, madame, you are hoppy today? Yes! I am so glad to see you. It has been a very long time." His ebony face showed mock disapproval.

"Yes, Antoine, I've been very busy." True, but Caribbean food would never be my daily fare.

"Ah, so hard, you work too hard. But today I have some nice fish. Fresh. Barely dead. The ocean is still dripping from his back. You will eat him and feel better. I have a beautiful table for you. The best in the house. Your friends, they are here."

Friends? Who else?

"Come. Come. Come."

There must have been a hundred people inside, sweating and eating under brightly colored umbrellas. I followed Antoine through the maze of tables to a raised platform in the far corner. Ryan sat silhouetted against a fake window hung with yellow and lavender curtains tied back to show a painted sunset. A ceiling fan revolved slowly above his head as he talked to a man in a linen sports jacket. Though his back was to me, I recognized the razor cut and perfect creases.

"Brennan." Ryan half rose from his chair. Catching my expression, his eyes narrowed in warning. Bear with me.

"Detective Lieutenant Ryan." Okay. But this better be good.

Claudel remained seated and nodded.

I took the seat next to Ryan. Antoine's wife appeared and, after the pleasantries, the detectives ordered beer. I asked for Diet Coke.

"So. What's this breakthrough?" No one could do condescending like Claudel.

"Why don't we order first?" Ryan the peace-maker.

Ryan and I exchanged thoughts on the weather. We agreed it was warm. When Janine returned I asked for the fish special. Jamaican plates for the detectives. I was beginning to feel the outsider.

"So. What have you come up with?" Ryan the moderator.

"The Métro."

"The Métro?"

"That narrows it to four million people. Two if we stick to males."

"Let her talk, Luc."

"What about the Métro?"

"Francine Morisette-Champoux lived six stops from the Berri-UQAM station."

"Now we're getting somewhere."

Ryan shot him a look that could have cut glass.

"So did Isabelle Gagnon. And Margaret Adkins."

"Hm."

Claudel said nothing.

"Trottier is too far out."

"Yes. And Damas is too close."

"The St. Jacques apartment is a few blocks away."

We ate in silence for a while. The fish was dry, the fries and dirty rice were greasy. Hard combination to get just right.

"It may be more complicated than simply the Métro stops."

"Oh?"

"Francine Morisette-Champoux and her husband had their home on the market. Listed with ReMax."

No one said anything.

"There was a sign outside Margaret Adkins's building. ReMax."

They waited for me to go on. I didn't. I reached into my purse, extracted the Gagnon photos, and placed one on the table. Claudel forked a fried plantain.

Ryan picked up the photo, studied it, then looked at me quizzically. I handed him the magnifying glass and pointed to an object barely visible at the far left edge of the photo. He examined it for a long time, then, saying nothing, he extended the picture and lens across the table.

Claudel wiped his hands, wadded the paper napkin, and tossed it onto his plate. Taking the photo, he repeated Ryan's actions. When he recognized the object his jaw muscles bunched. For a long time he stared at it, saying nothing.

"Neighbor?" Ryan asked.

"Looks like it."

"ReMax?"

"I think so. You can just see the R and part of the E. We can get the print blown up."

"Should be easy to track. The listing would only be four months old. Hell, in this economy it's probably still active." Ryan was already making notes.

"What about Damas?"

"I don't know." Wouldn't want to bother a victim's family. I didn't say it.

"Trottier?"

"No. I talked to Chantale's mother. She wasn't selling. Never listed the property."

"Could be the father."

We both turned to Claudel. He was looking at me, and this time his voice held no condescension.

"What?" Ryan.

"She spent a lot of time at the father's place. Could be he was selling." Endorsement?

"I'll check." Morc notes.

"She was going there the day she was killed," I said.

"She stayed there a couple of days every week." Patronizing, but not contemptuous. Progress.

"Where does he live?"

"Westmount. Billion-dollar condo on Barat, off Sherbrooke."

I tried to place that. Just over the border from Centre-ville. Not far from my condo.

"Just above the Forum?"

"Right."

"What Métro station?"

"Must be Atwater. It's just a couple of blocks up from there."

Ryan looked at his watch, waved to catch Janine's attention, then pantomimed a signature in the air. We paid, receiving handfuls of candy from Antoine.

The minute I reached my office I pulled out the map, located the Atwater station, and counted the stops to Berri-UQAM. One. Two. Three. Four. Five. Six. The phone rang as I was reaching for it.

28

ROBERT TROTTIER'S CONDO had been listed for a year and a half.

"Guess things are slow in that price range."

"I wouldn't know, Ryan. I've never been there."

"I've seen it on television."

"ReMax?"

"Royal Lepage."

"Ads?"

"He thinks so. We're checking."

"Sign outside?"

"Yes."

"Damas?" I asked.

She, her husband, and three kids lived with his parents. The senior Damases had owned their home since dirt was invented. Would die in it.

I thought about that for a while.

"What did Grace Damas do?"

"Raised kids. Crocheted doilies for the church.

Hopped around in part-time jobs. You ready for this? Once worked in a boucherie."

"Perfect." Who butchered the butcher?

"The husband?"

"Clean. Drives a truck." Pause. "Like his father before him."

Silence.

"Think it means anything?"

"The Métro or the listings?"

"Either."

"Hell, Brennan, I don't know." More silence. "Give me a scenario."

I'd been trying to concoct one.

"Okay. St. Jacques reads the real estate ads, picks an address. Then he stakes it out until he spots his victim. He stalks her, waits for his opportunity. Then the ambush."

"How does the Métro figure in?"

Think. "It's a sport to him. He's the hunter, she's the prey. The hidey-hole on Berger is his blind. He flushes her with the want ads, tracks her, then moves in for the kill. He only uses certain hunting areas."

"The sixth stop out."

"Got a better idea?"

"Why real estate notices?"

"Why? Vulnerable target, a woman home alone. Figures if she's selling she'll be there to show the property. Maybe he calls. The ad would give him an entrée."

"Why six?"

"I don't know. The guy's nuts."

Brilliant, Brennan.

"Must know the city pretty damn well."

We chewed on that.

"Métro worker?"

"Cabby?"

"Utilities?"

"Cop?"

There was an interval of tense silence.

"Brennan, I wouldn—"

"No."

"What about Trottier and Damas? They don't fit."

"No."

Silence.

"Gagnon was found in Centre-ville, Damas in St. Lambert, Trottier in St. Jerome. If our boy's a commuter, how does he handle that?"

"I don't know, Ryan. But it's four for five on both the ads and the Métro stops. Look at St. Jacques, or whoever this rodent is. His hole is right at Berri-UQAM, and he collected want ads. It's worth some follow-up."

"Yep."

"Might start with the St. Jacques collection, see what the guy saved."

"Yep."

Another thought occurred to me.

"What about profiling? We've got enough to give it a try now."

"Very trendy."

"Could help."

I could read his thoughts across the line.

"Claudel doesn't have to know. I could poke around unofficially, find out if it's worth pursuing. We've got crime scenes for Morisette-Champoux and Adkins, manner of death and body disposal for the others. I think they can work with that."

"Quantico?"

"Yeah."

He snorted. "Right. They're so backed up they won't return your call until the turn of the century."

"I know someone there."

"I'm sure you do." Sigh. "Why not. But just an inquiry at this point. Don't go committing us to anything. The request will have to come from Claudel or me."

A minute later I was dialing a Virginia area code. I asked for John Samuel Dobzhansky and waited. Mr. Dobzhansky was unavailable. I left a message.

I tried Parker Bailey. Another secretary, another message.

I called Gabby to find out her dinner plans. My own voice asked for a message.

Called Katy. Message.

Doesn't anybody stay in one place anymore?

I spent the rest of the afternoon on correspondence and student recommendations, listening for the phone. I wanted to talk to Dobzhansky. I wanted to talk to Bailey. A clock ticked inside my head, making it hard to concentrate. Countdown. How long until the next victim? At five I gave up and went home.

The condo was silent. No Birdie. No Gabby.

"Gab?" Maybe she was napping.

The guest room door was still closed. Birdie was asleep on my bed.

"You two really have it rough." I stroked his head. "Whoo. Time to clean your pan." The odor was noticeable.

"Too much on my mind, Bird. Sorry."

No acknowledgment.

"Where's Gabby?"

Blank stare. Stretch.

I replaced the litter. Birdie acknowledged by using it, pawing a large portion onto the floor.

"Come on, Bird, try to keep it in the pan. Gabby's not the neatest bathroom mate, but do your part." I looked at her jumble of cleansers and cosmetics. "I think she cleaned up a little."

I got a Diet Coke and changed into cutoffs. Plan dinner? Who was I kidding. We'd go out.

The answering machine blinked. One message. Me. I'd called around one. Hadn't Gabby heard it? Had she ignored it? Maybe she'd turned the phone off. Maybe she was sick. Maybe she wasn't here. I went to her door.

"Gab?"

I knocked softly.

"Gabby?"

Harder.

I opened the door and looked in. The usual Gabby mess. Jewelry. Papers. Books. Clothes everywhere. A bra hung from the back of a chair. I checked the closet. Shoes and sandals tossed in heaps. Amid it all, the neatly made bed. The incongruity of it struck me.

"Sonofabitch."

Birdie slithered past my legs.

"Was she here at all last night?"

He looked at me, jumped to the bed, circled twice, and settled. I dropped next to him, the familiar knot tightening in my stomach.

"She's done it again, Bird."

He spread his toes and began to lick.

"Not so much as a stinking note."

Birdie focused on inter-toe spaces.

"I will not think about this." I went to unload the dishwasher.

Ten minutes later I had calmed enough to dial her number. No answer. Of course. I tried the university. No answer.

I wandered into the kitchen. Opened the refrigerator. Closed it. Dinner? Reopened it. Diet Coke. Wandered to the living room, set the new Coke

DÉJÀ DEAD

next to the earlier can, clicked on the TV, surfed the channels, chose a sitcom I wouldn't watch. My mind raced from the murders to Gabby to my garden skull and back, unable to fix on anything. The cadence of dialogue and canned laughter provided background noise as my thoughts bounced around like atomic particles.

Anger at Gabby. Resentment at letting myself be used. Hurt that she would do it. Apprehension about her safety. Fear for a new victim. Frustration over my helplessness. I felt emotionally bruised, but couldn't stop beating myself.

I'm not sure how long I'd been there when the phone rang, the sound sending adrenaline pouring from wherever it rooms when not on duty.

Gabby!

"Hello."

"Tempe Brennan, please." A male voice. Familiar as my Midwest childhood.

"J.S.! God, am I glad to hear from you!"

John Samuel Dobzhansky. My first love. Counselors. Camp Northwoods. The romance outlasted that summer and the next, thrived until our freshman year of college. I went South, J.S. went North. I chose anthropology, met Pete. He trained in psychology, married, divorced. Twice. Years later we'd reconnected at the Academy. J.S. specialized in sexual homicide.

"You got that Camp Northwoods feeling?" he asked.

"Up in my head," I finished the line from the camp song. We both laughed.

"I wasn't sure if you'd want me to call at home, but you left the number so I figured I'd try."

"Glad you did. Thank you." Thank you. Thank you. "I want to pick your brain about a situation we've got up here. If that's okay?"

353

"Tempe, when will you stop disappointing me?" Feigned hurt.

We'd had dinner at Academy meetings, the possibility of a fling hanging heavy between us at first. Should we tamper with teenaged memories? Was the passion still there? Nothing verbalized, the idea waned bilaterally. Better to leave the past intact.

"What about the new love interest you were telling me about last year?"

"Gone."

"Sorry. J.S., we've had some murders here that I think are tied together. If I give you an overview, can you opine on whether we have a serial?"

"I can opine on anything." One of our old pet phrases.

I described the Adkins and Morisette-Champoux scenes, and outlined what had been done to the victims. I described how and where the other bodies were found, and how they'd been mutilated. Then I added my theories about the Métro and want ads.

"I'm having trouble convincing the cops these cases are connected. They keep saying there's no pattern. They're right to some extent. The victims are all different, one is shot, the others aren't. They lived all over the place. Nothing hooks together."

"Whoa. Whoa. Slow down. You're going about this all wrong. First of all, most of what you've described has to do with modus operandi."

"Yes."

"Similarities in MO can be useful, don't get me wrong, but disparities are extremely common. A perpetrator may gag or tie his victim with the phone cord at one scene, then bring his own rope to the next. He may stab or slash one victim, shoot or strangle the next, steal from one, not from another. I profiled one guy who used a different kind of weapon at every scene. You still there?"

"Yes."

"A criminal's MO is never static. It's like anything else, there's a learning curve. These guys get better with practice. They learn what works and what doesn't. They're continually improving their technique. Some more than others, of course."

"Comforting."

"Also, there are all kinds of random events that can affect what a perpetrator does, regardless of his best-laid plans. A phone rings. A neighbor shows up. A cord breaks. He has to improvise."

"I see."

"Don't misunderstand. Patterns in MO are useful, and we use that. But variations don't mean much."

"What *do* you use?"

"Ritual."

"Ritual?"

"Some of my colleagues call it a signature, or a calling card, and it's only seen at some crime scenes. Most perpetrators develop an MO because once a plan works a couple of times they gain confidence in it and believe it lowers their risk of getting caught. But with violent, repetitive offenders there's something else operating. These people are driven by anger. Their anger leads them to fantasize about violence, and eventually they act out the fantasies. But the violence isn't enough. They evolve rituals for expressing the anger. It's these rituals that give them away."

"What sort of rituals?"

"Usually they involve controlling, maybe humiliating the victim. You see, it isn't really the victim that's important. Her age, her appearance may be irrelevant. It's the need to express the anger. I did one guy whose victims ranged from seven to eighty-one years in age."

"So, what would you look for?"

"How does he encounter his victim? Does he jump her? Does he use a verbal approach? How does he control her once he's made contact? Does he assault her sexually? Does he do it before or after he kills her? Does he torture his victim? Does he mutilate the body? Does he leave anything at the scene? Take anything away?"

"But can't those things be affected by unexpected contingencies also?"

"Of course. But the critical thing is he does these things as part of his fantasy enactment, his anger dissipation ritual, not just to cover his ass."

"So, what do you think? Does what I described have a signature?"

"Off the record?"

"Of course."

"Absolutely."

"Really?" I began taking notes.

"I'd bet my ass on it."

"Your buns are safe, J.S. Do you think it's a sexual sadist?"

I heard a rattling as he switched the phone. "Sexual sadists are turned on by their victim's pain. They don't just want to kill, they want their victims to suffer. And—and this is critical—they're sexually aroused by it."

"And?"

"Part of your pattern says yes. Insertion of objects into the vagina or rectum is very common with these guys. Were your victims alive when this was done?"

"At least one. Hard to tell with the other two since the bodies were so decomposed."

"Sounds like sexual sadism is a possibility. The

real question remains, was the killer sexually aroused by his actions?"

I couldn't answer that. No semen was found on any of the victims. I said this.

"Useful, but doesn't rule out SS. I had one guy who'd masturbate in his victim's hand, cut it off, then grind it up in a blender. Never found semen at the scenes."

"How'd you get him?"

"One time his aim wasn't so good."

"Three of these women were dismembered. We know that for certain."

"That may show a pattern, but it's not proof of sexual sadism. Unless it was done before the victim's death. Serial killers, whether sexual sadists or not, are very cunning. They put a lot of planning into their crimes. Postmortem mutilation doesn't necessarily mean there's a sexual or sadistic component. Some cut the body up just to make it easier to hide."

"What about the mutilation? The hands?"

"Same answer. It's a pattern, it's overkill, but it may or may not be sexual. Sometimes it's just a way of rendering the victim powerless. I do see some indicators, however. You say the victims were unknown to their killer. They were savagely beaten. Three suffered object insertion, probably antemortem. That combination is characteristic."

I was writing furiously.

"Check whether the objects were brought to the scene or were already there. That could be part of this guy's signature, planned as opposed to opportunistic cruelty."

I noted it, starred it.

"What are some other characteristics of sexual sadism?"

"Patterned MO. Use of a pretext to make con-

KATHY REICHS

tact. A need to control and humiliate the victim. Excessive cruelty. Sexual arousal from the victim's fear and pain. Keeping victim memorabilia. The—"

"What was that last one?" I was writing so fast my hand was cramping.

"Memorabilia. Souvenirs."

"What kind of souvenirs?"

"Items from the murder scene, pieces of the victim's clothing, jewelry, that sort of thing."

"Newspaper clippings?"

"Sexual sadists love their own press."

"Would they keep records?"

"Maps, diaries, calendars, drawings, you name it. Some of them make tapes. The fantasy isn't just the kill. The stalk before and the reenactment afterward can be a big part of the turn-on."

"If they're so good at avoiding detection, why would they keep that stuff? Isn't it risky?"

"Most of them think they're superior to the cops. Too smart to get caught."

"What about body parts?"

"What *about* body parts?"

"Do they keep them?"

Pause. "Not common, but sometimes."

"So what do you think about the Métro and want ad idea?"

"The fantasies these guys act out can be incredibly elaborate and very specific. Some need special locations, exact sequences of events. Some sexual sadists need specific victim responses, so they script the whole thing, force the victim to say certain things, perform certain acts, wear certain clothes. But, Tempe, these behaviors aren't just typical of sexual sadists. They characterize a lot of personality disorders. Don't get hung up on the sexual sadist angle. What you want to look for is that signature, that calling card that only your killer leaves. That's

358

how you'll nail him, regardless of how psychiatrists classify him. Using the Métro and newspaper could figure into your boy's fantasy."

"J.S., based on what I've told you, what do you think?"

There was a long pause, a slow expulsion of breath.

"I think you've got a real nasty one up there, Tempe. Tremendous anger. Extreme violence. If it is this St. Jacques character, his using the victim's bank card bothers me. Either he's incredibly stupid, and it doesn't look that way, or he's getting sloppy for some reason. Maybe sudden financial pressure. Or he's getting bolder. The skull in your garden is a flag. He was sending a message. Maybe a taunt. Or, it's possible that at some level he wants to be caught. I don't like what you're telling me about how you figure in. And it looks like you *do* figure in. The picture. The skull. Based on what you've told me, looks more like he's taunting you."

I told him about the night at the monastery and the car that had tailed me.

"Christ, Tempe, if this guy's refocusing on you, don't play games. He's dangerous."

"J.S., if it was him on the monastery grounds, why didn't he just kill me then?"

"It goes back to what I was saying before. You probably surprised him out there, so he wasn't prepared to kill in the way he likes. He wasn't in control. Maybe he didn't have his kit. Maybe the fact that you were unconscious robbed him of the rush he gets at seeing his victim's fear."

"No death ritual."

"Exactly."

We chatted for a while, other places, old friends, the time before murder became part of our lives. When we hung up it was after eight.

I leaned back, stretched my arms and legs, and went limp. For some time I lay there, a rag doll recalling its past. Eventually, hunger roused me, and I went to the kitchen, warmed a tray of frozen lasagna and forced myself to eat it. Then I spent an hour reconstructing from my notes what J.S. had said. His parting words kept coming back to me.

"The intervals are getting shorter."

Yes, I knew that.

"He's upping the stakes."

I knew that too.

"He may now have his sights trained on you."

At ten I went to bed. I lay in the dark, staring at the ceiling, feeling alone and sorry for myself. Why did I carry the burden of these women's deaths? Did someone have me in the crosshairs of his psychopathic fantasy? Why wouldn't anyone take me seriously? Why was I getting old, eating frozen dinners in front of a television I didn't watch? When Birdie nestled at my knee, that tiny bit of contact triggered the tears I'd been holding back since talking to J.S. I cried into the pillowcase Pete and I had bought in Charlotte. Or, rather, I had bought while he stood around looking impatient.

Why had my marriage failed? Why was I sleeping alone? Why was Katy so discontented? Why had my best friend been inconsiderate of me again? Where was she? No. I wouldn't think about that. I don't know how long I lay there, feeling the emptiness of my life, listening for Gabby's key.

29

THE NEXT MORNING I GAVE
Ryan a summary of my discussion with J.S. A week
crept by. Nothing.

The weather stayed hot. Days, I worked through
bones. Remains found in a septic tank in Cancún
had been a tourist missing for nine years. Bones
scavenged by dogs had been a teenage girl before
homicide by a blunt instrument. A cadaver in a
box, hands severed, face mutilated beyond recognition, revealed only that it had been a white male,
skeletal age thirty-five to forty.

Nights, I visited the jazz festival, milling with the
sticky crowds that clogged Ste. Catherine and
Jeanne-Mance. I heard Peruvians, their music a
blend of woodwind and rain forest. I wandered
from Place des Arts to Complexe Desjardins, enjoying the saxophones and guitars and summer
nights. Dixieland. Fusion. R&B. Calypso. I willed
myself not to look for Gabby. I refused to fear for

the women about me. I listened to the music of
Senegal, Cape Verde, Rio, and New York, and, for
a while, I forgot. The five.

Then, on Thursday, a call came. LaManche.
Meeting on Tuesday. Important. Please be there.

I arrived not knowing what to expect, most certainly not what greeted me. Seated with LaManche
were Ryan, Bertrand, Claudel, Charbonneau, and
two detectives from St. Lambert. The director of
the lab, Stefan Patineau, sat at the far end of the
table, a crown prosecutor on his right.

They rose as one when I arrived, sending my
anxiety level into the cheap seats. I shook hands
with Patineau and the attorney. The others nodded,
their faces neutral. I tried to read Ryan's eyes, but
they would not meet mine. As I took the one remaining chair, my palms felt sweaty and the familiar knot had hold of my gut. Had this meeting been
called to discuss me? To review allegations made
against me by Claudel?

Patineau wasted no time. A task force was being
formed. The possibility of a serial killer would be
examined from every angle, all suspect cases investigated, every lead aggressively pursued. Known
sex offenders would be pulled in and questioned.
The six detectives would be assigned full time,
Ryan would coordinate. I would continue my normal casework, but serve as an ex-officio member
of the team. Space had been set aside downstairs,
all dossiers and relevant materials were being
moved to that location. Seven cases were under
consideration. The task force would hold its first
meeting that afternoon. We would keep Monsieur
Gauvreau and the prosecutor's office informed of
all progress.

Just like that. Done. I returned to my office,
more stunned than relieved. Why? Who? I'd been

arguing the serial killer theory for almost a month. What had happened to suddenly give it credence? Seven cases? Who were the other two?

Why ask, Brennan? You'll find out.

And I did. At one-thirty I entered a large room on the second floor. Four tables formed an island in the middle, portable chalk and bulletin boards lined the walls. The detectives were clumped at the back of the room, like buyers at a trade show booth. The board they were viewing held the familiar Montreal and Métro maps, colored pins jutting from each. Seven more boards stood side by side, each topped by a woman's name and picture. Five were as familiar as my own family, the others I didn't know.

Claudel favored me with a half second of eye contact, the others greeted me cordially. We exchanged comments about the weather, then moved to the table. Ryan distributed legal pads from a stack in the center, then launched right in.

"You all know why you're here, and you all know how to do your jobs. I just want to make sure of a few things at this point."

He looked from face to face, then gestured at a stack of folders.

"I want everyone to study these files. Go through them carefully. Digest everything in them. We're getting the information on computer, but it's slow. For now we'll use the old-fashioned way. If there's anything you think is relevant, anything at all, get it up on that victim's board."

Nods.

"We'll have an updated printout of the pervert parade today. Divide it up, roust these guys, see where they've been partying."

"Usually in their own shorts." Charbonneau.

"Could be one of them crossed the line, now finds his shorts lacking."

Ryan looked at each of us in turn.

"It's absolutely critical we work as a team. No individuals. No heroes. Talk. Exchange information. Bounce ideas off each other. That's how we're going to nail this bastard."

"If there is one." Claudel.

"If not, Luc, we'll clean house, nail a whole lot of bastards. Nothing lost."

Claudel tucked down the corners of his mouth and drew a series of short, quick lines on his tablet.

"It's equally important we be concerned about security," Ryan continued. "No leaks."

"Patineau going to announce our little civic group?" Charbonneau.

"No. In a sense, we're working undercover."

"Public hears the words serial killer, they'll go ape shit. Surprised they haven't already." Charbonneau.

"Apparently the press hasn't picked up on the connection. Don't ask me why. Patineau wants to keep it that way for now. That may change."

"Press has the memory of a gnat." Bertrand.

"Nah, that's the IQ score."

"They'd never make that cutoff."

"Okay. Okay. Let's go. Here's what we've got."

Ryan summarized each case. I listened mutely as my ideas, even my words, filled the air and were scribbled onto legal pads. Okay, some of Dobzhansky's ideas as well, but passed on by me.

Mutilation. Genital penetration. Real estate ads. Métro stops. Someone had been listening. What's more, someone had been checking. The boucherie where Grace Damas had once worked was a block off St. Laurent. Close to the St. Jacques apartment. Close to the Berri-UQAM Métro. It plotted. That made four for five. That's what had tipped the balance. That and J.S.

Following our talk, Ryan had convinced Patineau to forward a formal request to Quantico. J.S. had agreed to give the Montreal cases top priority. A flurry of faxes provided him with what he needed, and Patineau had a profile three days later. That had done it. Patineau had decided to move. *Voilà.* Task force.

I felt relieved, but also slighted. They'd taken my labor and left me to sweat. On walking into that meeting, I had feared personal censure, had not expected tacit acknowledgment of work well done. Nevertheless. I steadied my voice to hide my anger.

"So what does Quantico tell us to look for?"

Ryan pulled a thin folder from the stack, opened it, and read.

"Male. White. Francophone. Probably not educated beyond secondary level. Probably a history of NSO's . . ."

"C'est quoi, ça?" Bertrand.

"Nuisance sexual offenses. Peeping. Obscene phone calls. Indecent exposure."

"The cute stuff." Claudel.

"Dummy man." Bertrand.

Claudel and Charbonneau snorted.

"Shit." Claudel.

"My hero." Charbonneau.

"Who the hell's dummy man?" Ketterling, St. Lambert.

"Little maggot busts apartments so he can stuff the lady's nightie, then slash it. Been working his act about five years."

Ryan continued, selecting phrases from the report.

"Careful planner. Probably uses ruse to approach

victim. Possibly the real estate angle. Probably married . . ."

"*Pourquoi?*" Rousseau, St. Lambert.

"The hidey-hole. Can't bring the victims home to wifey."

"Or Mommy." Claudel.

Back to the report.

"Probably selects, prepares isolated location in advance."

"The basement?" Ketterling, St. Lambert.

"Hell, Gilbert sprayed the shit out of that place with Luminol. If there was any blood there, it would have lit up like Tomorrowland." Charbonneau.

Report. "Excessive violence and cruelty suggest extreme anger. Possible revenge orientation. Possible sadistic fantasies involving domination, humiliation, pain. Possible religious overlay."

"*Pourquoi, ça?*" Rousseau.

"The statue, the body dumps. Trottier was at a seminary, so was Damas."

For the next few moments no one said a word. The wall clock buzzed softly. In the corridor, a pair of high heels clicked closer, receded. Claudel's pen made short, tense strokes.

"*Beaucoup de* 'possibles' *et* 'probables.'" Claudel.

Claudel's continued resistance to the one-killer theory annoyed me.

"It's also *possible* and *probable* we're going to have another murder soon," I snapped.

Claudel's face hardened into its usual mask, which he pointed at his tablet. The lines in his cheeks tensed, but he said nothing.

Buzz.

"Does Dr. Dobzhansky have a long-term forecast?" I asked, calmer.

"Short term," Ryan said somberly and returned to the profile. "Indications of loss of control. Increasing boldness. Intervals shortening." He closed the folder and shoved it toward the center of the table. "Will kill again."

Silence again.

Eventually, Ryan looked at his watch. We all followed suit, like assembly line robots.

"So. Let's get into these files. Add anything you have that's not here. Luc, Michel, Gautier was CUM, so you guys might have more on that one."

Nods from Charbonneau and Claudel.

"Pitre fell to the SQ. I'll double-check her. The others are more recent, should be pretty complete."

Since I was all too familiar with the five recents, I started with Pitre and Gautier. The files had been open since '88 and '89 respectively.

Constance Pitre's semi-nude, badly decomposed body was found in an abandoned house at Khanawake, an Indian reserve upriver from Montreal. Marie-Claude Gautier was discovered behind the Vendôme Métro, a switching point for trains to the western suburbs. Both women had been savagely beaten, their throats slashed. Gautier had been twenty-eight, Pitre thirty-two. Neither had been married. Each lived alone. The usual suspects had been questioned, the usual leads pursued. Dead end in each case.

I spent three hours going over the files, which, compared to those I'd studied for the past six weeks, were relatively sparse. Both women had been prostitutes. Was that the reason for the limited investigations? Exploited in life, ignored in death? Good riddance? I refused to allow myself to pursue it.

I looked at family snapshots of each victim. Their faces were different, yet similar in some disturbing way. The yeasty white pallor, the lavish makeup, the cold, flat stare. Their expressions brought to recall my night on the Main, when I'd viewed the street production from a front-row seat. Resignation. Desperation. There I'd seen it live. Here it was in stills.

I spread the crime scene photos, knowing beforehand the story they'd tell. Pitre: the yard, the bedroom, the body. Gautier: the station, the bushes, the body. Pitre's head was almost severed. Gautier's throat had also been slashed, her right eye stabbed into pulpy mush. The extreme savagery of the attacks had prompted their inclusion in our investigation.

I read the autopsy, toxicology, and police reports. I dissected each interview and investigator's summary. I pulled out every detail of the victims' comings and goings, every particular of their lives and deaths. All the minutiae I could suck from each folder went onto a crude spreadsheet. It wasn't much.

I heard the others moving around, scraping chairs, exchanging banter, but I paid no attention. When I finally closed the files, it was past five. Only Ryan remained. I looked up to see him watching me.

"Wanna see the Gypsies?"

"What?"

"Heard you like jazz."

"Yeah, but the festival is over, Ryan." Heard from whom? How? Was this a social invitation?

"True. But the city isn't. Les Gitanes are playing in the Old Port. Great group."

"Ryan, I don't think so." But I *did* think. Had thought. That's why I'd refuse. Not now. Not until the investigation was over. Not until the animal was netted.

"Good enough." The electric eyes. "But you gotta eat."

That was true. Another frozen dinner, solo, was decidedly unappealing. No. Don't even give Claudel the appearance of impropriety.

"It's probably not a g—"

"We could chew over some of your thoughts on this stuff while we put away a pizza."

"Business meeting."

"Certainement."

Buzz.

Did I want to discuss the cases? Of course. Something about the added two didn't ring true. Even more, I was curious about the task force. Ryan had given us the official version; what were the real dynamics? Were there threads in the web I should know about? Avoid?

Buzz.

Would the others think twice? Of course not.

"Sure, Ryan. Where do you want to go?"

Shrug. "Angela's?"

Close to my condo. I thought of the 4 A.M. call last month, the "friend" he'd been with. You're paranoid, Brennan. The man wants a pizza. He knows you can park at home.

"Is that convenient for you?"

"Right on the way."

To what? I didn't ask.

"Fine. See you there in"—I looked at my watch—"thirty minutes?"

I stopped home, fed Birdie, barred myself from mirrors. No hair combing. No blusher. Business.

At six-fifteen Ryan sipped a cold beer, I a Diet Coke as we waited for a veggie supreme. No goat cheese on his half.

"You're making a mistake."

"I don't like it."

"Rigid."

"In touch with myself."

We exchanged small talk for a while, then I switched lanes. "Tell me about these other cases. Why Pitre and Gautier?"

"Patineau had me pull all unsolved SQ homicides that fit a certain profile. Back to '85. Basically the pattern you've been hammering on. Females, over-kill, mutilation. Claudel searched the CUM cases. Local PD's were asked to do the same. So far, these two have come up."

"Just the province?"

"Not exactly."

We fell silent as the waitress arrived, sliced, and served the pizza. Ryan ordered another Belle Gueule. I passed, mildly resentful. Your own fault, Brennan.

"Don't even think about touching my half."

"Don't like it." He drained his glass. "Do you know what goes through goats?"

I did, but blocked it.

"What do you mean, not exactly?"

"Initially, Patineau asked for a search of cases in and around Montreal. When the profile arrived from Quantico, he sent a composite description, our stuff and theirs, to the RCMP to see if the Mounties had similar cases in their files."

"And?"

"Negative. Looks like we've got a homeboy."

We ate in silence for a while.

Finally, "What's your take?"

I took my time answering.

"I only spent three hours with the new files, but somehow they don't seem to fit."

"The hooker angle?"

"That. But something else. The killings are violent, no question about that, but they're just too . . ."

I'd been trying to put a word to the feeling all afternoon, but hadn't found one. I dropped a piece of pizza to my plate, watched tomato and artichoke ooze off the soggy dough.

". . . messy."

"Messy?"

"Messy."

"Jesus, Brennan, what do you want? Did you see the Adkins apartment? Or Morisette-Champoux? Looked like Wounded Tree."

"Knee."

"What?"

"Knee. It was Wounded Knee."

"The Indians?"

I nodded.

"I don't mean blood. The Pitre and Gautier scenes looked, what . . . ?" Again, I groped for a word. "Disorganized. Unplanned. With the others, you get the sense this guy knew exactly what he was doing. Got into their homes. Brought his own weapon. Took it away with him. Never found one at the other scenes, right?"

He nodded.

"They recovered the knife with Gautier."

"No prints. That could suggest planning."

"It was winter. The guy probably wore gloves."

I swirled my Coke.

"The bodies look like they were just left. Quickly. Gautier was facedown. Pitre was lying on her side, her clothes were torn, her pants were at her ankles. Take another look at the Morisette-Champoux and Adkins photos. The bodies almost look posed. They were both lying on their backs, their legs were spread, their arms were positioned. Like dolls. Or ballerinas. Christ, Adkins looked like she'd been laid down while doing a pirouette. Their clothing wasn't torn, it was opened, neatly. It's as if he wanted to display what he'd done to them."

Ryan said nothing. The waitress appeared, wanting assurance we'd enjoyed our meal. Anything else? Just a check.

"I just get a different feeling with these other two cases. I could be dead wrong."

"That's what we're supposed to figure out."

Ryan took the check, raising a hand in a "don't argue" gesture. "This one's on me. Next one's yours."

He cut my protest short by reaching out to touch my upper lip. Slowly, he ran his index finger around the corner of my mouth, then held it up for my inspection.

"Goat," he said.

Fire ants would have had less effect on my face.

I arrived home to an empty apartment. No surprise. But I was becoming anxious about Gabby, and hoped she would reappear. Mainly so I could send her packing.

I lay on the couch and turned on the Expos game. Martinez had just beaned one off the batter. The announcer was going crazy. Tough moving back up to starter.

I watched until the announcer's voice faded to a hum and the noise in my head took over. How did Pitre and Gautier fit in? What did Khanawake mean? Pitre was Mohawk. The others had all been white. Four years ago the Indians had barricaded the Mercier Bridge, making life hell for commuters. Feelings between the reserve and its neighbors remained less then cordial. Was that significant?

Gautier and Pitre were hookers. Pitre had been busted several times. None of the other victims had

DÉJÀ DEAD

police records. Did that mean anything? If victims had been selected at random, what would be the odds that two out of seven would be hookers?

Had the Morisette-Champoux and Adkins scenes really shown premeditation? Was I imagining the staging? Was it accidental?

Was there a religious angle? That was one I hadn't really explored. If so, what did it mean?

Eventually, I drifted into uneasy sleep. I was on the Main. Gabby was beckoning to me from the upstairs window of a run-down hotel. The room behind her was dimly lit, and I could see figures moving about. I tried to cross the street to her, but women outside the hotel threw rocks when I moved. They were angry. A face appeared beside Gabby's, backlit against the room. It was Constance Pitre. She tried to put something over Gabby's head, a dress or gown of some sort. Gabby resisted, her gestures to me becoming more frantic.

A rock hit me in the gut, wrenching me hard into the present. Birdie stood on my stomach, tail in landing position, eyes fixed on my face.

"Thanks."

I dislodged him and swung to a sitting position. "What the hell did that mean, Bird?"

My dreams are not particularly disingenuous. My subconscious takes recent experience and throws it back at me, often in riddle form. Sometimes I feel like Arthur, frustrated with Merlin's cryptic answers. Just tell me! Think, Arthur. Think!

The rock-throwing. Obvious: Martinez's bean ball. Gabby. Obvious: She's on my mind. The Main. The hookers. Pitre. Pitre trying to dress Gabby. Gabby beckoning for help. A tingle of fear began to form.

Hookers. Pitre and Gautier were hookers. Pitre and Gautier are dead. Gabby works with hookers.

Gabby was being harassed. Gabby is gone. Could there be a connection? Could she be in trouble?

No. She used you, Brennan. She does it often. You always fall for it.

The fear would not recede.

What about the guy shadowing her? She seemed genuinely frightened.

She split. Not even a note. Thanks. Gotta go. Nothing.

Isn't that a bit much, even for Gabby? The fear became stronger.

"Okay, Dr. Macaulay, let's find out."

I went to the guest room and looked around. Where to begin? I had already gathered her belongings and heaped them on the closet floor. I hated to go through them.

Trash. It seemed less invasive. I dumped the wastebasket onto the desk. Tissues. Candy wrappers. Tinfoil. A sales slip from Limité. An ATM receipt. Three balls of crumpled paper.

I opened a yellow ball. Gabby's scrawl on lined paper:

"I'm sorry. I can't deal with this. I would never forgive myself if . . ."

It broke off there. A note to me?

I opened the other yellow ball:

"I will not succumb to this harassment. You are an irritant that must . . ."

Again, she'd given up. Or been interrupted. What had she been trying to say? To whom?

The other ball was white and larger. When I unwadded it, runaway fear shot through me, vaporizing all the unkind thoughts I'd been nurturing. I flattened the paper with trembling hands and stared.

What I saw was a pencil drawing, the central figure clearly female, her breasts and genitalia depicted in minute detail. The torso, arms, and legs were crudely sketched, the face an oval with features vaguely shadowed in. The woman's abdomen was open, the organs rising from it to circle the central figure. In the lower left-hand corner in a stranger's hand was written:

"Every move you make. Every step you take. Don't cut me."

30

I FELT COLD ALL OVER. OH, God, Gabby. What have you gotten into? Where are you? I looked at the mess around me. Was it normal Gabby chaos, or the aftermath of panicky flight?

I reread the unfinished notes. For whom were they intended? Me? Her stalker? I would never forgive myself if *what?* An irritant that must be *what?* I looked at the drawing and sensed what I'd felt when viewing Margaret Adkins's X rays. Foreboding. No. Not Gabby.

Calm down, Brennan. Think!

The phone. I tried Gabby's apartment and office. Answering machine. Voice mail. Bless the electronic age.

Think.

Where did her parents live? Trois-Rivières? 411. Only one Macaulay. Neal. An old woman's voice. French. So glad to hear from you. Been such a long time. How are you? No, they hadn't talked to Gabrielle in several weeks. No, that wasn't unusual. Young people, so busy. Is anything wrong? Assurances. Promises to visit soon.

Now what? I didn't know any of Gabby's current friends.

Ryan?

No. He's not your guardian. Anyway, what would you tell him?

Slow down. Think. I got a Diet Coke. Was I overreacting? I returned to the guest room and reexamined the sketch. Overreacting? Hell, I was underreacting. I checked a number, reached for the phone, and dialed.

"Y'allo."

"Hey, J.S. Tempe." I struggled to keep my voice steady.

"My God. Two calls in one week. Admit it. You can't stay away from me."

"It's been over a week."

"Anything under a month I interpret as irresistible attraction. What's up?"

"J.S., I . . ."

He caught the tremor in my voice and his demeanor changed, the flipness replaced by genuine concern.

"Are you okay, Tempe? What is it?"

"It's these cases I talked to you about last week."

"What's happened? I profiled the guy right away. Hope they realize that was your influence. Did they get my report?"

"Yes. You made the difference, actually. They've decided to form a task force. That part's moving right along."

I wasn't sure how to broach my anxiety about Gabby, didn't want to abuse our friendship.

"Could I ask you a few more questions? There's

something else I'm concerned about, and I really don't know wh—"

"Why do you even ask, Brennan? Fire away."

Where to begin? I should have made a list. My head was like Gabby's room, thoughts and images scattered haphazardly.

"This is something else."

"Yes. You said that."

"I guess I'm interested in what you call nuisance sexual offenders?"

"Okay."

"Would that include things like following someone, calling her, but not doing anything overtly threatening?"

"It could."

Start with the sketch.

"You told me last time that violent offenders often make records? Like tapes and drawings?"

"Right."

"Do nuisance offenders?"

"Do they what?"

"Make sketches and things."

"They might."

"Can the content of a drawing indicate the level of violence someone is capable of?"

"Not necessarily. For one person drawing could be a release valve, a way of acting out without actually engaging in violence. For another, it could be the trigger that sets him off. Or a reenactment of what he's already done."

Great.

"I found a drawing of a woman with her stomach slit and her guts spread out around her. What does that suggest?"

"The Venus de Milo has no arms. G.I. Joe has no dick. What does that mean? Art? Censorship?

Sexual deviance? Tough call when seen in a vacuum."

Silence. What should I tell him?

"Did this drawing come from the St. Jacques gallery?" he asked.

"No." I found it in my guest room trash. "You said offenders often escalate to higher and higher levels of violence, right?"

"Yeah. At first they might just engage in peeping, or obscene phone calls. Some stay with that, others move on to bigger challenges: self-exposure, stalking, even breaking and entering. For still others that's not enough; they progress to rape and even murder."

"So some sexual sadists might not actually be violent?"

"There you go with the sexual sadist business again. But in answer to your question, yes. Some of these guys play out their fantasies in other ways. Some use inanimate objects, or animals, some find consenting partners."

"Consenting partners?"

"A compliant partner, someone who'll permit whatever it is the fantasy requires. Subordination, humiliation, even pain. Could be a wife, a girlfriend, someone he pays."

"A prostitute?"

"Sure. Most prostitutes will do some role playing, within limits."

"That can defuse violent tendencies?"

"It can as long as she goes along. Same with a wife or girlfriend. It's often when the compliant partner gets fed up that things go bad. She's been his punching bag, then she pulls the plug, maybe even threatens to tell. He gets enraged, kills her, finds he enjoys it. On to the next."

Something he'd said was bothering me.

"Let's back up. What kind of inanimate objects?"

"Pictures, dolls, clothing. Anything, really. I had one guy used to beat the crap out of a life-size blowup of Flip Wilson in drag."

"I hate to ask."

"Deep-seated rage against blacks, gays, and women. Hat trick every time he jerked off."

"Of course."

I could hear the *Phantom of the Opera* in the background.

"J.S., if a guy does that, makes pictures or uses a doll, for instance, does that mean he probably won't kill?"

"Maybe, but again, who knows what's going to alter his curve and nudge him over that line? One day a naughty picture is enough, the next it's not."

"Could a guy do both?"

"Both what?"

"Flip-flop back and forth. Kill some victims, just stalk and harass others?"

"Sure. For one thing, a victim's behavior can alter the equation. He feels insulted or rejected by her. She says the wrong thing, turns left instead of right. She wouldn't even have to know. Don't forget, most serial killers have never met their victims. But these women star in the fantasy. Or he might see one woman in one role, cast another differently. Love your wife, then go out and kill. Cast one stranger as prey, another as friend."

"So, once someone starts killing, he could still revert to his earlier, less violent tactics on occasion?"

"He might."

"So someone who is seemingly just a nuisance could be a lot more?"

"Definitely."

"Someone who phones a victim, follows her, sends her gory sketches isn't necessarily harmless, even though he keeps his distance?"

"You are talking about St. Jacques, aren't you?"
Was I?

"Does it sound like him?"

"I just assumed we were discussing him. Or who-ever it was kept the bridal suite you guys tossed."

Open up your mind, let the fantasy unwind . . .

"J.S. I—It's gotten personal."

"What do you mean?"

I told him everything. Gabby. Her fear. Her exit. My anger, now my fear.

"Shit, Brennan, how do you get yourself into these things? Look, this guy sounds like bad news. Gabby's creep may or may not be St. Jacques, but it's possible. He stalks women. St. Jacques stalks women. He draws pictures of eviscerated females, doesn't exactly have a normal sex life, and carries a knife. St. Jacques, or whoever this devo is, is killing women, then cutting them up or disfiguring them. What do you think?"

Turn your face away from the garish light of day . . .

"When did she first notice this guy?" J.S. asked.
"I don't know."

"Before or after this whole thing broke?"
"I don't know."

"What *do* you know about him?"

"Not much. He hangs out with hookers, pays for sex, then plays a scene with lingerie. Carries a knife. Most of the women won't have anything to do with him."

"That sound good to you?"
"No."

"Tempe, I want you to report this to the guys you work with. Let them check it out. You say

Gabby is unpredictable, so it's probably nothing. She may have just taken off. But she's your friend. You've been threatened. The skull. The guy who followed you in the car."

"Maybe."

"Gabby was staying with you. She's disappeared. It warrants a look."

"Right. Claudel will rush right out and collar nightie man."

"Nightie man? You've been hanging with cops too long."

I stopped. Where had I gotten that? Of course. Dummy man.

"We have a fruitcake that breaks in, stuffs lingerie, stabs it, then leaves. Been at it for years. They call him dummy man."

"If he's been at it for years he can't be that dumb."

"No, no. It's what he makes with the lingerie. It's like a dummy."

Synapse. Or a doll.

Feel me, touch me . . .

J.S. said something, but my mind was veering off at warp speed. Dummy. Lingerie. Knife. A hooker named Julie who plays games with a nightie. A sketch of carnage with the words "don't cut me." News articles found in a Berger Street room, one about a break-in with a nightgown dummy, one with my picture, clipped and marked with an X. A skewered skull, grinning from my shrubbery. Gabby's face in 4 A.M. terror. A bedroom in chaos.

Help me make the music of the night . . .

"I've got to go, J.S."

"Tempe, promise me you'll do what I say. It's a long shot, but it could be that Gabby's creep is the sicko that kept the Berger Street nest. He could be your killer. If so, you're in danger. You're blocking him, so you're a threat to him. He had your picture. He may have put Grace Damas's skull in your yard. He knows who you are. He knows where you are."

I wasn't hearing J.S. In my mind I was already moving.

It took thirty minutes to cross Centre-ville, go up the Main, and find my alley spot. As I stepped over the splayed legs of a wino who sat slumped against the wall, his head bobbing to the muted thud of C&W coming through the brick, he smiled and raised a hand in a one-finger wave, then opened his palm and extended it toward me.

I dug in my pocket and gave him a loony. Maybe he'd watch my car.

The Main was a smorgasbord of night dwellers through which I nibbled a path. Panhandlers, hookers, druggies, and tourists. Accountants and salesmen jostled in clumps, reckless with binge merriment. For some it was a boisterous romp, for others a joyless reality. Welcome to the Hotel St. Laurent.

Unlike my last visit, this time I had a plan. I worked my way toward Ste. Catherine, hoping to find Jewel Tambeaux. Not so easy. Though the usual pack was gathered outside the Hotel Granada, Jewel wasn't part of it.

I crossed the street and considered the women. No one reached for a rock. I took this as a good sign. Now what? From my last social call on these ladies, I had a pretty good idea as to what I shouldn't do. That, however, gave me no clue as to what I should do.

I have a rule that has served me well in life. When in doubt, do nothing. If you're not sure, don't buy it, don't comment, don't commit. Sit tight. Deviation from this maxim has usually caused me regret. The red dress with the ruffled neck. The promise to debate Creationism. The angry letter fired off to the Vice Chancellor. This time I stuck to my policy.

I found a cement block, brushed off the broken glass, and sat. Knees drawn, eyes on the Granada, I waited. And waited. And waited.

For a while I was intrigued by the soap opera playing around me. As the Main Turns. Midnight came and went—1 A.M. Then 2. The script unwound its tale of seduction and exploitation. Maul My Children. The Young and the Hopeless. I played mental games, creating all sorts of clever titles.

By 3 A.M. screenwriting no longer held my interest. I was tired, discouraged, and bored. I knew surveillance was not glamorous, but I hadn't been prepared for just how numbing it was. I'd had enough coffee to fill an aquarium, prepared endless lists in my head, composed several letters I would never write, and played "guess the life story" of a great many citizens of Quebec. Hookers and johns had come and gone, but Jewel Tambeaux was not to be seen.

I stood and flexed backward, considered rubbing my anesthetized ass, decided against it. Next time, no cement. Next time no sitting up all night, watching for a hooker who could be in Saskatoon.

As I started to step off toward my car, a white Pontiac station wagon swung to the curb across the street. Orange Chihuly hair emerged, followed by a familiar face and halter.

Jewel Tambeaux slammed the Pontiac door, then leaned inside the passenger window to say something to the driver. A moment later the car sped off, and Jewel joined two women sitting on the hotel steps. In the pulsating neon they looked like a trio of housewives gossiping on a suburban stoop, their laughter sailing into the predawn air. After a moment, Jewel stood, hiked her spandex mini-skirt, and moved off up the block.

The Main was winding down, the action seekers gone, the scavengers just emerging. Jewel walked slowly, swinging her hips to some private rhythm. I angled across and fell in behind her.

"Jewel?"

She turned, her face a smiling question mark. I was not what she expected. Her eyes moved over my face, puzzled, disappointed. I waited for her to recognize me.

"Margaret Mead."

I smiled. "Tempe Brennan."

"Researching a book?" She moved her hand in a horizontal swath, indicating a title. "Ass on the Hoof, or My Life Among Hookers." Soft, Southern English, with a bayou cadence.

I laughed. "Might sell. May I walk with you?"

She shrugged and blew a puff of air, then turned and resumed her slow pelvic swing. I fell in beside her.

"You still looking for your friend, chère?"

"Actually, I was hoping to find you. I didn't expect you this late."

"Kindergarten's still open, sugar. Gotta *do* business to stay in business."

"True."

We walked a few steps in silence, my sneakers echoing her metallic clip.

"I've given up on finding Gabby. I don't think she wants to be found. She came to see me about a week ago, then took off again. I guess she'll turn up when she turns up."

I looked for a reaction. Jewel shrugged, said nothing. Her lacquered hair moved in and out of

shadow as we walked. Here and there a neon sign
blinked off as the last of the taverns closed their
doors, sealing in the smells of stale beer and cigarette smoke for another night.

"Actually, I'd like to talk to Julie."

Jewel stopped walking and turned to me. Her
face look tired, as though emptied by the night.
The life. She pulled a pack of Players from the V
in her halter, lit one, blew the smoke upward.

"Maybe you should go on home, cutie."

"Why do you say that?"

"You're still chasing killers, aren't you, chère?"
Jewel Tambeaux was no fool.

"I believe there's one out there, Jewel."

"And you think it's this cowboy Julie plays
with?"

"I'd sure like to talk to him."

She took a pull on her cigarette, tapped it with
a long red nail, then watched the sparks float to
the pavement.

"I told you last time, he's got the brains of a
liverwurst sandwich and the personality of roadkill,
but I doubt he's killed anybody."

"Do you know who he is?" I asked.

"No. These morons are about as scarce as pigeon
shit. I pay them about as much mind."

"You said this guy could be bad news."

"There really isn't much good news down here,
sugar."

"Has he been around lately?"

She considered me, then something else, turning
inward to an image or remembered thought at
which I could only guess. Some other bad news.

"Yeah. I've seen him."

I waited. She drew on her cigarette, watched a
car move slowly up the street.

"Haven't seen Julie."

She took another pull, closed her eyes and held the smoke, then sent it upward into the night.

"Or your friend Gabby."

An offering. Should I push?

"Do you think I could find him?"

"Frankly, sugar, I don't think you could find your own butt without a map."

Nice to be respected.

Jewel took one last drag, flipped the butt, and ground it with her shoe.

"Come on, Margaret Mead. Let's bag us some roadkill."

31

JEWEL WALKED WITH PUR-
pose now, her heels clicking a rapid tattoo on the
pavement. I wasn't sure where she was taking me,
but it had to beat my cement perch.

We went east two blocks, then left Ste. Catherine
and cut across an open lot. Jewel's apricot sculpture
moved smoothly through the dark while I stumbled
behind, threading my way through chunks of asphalt, aluminum cans, broken glass, and dead vegetation. How could she do that in stilettos?

We emerged on the far side, turned down an
alley, and entered a low wooden building with no
sign to indicate its calling. The windows were
painted black and strings of Christmas lights provided the only illumination, giving the interior the
reddish glow of a nocturnal animal exhibit. I wondered if that was the intent. Rouse the occupants
to late night action?

Discreetly, I glanced about. My eyes needed little

adjustment, since the amount of light inside differed only slightly from that outdoors. Staying with the Christmas theme, the decorator had gone with cardboard pine for the walls and cracked red vinyl for the stools, accessorizing with beer ads. Dark wooden booths lined one wall, cases of beer were stacked against another. Though the bar was almost empty, the air was heavy with the smell of cigarette smoke, cheap booze, vomit, sweat, and reefer. My cement block began to hold more appeal.

Jewel and the bartender exchanged nods. He had skin the color of day-old coffee and heavy brows. From under them, he tracked our movement.

Jewel walked slowly through the bar, checking each face with seeming disinterest. An old man called to her from a corner stool, waving a beer and gesturing to her to join him. She blew a kiss. He gave her the finger.

As we passed the first booth a hand reached out and grasped Jewel's wrist. With her other hand, she uncurled the fingers and laid the hand back in front of its owner.

"Playpen's closed, sugar."

I shoved my hands into my pockets and kept my eyes on Jewel's back.

At the third booth Jewel stopped, folded her arms, and shook her head slowly.

"*Mon Dieu*," she said, clicking her tongue against her upper teeth.

The booth's single occupant sat staring into a glass of watery brown liquid, elbows on the table, cheeks propped on curled fists. All I could see was the top of a head. Greasy brown hair divided unevenly along the crown and hung limply to either side of the face. White flecks littered the area of the part.

"Julie," said Jewel.

The face did not look up.

Jewel clicked again, then slid into the booth. I followed, grateful for the meager cover. The table-top was slick with something I didn't want to identify. Jewel leaned an elbow on its edge, jerked back with a wiping gesture. She dug out a cigarette, lit it, blew the smoke in an upward jet.

"Julie." Sharper.

Julie caught her breath and raised her chin.

"Julie?" The girl repeated her own name, sounding as if she'd been roused from sleep.

My heart slipped in an extra beat and my teeth grabbed for my lower lip.

Oh, God.

I was looking at a face that had lived no more than fifteen years. Its color could be described only in shades of gray. The pallid skin, the cracked lips, the vacant, recessed eyes with their somber underlining looked like those of someone long deprived of sunlight.

Julie stared at us without expression, as if our images were slow in forming in her brain, or recognition a complex exercise. Then.

"Can I have one, Jewel?" English. She reached a trembling hand across the table. The inside of her elbow looked purple in the room's muted glow. Slender gray worms crawled across the veins on her inner wrist.

Jewel lit a Player and handed it to her. Julie pulled the smoke deep into her lungs, held it, then blew it upward in a Jewel pantomime.

"Yeah. Oh yeah," she said. A tiny scrap of cigarette paper stuck to her lower lip.

She drew again, eyes closed, completely absorbed by the smoking ritual. We waited. Double tasking was not within Julie's capacity.

Jewel looked at me, eyes unreadable. I let her lead.

"Julie, darlin', you been workin'?"

"Some." The girl sucked another long drag, blew two streams of smoke from her nose. We watched them dissolve, silvery clouds in the reddish light.

Jewel and I were silent while Julie smoked. She didn't seem to question our being there. I doubted she questioned much of anything.

After a while she finished, stubbed out the butt, and looked at us. She seemed to consider what benefit our presence might hold.

"I haven't eaten today," she said. Like her eyes, her voice was flat and empty.

I glanced at Jewel. She shrugged and reached for another cigarette. I looked around. No menus. No blackboards.

"They got burgers."

"Would you like one?" How much cash did I bring?

"Banco does them."

"Okay."

She leaned from the booth and called to the bartender.

"Banco. Can I get a burger? With cheese?" She sounded six years old.

"You've got a tab, Jules."

"I'll get it," I said, sticking my head out of the booth.

Banco was leaning against the bar sink, arms folded across his chest. They looked like baobab branches.

"One?" He pushed off.

I looked at Jewel. She shook her head.

"One."

I turned back to the booth. Julie had slumped into the corner, her drink held loosely in two hands.

Her jaw hung slack, leaving her mouth partially open. The paper still rode her lower lip. I wanted to pick it off, but she seemed unaware. A microwave beeped, then hummed. Jewel smoked.

Shortly, the microwave gave four beeps, and Banco appeared with the burger, steaming in its plastic wrapper. He placed it in front of Julie and looked from Jewel to me. I ordered club soda. Jewel shook her head.

Julie tore the cellophane, then lifted the top to inspect the contents of the bun. Satisfied, she took a bite. When Banco brought my drink, I stole a peek at my watch. Three-twenty. I began to think Jewel would never speak again.

"Where you been workin', sugar?"

"Nowheres special." Through a mouthful of bun and burger.

"Haven't seen you lately."

"I was sick."

"You feelin' better now?"

"Mm."

"Working the Main?"

"Some."

"You still doing that little creep with the nightie?" Casual.

"Who?" She ran her tongue around the edge of the burger, like a child with an ice cream cone.

"Guy with the knife."

"Knife?" Absently.

"You know, chère, little man likes to stroke his tallywacker while you model his mama's sleep-wear?"

Julie's chewing slowed then stopped, but she didn't answer. Her face looked like putty, smooth, gray, and without expression.

Jewel's nails clicked against the tabletop. "Come

on, sugar, let's turn it up a notch. You know who I'm talking about?"

Julie swallowed, glanced up, then returned her attention to the burger.

"What about him?" She took a bite.

"Just wonderin' if he's still around."

"Who's she?" Garbled.

"Tempe Brennan. She's a friend of Dr. Macaulay. You know her, don't you, chère?"

"Something wrong with this guy, Jewel? He got the gon or AIDS or something? Why you asking about him?"

It was like interrogating a magic eight ball. If answers floated up at all they were random, not tied to specific questions.

"No, honey, I just wondered if he's still comin' around."

Julie's eyes met mine. They looked uninhabited.

"You work with her?" she asked me, her chin glistening with grease.

"Something like that," Jewel answered for me. "She'd like to talk to this nightie guy."

" 'Bout what?"

"Usual stuff," said Jewel.

"She a deaf-mute or something? Why can't she talk for herself?"

I started to speak, but Jewel wagged me silent.

Julie didn't seem to expect an answer. She finished the last of the burger and licked her fingers, one by one. Finally.

"What's with this guy? Jesus, he was talking about her, too."

Fear surged through every nerve in my body.

"Talking about who?" I blurted.

Julie regarded me, jaw slack, mouth half open as before. When not speaking or eating she seemed unable, or unwilling, to maintain its closure. I could see specks of food in her lower teeth.

"Why do you want to turn this guy?" she asked.

"Turn him?"

"He's the only steady bang I've got."

"She's not interested in turning anybody, she'd just like to talk to him." Jewel.

Julie sipped her drink. I tried again.

"What did you mean, 'he was talking about her, too'? Who was he talking about, Julie?" A look of bewilderment crossed her face, as if she'd already forgotten her words.

"Who was your regular talking about, Julie?" Jewel's voice was growing weary.

"You know, the old lady that hangs around, kinda butchy, with the nose ring and the weird hair?" She tucked one of her own lank strands behind an ear. "She's nice, though. She bought me doughnuts a couple of times. Isn't that who you're talking about?"

I ignored Jewel's warning squint.

"What was he saying about her?"

"He was pissed off at her or something. I don't know. I don't listen to what a trick says. I just fuck 'em and keep my ears and my mouth shut. It's healthier."

"But this guy's a regular."

"Kinda."

"Any particular times?" I couldn't help myself. Jewel gave me an "Okay, you're on your own" gesture.

"What is this, Jewel? Why's she asking me all this?" Again, she sounded like a child.

"Tempe wants to talk to him. That's all."

"I can really do without this guy getting busted. He's a creep, but it's regular money, and I need it real bad."

"I know, sugar."

Julie swirled the last of her drink then tossed it back. Her eyes avoided mine.

"And I'm not going to quit doing him. I don't care what anybody says. So he's weird, so what, it's not like he's going to kill me or nothing. Hell, I don't even have to fuck him. And what else would I do with my Thursdays? Take a class? Go to the opera? If I don't do him some other whore will."

It was the first emotion she'd shown, the adolescent bravado a contrast to her previous listlessness. I ached for her. But I feared for Gabby, and wouldn't let up.

"Have you seen Gabby lately?" I tried to sound softer.

"What?"

"Dr. Macaulay. Have you seen her recently?"

The lines between her eyes deepened, reminding me of Margot, though the shepherd probably had better short-term memory.

"The old lady with the nose ring," said Jewel, emphasizing the age indicator.

"Oh." Julie closed her mouth, then let it drop back open. "No. I've been sick."

Stay cool, Brennan. You almost have enough.

"Are you better now?" I asked.

She shrugged.

"Will you be okay?"

She nodded.

"Do you want anything else?"

She shook her head.

"Do you live close?" I hated using her like this, but I wanted a bit more.

"At Marcella's. You know, Jewel, over on St. Dominique? A lot of us crash there." She refused to look at me.

Yes. I had what I needed. Or would, very soon.

The burger and the booze and whatever else she'd taken were having their effect on Julie. The bravado ebbed, the apathy returned. She slumped in the corner of the booth, eyes staring out like the darkened circles on a gray-faced mime. She closed them and took a deep breath, swelling her bony chest inside its cotton tank. She looked exhausted.

Suddenly the Christmas glow was gone. Fluorescent brightness filled the bar and Banco was bellowing its imminent closing. The few remaining patrons moved toward the door, grumbling their dissatisfaction. Jewel tucked her Players into her halter and indicated we should follow. I checked my watch—4 A.M. I looked across at Julie and the guilt I'd been beating back all night surged up with full force.

In the unforgiving light Julie looked like a near cadaver, like someone slowly shuffling toward death. I wanted to wrap my arms around her and hold her for a moment. I wanted to take her home to Beaconsfield, or Dorval, or North Hatley, where she would eat fast food and go to the prom and order jeans from the Lands' End catalog. But I knew it would not happen. I knew Julie would be a statistic, and, sooner or later, she would be in the basement at Parthenais.

I paid the bill and we left the bar. The early morning air was moist and cool and carried the scents of river and brewery.

"Good night, ladies," said Jewel. "Don't y'all go out dancing now."

She wiggled her fingers, turned, and clicked rapidly up the alley. Without a word, Julie departed in the opposite direction. The vision of home and bed pulled like a magnet, but there was one more bit of information I had to have.

I hung back and watched Julie scurry up the

alley, assuming she'd be easy to follow. Wrong. When I looked up the alley, she was already disappearing around the next corner, and I had to race to catch up.

She took a zigzag path, cutting through lots and alleys to reach a run-down three-flat on St. Dominique, where she mounted the stairs, fumbled for a key, and disappeared through a peeling green door. I watched the tattered door curtain sway, then settle, barely disturbed by her indifferent slam. I noted the number.

Okay, Brennan. Bedtime. I was home in twenty minutes.

Under the covers, with Birdie at my knee, I formed a plan. It was easy to decide what *not* to do. Don't call Ryan. Don't spook Julie. Don't tip the little cretin with the knife and nightie act. Find out if it's St. Jacques. Find out where he lives. Or where his current hidey-hole is. Get something concrete. Then bring in the clod squad. You are here, boys. Bust this place.

It sounded so simple.

32

I DRAGGED THROUGH Wednesday in a fog of exhaustion. I hadn't intended to go to the lab but LaManche called, needing a report. Once there, I decided to stay. I sorted through old cases, sluggish and irritable, clearing those that Denis could discard. It's a task I hate, and one I'd been putting off for months. I lasted until 4 P.M. Once home I ate an early supper, took a long bath, and was under the covers by 8 o'clock.

When I woke on Thursday, sunlight was streaming into the bedroom, and I knew it was late. I stretched, rolled, and looked at the clock. Ten twenty-five. Good. I'd recouped some lost sleep. Phase One of the Plan. I had no intention of going to work.

I took my time getting up, running through a checklist of what I intended to do. From the moment I'd opened my eyes I felt charged, like a runner on marathon day. I wanted to set a pace. Control, Brennan. Run a smart race.

I went to the kitchen, made coffee, and read the *Gazette*. Thousands fleeing the war in Rwanda. Parizeau's Parti Québecois ten points ahead of Premier Johnson's Liberals. The Expos out of first place in the NL East. Laborers working during the annual construction holiday. No kidding. I never could understand the genius who thought that one up. In a country with four or five months of good weather for building, construction stops for two weeks in July while the workers go on holiday. Brilliant.

I had a second cup and finished the paper. So far so good. On to Phase Two. Mindless Activity.

I threw on shorts and a T and went to the gym. Thirty minutes on the StairMaster and a round on the Nautilus. Next, the Provigo, where I bought enough groceries to feed Cleveland. Back home I spent the afternoon mopping, scouring, dusting, and vacuuming. At one point I considered cleaning the refrigerator, but decided against it. Too extreme.

By 7 P.M. my nesting frenzy was sated. The place reeked of spray cleaners and lemon polish, the dining room table was covered with drying sweaters, and I had clean panties to last a month. I, on the other hand, looked and smelled as if I had been camping for weeks. I was ready to go.

The day had been sweltering and the evening promised no relief. I chose another shorts and T combo, accessorized with worn Nikes. Perfect. Not your street professional, but someone prowling the Main in search of recreational chemicals or a companion for the evening, or both. As I drove toward St. Laurent I ran through the Plan. Find Julie. Follow Julie. Find nightie man. Follow nightie man. Don't be seen. Simplicity itself.

I drove across Ste. Catherine, scanning the sidewalks on both sides. A few women had opened shop at the Granada, but there was no sign of Julie. I wouldn't expect her this early. I was allowing myself extra time to get into place.

The first glitch came when I turned into my alley. Like a genie from a bottle, a large woman materialized and bore down on me. She had Tammy Bakker makeup and the neck of a bull terrier. Though I couldn't catch all her words, there was no mistaking her message. I backed out and drove off in search of other parking arrangements.

I found a spot six blocks north, on a narrow side street lined with three-flats. Hot town. Summer in the city. Neighborhood watch was under way. Men's eyes tracked me from a balcony, others from a stoop, conversation suspended, beer cans resting on sweaty knees. Were they hostile? Curious? Disinterested? Very interested? I didn't stay in place long enough for anyone to approach. I locked the car and covered the distance to the end of the block at a brisk pace. Perhaps I was overly nervous, but I didn't want complications to sabotage my mission.

I breathed easier when I rounded the corner and entered the flow on St. Laurent. A clock in Le Bon Deli said eight-fifteen. Damn. I'd wanted to be in position by now. Should I modify the Plan? What if I missed her?

At Ste. Catherine I crossed St. Laurent and re-checked the crowd in front of the Granada. No Julie. Would she even come here? What route would she take? Damn. Why hadn't I started earlier? No time for indecision.

I hurried east, scanning the faces on both sides of the street, but the pedestrian flow had grown, making it harder to be sure she didn't slip past. I cut north at the vacant lot, retracing the path Jewel and I had taken two nights earlier. I hesitated at the alley bar, moved on, gambling again that Julie was not an early starter.

A few minutes later I stood hunched behind a utility pole on the far side of St. Dominique. The street was deserted and still. Julie's building showed no signs of life, windows dark, porch light dead, paint peeling grimly in the muggy dusk. The scene brought to mind photos I had seen of the Towers of Silence, platforms maintained by the Parsi sect in India on which they placed their dead to have the bones picked clean by vultures. I shivered in the heat.

Time crept by. I watched. An old woman trudged up the block, dragging a cart loaded with rags. She muscled her evening's take along the uneven pavement, then disappeared around a corner. The cart's tinny squeak-bump sound ebbed, then stilled. Nothing else disturbed the street's ragged ecosystem.

I looked at my watch—eight-forty. It had grown very dark. How long should I wait? What if she'd already left? Should I ring the bell? Damn. Why hadn't I gotten the time out of her? Why hadn't I gotten here earlier? Already the Plan was showing deficiencies.

Another expanse of time went by. A minute, maybe. I was debating leaving when a light went on in an upstairs room. Not long after, Julie emerged in bustier, mini-skirt, and over-the-knee boots. Her face, midriff, and thighs were splotches of white in the porch shadow. I drew back behind my pole.

She hesitated a moment, chin raised, arms wrapped around her midriff. She seemed to be testing the night. Then she plunged down the steps and walked quickly toward Ste. Catherine. I followed, trying to keep her in view, yet remain unnoticed.

At the corner she surprised me, turning left,

away from the Main. Good call on the Granada, Brennan, but where is she going? Julie wended her way quickly through the crowd, boot fringe swinging, oblivious to cat calls and wolf whistles. She was a good wender and I had to work to keep up.

The crowd grew smaller as we moved east, and eventually ceased being one. I'd been lengthening the distance between us in direct response to the thinning out of sidewalk people, but it was probably unnecessary. Julie seemed focused on a destination and disinterested in other foot traffic.

The streets not only grew emptier, the neighborhood changed flavor. We now shared Ste. Catherine with dandies in *GQ* haircuts, hardbodies in tanks and spray paint jeans, unisex couples, and the occasional transvestite. We had crossed into the gay village.

I followed Julie past coffeehouses, bookstores, and ethnic restaurants. Eventually she turned north, then east, then south onto a dead-end street of warehouses and seedy wooden buildings, many with corrugated metal covering the windows. Some had the appearance of having been upfitted for business space at street level, though they probably hadn't seen customers in years. Papers, cans, and bottles littered both curbs. The place looked like a set for the Jets and the Sharks.

Julie went straight to an entrance halfway up the block. She opened a dirty glass door covered with metal latticework, spoke briefly, then disappeared inside. I could see the glow of a beer sign through a window to the right. It was also armored with metal grillwork. A sign above the door said simply: BIÈRE ET VIN.

Now what? Was this the place of assignation, with a private room upstairs or in the back? Or was this a rendezvous bar they would leave together? I needed it to be the latter. If they left separately, their business concluded, the Plan was foiled. I wouldn't know what man to follow.

I couldn't just stand in front and wait. I spotted an even darker gap in the darkness across the street. An alleyway? I walked past the beer joint Julie had entered, and diagonaled toward the strip of blackness. It was a passageway between an abandoned barbershop and a storage company, about two feet wide and dark as a crypt.

Heart pounding, I slipped in and pressed against a wall, taking cover behind a cracked and yellowed barber pole that projected over the sidewalk. Several minutes passed. The air hung dead and heavy, the only movement my breathing. Suddenly, a rustling made me jump. I wasn't alone. As I was about to bolt, a dark blob shot from the trash at my feet and scurried toward the back of the passageway. My chest constricted, and once again a chill passed through me, despite the heat.

Ease back, Brennan. Just a rodent. Come on, Julie!

As if in response, Julie reappeared, followed by a man in dark sweats, L'UNIVERSITÉ DE MONTRÉAL arced across his chest. He cradled a paper bag in his left arm.

My pulse hammered even faster. Is it him? Is it the face in the ATM photo? Is it the Berger Street runner? I strained to see the man's features, but it was too dark and he was too far away. Would I recognize St. Jacques even if I got a good look? Doubtful. The photo had been too blurry, the man in the apartment too quick.

The pair looked straight ahead and didn't touch or speak. Like homing pigeons they retraced the path Julie and I had just taken, only digressing at

Ste. Catherine, where they continued south instead of turning west. They made several more turns, snaking through streets of run-down apartments and abandoned businesses, streets that were dark and sincerely unfriendly.

I trailed half a block behind, conscious of every scrape and crunch, wary of discovery. There was no cover. If they turned and saw me, I would have no excuse, no windows to shop, no doorways to enter, nothing to hide behind, physical or fictional. My only option would be to keep walking and hope to find a turnoff before Julie recognized me. They didn't look back.

We worked our way through a tangle of alleys and lanes, each emptier than the one before. At one point two men passed from the opposite direction, arguing in tense, hard voices. I prayed Julie and her john wouldn't follow the men with their eyes. They didn't. They kept on and disappeared around another corner. I sped up, fearful of losing them in the seconds they were out of sight.

My fears were well grounded. When I made the turn, they had vanished. The block was still and empty.

Shit!

I checked the buildings on both sides, running my eyes up and down each iron staircase, probing each entranceway. Nothing. Not a sign.

Damn!

I dashed up the sidewalk, furious with myself for losing them. I was halfway to the next corner when a door opened and Julie's regular stepped onto a rusted iron balcony just twenty feet ahead and to my right. He was at shoulder level, his back to me, but the sweatshirt looked the same. I froze, incapable of thought or action.

The man hawked a glob of phlegm and sent it

rocketing onto the sidewalk. Drawing the back of his hand across his mouth, he went back inside and closed the door, oblivious to my presence.

I stood as I was, legs rubbery, unable to move.

Great move, Brennan. Panic and rush the play! Why not light a flare and sound a siren?

The building into which he'd disappeared was one in a row that seemed to cling together for support. Take one out and the block would crumble. A sign identified it as LE ST. VITUS, and offered CHAMBRES TOURISTIQUES. Tourist rooms. Right.

Was this home or merely his trysting place? I resigned myself to more waiting.

Again I looked for a place to hide. Again I spotted what I thought was a gap on the far side of the street. Again I crossed and found that it was. Maybe I was showing a learning curve. Maybe I was lucky.

I took a breath and slipped into the darkness of my new passageway. It was like crawling into a Dumpster. The air was warm and heavy and smelled of urine and things gone bad.

I stood in the narrow space, shifting my weight from foot to foot. The belly-up spiders and roaches I'd seen entombed in the barber pole kept me from leaning against the wall. There was no question of sitting.

Time dragged by. My eyes never left the St. Vitus, but my thoughts traveled the galaxy. I thought of Katy. I thought of Gabby. I thought of Saint Vitus. Who was he anyway? How would he feel about having the rathole across the street named in his honor? Wasn't Saint Vitus a disease? Or was that Saint Elmo?

I thought of St. Jacques. The ATM photo was so poor you really couldn't see the face. The geezer was right. The guy's own mother wouldn't know him from that shot. Besides, he could have changed his hair, grown a beard, gotten glasses.

The Incas built a road system. Hannibal crossed the Alps. Seti occupied the throne. No one entered or left the St. Vitus. I tried not to think about what was unfolding in one of its rooms. I hoped the guy was a short timer. There's a first, Brennan.

There was no breeze in my tiny crevice, and the brick walls on either side still held the heat that had built up all day. My shirt grew clammy and clung to my skin. My scalp was sweaty damp, and an occasional bead broke free and trickled down my face or neck.

I shifted and watched and thought. The air was breathless. The sky flickered and rumbled softly. Celestial grumbling, nothing more. Now and then a car lighted the street, then passed on, casting it back into obscurity.

The heat and smell and confinement began to crowd in on me. I felt a dull pain in the space between my eyes, and the back of my throat was doing pre-nausea things. I thought about hanging it up. I tried squatting on my haunches.

Suddenly a form loomed over me! My mind exploded in a million directions. Was the passage open behind me? Stupid! I hadn't checked for an escape route!

The man stepped into the alley, fumbling for something at his waist. I looked down the corridor in back but it was pitch black. I was trapped!

Then it was like a physics experiment, with equal and opposite forces responding. I shot up and stumbled back on deadened legs. The man also staggered backward, a look of shock on his face. I could see he was Asian, though only his teeth and astonished eyes were clear in the murky shadows.

I pressed against the wall, as much for support

as for cover. He leered at me in a bewildered way, shook his head as though perplexed, then lurched off down the block, tucking his shirt and zipping his fly.

For a moment I just stood there, talking my heart rate down from the stratosphere.

A wino who only wanted to pee. He's gone.

What if it had been St. Jacques?

It wasn't.

You left yourself no out. You're being stupid. You're going to get yourself killed.

It was just a wino.

Go home. J.S. is right. Leave this to the cops.

They won't do it.

It's not your problem.

Gabby is.

She's probably in Ste. Adele.

Had me there.

Calmer, I resumed my surveillance. I thought some more about Saint Vitus. Saint Vitus's dance. That's it. It was widespread in the 1500s. People grew nervous and irritable, then their limbs started twitching. They thought it was a form of hysteria and hiked off to the saint. Then what about Saint Anthony? The fire. Saint Anthony's fire. Something to do with ergot in grain. Didn't it also make people act crazy?

I thought about cities I'd like to visit. Abilene. Bangkok. Chittagong. I'd always liked that name, Chittagong. Maybe I'd go to Bangladesh. I was in the D's when Julie came out of the St. Vitus and walked calmly up the block. I held my ground. She was no longer my mark.

I didn't have to hold for long. My prey was also leaving.

I gave him half a block, then dropped in behind. His movements reminded me of the trash rat. He scurried, shoulders hunched, head tucked, bag clutched to his chest. As I followed, I compared the figure ahead to the one I'd seen bolt from the Berger Street room. Not a good match as memory went, but St. Jacques had been too quick and his appearance too unexpected. This *could* be the same man, but I just hadn't gotten a good enough look the other time. This guy was definitely not moving as fast.

For the third time in as many hours I wove my way through a labyrinth of unlit side streets, tailing a quarry as close as I dared. I prayed he wouldn't stop off at another beer joint. I wasn't up to any more surveillance.

I needn't have worried. After snaking through a maze of tributary streets and side alleys, the man made one final turn and went directly to a bow-fronted graystone. It was like a hundred others I'd passed tonight, though a bit less seedy, the stone a little less dirty, the rusted stairs curving to doors slightly less in need of paint.

He took the stairs quickly, the metallic slap of his footfalls sharp against the air, then disappeared through an ornately carved door. A light went on almost immediately on the second floor of the bow, showing windows half open, curtains hanging limp and lifeless. A shadowy figure moved about the room, veiled by the graying lace.

I crossed the street and waited. No alley this time.

For a while the figure shifted back and forth, then it disappeared.

I waited.

It's him, Brennan. Outa here.

He could be visiting someone. Dropping something off.

You've got him. Let's go.

I checked my watch—eleven-twenty. Still early. Ten more minutes.

It took less. The figure reappeared, raised the windows to full open, and vanished again. Then the room went black. Bedtime!

I waited five minutes to be sure no one left the building, then needed no more convincing. Ryan and the boys could take it from here.

I noted the address and began winding my way back to the car, hoping I could find it. The air was still leaden, the heat as intense as midafternoon. Leaves and curtains hung motionless, as if laundered and left to dry. The neon of St. Laurent glowed over the tops of the darkened buildings, backlighting the maze of streets through which I hurried.

The clock on the dash said midnight when I pulled into the garage. I *was* improving. Home before dawn.

The noise didn't register at first. I was across the garage and singling out my key when it finally intruded on my conscious mind. I stood still to listen. A high-pitched beeping was coming from behind me, near the main auto entrance.

As I walked in that direction, trying to pinpoint its source, the tone clarified into a sharp, pulsating beat. When I drew near I could see that the noise came from a door to the right of the car ramp. Though the door appeared closed, the lock was only partly engaged, thus triggering the alarm.

I pushed, then pulled on the safety bar, slamming the door fully shut. The beeping stopped abruptly, leaving the garage deathly quiet. I reminded myself to mention the apparent malfunction to Winston.

The condo felt cool and fresh after my hours in hot, dirty crevices. For a moment I just stood in the hall, allowing the refrigerated air to roll over my hot skin. Birdie brushed back and forth against my leg, arching his back and purring in greeting. I looked down at him. Soft, white hairs clung to my sweaty legs. I stroked his head, fed him, and checked my messages. One hang-up. I headed for the shower.

As I lathered and relathered I ran over the events of the evening in my mind. What had I accomplished? Now I knew where Julie's lingerie loony lived. At least I assumed that's who he was since today was Thursday. So what? He might have nothing to do with the murders.

But I couldn't quite convince myself. Why? Why did I think this guy was hooked in? Why did I think it was my job to nail him? Why was I afraid for Gabby? Julie had been fine.

After my shower I was still keyed up and knew I wouldn't sleep, so I dug a chunk of Brie and a wedge of *tomme de chèvre de savoie* from the refrigerator and poured myself a ginger ale. Wrapping myself in a quilt, I stretched out on the couch, peeled an orange, and ate it with the cheese. Letterman couldn't hold my attention. Back to the debate.

Why did I just spend four hours packed in with spiders and rats to spy on some guy who likes to see whores in lingerie? Why not let the cops handle it?

It kept coming back to that. Why didn't I just tell Ryan what I knew and ask him to roust this guy?

Because it was personal. But not in the way I'd been telling myself. It wasn't just a threat in my garden, an attack on my safety or Gabby's. Something else was causing me to obsess over these cases, something deeper and more troubling. For the next hour, little by little, I admitted it to myself.

The truth was that, lately, I was scaring myself.

I saw violent death every day. Some woman killed by some man and thrown into a river, a wood, a dump. Some child's fractured bones uncovered in a box, a culvert, a plastic bag. Day after day I cleaned them up, examined them, sorted them out. I wrote reports. Testified. And sometimes I felt nothing. Professional detachment. Clinical disinterest. I saw death too often, too close, and I feared I was losing a sense of its meaning. I knew I couldn't grieve for the human being that each of my cadavers had been. That would empty my emotional reservoir for sure. Some amount of professional detachment was mandatory in order to do the work, but not to the extent of abandoning all feeling.

The deaths of these women had stirred something in me. I ached for their fear, their pain, their helplessness in the face of madness. I felt anger and outrage, and a need to root out the animal responsible for the slaughter. I felt for these victims, and my response to their deaths was like a lifeline to my feelings. To my own humanity and my celebration of life. I felt, and I was grateful for the feeling.

That's how it was personal. That's why I wouldn't stop. That's why I'd prowl the monastery grounds, and the woods, and the bars and back streets of the Main. I'd persuade Ryan to follow this up. I'd figure out Julie's client. I'd find Gabby. Maybe this was connected. Maybe not. No matter. One way or another, I'd flush out the sonofabitch responsible for this shedding of female blood, and I'd help shut him down. For good.

33

SPURRING THE INVESTIGA-
tion turned out to be harder than I thought. Partly
because of me.

By five-thirty on Friday afternoon my head and
my stomach ached from the endless cups of machine coffee. We'd been discussing the files for
hours. No one had turned up much, so we kept
rehashing the same things over and over, sifting
through the mountains of information, desperately
searching for something new. There was little.

Bertrand was working the realtor angle. Morisette-
Champoux and Adkins had listed their condos with
ReMax. So had Gagnon's neighbor. Huge firm,
three different offices, three separate agents. None
of them remembered the victims, or even the properties. Trottier's father had used Royal Lepage.

Pitre's former boyfriend was a doper who'd
killed a prostitute in Winnipeg. Could be a break.
Could be nothing. Claudel was on that.

The questioning of known sex offenders was continuing, coming up empty. Big surprise.

Teams of uniformed officers were canvassing the neighborhoods around the Adkins and Morisette-Champoux condos. Zero.

We had nowhere to turn so we were turning on one another. The mood was gloomy and patience was in short supply, so I bided my time, waiting for the right opening. They listened politely as I told them about the situation with Gabby, about the night in the car. I described the drawing, my conversation with J.S., and my surveillance of Julie.

When I finished, no one spoke. Seven women watched mutely from portable bulletin boards. Claudel's pen wove complex webs and grids. He'd been silent and withdrawn all afternoon, as if disconnected from the rest of us. My account made him even more sullen. The sound of the large electric clock began to dominate the room.

Buzzzz.

"And you have no idea if this is the same sack of shit we chased from Berger?" Bertrand.

I shook my head.

Buzzzz.

"I say we bust the cocksucker." Ketterling.

"For what?" Ryan.

Buzzzz.

"We could just be there for him, see how he deals with pressure." Charbonneau.

"If he is our boy that might spook him. The last thing we want is for him to panic and blow town." Rousseau.

"No. The last thing we want is for him to shove a plastic Jesus up someone else's sweet spot." Bertrand.

"The guy's probably just a wienie wagger."

"Or he could be Bundy with an underwear twist."

Buzzzz.

Round and round it went like that, zigging and zagging from French to English. Eventually, everyone was drawing Claudel lines.

Buzzzz.

Then.

"How unreliable *is* this Gabby?" Charbonneau.

I hesitated. Somehow daylight colored things differently. I'd sent these men on a chase before, and we still didn't know if it had been for wild geese.

Claudel looked up at me, eyes reptilian cold, and I felt the tightening in my stomach. This man despised me, wanted to destroy me. What was he doing behind my back? How far had his complaint gone? What if I was wrong?

And then I did something I would forever be unable to change. Deep down maybe I didn't think anything bad would really happen to Gabby. She'd always landed on her feet before. Maybe I just took the safe path. Who knows? I did not elevate concern for my friend's safety to the level of urgency. I backed off.

"She has taken off before."

Buzzzz.

Buzzzz.

Buzzzz.

Ryan was the first to respond.

"Like this? Without a word?"

I nodded.

Buzzzz.

Buzzzz.

Buzzzz.

Ryan's expression was grim. "All right. Let's get a name, run a check. But we'll keep it low profile for now. Without something else, we couldn't get a warrant anyway." He turned to Charbonneau. "Michel?"

Charbonneau nodded. We discussed a few other points, gathered our things, and broke.

In the many times I'd look back on that meeting, I'd always wonder if I could have altered later events. Why had I not sounded the cry over Gabby? Had the sight of Claudel dampened my resolve? Had I sacrificed the previous evening's zeal on the altar of professional caution? Had I compromised Gabby's survival rather than risk my professional standing? Would an all-out search begun that day have made any difference?

That night I went home and warmed a TV dinner. Swiss steak, I think. When the microwave beeped I removed the tray and peeled back the foil.

I stood there a moment, watching synthetic gravy congeal on synthetic mashed potatoes, feeling loneliness and frustration tune up for the overture. I could eat this and spend another night fighting back demons, with the cat and the sitcoms, or I could be the conductor of the evening's performance.

"Fuck this. Maestro . . . ?"

I threw the dinner into the trash and walked to Chez Katsura on Rue de la Montagne, where I treated myself to sushi and exchanged small talk with a card salesman from Sudbury. Then, declining his invitations, I moved on and caught the late showing of *The Lion King* at Le Faubourg.

It was ten-forty when I left the theater and took the escalator to the main level. The tiny mall was largely deserted, the vendors gone, their wares stowed and sealed in carts. I passed the bagel bakery, the frozen yogurt stand, the Japanese carryout, their shelves and counters stripped and barricaded behind collapsible security gates. Knives and saws hung in neat rows behind the butcher's empty cases.

The movie had been just what I needed. Singing hyenas, pounding African rhythms, and lion cub romance kept me from thinking of the murders for hours.

Well orchestrated, Brennan. Hakuna Matata.

I crossed Ste. Catherine and walked toward home. It was still hot and very humid. Mist haloed the streetlamps and hovered over the pavement, like steam from a hot tub on a cold winter night.

I saw the envelope as soon as I left the lobby and turned down my hall. It was wedged between the brass knob and the doorjamb. My first thought was Winston. Perhaps he needed to fix something and would be turning off the power or the water. No. He'd post a notice. A complaint about Birdie? A note from Gabby?

It wasn't. In fact, it wasn't a note at all. The envelope held two items, which lay on the table now, silent and terrible. I stared at them, heart pounding, hands trembling, knowing, yet refusing to admit their meaning.

The envelope contained a plastic ID. Gabby's name, date of birth, and *numéro d'assurance maladie* appeared in raised white letters below a red sunset on the left-hand side of the card. Her image was at the upper right, dreadlocks winging, something silver dangling from each ear.

The other item was a two-inch square cut from a large-scale city map. The map was in French, and showed streets and green spaces in an agonizingly familiar color code. I looked for landmarks or names that would help me pinpoint the neighborhood. Rue Ste. Hélène. Rue Beauchamp. Rue Champlain. I didn't know those streets. Could be Montreal, could be a score of other cities. I hadn't lived in Quebec long enough to know. The map contained no highways or features I could identify. Except one. A large black X covered the center of the map.

I stared numbly at the X. Terrible images formed in my mind but I fought them off, denying the one acceptable conclusion. It was a bluff. It was like the skull in the garden. This maniac was toying with me. Seeing how frightened he could make me.

I don't know how long I looked at Gabby's face, remembering it in other places, other times. A happy face in a clown hat at Katy's third birthday party. A face bathed in tears as she told me of her brother's suicide.

The house was silent around me, the universe at a standstill. Then horrible certainty overtook me.

It wasn't a bluff. Dear God, dear God, dear Gabby. I'm so very, terribly sorry.

Ryan picked up on the third ring.

"He's got Gabby," I whispered, knuckles white on the receiver, voice steady by sheer strength of will.

He wasn't fooled.

"Who?" he asked, sensing the underlying terror and going straight to the crux.

"I don't know."

"Where are they?"

"I—I don't know."

I heard the sound of a hand passing over a face.

"What do you have?"

He heard me out without interrupting.

"Shit."

Pause.

"Okay. I'll take the map in so ident can pinpoint the location, then we'll get a team out there."

"I can take the map in," I said.

"I think you should stay there. And I want a surveillance unit back on your building."

"I'm not the one in danger," I snapped. "This bastard's got Gabby! He's probably killed her already!"

My mask was crumbling. I fought to control the trembling in my hands.

"Brennan, I feel sick about your friend. I would help her in any way I could. Believe that. But you have to use your head. If this psychopath only got her purse but not her, she's probably okay, wherever she is. If he has her and has shown us where to find her, he will have left her in whatever state he wants her found. We can't change that. Meanwhile, someone put a note on your door, Brennan. The sonofabitch was in your building. He knows your car. If this guy is the killer, he won't hesitate to add you to his list. Respect for life is not among his personality traits, and he seems to have focused on yours right now."

He had a point.

"And I'll get somebody on the guy you followed."

I spoke slowly and softly. "I want ident to call me as soon as they pull up the location."

"Bren—"

"Is that a problem?" Not so softly.

It was irrational and I knew it, but Ryan was sensitive to my growing hysteria, or was it rage? Maybe he just didn't want to deal with me.

"No."

Ryan got the envelope around midnight, and the ident unit called an hour later. They lifted one print from the card. Mine. The X marked an abandoned lot in St. Lambert. An hour later I got a second call from Ryan. A patrol unit had checked the lot and all surrounding buildings. Nothing. Ryan had arranged for recovery in the morning. Including dogs. We were going back to the south shore.

"What time tomorrow?" I said, my voice shaking, my grief for Gabby already too dreadful to bear.

"I'll set it up for seven."

"Six."

"Six. Want a ride?"

"Thanks."

He hesitated. "She may be fine."

"Yeah."

I went through the normal bedtime motions, though I knew I wouldn't sleep. Teeth. Face. Hand lotion. Nightshirt. Then I wandered from room to room, trying not to think about the women on the bulletin boards. Murder scene photos. Autopsy descriptions. Gabby.

I adjusted a picture, repositioned a vase, picked fluff from the carpet. I felt cold, made myself a cup of tea, and turned down the air-conditioning. Minutes later, I shot it back up. Birdie withdrew to the bedroom, fed up with the pointless movement, but I couldn't stop myself. The feeling of helplessness in the face of impending horror was unbearable.

Around two, I stretched out on the couch, closed my eyes, and tried to will myself to relax. Concentrate on night sounds. AC compressor. Ambulance. Trickle of taps on the floor above. Water flowing through a pipe. Wood creaking. Walls settling.

My mind drifted to a visual mode. Images floated past, spinning and tumbling like parts of a Hollywood dream sequence. I saw Chantale Trottier's plaid jumper. Morisette-Champoux's gutted belly. The putrefied head that was Isabelle Gagnon. A severed hand. A mangled breast cupped in bone-white lips. A lifeless monkey. A statue. A plunger. A knife.

I couldn't help myself. I produced a cinema of death, tortured by the thought that Gabby had joined the cast. Darkness was fading into light when I got up to dress.

34

THE SUN HAD BARELY climbed above the horizon when we uncovered Gabby's body. Margot had gone directly to it, scarcely hesitating when released inside the plywood fence surrounding the property. She'd scented for a moment, then raced across the wooded lot, the saffron dawn tinging her fur and illuminating the dust around her feet.

The grave was hidden inside a crumbling house foundation. It was shallow, dug quickly, filled with haste. Standard. But then the killer had added a personal touch, outlining the burial with a carefully placed oval of bricks.

Her corpse lay on the ground now, zippered in its body bag. We'd sealed the scene with sawhorses and yellow tape, but it hadn't been necessary. The early hour and the plywood barrier had been protection enough. No one had come to gawk as we unearthed the body and went through our macabre routines.

I sat in a patrol unit, sipping cold coffee from a Styrofoam cup. The radio cackled and the usual motion swirled around me. I'd come to do my job, to be a professional, but found I couldn't do it. The others would have to manage. Perhaps later my brain would accept the messages it was currently rejecting. For now, I was numb and my brain was numb. I didn't want to see her in the trench, to replay the scene of the marbled and bloated body emerging as the layers of dirt were lifted off. I'd recognized the silver earrings instantly. Ganesh. I recalled an image of Gabby explaining about the little elephant. A friendly god. A happy god. Not a god of pain and death. Where were you, Ganesh? Why didn't you protect your friend? Why didn't *any* of her friends protect her? Agony. Push it away.

I'd done a visual ID on the body, then Ryan had taken charge of the scene. I watched as he conferred with Pierre Gilbert. They spoke a moment, then Ryan turned and walked in my direction.

He hitched his pant legs and squatted next to the open car door, one hand on the armrest. Though it was only midmorning, the temperature was already twenty-seven Celsius, and perspiration soaked his hair and armpits.

"I'm so sorry," he said.

I nodded.

"I know how hard this is."

No. You don't. "The body isn't too bad. I'm surprised, considering this heat."

"We don't know how long she's been here."

"Yes."

He reached over and took my hand. His palm left a small saddle of perspiration on the vinyl armrest. "There was noth—"

"Have you found anything?"

"Not much."

"No footprints, no tire tracks, nothing in this whole bloody field?"

He shook his head.

"Latents on the bricks?" I knew that was stupid even as I said it.

His eyes held mine.

"Nothing down in the pit?"

"There was one thing, Tempe. Lying on her chest." He hesitated a moment. "A surgical glove."

"A little sloppy for this guy. He never left anything before. Might be prints inside." I was fighting for control. "Anything else?"

"I don't think she was killed here, Tempe. She was probably transported from somewhere else."

"What is this place?"

"A tavern that closed down years ago. The property was sold, the building was knocked down, then the buyer went belly-up. The lot's been boarded up for six years."

"Who owns it?"

"You want a name?"

"Yes, a name," I snarled.

He checked his notebook. "Guy named Bailey."

Behind him I could see two attendants lift Gabby's remains onto a stretcher, then wheel it toward the coroner's van.

Oh, Gabby! I'm so sorry!

"Can I get you anything?" The ice blue eyes were studying my face.

"What?"

"Do you want a drink? Something to eat? Would you like to go home?"

Yes. And never come back.

"No. I'm fine."

For the first time I noticed the hand he'd placed over mine. The fingers were slender, but the hand itself was broad and angular. A dashed semicircle arced across his thumb knuckle.

"She wasn't mutilated."

"No."

"Why the bricks?"

"I've never been able to understand how these mutants think."

"It's a taunt, isn't it? He wanted us to find her, and he wanted to make a statement. There won't be any prints inside the glove."

He didn't say anything.

"This is different, isn't it, Ryan?"

"Yes."

The heat in the car was like molasses against my skin. I got out and lifted my hair to feel the breeze on my neck. There was none. I watched them secure the body bag with black canvas straps and slide it into the van. I felt a sob build in my chest and fought it back.

"Could I have saved her, Ryan?"

"Could any of us have saved her? I don't know." He let out a deep breath and squinted up into the sun. "Weeks ago, maybe. Probably not yesterday or the day before." He turned back and locked his gaze on me. "What I do know is we'll get this cocksucker. He's a dead man."

I spotted Claudel walking toward us, carrying a plastic evidence bag. He says one thing to me and I'll rip his goddamn lips off, I promised myself. I meant it.

"Very sorry," Claudel mumbled, avoiding my eyes. To Ryan. "We're about done here."

Ryan raised his eyebrows. Claudel gave him an "over there" head signal.

My pulse quickened. "What? What did you find?" Ryan placed a hand on each of my shoulders.

I looked at the bag in Claudel's hand. I could see a pale yellow surgical glove, dark brown stains mottling its surface. Protruding from the glove's rim was a flat object. Rectangle. White border. Dark background. A snapshot. Ryan's hands squeezed hard on my shoulders. I stared a question at him, already fearing the answer.

"Let's do this later."

"Let me see it." I reached out a trembling hand.

Claudel hesitated, extended the bag. I took it, grasped one glove finger through the plastic, and tapped gently until the photo slid free. I reoriented the bag and stared through the plastic.

Two figures, arms entwined, hair whipping, ocean breakers rolling behind. Fear gripped me. My breathing quickened. Calm. Stay calm.

Myrtle Beach—1992. Me. Katy. The bastard had buried a picture of my daughter with my murdered friend.

No one spoke. I watched Charbonneau approach from the grave site. He joined us, looked at Ryan, who nodded. The three men stood in silence. No one knew how to act, what to say. I didn't feel like helping them out. Charbonneau broke the silence.

"Let's go nail this sonofabitch."

"Got the warrant?" Ryan.

"Bertrand will meet us. They issued as soon as we found the . . . body." He looked at me, quickly away.

"Is our boy there now?"

"No one's gone in or out since they staked the place. I don't think we should wait."

"Yeah."

Ryan turned to me. "Judge Tessier bought probable cause and cut a warrant this morning, so we're going to bust the guy you tailed Thursday night. I'll drop y—"

"No way, Ryan. I'm in."

"Br—"

"In case you forgot, I just identified my best friend. She was holding a picture of me and my daughter. It may be this slimy piece of shit, or it may be some other psychopath that killed her, but I'm going to find out, and I'm going to do everything I can to fry his sorry ass. I will hunt him down and flush him out with or without you and your Merry Men." My finger was stabbing the air like a hydraulic piston. "I will be there! Starting now!"

My eyes burned and my chest began to heave. Don't cry. Don't you dare cry. I forced calmness over my hysteria. For a long time no one spoke.

"*Allons-y,*" said Claudel. Let's go.

35

BY NOON THE TEMPER-
ature and humidity were so high the city was ren-
dered lifeless. Nothing moved. Trees, birds, insects,
and humans held themselves as still as possible,
immobilized by the stifling heat. Most stayed out
of sight.

The drive was St. Jean Baptiste Day all over again.
The tense silence. The smell of air-conditioned sweat.
The fear in my gut. Only Claudel's surliness was ab-
sent. He and Charbonneau were meeting us there.

And the traffic was different. On our trip to Rue
Berger we had fought holiday crowds. Today we
breezed through empty streets, arriving at the suspect's place in less than twenty minutes. When we
turned the corner I could see Bertrand, Charbonneau, and Claudel in an unmarked car, Bertrand's
unit parked behind. The crime scene van was at
the end of the block, Gilbert behind the wheel, a
tech slumped against the passenger side window.

The three detectives got out as we walked toward them. The street was as I remembered it, though daylight showed it to be even plainer and more worn than it had appeared in the dark. My shirt was pasted to my clammy skin.

"Where's the stakeout team?" Ryan asked by way of greeting.

"They circled round back." Charbonneau.

"He in there?"

"No activity since they got here around midnight. He could be asleep inside."

"There's a back entrance?"

Charbonneau nodded. "Been covered all night. We've got units at each end of the block, and there's one on Martineau." He jerked a thumb toward the opposite side of the street. "If lover boy's in there, he's not going anywhere."

Ryan turned to Bertrand. "Got the paper?"

Bertrand nodded. "It's 1436 Séguin. Number 201. Come on down." He mimicked the game show invitation.

We stood a moment, sizing up the building as one would an adversary, preparing ourselves for assault and capture. Two black kids rounded the corner and started up the block, rap music blaring from an enormous boom box. They wore Air Jordans and pants big enough to house a nuclear family. Their T-shirts bore totems of violence, one a skull with melting eyeballs, the other the grim reaper with beach umbrella. Death on Vacation. The taller boy had shaved his scalp, leaving only an oval cap on top. The other had dreadlocks.

A mental flash of Gabby's dreadlocks. A stab of pain.

Later. Not now. I yanked my attention back to the moment.

We watched the boys enter a nearby building,

heard the rap truncated as a door closed behind them. Ryan looked in both directions, then back at us.

"We set?"

"Let's get the sonofabitch." Claudel.

"Luc, you and Michel cover the back. If he bolts, squash him."

Claudel squinted, tipped his head as though to speak, then shook it, exhaling sharply through his nose. He and Charbonneau moved off, turned back at Ryan's voice.

"We do this by the books." His eyes were hard. "No mistakes."

The CUM detectives crossed the street and disappeared around the graystone.

Ryan turned to me.

"Ready?"

I nodded.

"This could be the guy."

"Yes, Ryan, I know that."

"You all right?"

"Jesus, Ryan . . ."

"Let's go."

I felt a bubble of fear swell in my chest as we mounted the iron stairs. The outer door was unlocked. We entered a small lobby with a grimy tile floor. Mailboxes lined the right wall, circulars lay on the floor beneath them. Bertrand tried the inner door. It was also open.

"Great security," said Bertrand.

We crossed into a poorly lit corridor shrouded in heat and the smell of cooking grease. A threadbare carpet ran toward the back of the building and up a staircase to the right, secured at three-foot intervals by thin metal strips. Over it someone had laid a vinyl runner, at one time clear, now opaque with age and grime.

We climbed to the second floor, our feet making faint tapping sounds on the vinyl—201 was first on the right. Ryan and Bertrand placed themselves on either side of the dark wooden door, backs to the wall, jackets unbuttoned, hands resting loosely on their weapons.

Ryan motioned me beside him. I flattened myself against the wall, felt the rough plaster pluck at my hair. I took a deep breath, drawing in mildew and dust. I could smell Ryan's sweat.

Ryan nodded to Bertrand. The anxiety bubble swelled up into my throat.

Bertrand knocked.

Nothing.

He knocked again.

No response.

Ryan and Bertrand tensed. My breath was coming fast.

"Police. Open up."

Down the hall a door opened quietly. Eyes peered through a crack the width of a security chain.

Bertrand knocked harder, five sharp raps in the sweltering silence. Silence.

Then. *"Monsieur Tanguay n'est pas ici."*

Our heads whipped toward the sound of the voice. It was soft and high-pitched, and came from across the corridor.

Ryan gave Bertrand a stay-here gesture and we crossed. The eyes watched, their irises magnified behind thick lenses. They were barely four feet off the floor, and angled higher and higher as we approached.

The eyes shifted from Ryan to me and back, seeking the least threatening place to land. Ryan squatted to meet them at their level.

"Bonjour," he said.

"Hi."

"Comment ça va?"

"Ça va."

The child waited. I couldn't tell if it was a boy or girl.

"Is your mother home?"

Head shake.

"Father?"

"No."

"Anyone?"

"Who are you?"

Good, kid. Don't tell a stranger anything.

"Police." Ryan showed him his badge. The eyes grew even larger.

"Can I hold it?"

Ryan passed the badge through the crack. The child studied it solemnly, handed it back.

"Are you looking for Monsieur Tanguay?"

"Yes, we are."

"Why?"

"We want to ask him some questions. Do you know Monsieur Tanguay?"

The child nodded, offered nothing.

"What's your name?"

"Mathieu." Boy.

"When will your mother be home, Mathieu?"

"I live with my grammama."

Ryan shifted his weight and a joint cracked loudly. He dropped one knee to the floor, propped an elbow on the other, rested chin on knuckles, and looked at Mathieu.

"How old are you, Mathieu?"

"Six."

"How long have you lived here?"

The child looked puzzled, as though other possibilities had never occurred to him.

"Always."

"Do you know Monsieur Tanguay?"

Mathieu nodded.

"How long has he lived here?"

Shrug.

"When will your grammama be home?"

"She cleans for people." Pause. "Saturday." Mathieu rolled his eyes and nibbled his lower lip. "Just a minute." He disappeared into the apartment, reappeared in less than a minute. "Three-thirty."

"Sh . . . Shoot," said Ryan, uncoiling from his hunched position. He spoke to me, his voice tense, just above a whisper. "That asshole may be in there and we've got an unattended kid here."

Mathieu watched like a barn cat with a cornered rat, his eyes never leaving Ryan's face.

"Monsieur Tanguay's not here."

"Are you sure?" Ryan crouched again.

"He's gone away."

"Where?"

Another shrug. A chubby finger pushed his glasses up the bridge of his nose.

"How do you know he's away?"

"I'm taking care of his fish." A smile the size of the Mississippi lit his face. "He's got tetras, and angelfish, and white clouds." He used the English names. "They're fantastic!" *Fantastique!* Such a perfect word. Its English counterpart never quite matches it.

"When will Monsieur Tanguay be back?"

Shrug.

"Did Grammama write it on the calendar?" I asked.

The child regarded me, surprised, then disappeared as he had before.

"What calendar?" Ryan asked, looking up.

"They must keep one. He went to check something when he wasn't sure when Grammama would be home today."

Mathieu returned. "Nope."

Ryan stood. "Now what?"

"If he's right, we go in and toss the place. We've got a name, we'll run Monsieur Tanguay down. Maybe Grammama knows where he's gone. If not, we'll pop him as soon as he comes anywhere near here."

Ryan looked to Bertrand, pointed at the door.

Five more raps.

Nothing.

"Break it?" asked Bertrand.

"Monsieur Tanguay won't like it."

We all looked at the boy.

Ryan lowered himself a third time.

"He gets really mad if you do something bad," said Mathieu.

"It's important that we look for something in Monsieur Tanguay's apartment," explained Ryan.

"He won't like it if you break his door."

I squatted next to Ryan.

"Mathieu, do you have Monsieur Tanguay's fish in your apartment?"

Head shake.

"Do you have a key to Monsieur Tanguay's apartment?"

Mathieu nodded.

"Could you let us in?"

"No."

"Why not?"

"I can't come out when Grammama's gone."

"That's good, Mathieu. Grammama wants you to stay inside because she thinks it's safer for you. She's right, and you're a good boy to listen to her."

The Mississippi smile spread north again.

"Do you think we could use the key, Mathieu,

just for a few minutes? It's very important police business and you are correct that we shouldn't break the door."

"I guess that would be okay," he said. "Because you're police."

Mathieu darted out of sight, returned with a key. He pressed his lips together and looked straight at me as he held it through the crack.

"Don't break Monsieur Tanguay's door."

"We'll be very careful."

"And don't go in the kitchen. That's bad. You can't ever go in the kitchen."

"You close the door and stay inside, Mathieu. I'll knock when we've finished. Don't open the door until you hear my knock."

The small face nodded solemnly, then disappeared behind the door.

We rejoined Bertrand, who knocked again, called out. There was an awkward pause, then Ryan nodded, and I slipped the key into the lock.

The door opened directly into a small living room, its color scheme shades of maroon. Shelves stretched from floor to ceiling on two sides, the other walls were wood, every surface darkened by years of varnishing. Crushed red velvet looped across the windows, backed by graying lace, which blocked most of the sunlight. We stood absolutely still, listening and peering into the unlit room.

The only sound I heard was a faint buzzing, erratic, like electricity jumping a broken circuit. Bzzt. Bzzzzzt. Bzt. Bzt. It came from behind double doors ahead and to the left. Otherwise, the place was deathly quiet.

Poor choice of adverb, Brennan.

I looked around and furniture shapes emerged from the deep shadow, looking old and worn. The center of the room was occupied by a carved wooden table with matching chairs. A well-used couch sagged in the front bay, a Mexican blanket stretched across it. Opposite, a wooden trunk served as a stand for a Sony Trinitron.

Scattered about the room were small wooden tables and cabinets. Some were quite nice, not unlike pieces I'd unearthed at flea markets. I doubted any of these had been afternoon finds, purchased as bargains to strip and refinish. They looked as though they'd been in the place for years, ignored and unappreciated as successive tenants came and went.

The floor was covered by an aging dhurrie. And plants. Everywhere. They were tucked in corners and strung along baseboards and hung from hooks. What the occupant lacked in furnishings, he'd made up for in greenery. Plants dangled from wall brackets and rested on windowsills, tabletops, sideboards, and shelves.

"Looks like a fucking botanical garden," said Bertrand.

And smells, I thought. A musty odor permeated the air, a blend of fungus, and leaves, and damp earth.

Across from the main entrance a short hall led to a single closed door. Ryan gestured me back with the same move he'd used in the hall, then slid along the wall, shoulders hunched, knees bent, back pressed to the plaster. He inched up to the door, paused, then shot a foot hard against the wood.

The door flew in, hit the wall, and recoiled toward the frame, then came to rest half open. I strained for sounds of movement, my heart beating with the erratic buzzing. Bzzzzzzt. Bzt. Bzt. Bzzzzt. Da dum dum dum. Da dum. Da dum dum.

An eerie glow seeped from behind the half-open door, accompanied by a soft gurgling.

"Found the fish," said Ryan, moving through the door.

He flicked a switch with his pen and the room was thrown into brightness. Standard bedroom. Single bed, Indian print spread. Nightstand, lamp, alarm, nasal spray. Dresser, no mirror. Tiny bath to the rear. One window. Heavy drapes blocked a view of a brick wall.

The only uncommon items were the tanks that lined the back wall. Mathieu was right, they were *fantastique*. Electric blues, canary yellows, and black-and-white stripes darted in and out of rose and white coral and foliage of every shade of green imaginable. Each tiny ecosystem was illuminated in aquamarine and lulled by a rolling oxygen sonata.

I watched, mesmerized, feeling an idea about to form. Coaxing it. What? Fish? What? Nothing.

Ryan moved around me, using his pen to sweep back the shower curtain, open the medicine cabinet, poke among the food and nets surrounding the tanks. He used a hanky to open dresser drawers, then the pen to leaf through underwear, socks, shirts, and sweaters.

Forget the fish, Brennan. Whatever idea was in my mind, it was as elusive as the bubbles in the tanks, rising toward the surface only to disappear.

"Anything?"

He shook his head. "Nothing obvious. Don't want to piss off recovery, so I'm just doing a quick check. Let's case the other rooms, then I'll turn it over to Gilbert. Pretty clear Tanguay's elsewhere. We'll nail his ass, but in the meantime we might as well find out what he has here."

Back in the living room Bertrand was inspecting the TV.

"State of the art," he said. "Boy likes his tube."

"Probably needs a regular Cousteau fix," said

Ryan absently, body tense, eyes scanning the gloom around us. No one would surprise us today.

I wandered to the shelves containing the books. The range of topics was impressive, and, like the TV, the books looked new. I scanned the titles. Ecology. Ichthyology. Ornithology. Psychology. Sex. Lots of science, but the guy's taste was eclectic. Buddhism. Scientology. Archaeology. Maori art. Kwakiutl wood carving. Samurai warriors. World War II artifacts. Cannibalism.

The shelves held hundreds of paperbacks, including modern fiction, both French and English. Many of my favorites were present. Vonnegut. Irving. McMurtry. But the majority were crime fiction novels. Brutal murderers. Deranged stalkers. Violent psychopaths. Heartless cities. I could quote their cover blurbs without even reading them. There was also an entire shelf of nonfiction devoted to the lives of serial and spree killers. Manson. Bundy. Ramirez. Boden.

"I think Tanguay and St. Jacques belong to the same book club," I said.

"This butt wipe probably is St. Jacques," said Bertrand.

"No, this guy brushes his teeth," said Ryan.

"Yeah. When he's Tanguay."

"If he reads this stuff, his interests are incredibly broad," I said. "And he's bilingual." I glanced over the collection again. "And he's compulsive as hell."

"What are you now, Dr. Ruth?" asked Bertrand.

"Look at this."

They joined me.

"Everything's arranged by topic, alphabetically." I pointed to several shelves. "Then by author within each category, again alphabetically. Then by year of publication for each author."

"Doesn't everyone do that?"

Ryan and I looked at him. Bertrand was not a reader.

"Look how every book is aligned with the edge of the shelf."

"He does the same with his shorts and socks. Must use a square edge to stack them," said Ryan.

Ryan voiced my thoughts.

"Fits the profile."

"Maybe he just keeps the books for show. Wants his friends to think he's an intellectual," said Bertrand.

"I don't think so," I said. "They're not dusty. Also, look at the little yellow slips. He not only reads this stuff, he marks certain things to go back to. Let's point that out to Gilbert and his commandos so they don't lose the markers. Could be useful."

"I'll have them seal the books before they dust."

"Something else about Monsieur Tanguay."

They stared at the shelves.

"He reads some weird shit," said Bertrand.

"Besides the crime stories, what interests him most?" I asked. "Look at the very top shelf."

They looked again.

"Shit," said Ryan. "*Gray's Anatomy. Cunningham's Manual of Practical Anatomy. Color Atlas of Human Anatomy. Handbook of Anatomical Dissection. Medical Illustration of the Human Body.* Christ, look at this. *Sabiston's Principles of Surgery.* He's got more of this shit than a med school library. Looks like he's heavy into knowing what a body's got inside."

"Yeah, and not just the software. This squirrel's into the hardware."

Ryan reached for his radio. "Let's get Gilbert and his raiders up here. I'll tell the teams out back to go to ground and watch for Dr. Prick. We don't

DÉJÀ DEAD

want to spook him when he shows up. Christ,
Claudel's probably got his nuts in a half hitch by
now."

Ryan spoke into his handset. Bertrand continued
to skim the titles behind me.

Bzt. Bzzzzzzt. Bzzt. Bzt.

"Hey, this is your kind of stuff." He used a
hanky to withdraw something. "Looks like there's
just this one."

He laid a single volume of the *American Anthropologist* on the table. July 1993. I didn't have to
open it. I knew one entry on its table of contents.
"A major hit," she'd called it. "Fodder for promo-
tion to full professor."

Gabby's article. The sight of the *AA* hit me like
a snapped cable. I wanted out of there. I wanted
to be gone to a sunny Saturday where I was safe,
and no one was dead, and my best friend would be
calling with plans for dinner.

Water. Cold water on your face, Brennan.

I lurched toward the double doors and flipped
one open with my foot, looking for the kitchen.

BZZZZZT. BZZZZZT. BZT. BZZZZZZT.
BZT.

The room had no window. A digital clock to my
right gave off a luminous orange glow. I could
make out two white shapes and another pale
stretch at waist level. Refrigerator, stove, sink, I
assumed. I felt for a switch. The hell with procedure. They could sort out my prints.

The back of my hand pressed to my mouth, I
stumbled to the sink and splashed cold water on
my face. When I straightened and turned, Ryan
was standing in the doorway.

"I'm fine."

Flies shot around the room, startled at the sudden intrusion.

439

BZZT. BZT. BZZZZT.

"Mint?" He offered a roll of Life Savers.

"Thanks." I took one. "The heat."

"It's a cooker."

A fly careened off his cheek. "What the fu—" He swatted at the air. "What's this guy do in here?"

Ryan and I saw them at the same time. Two brown objects lay on the counter, halos of grease staining the paper towels on which they dried. Flies danced around them, landing and taking off in nervous agitation. A surgical glove lay to their left, a twin to the one we'd just unearthed. We went closer, fomenting the flies to excited flight.

I looked at each shriveled mass and thought of the roaches and spiders in the barber pole, their legs dried and constricted in rigor. These objects had nothing to do with arachnids, however. I knew instantly what they were, though I'd only seen the others in photos.

"They're paws."

"What?"

"Paws from some kind of animal."

"Are you sure?"

"Flip one over."

He did. With his pen.

"You can see the ends of the lower limb bones."

"What's he doing with them?"

"How the hell should I know, Ryan?" I thought of Alsa.

"Christ."

"Check the refrigerator."

"Oh, Christ."

The tiny corpse was there, skinned and wrapped in clear plastic. Along with several others.

"What are they?"

"Small mammals of some sort. Without the skin I can't tell. They're not horses."

"Thanks, Brennan."

Bertrand joined us. "What've you got?"

"Dead animals." Ryan's voice betrayed his aggravation. "And another glove."

"Maybe the guy eats roadkill," said Bertrand.

"Maybe. And maybe he makes lampshades out of people. That's it. I want this place sealed. I want every friggin' thing confiscated. Bag his cutlery, bag that blender, bag everything in the goddamn refrigerator. I want that disposal scraped and every inch of this place hosed with Luminol. Where the hell's Gilbert?"

Ryan moved toward a wall phone to the left of the door.

"Hold it. That phone got a redial button?"

Ryan nodded.

"Hit it."

"Probably get his priest. Or Grammama."

Ryan pushed the button. We listened to a seven-note melody followed by four rings. Then a voice answered, and the bubble of fear I'd been carrying all day rose to my head and I felt faint.

"Veuillez laissez votre nom et numéro de téléphone. Je vais vous rappelez le plutôt possible. Merci. Please leave your name and number and I'll return your call as soon as possible. Thanks. This is Tempe."

36

THE SOUND OF MY OWN voice hit me like a blow to the head. My legs buckled and my breath came in rapid gasps.

Ryan helped me to a chair, brought water, asked no questions. I have no idea how long I sat there, feeling nothing but emptiness. Eventually, my composure crept back, and I began to assess the reality.

He'd phoned me. Why? When?

I watched Gilbert don rubber gloves and slide his hand around the inside of the disposal. He drew something out and dropped it in the sink.

Was he trying to reach me? Or Gabby? What had he intended to say? Had he intended to speak at all, or just check whether I was there?

A photographer moved from room to room, his flash like a firefly in the gloomy flat.

The hang-ups. Was it he?

A tech in rubber gloves and coveralls taped books and sealed them into evidence bags, marking

442

each, then signing across the seal. Another brushed white powder across the red-black varnish of the shelves. A third emptied the refrigerator, removing packages in plain brown wrappers, and placing them in a cooler.

Had she died here, her last visual images the ones I now saw?

Ryan spoke to Charbonneau. Snatches of the conversation floated to me through the suffocating heat. Where's Claudel? Took off. Roust the superintendent. Find out about basements, storage areas. Get keys. Charbonneau left, returned with a middle-aged woman in housecoat and slippers. They disappeared again, accompanied by the book packer.

Again and again Ryan offered to take me home. There was nothing I could do, he told me gently. I knew that, but I couldn't leave.

Grammama arrived around four. She was neither hostile nor cooperative. Reluctantly, she provided a description of Tanguay. Male. Quiet. Brown hair, thinning. Medium everything. Could have fit half the men in North America. She had no idea where he was or how long he'd be gone. He'd left before, but never for long. She only noticed because Tanguay asked Mathieu to feed the fish. He was nice to Mathieu and gave him money when he cared for the fish. She knew little else about him, rarely saw him. She thought he worked, thought he had a car. Wasn't sure. Didn't care. Didn't want to get involved.

The recovery team spent all afternoon and late into the night dissecting the apartment. I didn't. By five I needed out. I accepted Ryan's offer of a ride and left.

We spoke little in the car. Ryan repeated what he'd said on the phone. I was to stay home. A team would watch my building around the clock. No late night sorties. No solo expeditions.

"Don't ride me, Ryan," I said, my voice betraying my emotional brittleness.

The rest of the drive was spent in strained silence. When we reached my building Ryan put the car in park and turned to me. I could feel his eyes on the side of my face.

"Listen, Brennan. I'm not trying to give you a hard time. This scum is going down. You can take that to the bank. I'd just like you to live to see it."

His concern touched me more than I was willing to admit.

They pulled out all stops. APB's went out to every cop in Quebec, to the Ontario Provincial Police, the RCMP, and the state forces in New York and Vermont. But Quebec is big, its borders easy to cross. Lots of places to hide or slip out.

In the days that followed I grappled with the possibilities. Tanguay could be lying low, biding his time. He could be dead. He could have taken off. Serial killers do that. Sensing danger, they pack up and relocate. Some are never caught. No. I refused to accept that.

Sunday I never left home. Birdie and I did what the French call *coconer*. We cocooned. I didn't get dressed, avoided the radio and television. I couldn't bear to see Gabby's photo, or hear the overdone descriptions of the victim and suspect. I made only three calls, first to Katy, then to my aunt in Chicago. Happy Birthday, Auntie! Eighty-four. Well done.

I knew Katy was in Charlotte, just wanted to reassure myself. No answer. Of course. Curse the distance. No. Bless the distance. I didn't want my daughter anywhere near the place a monster had held her picture. She would never know what I'd found.

The last call was to Gabby's mother. She was sedated, couldn't come to the phone. I spoke to Mr. Macaulay. Assuming they released the body, the funeral would be on Thursday.

For a time, I sat sobbing, my body rocking as though to a metronome. The demons that live in my bloodstream screamed for alcohol. Pleasure-pain, such a simple principle. Feed us. Numb us. Make it go away.

But I didn't. That would have been easy. You're down love-forty, so lob one in, shake hands at the net, and it's Miller time. Except this wasn't tennis. If I gave up in this game, I would lose my career, my friends, my self-respect. Hell, I might as well let St. Jacques/Tanguay do me in.

I would not give in. Not to the bottle, and not to the maniac. I owed it to Gabby. I owed it to myself and to my daughter. So I stayed sober and waited, desperately wishing I had Gabby to talk me through. I checked frequently to be sure the surveillance team was in place.

On Monday Ryan called around eleven-thirty. LaManche had completed the autopsy. Cause of death: ligature strangulation. Though the body was decomposed he'd found a groove buried deep in the flesh of Gabby's neck. Above and below it the skin was torn in a series of gouges and scratches. The vessels in the throat tissue showed hundreds of tiny hemorrhages.

Ryan's voice receded. I pictured Gabby desperately clawing to breathe, to live. Stop. Thank God we found her so quickly. I couldn't have faced the horror of Gabby on my autopsy table. The pain of losing her was unbearable enough.

". . . hyoid was broken. Also, whatever he used had links or loops or something, left a spiral pattern in the skin. "

"Was she raped?"

"He couldn't tell because of the decomposition. Negative for sperm."

"Time of death?"

"LaManche is giving it a minimum of five days. We know the upper limit is ten."

"Pretty wide window."

"Given this heat and the shallow burial, he thinks the body should be in worse shape."

Oh, God. She may not have died the day she disappeared.

"Have you checked her apartment?"

"No one saw her, but she'd been there."

"What about Tanguay?"

"Ready for this? The guy's a teacher. Small school out on the west island." I heard the rustle of paper. "St. Isidor's. Been there since 1991. He's twenty-eight. Single. For next of kin on his application he put 'none.' We're checking it. He's been living on Séguin since '91. Landlady thinks he was somewhere in the States before that."

"Prints?"

"Lots. We ran them, came up empty. Sent them south this morning."

"Inside the glove?"

"At least two readable and a smudged palm."

An image of Gabby. The plastic bag. Another glove. I jotted down a single word. Glove.

"He has a degree?"

"Bishops. Bertrand's out in Lennoxville now. Claudel's trying to roust someone at St. Isidor's, not having much luck. The caretaker is about a hundred and no one else is around. They're closed for the summer."

"Any names turn up in the apartment?"

"None. No pictures. No address books. No letters. Guy must live in a social vacuum."

A long silence as we mulled that over, then Ryan said,

"Might explain his unusual hobbies."

"The animals?"

"That. And the cutlery collection."

"Cutlery?"

"This squirrel had more blades than an orthopedic surgeon. Surgical tools mostly. Knives. Razors. Scalpels. Kept them stashed under the bed. Along with a box of surgical gloves. Original."

"A loner with a blade fetish. Great."

"And the standard porn gallery. Well thumbed."

"What else?"

"Guy's got a car." More rustling. "A 1987 Ford Probe. It's not in the neighborhood. They're looking for it. We got the driver's license photo this morning and sent that out too."

"And?"

"I'll let you judge for yourself, but I think Grammama was right. He's not memorable. Or maybe the Xerox/fax reproduction doesn't do him justice."

"Could it be St. Jacques?"

"Could be. Or Jean Chrétien. Or the guy that sells hot dogs on Rue St. Paul. Richard Petty's out. He's got a mustache."

"You're a laugh riot, Ryan."

"This guy doesn't even have a parking ticket. He's been a real good boy."

"Right. A real good boy who collects knives and porn and carves up small mammals."

Pause.

"What were they?"

"We're not sure yet. They're asking some guy over at U of M."

I looked at the word I'd written, swallowed hard.

"Any prints inside the glove we found with Gabby?" It was difficult to say her name.

"No."

"We knew there wouldn't be."

"Yeah."

I heard squad room noises in the background.

"I want to drop off a copy of this license photo so you'll have some idea what he looks like in case you meet him up close and personal. I still think it's better if you stick near home until we pop this asshole."

"I'm coming in. If ident is done with the gloves I want to take them over to biology. Then Lacroix."

"I think you sh—"

"Cut the macho crap, Ryan."

A breath drawn deeply, expelled.

"Are you holding out on me?"

"Brennan, what we know, you know."

"I'll be there in thirty minutes."

In less than half an hour I arrived at the lab. Ident had finished and sent the gloves to the biology section.

I looked at my watch—twelve-forty. I called the ident section at CUM headquarters to ask if I could see the photos taken at the St. Jacques apartment on Rue Berger. Lunchtime. The desk clerk would leave a message.

At one o'clock I walked over to the biology section. A woman with flyaway hair and a plump, Christmas angel face was shaking a glass vial. Two latex gloves lay on the counter behind her.

"*Bonjour,* Françoise."

"Ah. I thought I might see you today." The cherub eyes took on a worried expression. "I'm sorry. I don't quite know what to say to you."

"*Merci.* It's okay." I nodded at the gloves. "What have you got?"

"This one is clean. No blood." She gestured at Gabby's glove. "I'm just starting on the one from the kitchen. Would you like to watch?"

"Thank you."

"I've taken scrapings from these brown spots and rehydrated the sample in saline."

She examined the liquid and placed the vial in a test tube tray. Then she withdrew a glass pipette with a long, hollow projection, held it over a flame to seal it, and twisted off the tip.

"I'll test for human blood first."

Removing a tiny bottle from the refrigerator, she broke the seal and inserted the thin, tubular point of a fresh pipette. Like a mosquito sucking blood, the antiserum moved up the tiny pipeline. She sealed the other end with her thumb.

She then inserted the long beak of the pipette into the fire-sealed pipette, released her thumb, and allowed the antiserum to dribble out. She spoke as she worked.

"The blood knows its own proteins, or antigens. If it recognizes foreigners, antigens that don't belong, it tries to destroy them with antibodies. Some antibodies blow up foreign antigens, others clump them together. That clumping is called an agglutination reaction.

"Antiserum is created in an animal, usually a rabbit or a chicken, by injecting it with the blood of another species. The animal's blood recognizes the invaders and produces antibodies to protect itself. Injecting an animal with human blood produces human antiserum. Injecting it with goat blood produces goat antiserum. Horse blood produces horse antiserum.

"Human antiserum creates an agglutination reaction when mixed with human blood. Watch. If this is human blood a visible precipitate will form in the test tube, right where the sample solution and the antiserum meet. We'll compare to the saline as a control."

She tossed the pipette into a biological waste container and picked up the vial with the Tanguay sample solution. Using another pipette, she sucked the sample up the tube, released it into the antiserum, and set the pipette into a holder.

"How long will it take?" I asked.

"That depends on the strength of the antiserum. Anywhere from three to fifteen minutes. This is pretty good. Shouldn't be more than five or six minutes."

We checked it after five, Françoise holding the pipettes under the Luxolamp, a black card behind for background. We checked again after ten. Fifteen. Nothing. No white band appeared between the antiserum and the sample solution. The mixture stayed as clear as the control saline.

"So. It's not human. Let's see if it's animal."

She went back to the refrigerator and withdrew a tray of small bottles.

"Can you tell the exact species?" I asked.

"No. Usually just family. Bovid. Cervid. Canid."

I looked at the tray. Written next to each bottle was an animal name. Goat. Rat. Horse. I pictured the paws in Tanguay's kitchen.

"Let's try dogs."

Nothing.

"What about something like a squirrel or a gopher?"

She thought a minute then reached for a bottle. "Maybe rat."

In less than four minutes a tiny parfait had

formed in the tube, yellow above, clear below, a layer of foggy white between.

"*Voilà,*" said Françoise. "It's animal blood. Something small, a mammal, like a rodent or a ground hog or something. That's about all I'll be able to determine. I don't know if that helps you."

"Yes," I said. "That helps. May I use your phone?"

"*Bien sûr.*"

I dialed an extension down the hall.

"Lacroix."

I identified myself and explained what I wanted.

"Sure. Give me twenty minutes, I'm just finishing up a run."

I signed for the gloves, returned to my office, and spent the next half hour proofing and signing reports. Then I walked back to the corridor occupied by biology, and entered a door marked *Incendie et Explosifs*. Fire and Explosives.

A man in a lab coat stood in front of an enormous piece of machinery. A label identified it as an X-ray diffractometer. He didn't speak and I didn't say anything until he had removed a slide with a small white smear and placed it on a tray. Then he gave me eyes as soft as a Disney fawn, lids drooping, lashes curling back like petals on a daisy.

"*Bonjour,* Monsieur Lacroix. *Comment ça va?*"

"*Bien. Bien.* You have them?"

I held up two plastic bags.

"Let's get started."

He led me into a small room with an apparatus the size of a photocopier, two monitors, and a printer. A periodic chart of the elements hung on the wall above.

Lacroix laid the evidence bags on a counter and pulled on surgical gloves. Gingerly, he withdrew each suspect glove, inspected it, then laid it on its plastic bag. The gloves stretched across his hands looked identical to those on the counter.

"First we look for gross characteristics, details of manufacturing. Weight. Density. Color. How the rims are finished." He turned each glove over and over, examining as he spoke. "These two look quite similar. Same rim technique. See?"

I looked. The wrist of each glove ended in a border that rolled outward onto itself.

"They're not all like that?"

"No. Some roll in, some roll out. These are both outies. So. Now we see what's in them."

He carried Gabby's glove to the machine, raised the cover, and placed it on a tray inside.

"With very small samples I use those little holders." He pointed to a tray of small plastic tubes. "I stretch a square of polypropylene window film across the holder, then use press-on tabs to make a sticky spot to hold the fragment. That's not necessary with this. We'll just put the whole glove in."

Lacroix flipped a switch and the apparatus whirred to life. A box positioned on a pole in one corner lit up, the word X RAY white against a red background. A panel of buttons glowed, indicating the machine's condition. Red: X rays. White: Power. Orange: Shutter open.

For a few moments Lacroix adjusted dials, then he closed the cover and moved to a chair in front of the monitors.

"S'il vous plaît." He indicated the other chair.

A desert landscape appeared on the first monitor, a granular backdrop of synclines and anticlines, with shadows and boulders scattered here and there. Superimposed on that scene was a series of concentric circles, the two smallest and most central shaped like footballs. Two hashed lines intersected at right angles, forming a cross directly over the bull's-eye circles.

Lacroix adjusted the image by manipulating a joy stick. Boulders shifted in and out of the circles.

"That's the glove we're looking at, magnified eighty times. I'm just picking a target location. Each run samples an area of about three hundred microns, approximately the area inside the dotted circle. So you want to direct your X rays onto the best part of your sample."

He shifted the crosshairs a few more moments, then settled on a boulderless patch.

"There. That should be good."

He flipped a switch and the machine hummed.

"Now we're creating a vacuum. That'll take a couple of minutes. Then the scan. That's very quick."

"And this will determine what's in the glove."

"*Oui.* It's a form of X-ray analysis. X-ray microfluorescence can determine what elements are present in a sample."

The humming stopped and a pattern began to form on the right-hand monitor. A series of tiny red mounds sprouted across the bottom of the screen, then grew against a bright blue background, a thin yellow stripe up the middle of each. In the lower left-hand corner was an image of a keyboard, each key marked with the abbreviation for an element.

Lacroix typed in commands, and letters appeared on the screen. Some mounds remained small, others grew into tall peaks, like the giant termite castles I'd seen in Australia.

"*C'est ça.*" That's it. Lacroix pointed at a column on the far right. It rose from the bottom to the top of the screen, where its top was truncated. A smaller peak to its right climbed to a quarter of its height. Both were marked Zn.

"Zinc. That's standard. It's found in all these gloves."

He indicated a pair of peaks to the far left, one low, the other rising three quarters of the distance up the screen. "That low one is magnesium. Mg. The tall one marked Si is silicon." Farther to the right a double peak bore the letter S.

"Sulfur."

A Ca peak spired halfway up the screen.

"Quite a bit of calcium."

Beyond the calcium a gap, then a series of low mounds, foothills to the zinc pinnacle. Fe.

"A little iron."

He leaned back and summarized. "Pretty common cocktail. Lots of zinc, with silicon and calcium, the other major components. I'll print these, then let's test another spot."

We ran ten tests. All showed the same combination of elements.

"Right, then. The other glove."

We repeated the procedure with the glove from Tanguay's kitchen.

The peaks for zinc and sulfur were similar, but this glove contained more calcium, and had no iron, silicon, or magnesium. A small spike indicated the presence of potassium. It was the same on every run.

"What does this mean?" I asked, already certain of the answer.

"Each manufacturer uses a slightly different recipe for the latex. There will even be variation among gloves from the same company, but it will be within limits.

"So these gloves are not a pair?"

"They weren't even made by the same company."

He got up to remove the glove. My mind was stumbling over our finding.

"Would X-ray diffraction give more information?"

"What we've done, X-ray microfluorescence, tells what elements are present in an object. X-ray diffraction can describe the actual mixture of the elements. The chemical structure. For example, with microfluorescence we can know that something contains sodium and chloride. With diffraction we can tell that it is made up of sodium-chloride crystals.

"To oversimplify, in the X-ray diffractometer a sample is rotated and hit with X rays. The X rays bounce off the crystals, and their pattern of diffraction indicates the structure of those crystals.

"So one limitation with diffraction is that it can only be done on materials with a crystalline structure. That's about eighty percent of everything that comes in. Unfortunately, latex is not crystalline in structure. Diffraction probably wouldn't add much anyway. These gloves are definitely made by different manufacturers."

"What if they're just from different boxes? Surely individual batches of latex must vary."

He was silent for a moment. Then:

"Wait. Let me show you something."

He disappeared into the main lab and I could hear him talking to the technician. He reappeared with a stack of printouts, each composed of seven or eight sheets showing the familiar spire and steeple patterning. He unfolded each series and we looked at the variations in pattern.

"Each of these shows a sequence of tests done on gloves from a single manufacturer, but sampled from different boxes. There is variation, but the differences are never as great as those in the gloves we just analyzed."

I examined several series. The size of the peaks varied, but the components showed consistency.

"Now. Look at this."

He unfurled another series of printouts. Again, there were some differences, but overall the mix was the same.

Then I caught my breath. The configuration looked familiar. I looked at the symbols. Zn. Fe. Ca. S. Si. Mg. High zinc, silicon, and calcium content. Traces of the other elements. I laid the printout from Gabby's glove above the series. The pattern was almost identical.

"Monsieur Lacroix, are these gloves from the same manufacturer?"

"Yes, yes. That's my point. From the same box, probably. I just remembered this."

"What case is this?" My heart rate had picked up tempo.

"It came in just a few weeks ago." He flipped to the first sheet in the series. *Numéro d'événement:* 327468. "I can pull it up on the computer."

"Please."

Data filled the screen in seconds. I scanned it.

Numéro d'événement: 327468. Numéro de LML: 29427. Requesting Agency: CUM. Investigators: L. Claudel and M. Charbonneau. Recovery location: 1422 Rue Berger. Recovery date: 24/06/94.

An old rubber glove. Maybe the guy worried about his nails. Claudel! I thought he'd meant a glove for household cleaning! St. Jacques had a surgical glove! It matched the one in Gabby's grave!

I thanked Monsieur Lacroix, gathered the printouts, and left. I returned the gloves to property, my mind tearing through what I'd just learned. The glove from Tanguay's kitchen did not match the one buried with Gabby's body. Tanguay's prints were on it. The outside stains were animal blood. The glove found with Gabby was clean. No blood. No prints. St. Jacques had a surgical glove. It matched the one in Gabby's grave. Was Bertrand right? Were Tanguay and St. Jacques the same person?

A pink slip waited on my desk. CUM Ident had called. The photos of the Rue Berger flat had been archived on a CD-ROM disk. I could view it there or check it out. I called to request the latter, told them I'd be there shortly.

I fought my way to CUM headquarters, cursing the rush-hour traffic and the tourists that clogged the Old Port area. Leaving the car double-parked, I bolted the steps and went directly to the desk sergeant on the third floor. Amazingly, he had the disk. I signed it out, dashed back to the car, and stuffed it in my briefcase.

All the way home I kept looking over my shoulder, watching for Tanguay. Watching for St. Jacques. I couldn't stop myself.

37

I GOT HOME ABOUT FIVE-thirty and sat in the silence of the apartment, assessing what else I could do. Nothing. Ryan was right. Tanguay could be out there, waiting for his chance at me. I wouldn't make it easier for him.

But I had to eat. And keep busy.

As I let myself out the front door, I scanned the street. There. In the alley to the left of the pizza parlor. I nodded to the two uniforms and pointed in the direction of Ste. Catherine. I could see them confer, then one got out.

My street crosses Ste. Catherine, not far from Le Faubourg. As I walked toward the market I could sense the annoyance of the cop on my tail. No matter. The day was glorious. I hadn't noticed at the lab. The heat had broken and huge white clouds floated in a dazzling blue sky, casting islands of shadow over the day and its players. It felt good to be outside.

Veggies. At La Plantation I squeezed avocados, evaluated the color of bananas, chose broccoli, brussels sprouts, and baking potatoes with the concentration of a neurosurgeon. A baguette at the *boulangerie*. A chocolate mousse at the pâtisserie. I picked up pork chops, ground beef, and a *tourtière* at the boucherie.

"C'est tout?"

"No, what the hell. Give me a T-bone. Really thick." I held my thumb and index finger an inch apart.

As I watched him remove the saw from its hook, the cognitive itch began again. I tried to scratch it into a full-blown idea, but with no more success than I'd had before. The saw? Too obvious. Anyone can buy a chef's saw. The SQ had run that lead to a dead end, contacting every outlet in the province. Thousands had been sold.

What, then? I'd learned that trying to pry an idea out of the subconscious only drives it deeper. If I let it drift, eventually it will float to the surface. I paid for my meat and went home, with a brief detour at the Rue Ste. Catherine Burger King.

What greeted me was the last thing I wanted to see. Someone had called. For several minutes I sat on the edge of the couch, clutching my packages and staring at the tiny indicator light. One message. Was it Tanguay? Would he speak to me, or would I hear the sound of his listening, followed by a dial tone?

"You're being hysterical, Brennan. It's probably Ryan."

I dried my palm, reached out, and pushed the button. It wasn't Tanguay. It was worse.

"Hey, Mom. Y'all out having a good time? Hello? Are you there? Pick u-up." I could hear what sounded like traffic, as if she were calling from an outside phone. "Guess not. Well, I can't talk anyway. I'm on the road. On the road again . . ." She did a Willie Nelson imitation. "Pretty good, eh? Anyway, I'm coming to visit, Mom. You're right. Max is a pecker head. I don't need that." I heard a voice in the background. "Okay, just give me a minute," she said to whoever it was. "Listen, I got a chance to visit New York. The Big Apple. I hooked a free trip, so here I am. Anyway, I can get a ride to Montreal, so I'm coming up. See you soon!"

Click.

"No! Don't come here, Katy. No!" I spoke to the empty air.

I listened to the tape rewind. Jesus, what a nightmare! Gabby is dead. A psychopath placed a picture of Katy and me in her grave. Now Katy is on her way here. Blood pounded in my temples. My mind raced. I have to stop her. How? I don't know where she is.

Pete.

As his phone rang I had a flashback. Katy at three. At the park. I was talking to another mother, my eyes on Katy as she poured sand into plastic containers. Suddenly, she dropped her shovel and ran to the swings. She hesitated a moment, watching the iron pony swing back, then ran to it, her face exuberant with the feel of spring and the sight of the colorful mane and bridle moving through the air. I knew it would hit her and I could not stop it. It was happening again.

No answer on Pete's direct line.

I tried his switchboard number. A secretary told me he was away, taking a deposition. Of course. I left a message.

I stared at the answering machine. I shut my eyes and took several long, deep breaths, willing my heart to a slower pace. The back of my head felt as though it were clamped in a vise, and I was hot all over.

"This will not happen."

I opened my eyes to see Birdie gazing at me from across the room.

"This will not happen," I repeated to him.

He stared, his yellow eyes unblinking.

"I can do something."

He arched, placed all four paws in a tight little square, curled his tail, and sat, his eyes never leaving my face.

"I will do something. I will not just sit around and wait for this fiend to pounce. Not on my daughter."

I took the groceries to the kitchen and placed them in the refrigerator. Then I got out my laptop, logged in, and pulled up the spreadsheet. How long had it been since I'd started it? I checked the dates I'd entered. Isabelle Gagnon's body was found on June 2. Seven weeks. It seemed like seven years.

I went to the study and brought out my case files. Maybe the effort I'd spent photocopying wouldn't be wasted after all.

For the next two hours I scrutinized every photograph, every name, every date, literally every word in every interview and police report I had. Then I did it again. I went over and over the words, hoping to find some little thing I'd missed. The third time through I did.

I was reading Ryan's interview with Grace Damas's father when I noticed it. Like a sneeze that's been building, taunting but refusing to break, the message finally burst into my conscious thought.

A boucherie. Grace Damas had worked at a boucherie. The killer used a chef's saw, knew something about anatomy. Tanguay dissected animals.

Maybe there was a link. I looked for the name of the boucherie but couldn't find it.

I dialed the number in the file. A man answered.

"Mr. Damas?"

"Yes." Accented English.

"I'm Dr. Brennan. I'm working on the investigation of your wife's death. I wonder if I could ask you a couple of questions."

"Yes."

"At the time she disappeared, was your wife working outside the home?"

Pause. Then, "Yes."

I could hear a television in the background.

"May I ask where, please?"

"A bakery on Fairmont. Le Bon Croissant. It was just part time. She never worked full time, with the kids and all."

I thought that over. So much for my link.

"How long had she worked there, Mr. Damas?" I hid my disappointment.

"Just a few months, I think. Grace never lasted anywheres very long."

"Where did she work before that?" I dogged on.

"A boucherie."

"Which one?" I held my breath.

"La Boucherie St. Dominique. Belongs to a man in our parish. It's over on St. Dominique, just off St. Laurent, ya know?"

Yes. I pictured the rain against its windows.

"When did she work there?" I kept my voice calm.

"Almost a year, I guess. Most of '91, seems like. I can check. Think it's important? They never asked nothing about the dates before."

"I'm not sure. Mr. Damas, did your wife ever speak of someone named Tanguay?"

"Who?" Harsh.

"Tanguay."

An announcer's voice promised he'd be right back after the commercial break. My head throbbed and a dry scratching was beginning in my throat.

"No."

The vehemence startled me.

"Thank you. You've been very helpful. I'll let you know if there are any new developments."

I hung up and phoned Ryan. He'd left for the day. I tried his home number. No answer. I knew what I had to do. I made one call, picked up a key, and headed out.

La Boucherie St. Dominique was busier than the day I'd first noticed it. The same signs occupied its windows, but tonight the store was lit and open for business. There wasn't much. An old woman moved slowly down the glass case, her face flaccid in the fluorescent glare. I watched her double back and point to a rabbit. The stiff little carcass reminded me of Tanguay's sad collection. And Alsa.

I waited until the woman left, then approached the man behind the counter. His face was rectangular, the bones large, the features coarse. The arms that hung from his T-shirt looked surprisingly thin and sinewy in contrast. Dark splotches marred the white of his apron, like dried petals on a linen tablecloth.

"*Bonjour.*"

"*Bonjour.*"

"Slow tonight?"

"It's slow every night." English, accented like Damas's.

I could hear someone rattling utensils in a back room.

"I'm working on the Grace Damas murder investigation." I pulled out my ID and flashed it. "I need to ask you a few questions."

The man stared at me. In the back, a faucet went on, off.

"Are you the owner?"

Nod.

"Mr.?"

"Plevritis."

"Mr. Plevritis, Grace Damas worked here for a short time, did she not?"

"Who?"

"Grace Damas. Fellow parishioner at St. Demetrius?"

The scrawny arms folded across his chest. Nod.

"When was that?"

"About three, four years ago. I don't know exactly. They come and go."

"Did she quit?"

"Without notice."

"Why was that?"

"Hell if I know. Everyone was doing it about then."

"Did she seem unhappy, upset, nervous?"

"What do I look like, Sigmund Freud?"

"Did she have any friends here, anyone she was particularly close to?"

His eyes lighted on mine and a smile teased the corners of his mouth. "Close?" he asked, his voice oily as Valvoline. I returned his gaze, unsmiling.

The smile disappeared and his eyes left mine to wander the room.

"It's just me and my brother here. There's no one to get *close* with." He drew the word out, like an adolescent with a dirty joke.

"Did she have any peculiar visitors, anyone who might have been hassling her?"

"Look, I gave her a job. I told her what to do and she did it. I didn't keep track of her social life."

"I thought perhaps you might have noticed—"

"Grace was a good worker. I was mad as hell when she quit. Everyone splitting at the same time really left me with my nuts in a vise, so I was pissed. I admit it. But I don't hold a grudge. Later, when I heard she was missing, at church, ya know, I thought she'd taken off. Didn't really seem like her, but her old man can be pretty heavy sometimes. I'm sorry she got killed. But I really hardly remember her."

"What do you mean 'heavy'?"

A blank expression crossed his face, like a sluice gate dropping. He lowered his eyes and scratched with his thumbnail at something on the counter. "You'll have to talk to Nikos about that. That's family."

I could see what Ryan meant. Now what? Visual aids. I reached in my purse and pulled out the picture of St. Jacques.

"Ever see this guy?"

Plevritis leaned forward to take it. "Who is he?"

"Neighbor of yours."

He studied the face. "Not exactly a prizewinning photo."

"It was taken by a video camera."

"So was the Zapruder film, but at least you could see something."

I wondered at his reference but said nothing. Spare me another conspiracy buff. Then I saw something cross his face, a subtle squint that puckered then flattened his lower lids.

"What?"

"Well . . ." He stared at the photo.

"Yes?"

"This guy looks a little like the other shitrag that

465

bailed on me. But maybe that's because you put me in mind of him with all your questions. Hell, I don't know." He thrust the picture across the counter at me. "I gotta close up."

"Who? Who was that?"

"Look, it's a lousy picture. Looks like a lot of guys with bad hair. Don't mean nothing."

"What did you mean, someone else bailed on you? When?"

"That's why I was so cheesed off about Grace. The guy I had before her quit without so much as a good-bye, then Grace takes a walk, then not long after that this other guy. He and Grace were part-timers, but they were the only help I had. My brother was down in the States and I was running this place all by myself that year."

"Who was he?"

"Fortier. Lemme think. Leo. Leo Fortier. I remember 'cause I got a cousin named Leo."

"He worked here at the same time Grace Damas did?"

"Yeah. I hired him to replace the guy quit just before Grace started. I figured with two part-timers to split the hours, in case one didn't come in, I'd only be short-handed half the day. Then they both left. *Tabernac,* that was a mess. Fortier worked here maybe a year, year and a half, then just stopped coming. Never even turned in his keys. I had to start back at zero. I don't want to go through that again."

"What can you tell me about him?"

"That's an easy one. Nothing. He saw my sign, walked in off the street wanting to work part time. He fit in where I needed him, early morning to open, late night for closing and clean up, and he had experience cutting up meat. Turned out to be real good, actually. Anyway, I hired him. He had some other kind of job during the day. He seemed okay. Real quiet. Did his work, never opened his mouth. Hell, I never even knew where he lived."

"How did he and Grace get along."

"Hell if I know. He'd be gone when she came in, then he'd come back after she'd left for the day. I'm not sure they even knew each other."

"And you think the man in this picture looks like Fortier?"

"Him and every other guy with bad hair and an attitude about it."

"Do you know where Fortier is now?"

He shook his head.

"You know anyone named St. Jacques?"

"Nope."

"Tanguay?"

"Sounds like a bronzer for queers."

My head was pounding and my throat was starting to scratch. I left my card.

38

I ARRIVED HOME TO FIND Ryan fuming on my doorstep. He wasted no time.

"I just can't get through to you, can I? No one can. You're like one of those Ghost Dance Indians. Dress the dress and dance the dance and you're bulletproof."

His face was flushed, and I could see a tiny vessel throbbing in his temple. I thought it unwise to comment just yet.

"Whose car was it?"

"Neighbor."

"Do you find all this amusing, Brennan?"

I said nothing. The headache had spread from the back to encompass my entire cranium, and a dry cough told me my immune system was about to have callers.

"Is there anyone on this planet who can get through to you?"

"Would you like to come in for coffee?"

"What makes you think you can just sail off like that and leave everyone sucking wind? These guys don't exactly live to be out here protecting your sorry ass, Brennan. Why the hell didn't you call or page me?"

"I did."

"You couldn't wait ten minutes?"

"I didn't know where you were or how long it would be. I didn't think I'd be gone long. Hell, I wasn't."

"You could have left a message."

"I'd have left *War and Peace* if I'd known you were going to overreact like this." Not quite true. I knew.

"Overreact?" His voice went icy calm. "Let me review for you. Five, maybe seven women have been brutally murdered and mutilated in this town. The most recent was four weeks ago." He ticked points off on his fingers. "One of these women made a partial appearance in your garden. A nutcase had your picture in his spice collection. He's gone missing. A loner who collects knives and pornography, frequents hookers, and likes to slice and dice little animals dialed up your apartment. He'd been stalking your best friend. She is now dead. She was buried clutching a picture of you and your daughter. This loner has also gone missing."

A couple passed on the sidewalk, dropping their eyes and quickening their pace, embarrassed to witness a lovers' quarrel.

"Ryan, come inside. I'll make coffee." My voice sounded raspy and speech was starting to hurt.

He raised a hand in exasperation, fingers splayed, then dropped it to his side. I returned the keys to my neighbor, thanked her for the use of her car, and let Ryan and myself into the apartment.

"Decaf or high test?"

Before he could answer his beeper sounded, causing us both to jump.

"Better go with decaf. You know where the phone is."

I listened, rattling cups and pretending not to.

"Ryan." Pause. "Yeah." Pause. "No shit." Long pause. "When?" Pause. "Okay. Thanks. I'll be right there."

He came to the kitchen door and stood there, his face tense. My temperature, blood pressure, and pulse all began to rise. Stay calm. I poured two cups of coffee, forcing my hand not to tremble. I waited for him to speak.

"They got him."

My hand froze, the pot suspended in midair.

"Tanguay?"

He nodded. I returned the pot to its warmer. Carefully. I took out milk, poured a dollop in my cup, offered some to Ryan. Carefully. He shook his head. I put the carton back in the refrigerator. Carefully. I took a sip. Okay. Speak.

"Tell me."

"Let's sit."

We moved to the living room.

"They arrested him about two hours ago driving east on the 417. An SQ unit spotted the tag and pulled him.

"It's Tanguay?"

"It's Tanguay. Prints match."

"He was heading toward Montreal?"

"Apparently."

"What are they charging him with?"

"For now, possession of open alcohol in a moving vehicle. Jerk was thoughtful enough to crack a bottle of Jim Beam and leave it in the backseat. They also confiscated some skin magazines. He thinks that's the beef. They're letting him sweat for a while."

"Where was he?"

"Claims he has a cabin in the Gatineau. Inherited it from Daddy. Get this. He'd been fishing. Crime scene's sending out a team to take the place apart."

"Where is he now?"

"Parthenais."

"You're heading over there?"

"Yeah." He took a deep breath, expecting a fight. I had no desire to see Tanguay.

"Okay." My mouth was dry, and a languor was spreading through my body. Tranquillity? I hadn't felt that in a long time.

"Katy is coming," I said with a nervous laugh. "That's why I . . . why I went out tonight."

"Your daughter?"

I nodded.

"Bad timing."

"I thought I might find something. I . . . never mind."

For a few seconds neither of us spoke.

"I'm glad it's over." Ryan's anger was gone. He rose to his feet. "Would you like me to stop by after I've talked to him? Could be late."

Bad as I felt, there was no chance I'd sleep until I knew the outcome. Who was Tanguay? What would they find in his cabin? Had Gabby died there? Had Isabelle Gagnon? Grace Damas? Or had they been taken there, postmortem, merely to be butchered and packaged?

"Please."

When he'd gone I realized I'd forgotten to tell him about the gloves. I tried Pete again. Though Tanguay was in custody, I was still uneasy. I didn't want Katy anywhere near Montreal yet. Perhaps I'd go South.

This time I reached him. Katy had left several days earlier. She'd told her father I proposed the trip. True. And approved the plans. Not quite. He wasn't sure of the itinerary. Typical. She was traveling with friends from the university, driving to D.C. to stay with one set of parents, then to New York to visit the other friend's home. Then she planned to continue on to Montreal. Sounded okay to him. He was sure she'd call.

I started to tell him about Gabby and what had been going on in my life, but couldn't. Not yet. No matter. It was over. As usual he had to rush off to prepare for an early morning deposition, regretted he couldn't talk longer. What's new?

I felt too ill and weary even to take a bath. For the next few hours I sat wrapped in a quilt, shivering and staring at the empty fireplace, wishing I had someone to feed me soup, stroke my forehead, and say I would be better soon. I dozed and woke, drifting in and out of dream fragments, while microscopic beings multiplied in my bloodstream.

Ryan buzzed at one-fifteen.

"Jesus, you look awful, Brennan."

"Thanks." I rewrapped my quilt. "I think I'm getting a cold."

"Why don't we do this tomorrow?"

"No way."

He looked at me strangely then followed me in, threw his jacket on the couch, and sat.

"Name's Jean Pierre Tanguay. Twenty-eight. Homeboy. Grew up in Shawinigan. Never married. No kids. He has one sister living in Arkansas. His mother died when he was nine. Lot of hostility there. Father was a plasterer, pretty much raised the two kids. The old man died in a car wreck when Tanguay was in college. Apparently it hit him pretty hard. He dropped out of school, stayed with the sister for a while, then wandered around down in the States. You ready for this? While he was in Dixie he got a call from God. Wanted to be a Jesuit or something, but flunked the interview. Apparently they didn't think his personality was priestly enough. Anyway, he resurfaced in Quebec in '88 and managed to get back into Bishops. Finished his degree about a year and a half later."

"So he's been in the area since '88?"

"Yep."

"That would put him back here about the time Pitre and Gautier were murdered."

Ryan nodded. "And he's been here ever since."

I had to swallow before I spoke.

"What's he say about the animals?"

"Claims he teaches biology. We've checked that out. Says he's building a reference collection for his classes. Boils down the carcasses and mounts the skeletons."

"That would explain the anatomy books."

"Might."

"Where does he get them?"

"Roadkills."

"Oh, Christ, Bertrand was right." I could picture him skulking around at night, scraping up corpses and dragging them home in plastic bags.

"He ever work in a butcher shop?"

"He didn't say. Why?"

"What did Claudel find out from the people he works with?"

"Nothing we didn't know. Keeps to himself, teaches his classes. Nobody really knows him all that well. And they're not thrilled at a call late in the evening."

"Sounds like Grammama's profile."

"The sister says he's always been antisocial. Can't remember him having friends. But she's nine years older, doesn't remember much about him as a kid. She did throw us one interesting tidbit."

"Yes"

Ryan smiled. "Tanguay's impotent."

"The sister volunteered that?"

"She thought it might explain his antisocial tendencies. Sis thinks he's harmless, just suffers from low self-esteem. She's big into the self-help literature. Knows all the jargon."

I didn't reply. In my mind I was seeing lines from two autopsy reports.

"That makes sense. Adkins and Morisette-Champoux tested negative for sperm."

"Bingo."

"How did he become impotent?"

"Combination congenital and trauma. He was born a one-baller, then wrecked it in a soccer accident. Some freak thing where another player was carrying a pen. Tanguay caught it with his one good nut. Bye-bye spermatogenesis."

"And that's why he's a hermit?"

"Hey. Maybe Sis is right."

"Could explain his lack of sparkle with the girls." I thought of Jewel's comments. And Julie.

"And everyone else."

"Isn't it odd he'd choose teaching?" Ryan mused. "Why work in a setting where you have to interact with so many people? If you really feel inadequate, why not choose something less threatening, more private? Computers? Or lab work?"

"I'm not a psychologist, but teaching might be perfect. You don't interact with equals—you know, with adults; you interact with kids. You're the one in charge. You have the power. Your classroom is your little kingdom and the kids have to do what

you say. No way they're going to ridicule or sec-
ond-guess you."

"At least not to your face."

"Could be the perfect balance for him. Satisfy
his need for power and control by day, feed his
sexual fantasies at night."

"And that's the best-case scenario," I said.
"Think of the opportunities for voyeurism, or even
for physical contact that he has with those kids."

"Yeah."

We sat in silence for a while, Ryan's eyes sweeping the room much as they had in Tanguay's apartment. He looked exhausted.

"Guess the surveillance unit isn't necessary anymore," I said.

"Yeah." He stood.

I walked him to the door.

"What's your take on him, Ryan?"

He didn't answer right away. Then he spoke
very carefully.

"He claims he's innocent as Little Orphan
Annie, but he's nervous as hell. He's hiding something. By tomorrow we'll know what's in the little
country getaway. We'll use that and hit him with
the whole thing. He'll roll over."

When he left I took a heavy dose of cold medicine and slept soundly for the first time in weeks.
If I dreamed, I couldn't remember.

The next day I felt better, but not well enough
to go to the lab. Maybe it was avoidance, but I
stayed home. Birdie was the only one I wanted
to see.

I kept busy reading a student thesis and responding to correspondence I'd been ignoring for
weeks. Ryan called around one as I was unloading

the dryer. I knew from his voice things weren't going well.

"Crime scene turned the cabin inside out and came up empty. Nothing there to suggest the guy even cheats at solitaire. No knives. No guns. No snuff films. None of Dobzhansky's victim souvenirs. No jewelry, clothing, skulls, body parts. One dead squirrel in the refrigerator. That's it. Otherwise, zipp-o."

"Signs of digging?"

"Nothing."

"Is there a toolshed or a basement where he might have saws or old blades?"

"Rakes, hoes, wooden crates, an old chain saw, a broken wheelbarrow. Standard garden stuff. And enough spiders to populate a small planet. Apparently Gilbert's going to need therapy."

"Is there a crawl space?"

"Brennan, you're not listening."

"Luminol?" I asked, depressed.

"Clean."

"Newspaper clippings?"

"No."

"Is there anything to tie this place to the room we busted on Berger?"

"No."

"To St. Jacques?"

"No."

"To Gabby?"

"No."

"To *any* of the victims?"

He didn't answer.

"What do you think he does out there?"

"Fishes and thinks about his missing nut."

"What now?"

"Bertrand and I are going up to have a long talk with Monsieur Tanguay. Time to drop some names and start turning up the heat. I still think he'll give it up."

"Does it add up to you?"

"Maybe. Maybe Bertrand's idea isn't so bad. Maybe Tanguay's one of these split personalities. One side is the biology teacher who lives clean, fishes, and collects specimens for his students. The other side has uncontrollable rage against women and feels sexually inadequate, so he gets his rocks off stalking them and beating them to death. Maybe he keeps the two personalities apart, even to the extent of having a separate place for the stalker to enjoy his fantasies and admire his souvenirs. Hell, maybe Tanguay doesn't even know he's nuts."

"Not bad. Mr. Peepers and Mr. Creeper."

"Who?"

"Never mind. Old sitcom." I told him what I'd found out with Lacroix.

"Why didn't you tell me about this sooner?"

"You're a little hard to pin down, Ryan."

"So Rue Berger is definitely tied in."

"Why do you think there were no prints there?"

"Shit, Brennan, I don't know. Maybe Tanguay's just slick as black ice. If it's any comfort to you Claudel's already got this guy convicted."

"Why?"

"I'll let him tell you. Look, I've got to get up there."

"Keep in touch."

I finished my letters and decided to take them to the post office. I checked the refrigerator. My pork chops and ground beef wouldn't do for Katy. I smiled, remembering the day she announced she'd no longer eat meat. My fourteen-year-old zealot vegetarian. I thought she'd last three months. It had been over five years.

I made a mental list. Humus. Tabouli. Cheese. Fruit juices. No sodas for my Katy. How had I produced this child?

The scratch in my throat was back and I felt hot again, so I decided to stop by the gym. I'll blast these buggers with exercise and steam, I thought. One of us will come out the victor.

The exercise turned out to be a bad idea. After ten minutes on the StairMaster my legs trembled and perspiration poured down my face. I had to quit.

The steam had mixed results. It soothed my throat and released the bands that squeezed my forehead and facial bones. But as I sat there with the vapor swirling around me, my mind reached for something to play with. Tanguay. I ran through what Ryan had said, Bertrand's theory, J.C.'s prediction, and what I knew. Something about Tanguay bothered me. As my thoughts gathered speed I could feel myself tensing. The gloves. Why had I blocked their relevance before?

Did Tanguay's physical handicap really lead him to sexual fantasies that ended in violence? Was he really a man with a desperate need to control? Was killing the ultimate act of control for him? *I can just watch you, or I can hurt you or even kill you?* Did he also play out the fantasy with animals? With Julie? Then why murder? Did he keep the violence in check, then suddenly succumb to a need to act out? Was Tanguay the product of abandonment by his mother? His deformity? A bad chromosome? Something else?

And why Gabby? She didn't fit the picture. He knew her. She was one of the few who would talk to me. I felt a wave of anguish.

Yes. Of course she fit the picture. A picture that included me. I found Grace Damas. I identified Isabelle Gagnon. I was interfering, challenging his authority. His manhood. Killing Gabby vented his rage against me and reestablished his sense of control. What next? Did the picture mean he would have gone for my daughter?

A teacher. A killer. A man who likes to fish. A man who likes to mutilate. My mind continued to drift. I closed my eyes and felt heat trapped below the lids. Bright colors swam back and forth, like goldfish in a pond.

A teacher. Biology. Fishing.

Again the nagging. It was there. Come on. Come on. What? A teacher. A teacher. That's it. A teacher. Since 1991. St. Isidor's. Yes. Yes. We know that. So what? My head was too heavy to think. Then:

The CD-ROM. I'd forgotten all about it. I grabbed for my towel. Maybe there was something there.

39

I WAS PERSPIRING HEAVILY and felt weak all over, but I managed to drive. Bonehead move, Brennan. Microbes win this one. Reduce your speed. You don't want to be stopped. Get home. Find it. There's got to be something.

I flew along Sherbrooke, circled the block, and shot down the drive. The garage door was beeping again. Damn. Why can't Winston fix that? I parked the car and hurried to my apartment. Check the dates.

A satchel rested on the floor outside my door.

"Shit. Now what?"

I looked down at the backpack. Black leather. Made by Coach. Expensive. A gift from Max Ferranti. A gift to Katy. It was lying outside my door.

My heart froze in my chest.

Katy!

I opened the door and called her name. No answer. I punched in the security code and tried again. Silence.

I raced from room to room, searching for signs of my daughter, knowing I would find none. Did she remember to bring her key? If she had, she wouldn't have left her pack in the hall. She had been here, found me not home, left her pack, and gone somewhere.

I stood in the bedroom, trembling, a victim of virus and fear. Think, Brennan. Think! I tried. It wasn't easy.

She arrived and couldn't get in. She's gone for coffee, or window shopping, or to look for a phone. She'll call in a few minutes.

But if she didn't have the key, how did she get through the outer door into the corridor to my unit door? The garage. She must have come through the pedestrian door into the garage, the one that's not latching as it closes.

The phone!

I ran to the living room. No message. Could it be Tanguay? Did he have her?

That's impossible. He's in jail.

The teacher is in jail. But he's not the one. The teacher isn't the one. Or is he? Did he keep the Rue Berger room? Did he bury the glove with Katy's picture in Gabby's grave?

The fear sent a wave of nausea rising up my esophagus. I swallowed and my swollen throat screamed in protest.

Check the facts, Brennan. They may have been holidays.

I booted the computer with shaking hands, my fingers barely able to work the keys. The spreadsheet filled the screen. Dates. Times.

Francine Morisette-Champoux was killed in January. She died between 10 A.M. and noon. It was a Thursday.

Isabelle Gagnon disappeared in April, between 1 and 4 P.M. It was a Friday.

Chantale Trottier disappeared on an afternoon in October. She was last seen at her school in Centre-ville, miles from the west island.

They died or disappeared during the week. During the day. The school day. Trottier may have been abducted after school hours. The other two were not.

I grabbed the phone.

Ryan was out.

I slammed the receiver. My head felt like lead and my thoughts were coming in slow motion.

I tried another number.

"Claudel."

"Monsieur Claudel, this is Dr. Brennan."

He didn't answer.

"Where is St. Isidor's?"

He hesitated, and I didn't think he was going to answer.

"Beaconsfield."

"That's what, about thirty minutes from downtown?"

"Without traffic."

"Do you know what the school hours are?"

"What's this about?"

"Can I just have an answer?" I was pushing the envelope and about to crack. My voice must have told him.

"I can ask."

"Also, find out if Tanguay ever missed any days, if he called in sick or took personal leave, particularly on the days Morisette-Champoux and Gagnon were killed. They'll have a record. They'd have needed a substitute unless school was not in session for some reason."

"I'm going out there tom—"

"Now. I need it now!" I was poised on the edge of hysteria, toes clutching the end of the board. Don't make me jump.

I could hear his face muscles harden. Go ahead, Claudel. Hang up. I'll have your ass.

"I'll get back to you."

I sat on the edge of the bed, staring numbly at dust playing tag in a shaft of sunlight.

Move.

I went to the bathroom and splashed cold water on my face. Then I fished a plastic square from my briefcase and returned to the computer. The case was labeled with the Rue Berger address and the date 94/06/24. I raised the lid, removed a CD-ROM disk, and set it in the drive.

I opened a program for image viewing, bringing up a row of icons. I chose *Album* then *Open,* and a single album name appeared in the window. *Berger.abm.* I double-clicked and three rows of pictures filled the screen, each displaying six still photos of St. Jacques's apartment. A line at the bottom told me the album contained a hundred and twenty shots.

I clicked to maximize the first image. Rue Berger. The second and third showed the street from different angles. Next, the apartment building, front and back. Then the corridor leading to the St. Jacques apartment. Views of the apartment's interior started with image twelve.

I moved through the pictures, scrutinizing every detail. My head pounded. My shoulder and back muscles were like high-tension wires. I was back there again. The suffocating heat. The fear. The odors of filth and corruption.

Image by image I searched. For what? I wasn't sure. It was all there. The *Hustler* centerfolds. The newspapers. The city map. The staircase landing.

The filthy toilet. The greasy countertop. The Burger King cup. The bowl of SpaghettiOs.

I stopped, stared at the still life. File 102. A grimy plastic bowl. Fatty white rings congealing in red sludge. A fly, front legs clasped as if in prayer. An orange boulder rising from the sauce and pasta.

I squinted, leaned in. Could I be seeing what I thought I was seeing? There. Coursing across the orange chunk. My heart pounded. It couldn't be. We couldn't be that lucky.

I double-clicked, and a dotted line appeared. I dragged the cursor, and the line became a rectangle, its borders a string of rotating dots. I positioned the rectangle directly over the orange blob and zoomed in, magnifying the image again and again. Double. Triple. Up to eight times its actual size. I watched as the faint parabola I had spotted became an arched trail of dots and dashes.

I zoomed out and examined the entire arc.

"Oh, Jesus."

Using the image editor, I manipulated the brightness and contrast, modified the hue and saturation. I tried reversing the color, changing each pixel to its complement. I used a command to emphasize edges, sharpening the tiny trail against the orange background.

I leaned back and stared. It is. I inhaled deeply. Sweet Jesus, it really is.

With a trembling hand I reached for the phone.

A recorded message told me Bergeron was still on vacation. I was on my own.

I sifted the possibilities. I'd seen him do it several times. I could try. I had to know.

I looked up another number.

"Centre de Détention Parthenais."

"This is Tempe Brennan. Is Andrew Ryan there? He'd be with a prisoner named Tanguay."

"Un instant. Gardez la ligne."

Voices in the background. Come on. Come on.

"Il n'est pas ici."

Damn. I looked at my watch. "Is Jean Bertrand there?"

"Oui. Un instant."

More voices. Clatter.

"Bertrand."

I identified myself, explained what I'd found.

"No shit. What did Bergeron say?"

"He's on vacation until next Monday."

"Cheese, that's beautiful. Kind of like your false starts, eh? What do you want me to do?"

"Find a piece of plain Styrofoam and get Tanguay to bite down on it. Don't stick it too far into his mouth. I just need the front six teeth. Have him bite edge to edge so you get nice clean tooth marks, one arch on each side of the plate. Then I want you to take the Styrofoam downstairs to Marc Dallair in photography. He's way in back, behind ballistics. You got that?"

"Yeah. Yeah. How do I get Tanguay to agree to this?"

"That's your problem. Figure something out. If he's screaming innocent he should be delighted."

"Where am I supposed to come up with Styrofoam at four-forty in the afternoon?"

"Go buy yourself a bloody Big Mac, Bertrand. I don't know. Just get it. I've got to catch Dallair before he leaves. Get moving!"

Dallair was waiting for an elevator when my call came. He took it at the reception desk.

"I need a favor."

"Oui."

"Within the hour Jean Bertrand will bring bite mark specimens to your office. I need to have the image scanned into a Tif file and sent to me electronically as soon as possible. Can you do that?"

There was a long pause. In my mind I could see him glance at the elevator clock.

"Does this have to do with Tanguay?"

"Yes."

"Sure. I'll wait."

"Angle the light across the Styrofoam as close to parallel as possible to really bring the marks out. And be sure to include a scale, a ruler or something. And please make sure the image is exactly one to one."

"No problem. I think I have an ABFO ruler here somewhere."

"Perfect." I gave him my e-mail address and asked him to call when he'd sent the file.

Then I waited. Seconds crept by with glacial slowness. No phone. No Katy. The digits on the clock glowed green. I heard them change. Click, click, click as the rotors turned.

When the phone rang I grabbed it.

"Dallair."

"Yes." I swallowed and the pain was excruciating.

"I sent the file about five minutes ago. It's called *Tang.tif.* It's compressed, so you'll have to unencode. I'll stick here until you've downloaded, to be sure there's no problem. Just send a reply. And good luck."

I thanked him and hung up. Moving to the computer I logged into my mailbox at McGill. The *Mail Waiting!!!* message glowed brightly. Ignoring other unread mail, I downloaded the file Dallair had sent, and returned it to its graphic format. A dental imprint arched across the screen, each tooth clearly visible against a white background. To the left and below the impression was a right-angle ABFO ruler. I sent Dallair a reply and logged off.

Back in the imaging program, I called up *Tang.tif* and double-clicked it open. Tanguay's impression filled the screen. I retrieved the bite mark in the Rue Berger cheese, and tiled the two images side by side.

Next I converted both images to an RGB scale, to maximize the amount of information in the pictures. I adjusted tone, brightness, contrast, and saturation. Finally, using the image editor I sharpened the edges on the Styrofoam impression as I had with the indentations in the cheese.

For the type of comparison I planned to try, both images had to be to the same scale. I got out a needle point caliper and checked the ruler in the Tanguay photo. The distance between hash marks was exactly one millimeter. Good. The image was one to one.

There was no ruler in the Berger photo. Now what?

Use something else. Go back to the full image. There has to be a known.

There was. The Burger King cup touched the bowl adjacent to the cheese, its red and yellow logo clear and recognizable. Perfect.

I ran to the kitchen. Let it still be here! Throwing open the cabinet doors, I rummaged through the trash under the sink.

Yes! I washed off the coffee grounds and carried the cup to the computer. My hands trembled as I spread the calipers. The upright arm of the logo B measured exactly 4 millimeters across.

Selecting the resize function in the image editor I clicked on one edge of the B on the Rue Berger cup, dragged the cursor to the far border, and clicked again. Having chosen my calibration points

I told the program to resize the entire image so that the B measured exactly 4 millimeters across at that position. Instantly the picture changed dimension.

Both images were now one to one. I looked at them side by side on the computer screen. The impression Tanguay had given showed a complete dental arch, with eight teeth on each side of the midline.

Only five teeth had registered in the cheese. Bertrand was right. It was like a false start. The teeth had gripped, slid, or been retracted, then bitten a chunk from behind the mark I was now seeing.

I stared at the trail of indentations. I was sure it was an upper arch. I could see two long depressions to either side of the midline, probably the central incisors. Lateral to them were two similarly oriented but slightly shorter grooves. Farther out, on the left of the arcade, was a small, circular dent, probably made by the canine. No other teeth had registered.

I ran my sweaty palms down the sides of my shirt, arched my back, and took a deep breath.

Okay. Position.

Choosing the *Effect* function, I clicked on *Rotate,* and slowly maneuvered Tanguay's dental impression, hoping to achieve the same orientation as the mark in the cheese. Click by click I rotated the central incisors clockwise. Forward, then backward, then forward again, a few degrees at a time, my anxiousness and clumsiness prolonging the process. It took an entire growing season, but at last I was satisfied. Tanguay's front teeth lay at the same angle and position as their counterparts in the cheese.

Back to the *Edit* menu. *Stitch* function. I selected the cheese as the active image and the Tanguay impression as the floating image. I set the the transparency level at 30 percent, and Tanguay's bite mark grew cloudy.

I clicked on a spot directly between Tanguay's front teeth, and again on the corresponding gap in the cheese arcade, defining a stitch point on each image. Satisfied, I activated the *Place* function, and the image editor superimposed Tanguay's bite mark directly over that in the cheese. Too opaque. The cheese trail was completely obliterated.

I raised the transparency level to 75 percent, and watched the Styrofoam dots and dashes fade to ghostly transparency. I now had a clear view of the dents and hollows in the cheese through the impression made by Tanguay.

Dear God.

I knew instantly the bites were not by the same person. No amount of manual manipulation or fine tuning of the images could alter that impression. The mouth that had bitten into the Styrofoam had not left the marks in the cheese.

Tanguay's dental arch was too narrow, the curve at the front much tighter than that preserved in the cheese. The composite image showed a horseshoe overlying a partial semicircle.

More striking, the person eating cheese at the Rue Berger flat had an irregular break to the right of the normal midline gap, and the adjacent tooth shot off at a thirty-degree angle, making the tooth row look like a picket fence. The cheese eater had a badly chipped central incisor, and a sharply rotated lateral.

Tanguay's teeth were even and uninterrupted. His bite showed neither of these traits. He had not bitten that cheese. Either Tanguay had entertained a guest at Rue Berger, or the Rue Berger apartment had nothing to do with Tanguay at all.

40

WHOEVER USED RUE BERger had killed Gabby. The gloves matched. The strong probability was that Tanguay was not that person. His teeth had not bitten the cheese. St. Jacques was not Tanguay.

"Who the hell are you?" I asked, my voice raspy in the silence of my empty home. Fears for Katy erupted full force. Why hadn't she called?

I tried Ryan at home. No answer. I tried Bertrand. He'd gone. I tried the task force room. No one.

I went to the yard and peeked through the fence at the pizza parlor across the street. The alley was empty. The surveillance team had been pulled. I was on my own.

I ran through my options. What could I do? Not much. I couldn't leave. I had to be here if Katy came back. *When* Katy came back.

I looked at the clock—7:10 P.M. The files. Back

to the files. What else could I do from inside these walls? My refuge had become my prison.

I changed clothes and went to the kitchen. Though my head was swimming, I took no medication. My mind was dull enough without sedation. I'd blast the germs with vitamin C. I got a can of frozen orange juice from the freezer and dug for the opener. Damn. Where is it? Too impatient to look for long, I grabbed a steak knife and sawed the top of the cardboard can to remove the metal lid. Pitcher. Water. Stir. You can do it. Clean up the mess later.

Moments later I was settled on the couch, tightly quilted, tissues and juice within arm's reach. I played with my eyebrow to hold my nerves together.

Damas. I descended into the file, revisiting names, places, and dates I'd visited before. The Monastère St. Bernard. Nikos Damas. Father Poirier.

Bertrand had done a follow-up on Poirier. I re-read it, my mind resisting concentration. The good father checked out. I reviewed the original interview, looking for other names to chase after, like clues in a road rally scavenger hunt. Next I'd re-hash dates.

Who was the caretaker? Roy. Emile Roy. I dug for his statement.

It wasn't there. I went through everything in the jacket. Nothing. Surely someone had talked to him. I couldn't recall seeing the report. Why wasn't it here?

I sat for a moment, the friction of my breath the only sound in my universe. The pre-idea sensation was back, like an aura presaging a migraine. The sense that I was missing something was stronger than ever, but the elusive fact would not come into focus.

I went back to Poirier's statement. Roy tends the building and grounds. Fixes the furnace, shovels the snow.

Shovels snow? At age eighty? Why not? George Burns could do it. Past images drifted into my mind. I thought of the apparition I'd had, alone in the car, Grace Damas's bones lying behind me in the rain-soaked woods.

I thought of my other dream that night. The rats. Pete. Isabelle Gagnon's head. Her grave. The priest. What had he said? Only those who worked for the church could enter its gates.

Could that be it? Is that how he got onto the grounds of the monastery and Le Grand Séminaire? Is our killer someone who works for the church?

Roy!

Right, Brennan, an eighty-year-old serial killer.

Should I wait to hear from Ryan? Where the hell is he? I pulled out the phone book with trembling hands. If I can find the caretaker's number, I'll call.

There was one E. Roy listed in St. Lambert.

"*Oui.*" A gravelly voice.

Be careful. Take your time.

"Monsieur Emile Roy?"

"*Oui.*"

I explained who I was and why I was calling. Yes, I had the right Emile Roy. I asked about his duties at the monastery. For a long time he said nothing. I could hear him wheezing, the breath drawing in and out like air through a blowhole. Finally:

"I don't want to lose my job. I take good care of the place."

"Yes. Do you do it by yourself?"

I heard his breath catch, as though a pebble had clogged the blowhole.

"I just need a little help from time to time. It don't cost them nothing more. I pay for it myself, out of my wages." He was almost whining.

"Who helps you, Monsieur Roy?"

"My nephew. He's a good boy. Mostly he does the snow. I was going to tell Father, but . . ."

"What's your nephew's name?

"Leo. He's not going to get in no trouble, is he? He's a good boy."

The receiver felt slick in my palm.

"Leo what?"

"Fortier. Leo Fortier. He's my sister's grandson."

His voice receded. I was pouring sweat. I said the necessary things and hung up, my mind flailing, my heart racing.

Calm down. It could be a coincidence. Being a caretaker and a part-time butcher's helper doesn't make one a killer. Think.

I looked at the clock and reached for the phone. Come on. Be there.

She picked up on the fourth ring.

"Lucie Dumont."

Yes!

"Lucie, I can't believe you're still there."

"I had some trouble with a program file. I was just leaving."

"There's something I need, Lucie. It's extremely important. You may be the only one who can get it for me."

"Yes?"

"I want you to run a check on someone. Do whatever it is you do to pull up everything there is on this guy. Can you do that?"

"It's late and I wa—"

"This is critical, Lucie. My daughter may be in danger. I really need this!"

I made no attempt to hide the desperation in my voice.

"I can link through to the SQ files and see if he's there. I have clearance. What do you want to know?"

"Everything."

"What can you give me?"

"Just a name."

"Anything else?"

"No."

"Who is it?"

"Fortier. Leo Fortier."

"I'll call you back. Where are you?"

I gave her the number and hung up.

I paced the apartment, crazy with fear for Katy. Was it Fortier? Had his psychotic rage fixed on me because I had thwarted him? Had he killed my friend to vent this rage? Did he plan the same for me? For my daughter? How did he know about my daughter? Had he stolen the photo of Katy and me from Gabby?

The cold, numbing fear went deep into my soul. I had the worst thoughts I've ever known. I pictured Gabby's last moments, imagined what she must have felt. The phone exploded into my train of thought.

"Yes!"

"It's Lucie Dumont."

"Yes." My heart was pounding so hard I thought she might hear it.

"Do you know how old your Leo Fortier is?"

"Uh . . . thirty, forty."

"I came up with two; one has a date of birth 2/9/62, so he'd be about thirty-two. The other was born 4/21/16, so he'd be, what . . . seventy-eight."

"Thirty-two," I said.

"That's what I thought, so I ran him. He's got a big jacket. Goes back to juvenile court. No felonies, but a string of misdemeanor problems and psychiatric referrals."

"What kind of problems."

"Caught for voyeurism at age thirteen." I could hear her fingers clicking on the keyboard "Vandalism. Truancy. There was an incident when he was fifteen. Kidnapped a girl and kept her for eighteen hours. No charges. You want it all?"

"What about recent things?"

Click. Clickety. Click. I could picture her leaning into the monitor, her pink lenses bouncing back the green glow.

"The most recent entry is 1988. Arrested for assault. Looks like a relative, victim has the same name. No jail time. Did six months in Pinel."

"When did he get out?"

"The exact date?"

"Do you have it?"

"Looks like November 12, 1988."

Constance Pitre died in December of 1988. The room was hot. My body was slick with sweat.

"Does the file list the name of his attending psychiatrist at Pinel?"

"There's reference to a Dr. M. C. LaPerrière. Doesn't say who he is."

"Is his number there?"

She gave it to me.

"Where is Fortier now?"

"The file ends in 1988. You want that address?"

"Yes."

I was on the verge of tears as I punched in a number and listened to a phone ring on the far northern end of the island of Montreal. *Composer,* they say in French. *Composer le numéro.* Compose yourself, Brennan. I tried to think what to say.

"L'hôpital Pinel. Puis-je vous aider?" A female voice.

"Dr. LaPerrière, *s'il vous plaît."* Please let him still work there.

"Un instant, s'il vous plaît."

Yes! He was still on staff. I was put on hold, then led through the same ritual by a second female voice.

"Qui est sur la ligne, s'il vous plaît?"

"Dr. Brennan."

The sound of more empty air. Then.

"Dr. LaPerrière." A female voice, this one sounding tired and impatient.

"I'm Dr. Temperance Brennan," I said, fighting to keep the tremor from my voice, "forensic anthropologist at the Laboratoire de Médecine Légale, and I'm involved in the investigation of a series of murders which have taken place over the past several years in the Montreal area. We have reason to believe one of your former patients may be involved."

"Yes." Wary.

I explained about the task force, and asked what she could tell me about Leo Fortier.

"Dr. . . . Brennan, is it? Dr. Brennan, you know I can't discuss a patient file on the basis of a phone call. Without court authorization, that would be a breach of confidentiality."

Stay cool. You knew that would be the response.

"Of course. And that authorization will be forthcoming, but we are in an urgent situation, Doctor, and we cannot delay in speaking with you. And at this point that authorization really isn't necessary. Women are dying, Dr. LaPerrière. They're being brutally murdered and disfigured. The individual

doing this is capable of extreme violence. He muti-
lates his victims. We think he's someone with tremendous rage against women, and someone with
enough intelligence to plan and carry out these killings. And we think he'll strike again soon." I swallowed, my mouth dry from fear. "Leo Fortier is a
suspect, and we need to know whether, in your
opinion, there is anything in Fortier's history to
suggest he could fit this profile? The paperwork for
production of his records will catch up, but if you
have a recollection of this patient, information you
provide now may help us stop the killer before he
strikes again."

I had wrapped another quilt around myself, this
one a blanket of icy calm. I could not let her hear
the fear in my voice.

"I simply cannot . . ."

My blanket was slipping.

"I have a child, Dr. LaPerrière? Do you?"

"What?" Affront vied with the weariness.

"Chantale Trottier was sixteen years old. He
beat her to death, then cut her up and left her in
a dump."

"Jesus Christ."

Though I'd never met Marie Claude LaPerrière,
her voice painted a vivid scene, a triptych done in
metal gray, institutional green, and dirty brick.

I could picture her: middle-aged, disillusionment
etched deeply in her face. She worked for a system
in which she'd long ago lost faith, a system unable
to understand, much less curb, the cruelty of a society gone mad on its fringes. The gang bang victims.
The teenagers with vacant eyes and bleeding wrists.
The babies scalded and scarred by cigarette burns.
The fetuses floating in bloody toilet bowls. The old,
starved and tethered in their own excrement. The
women with their battered faces and pleading eyes.

Once, she'd believed she could make a difference. Experience had convinced her otherwise.

But she'd taken an oath. To what? For whom? The dilemma was now as familiar to her as her idealism had once been. I heard her take a deep breath.

"Leo Fortier was committed for a six-month period in 1988. During that time I was his attending psychiatrist."

"Do you remember him?"

"Yes."

I waited, heart pounding. I heard her click a lighter open and shut, then breathe deeply.

"Leo Fortier came to Pinel because he beat his grandmother with a lamp." She spoke in short sentences, treading carefully. "The old woman needed over a hundred stitches. She refused to press charges against her grandson. When Fortier's period of involuntary commitment ended, I recommended continued treatment. He refused."

She paused to select just the right words.

"Leo Fortier watched his mother die while his grandmother stood by. Grandma then raised him, engendering in him an extremely negative self-image that resulted in an inability to form appropriate social relationships.

"Leo's grandmother punished him excessively, but protected him from the consequences of his acts outside the home. By the time Leo was a teen, his activities suggest he was suffering severe cognitive distortion along with an overwhelming need to control. He'd developed an excessive sense of entitlement, and exhibited intense narcissistic rage when thwarted.

"Leo's need to control, his repressed love and hatred toward his grandmother, and his increasing social isolation led him to spend more and more time in his own fantasy world. He had also developed all the classic defense mechanisms. Denial, repression, projection. Emotionally and socially, he was extremely immature."

"Do you think he is capable of the behavior I have described?" I was surprised at how steady my voice sounded. Inside I was churning, terrified for my daughter.

"At the time I worked with Leo his fantasies were fixed and definitely negative. Many involved violent sexual behaviors."

She paused and I heard another deep breath.

"In my opinion, Leo Fortier is a very dangerous man."

"Do you know where he lives now?" This time my voice trembled.

"I have had no contact with him since his release."

I was about to say good-bye when I thought of another question. "How did Leo's mother die?"

"At the hands of an abortionist," she answered.

When I hung up, my mind was racing. I had a name. Leo Fortier worked with Grace Damas, had access to church properties, and was extremely dangerous. Now what?

I heard a soft rumble and noticed that the room had turned purple. I opened the French doors and looked out. Heavy clouds had gathered over the city, casting the evening into premature darkness. The wind had shifted and the air was dense with the smell of rain. Already the cypress was whipping to and fro, and leaves were dancing along the ground.

One of my earliest cases unexpectedly came to mind. Nellie Adams, five years old, missing. I'd heard it on the news. There had been a violent thunderstorm the day she was reported missing. I'd thought of her that night from the safety of my bed. Was she out there, alone and terrified in that storm? Six weeks later I'd identified her from a skull and rib fragments.

Please, Katy! Please come back now!

Stop it! Call Ryan.

Lightning flickered on the wall. I latched the doors shut and walked over to a lamp. Nothing. The timer, Brennan. It's set for eight. It's still too early.

I slid my hand behind the couch and flicked the timer button. Nothing. I tried the wall switch. Nothing. I felt my way along the wall and rounded the corner into the kitchen. The lights would not respond. With growing alarm, I stumbled down the hall and into the bedroom. The clock was dark. No power. I stood for a moment, my mind grasping at explanations. Had there been a lightning strike? Had the wind felled branches onto a feeder line?

I realized the apartment was unnaturally quiet, and closed my eyes to listen. A mélange of sounds filled the vacuum left by stilled appliances. The storm outside. My own heartbeat. And then, something else. A faint click. A door closing? Birdie? Where was it? The other bedroom?

I crossed to the bedroom window. Lights glowed along the street and from the apartments on De Maisonneuve. I ran back down the hall to the courtyard doors. I could see the lights in my neighbors' windows gleaming through the rain. It was just me! Only my power was off! Then I remembered: the safety alarm had not beeped when I opened the French doors. I had no security system!

I jumped for the telephone.

The line was dead.

41

I HUNG UP AND MY EYES swept through the dimness around me. No threatening form met them, but I could sense another presence. I trembled and then tensed, my thoughts running through my options like a deck of cards.

Stay calm, I told myself. Make a break for it through the French doors into the garden.

But the garden gate was locked and the key was in the kitchen. I pictured the fence. Could I scale it? If not, at least in the garden I'd be outside and someone might hear me scream. *Would* anyone hear? The storm was raging out there.

I strained to hear the slightest sound, my heart banging against my ribs like a moth against a screen. My mind flew in a thousand directions. I thought of Margaret Adkins, of Pitre and the others, of their slashed throats, their sightless, staring eyes.

Take action, Brennan. Make a move! Don't wait

to be his victim! My fear for Katy was making rational thought difficult. What if I get away and he waits for her? No, I told myself, he won't wait for anything. He needs to be in control. He'll disappear and plan for next time.

I swallowed and nearly screamed in pain, my throat parched from illness and fear. I decided to run, to throw open the French doors, and fling myself into the rain and freedom. My body rigid, every muscle and tendon taut, I sprang for the door. In five steps I rounded the couch and was there, one hand on the handle, the other turning the latch. The brass felt cold in my feverish fingers.

From nowhere a hand like a ham whipped across my face and jerked me back, pressing my skull against a body solid as concrete, crushing my lips and twisting my jaw out of alignment. The hard palm covered my mouth, and a familiar scent filled my nostrils. The hand felt unnaturally smooth and slippery. From the corner of my eye I saw a glint of metal, and felt something cold against my right temple. My fear was like white noise, overpowering my mind and obliterating everything beyond my body and his.

"Well, Dr. Brennan. I believe we have a date this evening." Spoken in English, but with a French pronunciation. Soft and low, like a love song with the lyrics recited.

I struggled, my body twisting, my hands flailing. His grip was like a vise. Desperate, I lashed out and clawed the air.

"No, no. Don't fight. You're with me tonight. There's no one else in the world but us." I could feel his heat against my neck as he pressed me back against him. Like his hand, his body felt oddly smooth and compact. Panic overwhelmed me. I felt helpless.

I couldn't think. I couldn't speak. I didn't know whether to beg, to fight, to reason with him. He held my head immobile, his hand mashing my lips against my teeth. I could taste blood in my mouth.

"Nothing to say? Well, we'll talk later." As he spoke he did something odd with his lips, wetting them then sucking them back against his teeth.

"I brought you something." I felt his body twist, and the hand came off my mouth. "A present."

A slithery metallic sound, then he pulled my head forward and slid something cold past my face and onto my neck. Before I could react, his arm jerked and I was yanked into a place far beyond thinking, a place of bursting light and choking and gagging. At this point I could do nothing but categorize my pain according to the moves he made.

He released, then pulled up hard on the chain once more, crushing my larynx and twisting my jaw and vertebrae. The pain was unendurable.

I clawed and gasped for air and he spun me, grabbed my hands, and circled my wrists with another chain. He pulled it tight with one sharp tug, clipped it to the neck chain, then yanked and held both high above his head. Fire roared through my lungs and my brain begged for air. I fought to remain conscious, tears running down my face.

"Oh, did that hurt? I'm sorry."

He lowered the chain and my tortured throat gasped for breath.

"You look like a big fish dangling there, sucking for air."

I was facing him now, his eyes but inches from mine. Through my pain I registered little. His could have been anyone's face, an animal's face. The corners of his mouth quivered, as though teased by an inner joke. He circled my lips with the tip of a knife.

My mouth was so dry my tongue stuck to it when I tried to talk. I swallowed.

"I'd li—"

"Shut up! You shut your fucking mouth! I know what you'd like. I know what you think about me. I know what you all think about me. You think I'm some kind of genetic freak that ought to be exterminated. Well, I'm as good as anybody. And I'm in charge here."

He gripped the knife so hard his hand trembled. It looked ghostly pale in the gloom of the hallway, the knuckles bulging white and round. Surgical gloves! That's what I'd smelled. The blade bit into my cheek, and I could feel warmth trickle down my chin. I felt utterly without hope.

"Before I'm through you'll be tearing your panties off, you'll want me so bad. But that's later, *Doctor* Brennan. For now, you speak when I tell you to."

He was breathing hard, his nostrils white. His left hand toyed with the choke chain, wrapping and rewrapping the links around his palm.

"Now. Tell me." Calm again. "What are you thinking?" His eyes looked cold and hard, like some Mesozoic mammal.

"You think I'm crazy?"

I held my tongue. Rain pounded the window behind him.

He pulled in the chain, drawing my face close to his. His breath brushed the sweat on my skin.

"Worried about your daughter?"

"What do you know about my daughter?" I choked.

"I know everything about you, Dr. Brennan." His voice was low and syrupy again. It felt like something obscene crawling in my ear. I swallowed through my pain, needing to speak, not wanting to provoke him. His moods were swinging like a hammock in a hurricane.

"Do you know where she is?"

"I might." He raised the chain again, this time slowly, forcing my chin into full extension, then he drew the knife across my throat in a slow backhand motion.

Lightning flashed and his hand jumped. "Tight enough?" he asked.

"Please—" I gagged.

He eased off on the chain, allowing me to drop my chin. I swallowed and took a deep breath. My throat was on fire and my neck was bruised and swollen. I raised my hands to rub it, and he jerked them down with the wrist chain. His mouth did another rodent twitch.

"Nothing to say?" He stared at me, his eyes black and all pupil. The lower lids quivered, like his lips.

Terrified, I wondered what the others had done. What Gabby had done.

He lifted the chain above my head and began to increase the tension, a child torturing a puppy. A homicidal child. I remembered Alsa. I remembered the marks in Gabby's flesh. What had J.S. said? How could I use it?

"Please. I'd like to talk to you. Why don't we go somewhere where we can have a drink and—?"

"Bitch!"

His arm snapped and the chain tightened savagely. Flames shot through my head and neck. I raised my hands in reflex, but they were cold and useless.

"The great *Doctor* Brennan doesn't drink, does she? Everyone knows that."

Through my tears I could see his lids jump

wildly. He was reaching the edge. Oh, God! Help me!

"You're like all the others. You think I'm a fool, don't you?"

My brain was sending two messages: Get away! Find Katy!

He held me while the wind moaned and rain lashed the windows. Far away I heard a horn honk. The smell of his sweat mingled with my own. His eyes, glassy with madness, bore into my face. My heart was beating wildly.

Then something plupped in the silence of the bedroom, and his lids tightened momentarily as he paused. Birdie appeared in the doorway and emitted a noise between a squeak and a growl. Fortier's eyes shifted to the white shadow and I took my chance.

I shot my leg out and brought it up between his legs, concentrating all my fear and hatred in the force of that blow. My shin slammed hard into his crotch. He screamed and doubled over. I jerked the chain ends from his hand, spun, and flung myself down the hall, terror and desperation propelling me forward. I felt as if I were moving in slow motion.

He recovered quickly, his scream of pain converted into a howl of anger.

"Bitch!"

I pitched down the narrow hall, nearly tripping over the dragging chain.

"You're dead, bitch!"

I could hear him behind me, lurching through the dark, breathing like a desperate animal. *"You're mine! You won't get away!"*

I staggered around the corner, twisting my hands, fighting to loosen the wrist chain. Blood pounded in my ears. I was a robot, my sympathetic nervous system working the controls.

"Cunt!"

He was between me and the front door, forcing me to cut through the kitchen! One thought drove me: Get to the French doors!

My right hand slipped free of the chain.

"Whore! You're mine!"

Two steps into the kitchen the pain slammed into me again and I thought my neck had snapped. My left arm flew up and my head whipped back. He had gotten a hand on the trailing neck chain. I felt my insides heave as my air supply was again choked off.

With my unbound hand I tried to free my throat, but the harder I clawed the tighter he pulled. I twisted and pulled, but the chain only cut deeper.

Slowly, he reeled in the chain, drawing me back toward him. I could smell his frenzy, feel his body tremble in the shake of the chain. Loop by loop he shortened my leash. I began to feel dizzy, and thought I was fainting.

"You'll pay for that, bitch." His voice was a hiss.

My face and fingertips tingled from lack of oxygen, and my ears filled with a hollow ringing. The room began to heave about me. A spatter of dots formed in the middle of my field of vision, coalesced, then spread outward as a black cumulus. Through the growing cloud I saw ceramic tile rise toward me, as if in slow motion. I watched my hands reach out as I floated forward, an insensible host tumbling with its parasite rider.

As we pitched forward, my stomach struck a section of counter, and my head slammed into an overhead cabinet. He lost his grip on the chain, but pushed up hard behind me.

He spread his legs and molded his body against

mine, pressing me against the counter. The edge of the dishwasher cut painfully across my left pelvic bone, but I could breathe.

His chest heaved, and every fiber of his tissue felt taut, like a slingshot stretched to deliver. With a looping wrist motion he retrieved his grip on the chain and forced my head into a backward arch. Then he reached across my throat and placed the tip of the knife under the angle of my jaw. My carotid throbbed against cold steel. I felt his breath on my left cheek.

He held me for an eternity, head back, hands straight out and useless, like a carcass dangling on a hook. I seemed to be watching myself from across a wide gulf, a spectator, horrified but powerless to help.

I got my right hand onto the counter, trying to push against it to elevate myself and slacken the chain. Then I touched something on the countertop. The orange juice container. The knife.

Silently, my fingers wrapped around the handle. I moaned and tried to sob. Divert his attention.

"Quiet, bitch! We're going to play a game now. You like games, don't you?"

Carefully I rotated the knife, gagging loudly to cover the tiniest scrape.

My hand trembled, hesitated.

Then I saw the women again, saw what he'd done to them. I felt their terror and knew their final desperation.

Do it!

Adrenaline spread through my chest and limbs like lava rolling down a mountainside. If I was going to die, it would not be like a rat in a hole. I would die charging the enemy, guns blazing. My mind refocused and I became an active participant in my own fate. I gripped the knife, blade upward, and estimated the angle. Then I thrust across my body and over my left shoulder with all the strength that fear, desperation, and vengeance could muster.

The point struck bone, slipped a little, then plunged into mushy softness. His earlier scream was nothing compared with what now ripped from his throat. As he lurched backward his left hand dropped and his right hand passed across my throat. The chain end slithered to the floor, releasing its death hold.

I felt a dull ache across my throat, then something wet. It didn't matter. All I wanted was air. I gulped hungrily, reaching up to loosen the links and feeling what I knew must be my own blood.

From behind me, another scream, high-pitched, primal, like the death cry of a feral animal. Panting and holding the counter for support, I turned to look.

He stumbled backward across the kitchen, one hand to his face, the other thrown out in an attempt at balance. Horrible sounds gurgled from his open mouth as he slammed against the far wall and slid slowly to the floor. The outthrust hand left a black streak snaking down the plaster. For a moment his head rolled back and forth, then a thin moan rose from his throat. His hands dropped and his head settled, chin down, eyes fixed on the floor.

I stood frozen in the sudden stillness, the only sounds my rasping breath and his fading whimpers. Through my pain, my surroundings began to register. Sink. Stove. Refrigerator, deathly still. Something slippery underfoot.

I stared at the form slumped inert on my kitchen floor, legs splayed forward, chin on chest, back propped against the wall. In the dimness I could see a dark smear trailing down his chest toward his left hand.

Lightning sparked like a welder's torch, and illuminated my handiwork.

His body looked sleek, smoothed by the peacock blue membrane that encased it. A blue and red cap stretched across his scalp, flattening his hair and turning his head into a featureless oval.

The handle of the steak knife rose from his left eye like a flag pin on a putting green. Blood streamed down his face and throat, darkening the spandex on his chest. He had stopped moaning.

I gagged and the flotilla of spots sailed back into my field of vision. My knees buckled and I tried to lean against the counter.

I tried to breathe more deeply and raised my hands to my throat to remove the chain. I felt a warm slipperiness. I lowered one hand and stared. Oh yes. I'm bleeding.

I was moving toward the door, thinking of Katy, of getting help, when a sound froze me in place. The slither of steel links! The room flickered white, black.

Too beaten to run, I turned. A dark silhouette moved silently toward me.

I heard my own voice, then saw a thousand spots, and the black cloud rolled over everything.

Sirens wailing in the distance. Voices. Pressure on my throat.

I opened my eyes to light and movement. A form loomed over me. A hand pressed something against my neck.

Who? Where? My own living room. Memory. Panic. I struggled to sit up.

"Attention. Attention. Elle se leve."

Hands pressed me gently down.

Then, a familiar voice. Unexpected. Out of context.

"Don't move. You've lost a lot of blood. There is an ambulance on the way."

Claudel.

"Where. I . . . ?"

"You're safe. We've got him."

"What's left of him." Charbonneau.

"Katy?"

"Lie back. You've got a gash on your throat and right neck and if you move your head, it bleeds. You've lost a good amount of blood and we don't want you to lose any more."

"My daughter?"

Their faces floated above me. A bolt of lightning flared, turning them white.

"Katy?" My heart pounded. I couldn't breathe.

"She's fine. Anxious to see you. Friends are with her."

"Tabernac." Claudel moved away from the couch. *"Où est cette ambulance?"*

He strode into the hall, glanced at something on the kitchen floor, then back at me, an odd expression on his face.

A siren's wail grew louder, filled my tiny street. Then a second. I saw red and blue pulse outside the French doors.

"Relax now," said Charbonneau. "They're here. We'll see your daughter is looked after. It's over."

42

THERE'S STILL A GAP IN MY official memory files. The next two days are there, but they're fuzzy and out of synch, a disjointed collage of images and feelings that come and go, but have no rational pattern.

A clock with numbers that were never the same. Pain. Hands tugging, probing, lifting my eyelids. Voices. A light window. A dark window.

Faces. Claudel in harsh fluorescence. Jewel Tambeaux silhouetted against a white hot sun. Ryan in yellow lamplight, slowly turning pages. Charbonneau dozing, TV blue flickering across his features.

I had enough pharmaceuticals in me to numb the Iraqi army, so it's hard to sort drugged sleep from waking reality. The dreams and memories spin and swirl like a cyclone circling its eye. No matter how often I retrace my steps through that time, I cannot sort out the images.

Coherence returned on Friday.

I opened my eyes to bright sunlight, saw a nurse adjusting an IV drip, and knew where I was. Someone to my right was making soft clicking noises. I turned my head and pain shot through it. A dull throbbing in my neck told me further movement was ill advised.

Ryan sat in a vinyl chair, entering something into a pocket organizer.

"Am I going to live?" My words sounded slurred.

"*Mon Dieu.*" Smiling.

I swallowed and repeated the question. My lips felt stiff and swollen.

The nurse reached for my wrist, placed her fingertips on it, focused on her watch.

"That's what they say." Ryan slid the organizer into his shirt pocket, rose, and crossed to the bed. "Concussion, laceration of the right neck and throat region with significant loss of blood. Thirty-seven stitches, each carefully placed by a fine plastic surgeon. Prognosis: she'll live."

The nurse gave him a disapproving glance. "Ten minutes," she said, and left.

A flash of memory shot fear through the layer of drugs.

"Katy?"

"Relax. She'll be here in a while. She was in earlier, but you were out cold."

I looked a question mark at him.

"She showed up with a friend just before you left in the ambulance. Some kid she knows at McGill. She'd been dropped at your place sans key that afternoon, but talked her way through the outer door. Seems some of your neighbors aren't exactly security conscious." He hooked a thumb inside his belt. "But she couldn't get into your unit. She called you at the office, but no score. So she left her pack to flag you that she was in town, and reconnected with her friend. Sayonara, Mom.

"She meant to get back by dinnertime, but the storm hit, so the two of them hung tight at Hurley's and sipped a few. She tried to call, but couldn't get through. She nearly blew a valve when she arrived, but I was able to calm her down. One of the victim assistance officers is staying in close touch with her, making sure she knows what's up. Several people here offered to take her in, but she preferred to crash with her friend. She's been here every day and is going snake wanting to see you."

Despite my best efforts, tears of relief. A tissue and a kind look from Ryan. My hand looked strange against the green hospital blanket, as though it belonged to someone else. A plastic bracelet circled my wrist. I could see tiny flecks of blood under my nails.

More memory bytes. Lightning. A knife handle.

"Fortier?"

"Later."

"Now." The ache in my neck was intensifying. I knew I wouldn't feel like conversation for long. Also, Florence Nightingale would be back soon.

"He lost a lot of blood, but modern medicine saved the bastard. As I understand it, the blade slashed the orbit but then slid into the ethmoid without penetrating the cranium. He will lose his eye, but his sinuses should be great."

"You're a riot, Ryan."

"He got into your building through the faulty garage door, then picked your lock. No one was home, so he disabled the security system and the power. You didn't notice since your computer goes to battery when the power fails, and the regular phone isn't tied in to the electricity, just the portable. He must have cut the phone line right after you made your last call. He was probably in there when Katy tried the door and left her pack."

Another icicle of fear. A crushing hand. A choke collar.

"Where is he now?

"He's here."

I struggled to sit up and my stomach felt as if it were doing the same. Ryan gently pushed me back against the pillow.

"He's under heavy guard, Tempe. He's not going anywhere."

"St. Jacques?" I heard a tremor in my voice.

"Later."

I had a thousand questions, but it was too late. I was slipping back into the hollow where I'd been curled the past two days.

The nurse returned and shot Ryan a withering look. I didn't see him leave.

The next time I woke Ryan and Claudel were talking quietly by the window. It was dark outside. I'd been dreaming of Jewel and Julie.

"Was Jewel Tambeaux here earlier?"

They turned in my direction.

"She came on Thursday." Ryan.

"Fortier?"

"They've taken him off critical."

"Talking?"

"Yes."

"Is he St. Jacques?"

"Yes."

"And?"

"Maybe this should wait until you're stronger."

"Tell me."

The two exchanged glances, then approached. Claudel cleared his throat.

"Name's Leo Fortier. Thirty-two years old. Lives

off the island with his wife and two kids. Drifts from job to job. Nothing steady. He and Grace Damas had an affair back in 1991. Met at a butcher shop where they both worked."

"La Boucherie St. Dominique."

"Oui." Claudel gave me an odd look. "Things start going bad. She threatens to blow the whistle to wifey, starts dunning lover boy for money. He's had it, so he asks her to meet him at the shop after hours, kills her, and cuts her body up."

"Risky."

"The owner's out of town, place is closed up for a couple of weeks. All the equipment is there. Anyway, he cuts her up, hauls her out to St. Lambert, and buries her on the monastery grounds. Seems his uncle is custodian. Either the old man gave him a key or Fortier helped himself."

"Emile Roy."

"Oui."

Again the look.

"That isn't all," said Ryan. "He used the monastery to do Trottier and Gagnon. Took them there, killed them, dismembered their bodies in the basement. He cleaned up after himself, so Roy wouldn't suspect, but when Gilbert and the boys gave the cellar a Luminol spray this morning it lit up like halftime at the Orange Bowl."

"That's how he also had access to Le Grand Séminaire," I said.

"Yeah. Says he got that idea when he was following Chantale Trottier. Her father's condo is right around the corner. Roy keeps a board at the monastery with all kinds of church keys hanging on hooks, neatly marked. Fortier just lifted the one he wanted."

"Oh. And Gilbert has a chef's saw for you. Says it glows." Ryan.

He must have seen something in my face.

"When you're feeling better."

"I can hardly wait." I was trying, but my bruised brain was withdrawing again.

The nurse came in.

"This is police business," Claudel said.

She folded her arms and shook her head.

"Merde."

She ushered them out quickly, but returned in a moment. With Katy. My daughter crossed the room without a word and clasped both my hands in hers. Tears filled her eyes.

Softly, "I love you, Mom."

For a moment I just looked at her, a thousand emotions boiling inside me. Love. Gratitude. Helplessness. I cherished this child as no other being on earth. I desperately wished for her happiness. Her safety. I felt completely unable to assure her of either. I could feel tears of my own.

"And I love you, darling."

She dragged a chair close and sat alongside my bed, not releasing my hands. The fluorescent light gleamed a halo of blond around her head.

She cleared her throat. "I'm staying at Monica's. She's commuting to McGill for summer school and living at home. Her family is taking good care of me." She paused, unsure what to say, what to hold back. "Birdie is with us."

She looked toward the window, back at me.

"There's a policewoman who talks to me twice a day and will bring me here whenever I want." She leaned forward, resting her forearms on the bed. "You haven't been awake very much."

"I plan to do better."

A nervous smile. "Dad calls every day to make sure I don't need anything and to ask about you."

Guilt and loss joined the emotions that were churning in me. "Tell him I'm fine."

The nurse returned quietly and stood next to Katy, who took her cue. "I'll be back tomorrow."

It was morning when I got the next installment on Fortier.

"He's been a nuisance sex offender for years. Got a sheet going back to 1979. Kept a girl locked up for a day and a half when he was fifteen, but nothing ever came of it. The grandmother kept it out of court, no arrest record. Mostly, he'd pick out a woman, follow her, keep records of her activities. He finally got busted for assault in 1988—"

"The grandmother."

Another Claudel look. I noticed his silk tie was the exact mauve of his shirt.

"*Oui.* An evaluation by a court-appointed psychiatrist at that time described him as paranoid and compulsive." He turned to Ryan. "What else did that shrink write? Tremendous anger, potential for violence, especially against women."

"So he got six months and walked. Typical."

This time Claudel just stared at me. He pinched his eyes at the bridge of his nose and continued.

"Except for the kid and Granny, Fortier up to that point hasn't really done much beyond nuisance stuff. But he gets a real rush killing Grace Damas, decides to move on to bigger things. It's right after that he rents his first hidey-hole. The one on Berger was only his latest."

"Didn't want to share his hobby with the little woman at home." Ryan.

"Where did he get the rent money with only a part-time job?"

"Wife works. He probably squeezed it from her, told her some lie. Or maybe he had another hobby we don't know about. We're sure going to find out."

Claudel continued in his detached, case-discussing voice.

"The next year he begins stalking in earnest, going about it systematically. You were right about the Métro. He's got a thing about the number six. He starts out riding six stops, then follows a woman that fits his profile. His first random hit is Francine Morisette-Champoux. Our boy gets on at Berri-UQAM, gets off at Georges-Vanier and follows her home. He tracks her for several weeks, then makes his move."

I thought of her words and felt a rush of anger. She wanted to feel safe. Untouchable in her home. The ultimate female fantasy. Claudel's voice reconnected.

"But the free stalk is too risky, not controlled enough for him. He gets the idea of using real estate signs from the one on the Morisette-Champoux condo. It's the perfect in."

"Trottier?" I felt sick.

"Trottier. This time he takes the green line, rides his six stops, and gets off at Atwater. He walks around until he spots a sign. Daddy's condo. He watches, takes his time, sees Chantale come and go. Says he spotted the Sacré Cœur logo on her uniform, even went to the school some days. Then the ambush."

"By this time he'd also found a safer killing spot," added Ryan.

"The monastery. Perfect. How did he get Chantale to go with him?"

"One day he waits until he knows she's alone, rings the bell, asks to see the condo. He's a potential buyer, right? But she won't let him in. A few days later he pulls up next to her as she's leaving school. What a coincidence. Claims he had an appointment with her father, but no one showed up. Chantale knows how badly the old man wants to sell the place, so she agrees to walk him through. The rest we know."

The fluorescent tube above my bed buzzed softly. Claudel went on.

"Fortier doesn't want to risk another body on the monastery grounds, so he drives her all the way up to St. Jerome. But he doesn't like that either. It's too long in the car. What if he got stopped? He's seen the seminary, remembers the key. Next time he'll do even better."

"Gagnon."

"Learning curve."

"*Voilà.*"

At that moment the nurse appeared, a younger, gentler version of my weekday keeper. She read my chart, felt my head, took my pulse. For the first time I noticed that the IV was gone from my arm.

"Are you getting tired?"

"I'm fine."

"You can have another painkiller if you need it."

"Let's see how it goes," I said.

She smiled and left.

"What about Adkins?"

"He gets agitated when he talks about Adkins," said Ryan. "Closes up. It's almost as if he's proud of the others, but feels different about her."

A medicine cart passed in the corridor, rubber wheels gliding silently over tile.

Why didn't Adkins fit the pattern?

A robotic voice urged someone to dial 237.

Why so messy?

Elevator doors opened, whooshed shut.

"Think about this," I said. "He's got the place on Berger. His system is working. He finds his victims with the Métro and the 'for sale' signs, then he tracks them until the right moment. He has a safe place to kill and a safe place to dump the bodies. Maybe it's working too well. Maybe the rush isn't there anymore, so he has to up the stakes. He decides to go back into the victim's home, like he did with Morisette-Champoux."

I remembered the photos. The disheveled warm-up suit. The dark red pool around the body.

"But he gets sloppy. We found out he called ahead to make an appointment with Margaret Adkins. What he didn't count on was the husband phoning during his visit. He has to kill her quickly. He has to cut her fast, mutilate her with something close at hand. He pulls it off, gets away, but it's rushed. He's not in control."

The statue. The severed breast.

Ryan nodded.

"Makes sense. The kill is just the final act in his fantasy of control. I can kill you or let you live. I can hide your body or display it. I can deprive you of your gender by mutilating your breasts or vagina. I can render you powerless by cutting off your hands. But then the husband calls and threatens his whole fantasy satisfaction."

"Spoiled the rush." Ryan.

"He never used stolen items before Adkins. Maybe he used her bank card afterward to reassert control."

"Or maybe he had a cash flow problem, needed to blow something up his nose and had no purchasing power." Claudel.

"It's weird. Can't shut him up on the others, but he turns into a potted palm on Adkins." Ryan.

For a while no one said anything.

"Pitre and Gautier?" I asked, avoiding what I really had to know.

"Claims they're not his."

Ryan and Claudel exchanged words. I didn't hear them. A chill spread and filled my rib cage, a question taking form. It coalesced, hung there, then slithered up and forced itself into language.

"Gabby?"

Claudel dropped his eyes.

Ryan cleared his throat.

"You've had a—"

"Gabby?" I repeated. Tears burned the insides of my eyelids.

Ryan nodded.

"Why?"

No one spoke.

"It's because of me, isn't it?" I fought to keep my voice even.

"This fuckhead's a nutcase," said Ryan. "He's crazy for control. He won't open up much about his childhood, but he's got so much rage against the grandmother you have to scrape it off your teeth when you leave the room. Blames all of his problems on her. Keeps saying she ruined him. From what we've learned, she was a very domineering woman, and fanatically religious. His feelings of powerlessness probably stem from whatever went on between them."

"Meaning the guy's a real loser with women and blames it on the old lady," added Claudel.

"What does this have to do with Gabby?"

Ryan seemed reluctant to continue.

"At first Fortier gets a sense of control through peeping. He can watch his victims, track them, learn all about them, and they aren't even aware of him. He keeps his notebooks and clippings and runs a fantasy show in his head. An added bonus is that there's no risk of rejection. But eventually, that's not enough. He kills Damas, finds he likes it, and decides on a career move. He starts kidnapping and killing his victims. The ultimate control. Life and death. He's in charge and unstoppable."

I stared into the flame blue irises.

"Then you come along and dig up Isabelle Gagnon."

"I'm a threat," I said, anticipating where he was going.

"His perfect MO is jeopardized, he feels a threat. And Dr. Brennan is the cause. You may topple the whole fantasy in which he's the supreme player."

I ran over the events of the past six weeks.

"I dig up and identify Isabelle Gagnon in early June. Three weeks later Fortier kills Margaret Adkins, and the next day we show up on Rue Berger. Three days after that I find Grace Damas's skeleton."

"You've got it."

"He's furious."

"Exactly. The hunt is his way of acting out his contempt for women—"

"Or his anger at Granny." Claudel.

"Maybe. Anyway, he sees you as blocking him."

"And I'm a woman."

Ryan reached for a cigarette, remembered where he was.

"Also, he made a mistake. Adkins was sloppy. Using the bank card almost cost him."

"So he needs someone to blame."

"This guy can't admit he's screwed up. And he definitely can't deal with a woman catching him out."

"But why Gabby? Why not me?"

"Who knows? Chance? Timing? Maybe she walked out before you did."

"I don't think so," I said. "It's obvious he'd been

stalking me for some time. He put the skull in my yard?"

Nods.

"He could have waited, then grabbed me like he did the others."

"This is one sick fucker." Claudel.

"Gabby wasn't like the others, she wasn't a random-stranger killing. Fortier knew where I lived. He knew she was staying with me."

I was talking more to myself than to Ryan and Claudel. An emotional aneurysm, formed over the past six weeks and held in check by force of will, was threatening to burst.

"He did it on purpose. The psycho prick wanted me to know. It was a message, like the skull."

My voice was rising but I couldn't hold it back. I pictured an envelope on my door. An oval of bricks. Gabby's bloated face with its tiny silver gods. A picture of my daughter.

The thin wall of my emotional balloon ruptured, and weeks of pent-up grief and tension rushed through the puncture.

Razors of pain shot through my throat but I screamed, "No! No! No! You goddamn sonofabitch!"

I heard Ryan speak sharply to Claudel, felt his hands on my arms, saw the nurse, felt the needle. Then nothing.

43

RYAN CAME TO SEE ME AT home on Wednesday. The earth had turned seven times since my night in hell, and I'd had time to construct an official version for myself. But there were holes I wanted to fill.

"Has Fortier been charged?"

"Monday. Five counts of first degree."

"Five?"

"Pitre and Gautier are probably unrelated."

"Tell me something. How did Claudel know Fortier would show up here?"

"He didn't, really. From your questions about the school, he realized Tanguay couldn't be the perp. He checked, found out the kids are in at eight, out at three-fifteen. Tanguay earned a perfect attendance ribbon. Hadn't missed a day since he started, and there were no school holidays on the days you asked about. Also he'd learned about the glove business.

"He knew you were exposed, so he hauled ass back to your place to keep watch until he could get a unit back on site. Got here, tried the phone and found it dead. He vaulted the garden gate and found the French doors unlocked. You two were too busy dancing to hear him. He would have broken the glass, but you must have gotten the latch open when you tried to split."

Claudel. My rescuer again.

"Anything new turn up?"

"They found an athletic bag in Fortier's car with three choke collars, a couple of hunting knives, a box of surgical gloves, and a set of street clothes."

I packed as he talked, perched on the end of my bed.

"His kit."

"Yes. I'm sure we'll tie the Rue Berger glove and the one with Gabby to the box in his car."

I pictured him that night, Spiderman smooth, gloved hands bone white in the darkness.

"He'd wear the cycling suit and gloves whenever he went out to play. Even at Berger. That's why we always came up empty. No hairs, no fibers, no latents."

"No sperm."

"Oh yeah. He also had a box of condoms."

"Perfect."

I went to the closet for my old sneakers, tucked them into the duffel.

"Why did he do it?"

"I doubt we'll ever know. Apparently the grandmother could have run the showers and sifted the gold crowns out of the ovens."

"Meaning?"

"She was tough. And fanatic."

"About?"

"Sex and God. Not necessarily in that order."

"For example?"

"Gave little Leo an enema and dragged him to church every morning. To cleanse body and soul."

"The daily Mass and swish protocol."

"We talked to a neighbor who remembers one time the kid was wrestling on the floor with the family dog. The old biddy nearly stroked out because the schnauzer had a hard-on. Two days later the pup turned up with a belly full of rat poison."

"Did Fortier know?"

"He doesn't talk about it. He does talk about a time he was seven and she caught him jacking off. Granny tied little Leo's wrists to her own and dragged him around for three days. He's got spiders in his head when it comes to hands."

I paused in the middle of folding a sweater.

"Hands."

"Yeah."

"That's not all. There was also an uncle, a priest who'd been forced to take early retirement. Hung around the house in his bathrobe, probably abused the kid. It's another topic he goes mute on. We're checking it out."

"Where is the grandmother now?"

"Dead. Right before he killed Damas."

"The trigger?"

"Who knows."

I started going through bathing suits, gave up, stuffed them all in the duffel.

"What about Tanguay?"

Ryan shook his head and expelled a long breath. "Looks like he's just another citizen with a seriously impaired approach to sex."

I stopped sorting socks and looked at him.

"He's mainline fruitcake, but probably harmless."

"Meaning?"

"He was a biology teacher. Collected roadkill, boiled the carcasses down and mounted the skeletons. He was building a display for his classroom."

"The paws?"

"Dried them for a vertebrate paw collection."

"Did he kill Alsa?"

"He claims he found her dead on the street near UQAM and brought her home for the collection. He'd just cut her up when he read the article in the *Gazette*. Scared him, so he stuffed her in a bag and left her at the bus station. We'll probably never know how she got out of the lab."

"Tanguay *is* Julie's client, isn't he?"

"None other. Gets his jolt by hiring a hooker to dress in Mama's nightie. And . . ."

He hesitated.

"And?"

"You ready for this? Tanguay was dummy man."

"No. The bedroom burglar?"

"You got it. That's why his butt was sucked right up his throat when we were questioning him. He thought we'd hauled him on that. The dumb little bastard came out with it all by himself. Apparently, when he couldn't score on the street, he'd use plan B."

"Break in and crank up on someone else's jammies."

"You've got it. Better than bowling."

There was something else that had been bothering me.

"The phone calls?"

"Plan C. Phone a woman, hang up, feel your genitals twinkle. Typical peeper stuff. He had a list of numbers."

"Any theories on how he got mine?"

"Probably lifted it from Gabby. He was peeping her."

"The picture I found in my wastebasket?"

"Tanguay. He's into aboriginal art. It was a copy of something he saw in a book. Did it to give to Gabby. Wanted to ask her not to cut him out of the project."

I looked at Ryan. "Pretty ironic. She thought she had a stalker when she actually had two."

I felt my eyes well with tears. The emotional scar tissue was forming, but was still embryonic. It would take time until I could think of her.

Ryan rose and stretched. "Where's Katy?" he asked, changing the subject.

"Gone for suntan lotion." I pulled the drawstring on the duffel and dropped it to the floor.

"How's she doing?"

"She seems fine. Looks after me like a private duty nurse."

Unconsciously, I scratched at the stitches in my neck.

"But it may trouble her more than she lets on. She knows about violence, but it's evening news violence, in South L.A. and Tel Aviv and Sarajevo. It's always been something that happens to other people. Pete and I purposely sheltered her from what I do, kept Katy apart from my work. Now it's real and close and personal. She's had her world tipped, but she'll come around."

"And you?"

"I'm fine. Really."

We stood in silence and studied each other. Then he reached for his jacket and folded it over his arm.

"Going to a beach?" His affected indifference was not quite convincing.

"Every one we can find. We've dubbed it 'The Great Sand and Surf Quest.' First Ogonquit, then a swing down the coast. Cape Cod. Rehobeth. Cape

May. Virginia Beach. Our only plan is to be at Nags Head on the fifteenth."

Pete had arranged that. He planned to be there.

Ryan placed a hand on my shoulder. His eyes spoke of more than professional interest.

"Are you coming back?"

I'd been asking myself all week. Am I? To what? The work? Could I go through this again with yet another twisted psychopath? To Quebec? Could I bear to let Claudel carve me up and serve me to some hearing commission? What about my marriage? That wasn't in Quebec. What would I do about Pete? What would I feel when I saw him?

I'd made only one decision: I wouldn't think about it for now. I'd vowed to put tomorrow's uncertainties aside and leave my time with Katy unblemished.

"Of course," I said. "I'll have to finish my reports, then testify."

"Yeah."

A tense silence. We both knew it was a nonanswer.

He cleared his throat and reached into his jacket pocket.

"Claudel asked me to give this to you."

He held out a brown envelope with the CUM logo on the upper left-hand corner.

"Great."

I stuck it in my pocket and followed him to the door. Not now.

"Ryan."

He turned.

"Can you do this day after day, year after year, and not lose faith in the human species?"

He didn't answer right away, seemed to focus on a point in space between us. Then his eyes met mine.

"From time to time the human species spawns predators that feed on those around them. They're not the species. They're mutations of the species. In my opinion these freaks have no right to suck oxygen from the atmosphere. But they're here, so I help cage them up and put them where they can't hurt others. I make life safer for the folks who get up, go to work each day, raise their kids or their tomatoes, or their tropical fish, and watch the ball game in the evening. *They* are the human species."

I watched him walk away, admiring once again the way he filled his 501's. And brains, too, I thought as I closed the door. Maybe, I said to myself, smiling. May, by God, be.

Later that evening Katy and I went for ice cream, then drove up the mountain. Sitting on my favorite overlook we could see the whole valley, the St. Lawrence a black cutout in the distance, Montreal a twinkling panorama spreading from its edges.

I looked down from my bench, like a passenger on Mr. Toad's Wild Ride. But the ride was finally over. Perhaps I'd come to say good-bye.

I finished my cone and jammed the napkin in my pocket. My hand touched Claudel's envelope.

Hell, why not.

I opened it and withdrew a handwritten note. Odd. It was not the formal complaint I'd expected. The message was written in English.

Dr. Brennan,
You are right. No one should die in anonymity. Thanks to you, these women did not. Thanks to you, Leo Fortier's killing days are over.
We are the last line of defense against them:

the pimps, the rapists, the cold-blooded killers.
I would be honored to work with you again.
                                    Luc Claudel

Higher up the mountain, the cross glowed softly, sending its message out over the valley. What was it Kojak said? Somebody loves ya, baby.

Ryan and Claudel had it figured. And we were the last line.

I looked at the city below. Hang in there. Somebody loves ya.

"À la prochaine," I said to the summer night.

"What's that?" asked Katy.

" 'Until the next time.' "

My daughter looked puzzled.

"Let's go to the beach."

Scribner proudly presents

CROSS BONES

Kathy Reichs

Available in hardcover
from Scribner
June 28, 2005

Turn the page for a preview of
Cross Bones . . .

By four, what remained of Avram Ferris's face was back in position, and Y-shaped stitching held his belly and chest. Ferris, a fifty-six-year-old Orthodox Jew, had gone missing a week earlier. His body had been discovered yesterday in a storage closet in his place of business. Death by self-inflicted gunshot wound was the on-scene assessment, but the man's family adamantly rejected suicide as the cause of death. The photographer had five rolls of film. My boss, Pierre LaManche, had a ream of diagrams and notes. I had four tubs of bloody shards.

I was cleaning bone fragments, when Ryan appeared in the corridor outside my lab. I watched his approach through the window above my sink.

Craggy face, eyes too blue for his own good.

Or mine.

Seeing me, Ryan pressed his palms and nose to the glass. I flicked water at him.

He pushed back and pointed at my door. I mouthed "open" and waved him through, a goofy smile spreading across my face

OK. Maybe Ryan isn't so bad for me.

But I had reached that opinion only recently.

For almost a decade Ryan and I had butted heads in an on-again, off-again non-relationship. Up-down. Yes-no. Hot-cold.

Hot-hot.

I've been attracted to Ryan since the get-go, but there have been more obstacles to acting on that attraction than there were signers of the Declaration.

I believe in the separation of job and play. No water cooler romance for this señorita. No way.

Ryan works homicide. I work the morgue. Professional exclusion clause applies. Obstacle one.

Ryan was widely known as the squad-room Lothario. Stud muffin exclusion clause applies. Obstacle two.

But Ryan sweet-talked the loopholes, and, after years of resistance, I finally jumped through.

"How's it going, cupcake?" he asked, coming through the door.

"Good." I added a fragment to those drying on the corkboard.

"That the chimney stiff?" Ryan was eyeing the box holding Charles Bellemare.

"Happy trails for the Cowboy," I said.

"Guy take a hit?"

I shook my head. "Looks like he leaned to when he should have leaned fro. No idea why he was sitting on a chimney ledge." I stripped off my gloves and squeezed soap onto my hands. "Who's the blond guy downstairs?"

"Birch. He'll be working Ferris with me."

"New partner?"

Ryan shook his head. "Loan-over. You think Ferris offed himself?"

I turned and shot Ryan a you-know-better-than-that look.

Ryan gave me an expression of choirboy innocence. "Not trying to rush you."

Yanking paper towels from the holder, I said, "Tell me about him."

Ryan nudged Bellemare aside and rested one haunch on my worktable.

"Family's Orthodox."

"Really?" Mock surprise.

"The Fab Four were here to ensure a kosher autopsy."

"Who were they?" I wadded and tossed the paper towels.

"Rabbi, members of the temple, one brother. You want names?"

I shook my head.

"Ferris was a bit more secular than his kin. Operated an import business from a warehouse out near Mirabel airport. Told the wife he'd be out of town on Thursday and Friday. According to—" Ryan pulled out and glanced at a spiral pad.

"Miriam," I supplied.

"Right." Ryan gave me an odd look. "According to Miriam, Ferris was trying to expand the business. He called around four on Wednesday, said he was heading out, and that he'd be back late on Friday. When he didn't arrive by sundown, Miriam figured he'd been delayed and preferred not to drive on the Sabbath."

"Had that happened before?"

Ryan nodded. "Ferris wasn't in the habit of phoning home. When he hadn't shown up Saturday, Miriam started working the speed dial. No one in the family had seen him. Neither had his secretary. Miriam didn't know which accounts he was planning to hit, so she decided to sit tight. Sunday morning she checked the warehouse. Sunday afternoon she filed a missing persons report. Cops said they'd investigate if hubby hadn't surfaced by Monday morning."

"Grown man extending his business trip?"

Ryan shrugged one shoulder. "Happens."

"Ferris never left Montreal?"

"LaManche thinks he died not long after his call to Miriam."

"Miriam's story checks out?"

"So far."

"The body was found in a closet?"

Ryan nodded. "Blood and brains all over the walls."

"What kind of closet?"

"Small storage space off an upstairs office."

"Why would cats be in there with him?"

"The door's outfitted with one of those little two-way flaps. Ferris kept food and litter in there."

"He gathered the cats to shoot himself?"

"Maybe they were in there when he took the bullet, maybe they slipped in later. Ferris may have died sitting on a stool, then tumbled off. Somehow his feet ended up jamming the kitty door."

I thought about that.

"Miriam didn't check the closet when she visited on Saturday?"

"No."

"She didn't hear scratching or meowing?"

"The Missus is *not* a cat lover. That's why Ferris kept them at work."

"She didn't notice any odor?"

"Apparently Ferris wasn't real fastidious about feline toilette. Miriam said if she'd smelled anything she'd have figured it was kitty litter."

"She didn't find the building overly warm?"

"Nope. But if a cat brushed the thermostat after her visit, Ferris would still have been cooking from Sunday till Tuesday."

"Did Ferris have other employees besides the secretary?"

"Nope." Ryan consulted the notes in his spiral. "Courtney Purviance. Miriam calls her a secretary. Purviance prefers the term *associate*."

"Is the wife downgrading, or the help upgrading?"

"More likely the former. Appears Purviance played a pretty big role in running the business."

"Where was Purviance on Wednesday?"

"Left early. Bad sinuses."

"Why didn't Purviance find Ferris on Monday?"

"Monday was some kind of Jewish holiday. Purviance was home eating seder and planting trees."

"Tu Bishvat, the festival of trees. Was anything missing?"

"Purviance insists there's nothing in the place worth stealing. Computer's old. Radio's older. Inventory's not valuable. But she's checking."

"How long has she worked for Ferris?"

"Since ninety-eight."

"Anything suspicious in Ferris's background? Known associates? Enemies? Gambling debts? Jilted girlfriend? Boyfriend?"

Ryan shook his head.

"Anything to suggest he was suicidal?"

"I'm digging, but so far zip. Stable marriage. Took the little woman to Boca in January. Business wasn't blazing, but it was producing a steady living. Especially since Purviance hired on, a fact she's not hesitant to mention. No signs of depression."

I remembered Kessler and slipped the photo from the pocket of my lab coat.

"A gift from one of the Fab Four." I held it out. "He thinks it's the reason Ferris is dead."

"Meaning?"

"He thinks it's the reason Ferris is dead."

"You can be a real pain in the ass, Brennan."

"I work at it."

Ryan studied the photo.

"Which of the Fab Four?"

"Kessler."

Floating a brow, Ryan laid down the photo and flipped a page in his spiral.

"You sure?"

"That's the name he gave me."

When Ryan looked up the brow had settled.

"No one named Kessler was cleared for that autopsy."

"I'm certain Kessler's the name he gave."

"He was an authorized observer?"

"As opposed to one of the multitudes of Hasidim who haunt these halls?"

Ryan ignored my sarcasm.

"Did Kessler say that's why he was here?"

"No." For some reason Ryan's questions were irking me.

"You'd seen Kessler earlier in the autopsy room?"

"I—"

I'd been distressed over Miriam and Dora Ferris, then distracted by Pelletier's call. Kessler had glasses, a beard, and a black suit. My mind had settled for a cultural stereotype.

I wasn't irked at Ryan. I was irked at myself.

"I just assumed."

"Let's take it from the top."

I told Ryan about the incident in the downstairs corridor.

"So Kessler was in the hall when you left the family room."

"Yes."

"Did you see where he came from?"

"No."

"Where he went?"

"I thought he was going to join Dora and Miriam."

"Did you actually see him enter the family room?"

"I was speaking to Pelletier." It came out sharper than I intended.

"Don't be defensive."

"That was not defensive," I said defensively, and did a two-handed pull to unsnap my lab coat. "That was enlargement of detail."

Ryan picked up Kessler's print.

"What am I looking at?"

"A skeleton."

Ryan's eyes rolled up.

"Kessler—" I stopped. "The mysterious bearded stranger told me it came from Israel."

"The photo *came from* Israel, or was shot there?"

Another screw-up on my part.

"The picture's over forty years old. It's probably meaningless."

"When someone says it caused a death, it's not meaningless."

I reddened.

Ryan flipped the photo as I had. "What's *M de 1 H*?"

"You think that's an *M*?"

Ryan ignored my question.

"What was going on in October of sixty-three?" he asked more of himself than of me.

"Oswald's thoughts were on JFK."

"Brennan, you can be a real—"

"We've established that."

Crossing to Ryan, I reversed the photo and pointed at the object to the left of the leg bones.

"See that?" I asked.

"It's a paintbrush."

"It's a cocked-up north arrow."

"Meaning?"

"Old archaeologist's trick. If you don't have an official marker to indicate scale and direction, place something in the shot and point it north."

"You think this was taken by an archaeologist?"

"Yes."

"What site?"

"A site with burials."

"Now we're getting somewhere."

"Look, this Kessler's probably a crackpot. Find him and grill him. Or talk to Miriam Ferris." I flapped a hand at the print. "Maybe she knows why her husband was freaked over this thing." I slipped off my lab coat. "If he *was* freaked over the thing."

Ryan studied the photo for a full minute. Then he looked up and said,

"Think any of your paleo-pals might recognize this?"

"I can make a few calls."

"Couldn't hurt."

At the door Ryan turned and flashed his brows.

"See you later?"

"Wednesday's my Tai Chi night."

"Tomorrow?"

"You're on."

The next morning, I spent my first hour in the lab identifying, marking, and inventorying the fragments from Avram Ferris's head. I wasn't yet undertaking an in-depth examination, but I was noticing details.

At nine twenty, I returned to my office and phoned Jacob Drum, a colleague at UNC-Charlotte. His voice mail answered. I left a message asking that he return my call.

I'd been with the fragments another hour when the phone rang.

"Hey, Tempe."

"Hey, Jake."

"Won't get above fifty in Charlotte today. Cold up there?"

In winter, southerners delight in querying Canadian weather. In summer, interest plummets.

"It's cold." The predicted high was in negative figures.

"Going where the weather suits my clothes."

"Off to dig?" Jake was a biblical archaeologist who'd been excavating in the Middle East for almost three decades.

"Yes, ma'am. Doing a first-century synagogue. Crew's set. Got my regulars in Israel, meeting up with a field supervisor in Toronto on Saturday. Just finalizing my own travel arrangements now. Do you have any idea how rare these things are? There are first-century synagogues at Masada and Gamla. That's about it."

"Sounds like a terrific opportunity. Listen, I'm glad I caught you. Got a favor to ask."

"Shoot."

I described Kessler's print, leaving out specifics as to how I'd obtained it.

"Pic was shot in Israel?"

"I'm told it came from Israel."

"It dates to the sixties?"

"October '63 is written on the back. And some kind of notation. Maybe an address."

"Pretty vague."

"Yes."

"I'll be glad to check it out."

"I'll scan the image and send it by email."

"I'm not optimistic."

"I appreciate your willingness to take a look."

"You gotta come dig with us, Tempe. Get back to your archaeological roots."

"There's nothing I'd like better, but I can't take off now."

"One of these days."

"One of these days."

After our call, I hurried to the imaging section, scanned Kessler's photo, and transferred the .jpg file to the computer in my lab. Then I hurried back, logged on, and transmitted the image to Jake's inbox at UNCC.

Back to Ferris's shattered head.

Cranial fractures show tremendous variability in patterning. The successful interpretation of any given pattern rests on an understanding of the biomechanical properties of bone, combined with a knowledge of the intrinsic and extrinsic factors involved in fracture production.

Simple, right? Like quantum physics.

Though bone seems rigid, it actually has a certain amount of elasticity. When subjected to stress, a bone yields and changes shape. When its limits of elastic deformation are exceeded, the bone fails, or fractures.

That's the biomechanical bit.

In the head, fractures travel the paths of least resistance. These paths are determined by things such as vault curvature, bony buttressing, and sutures, the squiggly junctures between individual bones.

Those are the intrinsic factors.

Extrinsic factors include the size, speed, and angle of the impacting object.

Think of it this way. The skull is a sphere with bumps and curves and gaps. There are predictable ways in which that sphere fails when walloped by an impacting object. Both a .22-caliber bullet and a two-inch pipe are impacting objects. The bullet's just moving a whole lot faster and striking a smaller area.

You get the idea.

Despite the massive damage, I knew I was seeing an atypical pattern in Ferris's head. The more I looked, the more uneasy I grew.

I was placing an occipital fragment under the microscope, when the phone rang. It was Jake Drum. This time there was no leisurely "hey."

"Where did you say you got this photo?"

"I didn't. It—"

"Who gave it to you?"

"A man named Kessler. But—"

"Do you still have it?"

"Yes."

"How long will you be in Montreal?"

"I'm leaving for a quick trip to the States on Sunday, but—"

"If I divert to Montreal Saturday, can you show me the original?"

"Yes. Jake—"

"I've got to phone the airlines." His voice was so taut it could have moored the Queen Mary. "In the meantime, hide that print."

Purchase a hardcover copy of Kathy Reichs's newest novel

CROSS BONES

Available June 2005 and receive a $2.00 rebate by mail.

Mail the original store receipt for
Cross Bones
(ISBN 0-7432-3348-4)
dated on or before August 31, 2005,
along with your name, address, and zip code to:

> Simon & Schuster
> Marketing Department/KR
> 1230 Avenue of the Americas, 12th floor
> New York, NY 10020

SCRIBNER
A Division of Simon & Schuster
A VIACOM COMPANY

www.simonsays.com

12275